Collector's Library

SPINECHILLERS

*Tales for Hallowe'en
and Other Dark Nights*

SPINECHILLERS

*Tales for Hallowe'en and
Other Dark Nights*

Selected and with an Introduction by
DAVID STUART DAVIES

Collector's Library

This edition published in 2012 by
Collector's Library
an imprint of CRW Publishing Limited
69 Gloucester Crescent, London NW1 7EG

ISBN   978 1 907360 69 5

Typeset in Great Britain by Antony Gray
Printed and bound in China by Imago

1

Contents

INTRODUCTION

Hallowe'en is, of course, the night when all the ghosts, ghouls and long-legged beasties come out to taunt us poor mortals – taunt us and worse. The term is short for All Hallows' Eve, which is 31 October, the night before All Saints' Day. The festival was Celtic in origin, but it was taken over by the Christian Church and first called 'Hallowe'en' in the sixteenth century. Traditionally, it was believed that the souls of the departed wandered the earth until All Saints' Day, and All Hallows' Eve provided one last chance for the dead to gain vengeance on their enemies before moving on to the next world. In more recent times, it has become an evening when youngsters dress up as witches, vampires, demons and monsters in various horrendous guises and visit their neighbours to play a trick or exact a treat. It is also the night for telling scary stories. And that is what this volume is all about: scary stories. Of course, in truth, any dark night will do. Any dark night when the clouds hide the moon and the mist rises, the wind blows eerily under the eaves and skeletal branches tap at the windows like the bony fingers of some dead hand seeking entry.

Since the beginning of time man has been fascinated by fear: wary of it in reality but entertained by it in fiction. From tales told around a campfire to graphic gruesome visions viewed from the edge of a cinema seat as some unnatural and ghoulish event unfolds on the screen, we love being scared. Our imagination allows us, for a brief time, to suspend belief and enter these nightmare worlds. The pulse quickens, the goose-pimples rise – as does the hair on the back of the neck – and the eyes shine with a curious blend of fear and pleasure. And I believe that it is in reading stories that one receives the richest rewards in this compulsive pursuit of the thrill associated with fear. One's own imagination is capable of far greater horrors and chills than any film or television programme can generate. Stimulated by the words on the page, the mind can construct the most fearsome of visions. The writer's narratives are your springboard into the terror beyond. There are no more macabre or arcane visions than those conjured by your own imagination.

It was in the nineteenth century that the supernatural tale first became a respected and a popular genre. This was a period when medical science was making giant strides, and while man's physical status was being explored, examined and explained, people also began to question more objectively the notion of mortality and in particular what really happens after death. This increased speculation brought about the rise of whole tribes of spiritualists, mediums and clairvoyants ready to provide answers. They could talk to the dead, raise spirits and bring messages back from 'the other side', claiming to have proof of existence beyond the grave.

In literature, stories of ghosts, vampires and other undead fiends became voguish. No self-respecting author failed to dabble in the genre. These early scribes began a tradition – the tradition of evoking horror in a bid to entertain the reader – that still exists today, although it has to be said that the modern practitioners on the whole tend to go straight for the gory and the gruesome, the stomach-churning shock element, rather than opting to build a more subtle, creeping sense of fear.

Quite a number of the contributors to this current brew of chilling stories were masterful exponents of the scary tale in the nineteenth century and among them were a surprising number of female authors who took pleasure and exhibited great skill in the process – writers such as Edith Wharton, Elizabeth Gaskell, Mary E. Braddon, Edith Nesbit, Vernon Lee and Charlotte Riddell. It was as though their feminine sensitivity was especially attuned to the notion of ghosts and troubled spirits. Other contributors – such as Bernard Capes, Barry Pain, Robert Barr and E. F. Benson – came a little later, but they were true to the mood, ethos and tradition of the pioneers of the genre. They emulated and occasionally surpassed their predecessors.

While it would be fair to say that the majority of the tales in this collection deal with ghosts, either malign or benevolent, there are a handful of tales which are just simply strange and wonderfully unnerving in their strangeness. Take the opening story, 'Markheim', by Robert Louis Stevenson, for example. There is a growing sense of inevitability about the denouement as the narrative progresses, and yet when one has finished reading, niggling questions remain as to what actually happened in that room with the dead man. Similarly, 'August Heat' by W. F. Harvey is a wonderfully unsettling piece involving cruel coincidences and the uncompromising hand of fate rather than any intrusion of a supernatural presence. Ironically, it is a story that can haunt the mind long after one has closed the book.

Werewolves and vampires also make guest appearances (see 'The White Wolf of the Hartz Mountains' by Captain Frederick Marryat, 'Mrs Amworth' by E. F. Benson and 'The Mask' by Bernard Capes), as well a strange array of the returning dead. For me, perhaps the most chilling encounter with ghosts is found in Amyas Northcote's deceptively gentle tale 'Brickett Bottom'. The unsettling sense of dread is engendered so simply, in such a restrained manner, that the horror of the scenario increases in intensity as a result.

In assembling a volume of stories which are all designed to frighten the reader in a pleasurable fashion, one must aim for variety. A sameness of narrative would be certain to lessen any effect. One must keep surprising the reader and presenting him with something fresh. Regard this anthology then rather like a large box of delectable chocolates, individually wrapped in glittering paper but giving no hint as to flavour or content. Each one is unique, harbouring a very individual taste. It is now time for you to dip into this dark confection and judge for yourself.

ABOUT THE AUTHORS

E. F. Benson (1867–1940)

It is not given to many writers to find fame and success in two very different literary genres, but that is what Edward Frederic Benson achieved. He wrote over a hundred books in his lifetime, including his extremely successful social satires, the Mapp & Lucia novels. However, it was for his ghost stories that E. F. Benson was best known when he was alive. Even within this narrow category of fiction, Benson was able to vary widely both his style and his focus. His range was far broader and more adventurous than that of any other writer of supernatural fiction. It is true to say that in general women do not feature prominently in Benson's stories but when they do their role is both sinister and ominous. Perhaps the best example of this is the eponymous figure in 'Mrs Amworth', who, our bachelor narrator informs us, seems a cheerful soul with a loud jolly laugh, but who we discover to be in fact a particularly nasty undead creature who has a penchant for adolescent boys.

Robert Louis Stevenson (1850–94)

Perhaps best remembered for his rousing adventure yarns like *Treasure Island*, *Kidnapped* and *The Black Arrow*, Stevenson also had a passion for the dark and weird tale. He was after all the author of *The Strange Case of Dr Jekyll and Mr Hyde*. He constantly found himself drawn to telling tales of the un-natural and the supernatural. 'Markheim' has been described as a ghost story, but it is not quite that for there are uncertainties connected with the nature and identity of the strange visitor. Nevertheless, 'Markheim' is not only a beautifully constructed story but it is also a highly perceptive psychological study of the power of guilt. In a very Dickensian way, Stevenson weaves a wonderfully claustrophobic quilt of words that threatens to stifle not only Markheim but the reader too.

Captain Frederick Marryat (1792–1848)

As a young officer in the Royal Navy, Marryat had a heroic career. He resigned his commission in 1830 to take up writing full time. Most of his works of fiction concern the sea and sailing, such as the popular *Mr Midshipman Easy*, although he is perhaps best remembered for the children's classic novel *Children of the New Forest*, which is set at the time of the English Civil War. 'The White Wolf of the Hartz Mountains' is one of Marryat's rare excursions into the realms of the supernatural. This story is an episode from the author's novel *The Phantom Ship* (1839) and features that most unusual of demonic creatures – a female werewolf.

Robert Barr (1850–1912)

Although British born, Barr spent his early years in Canada. He made his name there as a journalist and then returned to Britain in 1881. He was co-founder of *The Idler*, with Jerome K. Jerome. Most of his literary output was in the crime genre, then seriously in vogue. When Arthur Conan Doyle's Sherlock Holmes stories were becoming well known, Barr published the first Holmes parody, 'The Adventures of Sherlaw Kombs' (1892). Despite the jibe at the growing Holmes phenomenon, Barr and Doyle remained on very good terms. Doyle describes him in his *Memories and Adventures* as 'a volcanic Anglo- or rather Scot-American, with a violent manner, a wealth of strong adjectives, and one of the kindest natures underneath it all'. Barr's contributions to macabre fiction were few but memorable. 'The Vegeance of the Dead' is among his most successful efforts.

Edith Wharton (1862–1937)

Born in America, Edith Wharton was an author of great skill. In novels such as *The Age of Innocence* and *The House of Mirth* she explored the lives and social milieu of New York's upper class. She was awarded the Pulitzer Prize in 1921. She was also an excellent writer of ghost stories and these short tales spanned her entire career, beginning with 'The Lady's Maid's Bell' in 1904 and concluding with 'All Souls' in 1937, the year of her death. Her interest in the supernatural began when she was a little girl and had been given a book of children's ghost stories to read. These tales took such a grip on her imagination that they threw her into 'a state of chronic fear'. She never forgot the sensation and became fascinated with the task of eliciting the same sort of response in her reader. 'A Bottle of Perrier' is one of her most successful exercises in stimulating fear.

Bernard Capes (1854–1918)

Once highly regarded, Capes was a prolific author of popular fiction, mostly historical romances and mysteries, whose work unaccountably slipped into obscurity immediately after his death. In recent years aficionados of the ghost story have rediscovered him and gradually his fiction is being recognised for its richness and originality. Sadly, there was no one collection of his supernatural tales published in his lifetime. Most of these spooky narratives first appeared in the various periodicals of the day. G. K Chesterton was an admirer of his ghost stories and observed that Capes could write 'a penny dreadful so as to make it worth a pound'. 'The Mask' is a fine example of his style and power. It is a deceptively leisurely tale about a vampiric portrait and in telling it he expertly ratchets up the tension in a way that is almost imperceptible.

Elizabeth Gaskell (1810–65)

Gaskell is best known for her novels *Cranford* (1853) and *North and South* (1854), which explored the social issues of the day. Encouraged by Charles Dickens, she began contributing ghost stories to his publications. She often took her plots from snatches of gossip or old wives' tales that she had heard. While on the surface her work has a certain quaintness and a reticence of expression, the stories are well constructed and strong on atmosphere. Surprisingly, 'The Grey Woman' is one of her lesser known works and rarely finds its way into anthologies.

F. Marion Crawford (1854–1909)

Francis Marion Crawford is another of those writers who was very popular in their day but have since slipped completely from the consciousness of the general public. He was born of ex-patriate American parents in Italy where he spent most of his life. He wrote more than forty books, mainly historical dramas infused with an element of fantasy or heightened romanticism. His output of purely supernatural fiction was comparatively small but where the quantity is lacking the quality is not. 'For the Blood is the Life' is generally considered one of the best vampire tales ever commited to paper. Poetic in mood, subtle in presentation, it is gripping and exciting while avoiding the clichés common to such stories.

Amyas Northcote (1864–1923)

Northcote remains a shadowy figure. Little is known about him other than that he was the seventh son of the 1st Earl of Iddesleigh (Chancellor of the Exchequer under Disraeli). Shortly after his father died, he emigrated to America where he set up business in Chicago. He returned to Britain at the turn of the century. He had developed an interest in writing while in the States and in 1921 he produced a slim volume of ghost stories, *In Ghostly Company*. Sadly it proved to be Amyas Northcote's only published volume of any kind. He died very suddenly just eighteen months after the book appeared. The star story of the collection is 'Brickett Bottom', which was championed by the distinguished scholar of the supernatural Montague Summers, who featured it in his classic *The Supernatural Omnibus* in 1931. Jack Adrian, one of the major commentators on the British ghost story, thought that 'Brickett Bottom' 'is far better than simply a good tale told; it plumbs the most profound depths of horror and despair.'

W. F. Harvey (1885–1937)

Born into a wealthy Quaker family in Yorkshire, William Fryer Harvey grew up with a highly developed social conscience; he was a qualified doctor, a war veteran and a loving family man – and yet he took pleasure in creating a series of deeply disturbing and frightening tales. Harvey's stories are remarkable for their subtlety and restraint. 'August Heat' is a fine example of his considerable skill. To begin with, because of its unique qualities, the story cannot be fitted into a specific genre; the scenario is presented in a wonderful dream-like fashion that helps the reader share the sense of unreality felt by the central character. This story is a little gem.

E. G. Swain (1861–1938)

Swain was born in Cheshire. He was ordained in 1885 and in 1892 became Chaplain of King's College, Cambridge, where M. R. James was already the Dean. In 1905, he accepted the living of Stanground, near Peterborough. As 'Stoneground', the parish and Swain's own church of St John the Baptist became the setting for his volume of ghostly stories published in 1912. The tales are set in and around a church and parish on the edge of the fens. The protagonist, the Rector of Stoneground, the Reverend Roland Batchel, is a kindly, humane bachelor and amateur antiquarian, not unlike Swain himself. The writer's style is very much influenced by that of James, to whom he dedicated the book. 'Bone to his Bone' is one of the best stories in this collection.

Mary E. Braddon (1837–1915)

After a brief career on the stage, Mary Braddon took up writing to earn her living. She tackled many genres, including domestic fiction, mystery and adventure. She is best known for her novel *Lady Audley's Secret* (1862) which helped her to become one of the most popular novelists of her day. She was a prolific writer and though her supernatural tales are but a small part of her overall output, they are very effective. Always choosing the short-story format for these narratives, she often focused on sexual and emotional matters presented in supernatural terms. 'The Cold Embrace' is a fine example of this approach, dealing as it does with unrequited love and the dramatic and scary outcome of a damaged relationship.

R. H. Benson (1871–1914)

Robert Hugh Benson was the youngest of the trio of Benson brothers (the others were Arthur Christopher and Edward Frederic) who all achieved some success and fame through writing. And remarkably all three brothers wrote a great deal of supernatural fiction. Robert initially achieved notoriety by means of a scandal. He was ordained as a priest in the Church of England by his father (then Archbishop of Canterbury) in 1896 but several years later, after his father's death, he renounced this faith and became a Roman Catholic priest. R. H. Benson's tales are heavily influenced by his Catholic fervour, but he also managed to instil into his prose a sense of cool menace, as here in 'The Traveller'. His observations about ghost-story fiction and the effects it attempts to achieve are very perceptive and telling: 'It is like looking at the backs of a crowd; they are attending to something else, not us at all. Just occasionally we catch the eye of someone who turns round – but that is all.'

Sir Max Beerbohm (1872–1956)

Henry Maximilian Beerbohm, the youngest of nine children of a Lithuanian-born grain merchant, was a dilettante, a caricaturist of great note and a dabbler in fiction. He was a friend of Aubrey Beardsley, George Bernard Shaw and Oscar Wilde and matched them in wit and flamboyance. His greatest achievement as an author was his novel *Zuleika Dobson* (1911), a satire of undergraduate life at Oxford. Indeed, our story, 'A.V. Laider', begins as a social satire in a louche and witty fashion but then develops in an intriguing way as we, along with the narrator, become fascinated by Mr Laider's terrible story.

Vernon Lee (1856–1935)

Vernon Lee (the pseudonym of Violet Paget) lived during much of her writing career in Italy. She was highly respected in her lifetime as a cultural historian, poet, novelist and aesthetician and as the author of a small number of notable supernatural stories. A great champion of eighteenth-century classical culture, its music, architecture and art, she wrote several important books on the subject. It is this rich Italian background that provides the backdrop for our story 'A Wicked Voice', an ingenious tale of ghostly revenge and vindictiveness.

Amelia B. Edwards (1831–1892)

Like Elizabeth Gaskell, Amelia Edwards was a friend of Charles Dickens and published a number of stories in his magazines. Apart from her writing activities, like many of the dynamic women of her era she had many strings to her bow. She was one of the founders and Honorary Secretary of the Egypt Exploration Fund, a pioneer archaeological society. Her travel books, *A Thousand Miles up the Nile* (1877) and *Pharoahs, Fellahs and Explorers* (1891), became key texts in the study of Egyptology. She was also an accomplished exponent of the Victorian ghost story and was not afraid to use shocking ideas to spice up a spooky brew. 'In the Confessional' is typical of her approach – a juicy story of hatred, betrayal and jealousy with murderous consequences.

Ambrose Bierce (1842–1914?)

Of all the writers of ghost and horror stories, Ambrose Gwinett Bierce is perhaps the most colourful. He was a dark, cynical and pessimistic character who had a grim vision of fate and the unfairness of life which he channelled into his fiction. The tenth of thirteen children, he was born in a log cabin in Ohio in June 1842. He became a journalist and a respected author of bizarre and horror fiction. He is perhaps best known for his satirical work, *The Devil's Dictionary* (1906). Bierce's life ended in mystery: he disappeared in Mexico in 1914 and was never heard of again. 'The Moonlit Road' tells a ghost story from three perspectives, including that of the dead victim. It slowly unravels a tragedy which even when untangled is not really fully explained. There is also in the telling a great sadness which reflects Bierce's own miserable view of existence.

Henry James (1843–1916)

James, an American long domiciled in England, has the distinction of having written one of the greatest ghost novellas of all time, *The Turn of the Screw*. It was perhaps inevitable that James should turn his hand to writing tales of the supernatural in which to examine the psychological and emotional effects of hauntings, for his father, Henry James senior, experienced a terrifying paranormal incident and underwent a religious conversion to Spiritualism. Also, the author's brother, William James, a distinguished philosopher and psychologist, founded the American Society of Psychical Research, which investigated ghostly and other paranormal phenomena. The mood of uncertainty and mistrust charged with an undercurrent of sexual tension so strong in *The Turn of the Screw* is also potent in 'The Friends of the Friends'.

Jerome K. Jerome (1859–1927)

Jerome Klapka Jerome is generally regarded as a writer of humorous fiction. His novel *Three Men in a Boat* (1889) is one of the great comic novels in British literature. Some of his forays into supernatural fiction were also tinged with wit and satire and therefore it is somewhat surprising to encounter his story 'Silhouettes', a very dark, very gloomy and challenging read, totally bereft of any levity at all. The epithet which best describes this tale, recollected from a grim and mysterious childhood, is 'strange'. The intriguing narrative has a hypnotising effect on the reader, drawing him in and yet tantalisingly failing to explain the dark mystery at its heart.

Barry Pain (1864–1928)

Like his friend Jerome K. Jerome, Barry Pain was also a journalist and humourist who occasionally crossed the literary tracks on to the dark side. Pain is perhaps best remembered for the Eliza books about the comical trials and tribulations of a suburban housewife, but his supernatural fiction deserves equal attention. He seemed to take pleasure in presenting the reader with a scenario that was not quite a ghost story and not quite a supernatural tale, but yet was both macabre and unsettling. 'The Glass of Supreme Moments' defies categorisation. While it has elements of a grim moral fairy tale, it is also a bleak fantasy with strange powers to comfort and unnerve the reader at one and the same time.

Richard Marsh (1857–1915)

Richard Marsh was the pseudonym of the British author born Richard Bernard Heldmann. He was a writer of ghost stories and Victorian thrillers. His best known work, the horror novel *The Beetle* (1897), was published in the same year as Bram Stoker's *Dracula* and was initially even more popular. He began writing short stories under his real name, changing it to 'Richard Marsh' in 1893. Marsh died a few months after the birth of his grandson Robert Aikman, who himself grew up to be a respected weaver of supernatural fiction. 'The Fifteenth Man' is a simple but fast moving and compelling ghost story with the rare setting of a rugby match.

Charlotte Riddell (1832–1906)

Charlotte Elizabeth Lawson Cowan, later known as Mrs Riddell, wrote some of the most startling and original ghost stories of the period. She was the author of well over forty novels and numerous short stories – so numerous, in fact, that she herself lost track of the number, for she wrote many anonymously and under various pseudonyms in addition to those bearing her own name. The year 1882 saw the publication of *Weird Tales*, a rich set of ghost stories from which comes the tale chosen for this volume. Critics of the genre regard this collection as presenting some of the best ghost stories ever written. Part of this excellence lies in Riddell's ability to vary the type and scope of the hauntings. It is a facility that provides a freshness and a surprise element to her plots. Riddell was also adept at evoking a sense of place and this is evident in 'The Old House in Vauxhall Walk'. Of course, the house, which is so beautifully and expertly described in its neglect and decay, harbours ghostly secrets and horrors.

E. F. BENSON

Mrs Amworth

The village of Maxley, where, last summer and autumn, these strange events took place, lies on a heathery and pine-clad upland of Sussex. In all England you could not find a sweeter and saner situation. Should the wind blow from the south, it comes laden with the spices of the sea; to the east high downs protect it from the inclemencies of March; and from the west and north the breezes which reach it travel over miles of aromatic forest and heather. The village itself is insignificant enough in point of population, but rich in amenities and beauty. Halfway down the single street, with its broad road and spacious areas of grass on each side, stands the little Norman Church and the antique graveyard long disused: for the rest there are a dozen small, sedate Georgian houses, red-bricked and long-windowed, each with a square of flower-garden in front, and an ampler strip behind; a score of shops, and a couple of score of thatched cottages belonging to labourers on neighbouring estates, complete the entire cluster of its peaceful habitations. The general peace, however, is sadly broken on Saturdays and Sundays, for we lie on one of the main roads between London and Brighton and our quiet street becomes a racecourse for flying motor cars and bicycles.

A notice just outside the village begging them to go slowly only seems to encourage them to accelerate their speed, for the road lies open and straight, and there is really no reason why they should do otherwise. By way of protest, therefore, the ladies of Maxley cover their noses and mouths with their handkerchiefs as they see a motor car approaching, though, as the street is asphalted, they need not really take these precautions against dust. But late on Sunday night the horde of scorchers has passed, and we settle down again to five days of cheerful and leisurely seclusion. Railway strikes which agitate the country so much leave us undisturbed because most of the inhabitants of Maxley never leave it at all.

I am the fortunate possessor of one of these small Georgian houses, and consider myself no less fortunate in having so interesting and stimulating a neighbour as Francis Urcombe, who, the most confirmed of Maxleyites, has not slept away from his house, which stands just opposite to mine in the village street, for nearly two years, at which date, though still in middle life, he resigned his Physiological Professorship at Cambridge University and devoted himself to the study of those occult and curious phenomena which seem equally to concern the physical and the psychical sides of human nature. Indeed his retirement was not unconnected with his passion for the strange uncharted places that lie on the confines and borders of science, the existence of which is so stoutly denied by the more materialistic minds, for he advocated that all medical students should be obliged to pass some sort of examination in mesmerism, and that one of the tripos papers should be designed to test their knowledge in such subjects as appearances at time of death, haunted houses, vampirism, automatic writing, and possession.

'Of course they wouldn't listen to me,' ran his account of the matter, 'for there is nothing that these seats of learning are so frightened of as knowledge, and the road to knowledge lies in the study of things like these. The functions of the human frame are, broadly speaking, known. They are a country, anyhow, that has been charted and mapped out. But outside that lie huge tracts of undiscovered country, which certainly exist, and the real pioneers of knowledge are those who, at the cost of being derided as credulous and superstitious, want to push on into those misty and probably perilous places. I felt that I could be of more use by setting out without compass or knapsack into the mists than by sitting in a cage like a canary and chirping about what was known. Besides, teaching is very bad for a man who knows himself only to be a learner: you only need to be a self-conceited ass to teach.'

Here, then, in Francis Urcombe, was a delightful neighbour to one who, like myself, has an uneasy and burning curiosity about what he called the 'misty and perilous places'; and this last spring we had a further and most welcome addition to our pleasant little community, in the person of Mrs Amworth, widow of an Indian civil servant. Her husband had been a judge in the North-West Provinces, and after his death at Peshawar she came back to England, and after a year in London found herself starving for the ampler air and sunshine of the country to take the place of the fogs and griminess of town. She had, too, a special reason for settling in Maxley, since her ancestors up till a hundred years ago had long been native to the place, and in the old churchyard, now disused, are many gravestones bearing her maiden name of Chaston. Big and energetic, her vigorous and genial personality speedily woke Maxley up to a higher degree of sociality than it had ever known. Most of us were bachelors or spinsters or elderly folk not much inclined to exert ourselves in the expense and effort of hospitality, and hitherto the gaiety of a small tea-party, with bridge afterwards and goloshes (when it was wet) to trip home in again for a solitary dinner, was about the climax of our festivities. But Mrs Amworth showed us a more gregarious way, and set an example of luncheon-parties and little dinners, which we began to follow. On other nights when no such hospitality was on foot, a lone man like myself found it pleasant to know that a call on the telephone to Mrs Amworth's house not a hundred yards off, and an enquiry as to whether I might come over after dinner for a game of piquet before bedtime, would probably evoke a response of welcome. There she would be, with a comrade-like eagerness for com-panionship, and there was a glass of port and a cup of coffee and a cigarette and a game of piquet. She played the piano, too, in a free and exuberant manner, and had a charming voice and sang to her own accompani-ment; and as the days grew long and the light lingered late, we played our game in her garden, which in the course of a few months she had turned from being a nursery for slugs and snails into a glowing patch of luxuriant blossoming. She was always cheery and jolly; she was interested in everything, and in music, in gardening, in games of all sorts was a competent performer. Everybody (with one exception) liked her, everybody felt her to bring with her the tonic of a sunny day. That one exception was Francis Urcombe; he, though he confessed he did not like her, acknowledged that he was vastly interested in her. This always seemed strange to me, for pleasant and jovial as she was, I could see nothing in her that could call forth conjecture or intrigued surmise, so healthy and unmysterious a figure did she present. But of the genuineness of Urcombe's interest there could be no doubt; one could see him watching and scrutinising her. In matter of age, she frankly volunteered the information that she was forty-five; but her briskness, her activity, her unravaged skin, her coal-black hair, made it difficult to believe that she was not adopting an unusual device, and adding ten years on to her age instead of subtracting them.

Often, also, as our quite unsentimental friendship ripened, Mrs Amworth would ring me up and propose her advent. If I was busy writing, I was to give her, so we definitely bargained, a frank negative, and in answer I could hear her jolly laugh and her wishes for a successful evening of work. Sometimes, before her proposal arrived, Urcombe would already have stepped across from his house opposite for a smoke and a chat, and he, hearing who my intending visitor was, always urged me to beg her to come. She and I should play our piquet, said he, and he would look on, if we did not object, and learn something of the game. But I doubt whether he paid much attention to it, for nothing could be clearer than that, under that penthouse of forehead and thick eyebrows, his attention was fixed not on the cards, but on one of the players. But he seemed to enjoy an hour spent thus, and often, until one particular evening in July, he would watch her with the air of a man who has some deep problem in front of him. She, enthusiastically keen about our game, seemed not to notice his scrutiny. Then came that evening, when, as I see in the light of subsequent events, began the first twitching of the veil that hid the secret horror from my eyes. I did not know it then, though I noticed that thereafter, if she rang up to propose coming round, she always asked not only if I was at leisure, but whether Mr Urcombe was with me. If so, she said, she would not spoil the chat of two old bachelors, and laughingly wished me good-night.

Urcombe, on this occasion, had been with me for some half-hour before Mrs Amworth's appearance, and had been talking to me about the medieval beliefs concerning vampirism, one of those borderland subjects which he declared had not been sufficiently studied before it had been consigned by the medical profession to the dust-heap of exploded super-stitions. There he sat, grim and eager, tracing, with that pellucid clearness which had made him in his Cambridge days so admirable a lecturer, the history of those mysterious visitations. In them all there were the same general features: one of those ghoulish spirits took up its abode in a living man or woman, conferring supernatural powers of bat-like flight and glutting itself with nocturnal blood-feasts. When its host died it continued to dwell in the corpse, which remained undecayed. By day it rested, by night it left the grave and went on its awful errands. No European country in the Middle Ages seemed to have escaped them; earlier yet, parallels were to be found, in Roman and Greek and in Jewish history.

'It's a large order to set all that evidence aside as being moonshine,' he said. 'Hundreds of totally in-dependent witnesses in many ages have testified to the occurrence of these phenomena, and there's no explanation known to me which covers all the facts. And if you feel inclined to say, "Why, then, if these are facts, do we not come across them now?" there are two answers I can make you. One is that there were diseases known in the Middle Ages, such as the black death, which were certainly existent then and which have become extinct since, but for that reason we do not assert that such diseases never existed. Just as the black death visited England and decimated the population of Norfolk, so here in this very district about three hundred years ago there was certainly an outbreak of vampirism, and Maxley was the centre of it. My second answer is even more convincing, for I tell you that vampirism is by no means extinct now. An outbreak of it certainly occurred in India a year or two ago.'

At that moment I heard my knocker plied in the cheerful and peremptory manner in which Mrs Amworth is accustomed to announce her arrival, and I went to the door to open it.

'Come in at once,' I said, 'and save me from having my blood curdled. Mr Urcombe has been trying to alarm me.'

Instantly her vital, voluminous presence seemed to fill the room.

'Ah, but how lovely!' she said. 'I delight in having my blood curdled. Go on with your ghost-story, Mr Urcombe. I adore ghost-stories.'

I saw that, as his habit was, he was intently observing her.

'It wasn't a ghost-story exactly,' said he. 'I was only telling our host how vampirism was not extinct yet. I was saying that there was an outbreak of it in India only a few years ago.'

There was a more than perceptible pause, and I saw that, if Urcombe was observing her, she on her side was observing him with fixed eye and parted mouth. Then her jolly laugh invaded that rather tense silence.

'Oh, what a shame!' she said. 'You're not going to curdle my blood at all. Where did you pick up such a tale, Mr Urcombe? I have lived for years in India and never heard a rumour of such a thing. Some story-teller in the bazaars must have invented it: they are famous at that.'

I could see that Urcombe was on the point of saying something further, but checked himself.

'Ah! very likely that was it,' he said.

But something had disturbed our usual peaceful sociability that night, and something had damped Mrs Amworth's usual high spirits. She had no gusto for her piquet, and left after a couple of games. Urcombe had been silent too, indeed he hardly spoke again till she departed.

'That was unfortunate,' he said, 'for the outbreak of – of a very mysterious disease, let us call it, took place at Peshawar, where she and her husband were. And – '

'Well?' I asked.

'He was one of the victims of it,' said he. 'Naturally I had quite forgotten that when I spoke.'

The summer was unreasonably hot and rainless, and Maxley suffered much from drought, and also from a plague of big black night-flying gnats, the bite of which was very irritating and virulent. They came sailing in of an evening, settling on one's skin so quietly that one perceived nothing till the sharp stab announced that one had been bitten. They did not bite the hands or face, but chose always the neck and throat for their feeding-ground, and most of us, as the poison spread,

assumed a temporary goitre. Then about the middle
of August appeared the first of those mysterious cases
of illness which our local doctor attributed to the
long-continued heat coupled with the bite of these
venomous insects. The patient was a boy of sixteen or
seventeen, the son of Mrs Amworth's gardener, and
the symptoms were an anaemic pallor and a languid
prostration, accompanied by great drowsiness and an
abnormal appetite. He had, too, on his throat two
small punctures where, so Dr Ross conjectured, one
of these great gnats had bitten him. But the odd thing
was that there was no swelling or inflammation round
the place where he had been bitten. The heat at this
time had begun to abate, but the cooler weather failed
to restore him, and the boy, in spite of the quantity of
good food which he so ravenously swallowed, wasted
away to a skin-clad skeleton.

I met Dr Ross in the street one afternoon about
this time, and in answer to my enquiries about his
patient he said that he was afraid the boy was dying.
The case, he confessed, completely puzzled him: some
obscure form of pernicious anaemia was all he could
suggest. But he wondered whether Mr Urcombe
would consent to see the boy, on the chance of his
being able to throw some new light on the case, and
since Urcombe was dining with me that night, I
proposed to Dr Ross to join us. He could not do this,
but said he would look in later. When he came,
Urcombe at once consented to put his skill at the
other's disposal, and together they went off at once.
Being thus shorn of my sociable evening, I telephoned
to Mrs Amworth to know if I might inflict myself
on her for an hour. Her answer was a welcoming
affirmative, and between piquet and music the hour

lengthened itself into two. She spoke of the boy who was lying so desperately and mysteriously ill, and told me that she had often been to see him, taking him nourishing and delicate food. But today – and her kind eyes moistened as she spoke – she was afraid she had paid her last visit. Knowing the antipathy between her and Urcombe, I did not tell her that he had been called into consultation; and when I returned home she accompanied me to my door, for the sake of a breath of night air, and in order to borrow a magazine which contained an article on gardening which she wished to read.

'Ah, this delicious night air,' she said, luxuriously sniffing in the coolness. 'Night air and gardening are the great tonics. There is nothing so stimulating as bare contact with rich mother earth. You are never so fresh as when you have been grubbing in the soil – black hands, black nails, and boots covered with mud.' She gave her great jovial laugh.

'I'm a glutton for air and earth,' she said. 'Positively I look forward to death, for then I shall be buried and have the kind earth all round me. No leaden caskets for me – I have given explicit directions. But what shall I do about air? Well, I suppose one can't have everything. The magazine? A thousand thanks, I will faithfully return it. Good-night: garden and keep your windows open, and you won't have anaemia.'

'I always sleep with my windows open,' said I.

I went straight up to my bedroom, of which one of the windows looks out over the street, and as I undressed I thought I heard voices talking outside not far away. But I paid no particular attention, put out my lights, and falling asleep plunged into the depths of a most horrible dream, distortedly suggested no doubt, by my last words with Mrs Amworth. I dreamed that I woke, and found that both my bedroom windows were shut. Half-suffocating I dreamed that I sprang out of bed, and went across to open them. The blind over the first was drawn down, and pulling it up I saw, with the indescribable horror of incipient nightmare, Mrs Amworth's face suspended close to the pane in the darkness outside, nodding and smiling at me. Pulling down the blind again to keep that terror out, I rushed to the second window on the other side of the room, and there again was Mrs Amworth's face. Then the panic came upon me in full blast; here was I suffocating in the airless room, and whichever window I opened Mrs Amworth's face would float in, like those noiseless black gnats that bit before one was aware. The nightmare rose to screaming point, and with strangled yells I awoke to find my room cool and quiet with both windows open and blinds up and a half-moon high in its course, casting an oblong of tranquil light on the floor. But even when I was awake the horror persisted, and I lay tossing and turning. I must have slept long before the nightmare seized me, for now it was nearly day, and soon in the east the drowsy eyelids of morning began to lift.

I was scarcely downstairs next morning – for after the dawn I slept late – when Urcombe rang up to know if he might see me immediately. He came in, grim and preoccupied, and I noticed that he was pulling on a pipe that was not even filled.

'I want your help,' he said, 'and so I must tell you first of all what happened last night. I went round with the little doctor to see his patient, and found him just alive, but scarcely more. I instantly diagnosed in my own mind what this anaemia, unaccountable by any other explanation, meant. The boy is the prey of a vampire.'

He put his empty pipe on the breakfast-table, by which I had just sat down, and folded his arms, looking at me steadily from under his overhanging brows.

'Now about last night,' he said. 'I insisted that he should be moved from his father's cottage into my house. As we were carrying him on a stretcher, whom should we meet but Mrs Amworth? She expressed shocked surprise that we were moving him. Now why do you think she did that?'

With a start of horror, as I remembered my dream that night before, I felt an idea come into my mind so preposterous and unthinkable that I instantly turned it out again.

'I haven't the smallest idea,' I said.

'Then listen, while I tell you about what happened later. I put out all light in the room where the boy lay, and watched. One window was a little open, for I had forgotten to close it, and about midnight I heard something outside, trying apparently to push it farther open. I guessed who it was – yes, it was full twenty feet from the ground – and I peeped round the corner of the blind. Just outside was the face of Mrs Amworth and her hand was on the frame of the window. Very softly I crept close, and then banged the window down, and I think I just caught the tip of one of her fingers.'

'But it's impossible,' I cried. 'How could she be floating in the air like that? And what had she come for? Don't tell me such – '

Once more, with closer grip, the remembrance of my nightmare seized me.

'I am telling you what I saw,' said he. 'And all night long, until it was nearly day, she was fluttering outside, like some terrible bat, trying to gain admittance. Now put together various things I have told you.'

He began checking them off on his fingers.

'Number one,' he said: 'there was an outbreak of disease similar to that which this boy is suffering from at Peshawar, and her husband died of it. Number two: Mrs Amworth protested against my moving the boy to my house. Number three: she, or the demon that inhabits her body, a creature powerful and deadly, tries to gain admittance. And add this, too: in medieval times there was an epidemic of vampirism here at Maxley. The vampire, so the accounts run, was found to be Elizabeth Chaston . . . I see you remember Mrs Amworth's maiden name. Finally, the boy is stronger this morning. He would certainly not have been alive if he had been visited again. And what do you make of it?'

There was a long silence, during which I found this incredible horror assuming the hues of reality.

'I have something to add,' I said, 'which may or may not bear on it. You say that the – the spectre went away shortly before dawn.'

'Yes.'

I told him of my dream, and he smiled grimly.

'Yes, you did well to awake,' he said. 'That warning came from your subconscious self, which never wholly slumbers, and cried out to you of deadly danger. For two reasons, then, you must help me: one to save others, the second to save yourself.'

'What do you want me to do?' I asked.

'I want you first of all to help me in watching this boy, and ensuring that she does not come near him.

Eventually I want you to help me in tracking the thing down, in exposing and destroying it. It is not human: it is an incarnate fiend. What steps we shall have to take I don't yet know.'

It was now eleven of the forenoon, and presently I went across to his house for a twelve-hour vigil while he slept, to come on duty again that night, so that for the next twenty-four hours either Urcombe or myself was always in the room where the boy, now getting stronger every hour, was lying. The day following was Saturday and a morning of brilliant, pellucid weather, and already when I went across to his house to resume my duty the stream of motors down to Brighton had begun. Simultaneously I saw Urcombe with a cheerful face, which boded good news of his patient, coming out of his house, and Mrs Amworth, with a gesture of salutation to me and a basket in her hand, walking up the broad strip of grass which bordered the road. There we all three met. I noticed (and saw that Urcombe noticed it too) that one finger of her left hand was bandaged.

'Good-morning to you both,' said she. 'And I hear your patient is doing well, Mr Urcombe. I have come to bring him a bowl of jelly, and to sit with him for an hour. He and I are great friends. I am overjoyed at his recovery.'

Urcombe paused a moment, as if making up his mind, and then shot out a pointing finger at her.

'I forbid that,' he said. 'You shall not sit with him or see him. And you know the reason as well as I do.'

I have never seen so horrible a change pass over a human face as that which now blanched hers to the colour of a grey mist. She put up her hand as if to shield herself from that pointing finger, which drew the sign of the cross in the air, and shrank back cowering on to the road. There was a wild hoot from a horn, a grinding of brakes, a shout – too late – from a passing car, and one long scream suddenly cut short. Her body rebounded from the roadway after the first wheel had gone over it, and the second followed. It lay there, quivering and twitching, and was still.

She was buried three days afterwards in the cemetery outside Maxley, in accordance with the wishes she had told me that she had devised about her interment, and the shock which her sudden and awful death had caused to the little community began by degrees to pass off. To two people only, Urcombe and myself, the horror of it was mitigated from the first by the nature of the relief that her death brought; but, naturally enough, we kept our own counsel, and no hint of what greater horror had been thus averted was ever let slip. But, oddly enough, so it seemed to me, he was still not satisfied about something in con-nection with her, and would give no answer to my questions on the subject. Then as the days of a tranquil mellow September and the October that followed began to drop away like the leaves of the yellowing trees, his uneasiness relaxed. But before the entry of November the seeming tranquillity broke into hurricane.

I had been dining one night at the far end of the village, and about eleven o'clock was walking home again. The moon was of an unusual brilliance, rendering all that it shone on as distinct as in some etching. I had just come opposite the house which Mrs Amworth had occupied, where there was a board up telling that it was to let, when I heard the click of her front gate, and next moment I saw, with a sudden chill and quaking of my very spirit, that she stood there. Her profile, vividly illuminated, was turned to me, and I could not be mistaken in my identification of her. She appeared not to see me (indeed the shadow of the yew hedge in front of her garden enveloped me in its blackness) and she went swiftly across the road, and entered the gate of the house directly opposite. There I lost sight of her completely.

My breath was coming in short pants as if I had been running – and now indeed I ran, with fearful backward glances, along the hundred yards that separated me from my house and Urcombe's. It was to his that my flying steps took me, and next minute I was within.

'What have you come to tell me?' he asked. 'Or shall I guess?'

'You can't guess,' said I.

'No; it's no guess. She has come back and you have seen her. Tell me about it.'

I gave him my story.

'That's Major Pearsall's house,' he said. 'Come back with me there at once.'

'But what can we do?' I asked.

'I've no idea. That's what we have got to find out.'

A minute later, we were opposite the house. When I had passed it before, it was all dark; now lights gleamed from a couple of windows upstairs. Even as we faced it, the front door opened, and next moment Major Pearsall emerged from the gate. He saw us and stopped.

'I'm on my way to Dr Ross,' he said quickly. 'My wife has been taken suddenly ill. She had been in bed an hour when I came upstairs, and I found her white as a ghost and utterly exhausted. She had been to sleep, it seemed – but you will excuse me.'

'One moment, Major,' said Urcombe. 'Was there any mark on her throat?'

'How did you guess that?' said he. 'There was: one of those beastly gnats must have bitten her twice there. She was streaming with blood.'

'And there's someone with her?' asked Urcombe.

'Yes, I roused her maid.'

He went off, and Urcombe turned to me. 'I know now what we have to do,' he said. 'Change your clothes, and I'll join you at your house.'

'What is it?' I asked.

'I'll tell you on our way. We're going to the cemetery.'

He carried a pick, a shovel, and a screwdriver when he rejoined me, and wore round his shoulders a long coil of rope. As we walked, he gave me the outlines of the ghastly hour that lay before us.

'What I have to tell you,' he said, 'will seem to you now too fantastic for credence, but before dawn we shall see whether it outstrips reality. By a most fortunate happening, you saw the spectre, the astral body, whatever you choose to call it, of Mrs Amworth, going on its grisly business, and therefore, beyond doubt, the vampire spirit which abode in her during life animates her again in death. That is not exceptional – indeed, all these weeks since her death I have been expecting it. If I am right, we shall find her body undecayed and untouched by corruption.'

'But she has been dead nearly two months,' said I.

'If she had been dead two years it would still be so, if the vampire has possession of her. So remember:

whatever you see done, it will be done not to her, who in the natural course would now be feeding the grasses above her grave, but to a spirit of untold evil and malignancy, which gives a phantom life to her body.'

'But what shall I see done?' said I.

'I will tell you. We know that now, at this moment, the vampire clad in her mortal semblance is out; dining out. But it must get back before dawn, and it will pass into the material form that lies in her grave. We must wait for that, and then with your help I shall dig up her body. If I am right, you will look on her as she was in life, with the full vigour of the dreadful nutriment she has received pulsing in her veins. And then, when dawn has come, and the vampire cannot leave the lair of her body, I shall strike her with this' – and he pointed to his pick – 'through the heart, and she, who comes to life again only with the animation the fiend gives her, she and her hellish partner will be dead indeed. Then we must bury her again, delivered at last.'

We had come to the cemetery, and in the brightness of the moonshine there was no difficulty in identifying her grave. It lay some twenty yards from the small chapel, in the porch of which, obscured by shadow, we concealed ourselves. From there we had a clear and open sight of the grave, and now we must wait till its infernal visitor returned home. The night was warm and windless, yet even if a freezing wind had been raging I think I should have felt nothing of it, so intense was my preoccupation as to what the night and dawn would bring. There was a bell in the turret of the chapel, that struck the quarters of the hour, and it amazed me to find how swiftly the chimes succeeded one another.

42

The moon had long set, but a twilight of stars shone in a clear sky, when five o'clock of the morning sounded from the turret. A few minutes more passed, and then I felt Urcombe's hand softly nudging me; and looking out in the direction of his pointing finger, I saw that the form of a woman, tall and large in build, was approaching from the right. Noiselessly, with a motion more of gliding and floating than walking, she moved across the cemetery to the grave which was the centre of our observation. She moved round it as if to be certain of its identity, and for a moment stood directly facing us. In the greyness to which now my eyes had grown accustomed, I could easily see her face, and recognise its features.

She drew her hand across her mouth as if wiping it, and broke into a chuckle of such laughter as made my hair stir on my head. Then she leaped on to the grave, holding her hands high above her head, and inch by inch disappeared into the earth. Urcombe's hand was laid on my arm, in an injunction to keep still, but now he removed it.

'Come,' he said.

With pick and shovel and rope we went to the grave. The earth was light and sandy, and soon after six struck we had delved down to the coffin lid. With his pick he loosened the earth round it, and, adjusting the rope through the handles by which it had been lowered, we tried to raise it. This was a long and laborious business, and the light had begun to herald day in the east before we had it out, and lying by the side of the grave. With his screwdriver he loosed the fastenings of the lid, and slid it aside, and standing there we looked on the face of Mrs Amworth. The eyes, once closed in death, were open, the cheeks were flushed with colour, the red, full-lipped mouth seemed to smile.

'One blow and it is all over,' he said. 'You need not look.'

Even as he spoke he took up the pick again, and, laying the point of it on her left breast, measured his distance. And though I knew what was coming I could not look away . . .

He grasped the pick in both hands, raised it an inch or two for the taking of his aim, and then with full force brought it down on her breast. A fountain of blood, though she had been dead so long, spouted high in the air, falling with the thud of a heavy splash over the shroud, and simultaneously from those red lips came one long, appalling cry, swelling up like some hooting siren, and dying away again. With that, instantaneous as a lightning flash, came the touch of corruption on her face, the colour of it faded to ash, the plump cheeks fell in, the mouth dropped.

'Thank God, that's over,' said he, and without pause slipped the coffin lid back into its place.

Day was coming fast now, and, working like men possessed, we lowered the coffin into its place again, and shovelled the earth over it . . . The birds were busy with their earliest pipings as we went back to Maxley.

ROBERT LOUIS STEVENSON

Markheim

'Yes,' said the dealer, 'our windfalls are of various kinds. Some customers are ignorant, and then I touch a dividend on my superior knowledge. Some are dishonest,' and here he held up the candle, so that the light fell strongly on his visitor, 'and in that case,' he continued, 'I profit by my virtue.'

Markheim had but just entered from the daylight streets, and his eyes had not yet grown familiar with the mingled shine and darkness in the shop. At these pointed words, and before the near presence of the flame, he blinked painfully and looked aside.

The dealer chuckled. 'You come to see me on Christmas Day,' he resumed, 'when you know that I am alone in my house, put up my shutters, and make a point of refusing business. Well, you will have to pay for that; you will have to pay for my loss of time, when I should be balancing my books; you will have to pay, besides, for a kind of manner that I remark in you today very strongly. I am the essence of discretion, and ask no awkward questions; but when a customer cannot look me in the eye, he has to pay for it.' The dealer once more chuckled; and then, changing to his usual business voice, though still with a note of irony, 'You can give, as usual, a clear account of how you came into the possession of the object?' he continued. 'Still your uncle's cabinet? A remarkable collector, sir!'

And the little pale, round-shouldered dealer stood

almost on tiptoe, looking over the top of his gold spectacles, and nodding his head with every mark of disbelief. Markheim returned his gaze with one of infinite pity, and a touch of horror.

'This time,' said he, 'you are in error. I have not come to sell, but to buy. I have no curios to dispose of; my uncle's cabinet is bare to the wainscot; even were it still intact, I have done well on the Stock Exchange, and should more likely add to it than otherwise, and my errand today is simplicity itself. I seek a Christmas present for a lady,' he continued, waxing more fluent as he struck into the speech he had prepared; 'and certainly I owe you every excuse for thus disturbing you upon so small a matter. But the thing was neglected yesterday; I must produce my little compliment at dinner; and, as you very well know, a rich marriage is not a thing to be neglected.'

There followed a pause, during which the dealer seemed to weigh this statement incredulously. The ticking of many clocks among the curious lumber of the shop, and the faint rushing of the cabs in a near thoroughfare, filled up the interval of silence.

'Well, sir,' said the dealer, 'be it so. You are an old customer after all; and if, as you say, you have the chance of a good marriage, far be it from me to be an obstacle. Here is a nice thing for a lady now,' he went on, 'this hand-glass – fifteenth-century, warranted; comes from a good collection, too; but I reserve the name, in the interests of my customer, who was just like yourself, my dear sir, the nephew and sole heir of a remarkable collector.'

The dealer, while he thus ran on in his dry and biting voice, had stooped to take the object from its place; and, as he had done so, a shock had passed through Markheim, a start both of hand and foot, a sudden leap of many tumultuous passions to the face. It passed as swiftly as it came, and left no trace beyond a certain trembling of the hand that now received the glass.

'A glass,' he said hoarsely, and then paused, and repeated it more clearly. 'A glass? For Christmas? Surely not?'

'And why not?' cried the dealer. 'Why not a glass?'

Markheim was looking upon him with an indefinable expression. 'You ask me why not?' he said. 'Why, look here – look in it – look at yourself! Do you like to see it? No! nor I – nor any man.'

The little man had jumped back when Markheim had so suddenly confronted him with the mirror; but now, perceiving there was nothing worse on hand, he chuckled. 'Your future lady, sir, must be pretty hard favoured,' said he.

'I ask you,' said Markheim, 'for a Christmas present, and you give me this – this damned reminder of years, and sins and follies – this hand-conscience! Did you mean it? Had you a thought in your mind? Tell me. It will be better for you if you do. Come, tell me about yourself. I hazard a guess now, that you are in secret a very charitable man?'

The dealer looked closely at his companion. It was very odd, Markheim did not appear to be laughing; there was something in his face like an eager sparkle of hope, but nothing of mirth.

'What are you driving at?' the dealer asked.

'Not charitable?' returned the other, gloomily. 'Not charitable; not pious; not scrupulous; unloving, unbeloved; a hand to get money, a safe to keep it. Is that all? Dear God, man, is that all?'

'I will tell you what it is,' began the dealer, with some sharpness, and then broke off again into a chuckle. 'But I see this is a love match of yours, and you have been drinking the lady's health.'

'Ah!' cried Markheim, with a strange curiosity. 'Ah, have you been in love? Tell me about that.'

'I,' cried the dealer. 'I in love! I never had the time, nor have I the time today for all this nonsense. Will you take the glass?'

'Where is the hurry?' returned Markheim. 'It is very pleasant to stand here talking; and life is so short and insecure that I would not hurry away from any pleasure – no, not even from so mild a one as this. We should rather cling, cling to what little we can get, like a man at a cliff's edge. Every second is a cliff, if you think upon it – a cliff a mile high – high enough, if we fall, to dash us out of every feature of humanity. Hence it is best to talk pleasantly. Let us talk of each other: why should we wear this mask? Let us be confidential. Who knows, we might become friends?'

'I have just one word to say to you,' said the dealer. 'Either make your purchase, or walk out of my shop!'

'True, true,' said Markheim. 'Enough fooling. To business. Show me something else.'

The dealer stooped once more, this time to replace the glass upon the shelf, his thin blond hair falling over his eyes as he did so. Markheim moved a little nearer, with one hand in the pocket of his greatcoat; he drew himself up and filled his lungs; at the same time many different emotions were depicted together on his face – terror, horror, and resolve, fascination and a physical repulsion; and through a haggard lift of his upper lip, his teeth looked out.

'This, perhaps, may suit,' observed the dealer. And

then, as he began to re-arise, Markheim bounded from behind upon his victim. The long, skewer-like dagger flashed and fell. The dealer struggled like a hen, striking his temple on the shelf, and then tumbled on the floor in a heap.

Time had some score of small voices in that shop – some stately and slow as was becoming to their great age; others garrulous and hurried. All these told out the seconds in an intricate chorus of tickings. Then the passage of a lad's feet, heavily running on the pavement, broke in upon these smaller voices and startled Markheim into the consciousness of his sur- roundings. He looked about him awfully. The candle stood on the counter, its flame solemnly wagging in a draught; and by that inconsiderable movement the whole room was filled with noiseless bustle and kept heaving like a sea; the tall shadows nodding, the gross blots of darkness swelling and dwindling as with respiration, the faces of the portraits and the china gods changing and wavering like images in water. The inner door stood ajar, and peered into that leaguer of shadows with a long slit of daylight like a pointing finger.

From these fear-stricken rovings, Markheim's eyes returned to the body of his victim, where it lay, both humped and sprawling, incredibly small and strangely meaner than in life. In these poor, miserly clothes, in that ungainly attitude, the dealer lay like so much sawdust. Markheim had feared to see it, and, lo! it was nothing. And yet, as he gazed, this bundle of old clothes and pool of blood began to find eloquent voices. There it must lie; there was none to work the cunning hinges or direct the miracle of locomotion – there it must lie till it was found. Found! ay, and then? Then would this dead flesh lift up a cry that would ring over England, and fill the world with the echoes of pursuit. Ay, dead or not, this was still the enemy. 'Time was that when the brains were out,' he thought; and the first word struck into his mind. Time, now that the deed was accomplished – time, which had closed for the victim, had become instant and momentous for the slayer.

The thought was yet in his mind, when, first one and then another, with every variety of pace and voice – one deep as the bell from a cathedral turret, another ringing on its treble notes the prelude of a waltz – the clocks began to strike the hour of three in the afternoon.

The sudden outbreak of so many tongues in that dumb chamber staggered him. He began to bestir himself, going to and fro with the candle, beleaguered by moving shadows, and startled to the soul by chance reflections. In many rich mirrors, some of home design, some from Venice or Amsterdam, he saw his face repeated and repeated, as it were an army of spies; his own eyes met and detected him; and the sound of his own steps, lightly as they fell, vexed the surrounding quiet. And still, as he continued to fill his pockets, his mind accused him with a sickening iteration of the thousand faults of his design. He should have chosen a more quiet hour; he should have prepared an alibi; he should not have used a knife; he should have been more cautious, and only bound and gagged the dealer, and not killed him; he should have been more bold, and killed the servant also; he should have done all things other-wise. Poignant regrets, weary, incessant toiling of the mind to change what was unchangeable, to plan what was now useless, to be the architect of the irrevocable past. Meanwhile, and behind all this activity, brute terrors, like the scurrying of rats in a deserted attic, filled the more remote chambers of his brain with riot; the hand of the constable would fall heavy on his shoulder, and his nerves would jerk like a hooked fish; or he beheld, in galloping defile, the dock, the prison, the gallows, and the black coffin.

Terror of the people in the street sat down before his mind like a besieging army. It was impossible, he thought, but that some rumour of the struggle must have reached their ears and set on edge their curiosity; and now, in all the neighbouring houses, he divined them sitting motionless and with uplifted ear – solitary people, condemned to spend Christmas dwelling alone on memories of the past, and now startingly recalled from that tender exercise; happy family parties struck into silence round the table, the mother still with raised finger – every degree and age and humour, but all, by their own hearths, prying and hearkening and weaving the rope that was to hang him. Sometimes it seemed to him he could not move too softly; the clink of the tall Bohemian goblets rang out loudly like a bell; and alarmed by the bigness of the ticking, he was tempted to stop the clocks. And then, again, with a swift transition of his terrors, the very silence of the place appeared a source of peril, and a thing to strike and freeze the passer-by; and he would step more boldly, and bustle aloud among the contents of the shop, and imitate, with elaborate bravado, the movements of a busy man at ease in his own house.

But he was now so pulled about by different alarms that, while one portion of his mind was still alert and cunning, another trembled on the brink of lunacy.

One hallucination in particular took a strong hold on his credulity. The neighbour hearkening with white face beside his window, the passer-by arrested by a horrible surmise on the pavement – these could at worst suspect, they could not know; through the brick walls and shuttered windows only sounds could penetrate. But here, within the house, was he alone? He knew he was; he had watched the servant set forth sweethearting, in her poor best, 'out for the day' written in every ribbon and smile. Yes, he was alone, of course; and yet, in the bulk of empty house above him, he could surely hear a stir of delicate footing; he was surely conscious, inexplicably conscious of some presence. Ay, surely; to every room and corner of the house his imagination followed it; and now it was a faceless thing, and yet had eyes to see with; and again it was a shadow of himself; and yet again behold the image of the dead dealer, re-inspired with cunning and hatred.

At times, with a strong effort, he would glance at the open door which still seemed to repel his eyes. The house was tall, the skylight small and dirty, the day blind with fog; and the light that filtered down to the ground storey was exceedingly faint, and showed dimly on the threshold of the shop. And yet, in that strip of doubtful brightness, did there not hang wavering a shadow?

Suddenly, from the street outside, a very jovial gentleman began to beat with a staff on the shop door, accompanying his blows with shouts and railleries in which the dealer was continually called upon by name. Markheim, smitten into ice, glanced at the dead man. But no! he lay quite still; he was fled away far beyond earshot of these blows and shoutings;

he was sunk beneath seas of silence; and his name, which would once have caught his notice above the howling of a storm, had become an empty sound. And presently the jovial gentleman desisted from his knocking and departed.

Here was a broad hint to hurry what remained to be done, to get forth from this accusing neighbourhood, to plunge into a bath of London multitudes, and to reach, on the other side of day, that haven of safety and apparent innocence – his bed. One visitor had come; at any moment another might follow and be more obstinate. To have done the deed, and yet not to reap the profit, would be too abhorrent a failure. The money – that was now Markheim's concern; and as a means to that, the keys.

He glanced over his shoulder at the open door, where the shadow was still lingering and shivering; and with no conscious repugnance of the mind, yet with a tremor of the belly, he drew near the body of his victim. The human character had quite departed. Like a suit half stuffed with bran, the limbs lay scattered, the trunk doubled, on the floor; and yet the thing repelled him. Although so dingy and inconsiderable to the eye, he feared it might have more significance to the touch. He took the body by the shoulders, and turned it on its back. It was strangely light and supple, and the limbs, as if they had been broken, fell into the oddest postures. The face was robbed of all expression; but it was as pale as wax, and shockingly smeared with blood about one temple. That was, for Markheim, the one displeasing circumstance. It carried him back, upon the instant, to a certain fair-day in a fishers' village: a grey day, a piping wind, a crowd upon the street, the blare of brasses, the booming of drums,

the nasal voice of a ballad singer; and a boy going to
and fro, buried over head in the crowd and divided
between interest and fear, until, coming out upon
the chief place of concourse, he beheld a booth
and a great screen with pictures, dismally designed,
garishly coloured – Brownrigg with her apprentice,
the Mannings with their murdered guest, Weare in
the death-grip of Thurtell, and a score besides of
famous crimes. The thing was as clear as an illusion;
he was once again that little boy; he was looking
once again, and with the same sense of physical
revolt, at these vile pictures; he was still stunned by
the thumping of the drums. A bar of that day's music
returned upon his memory; and at that, for the first
time, a qualm came over him, a breath of nausea,
a sudden weakness of the joints, which he must
instantly resist and conquer.

He judged it more prudent to confront than to flee
from these considerations, looking the more hardily
in the dead face, bending his mind to realise the
nature and greatness of his crime. So little a while ago
that face had moved with every change of sentiment,
that pale mouth had spoken, that body had been all
on fire with governable energies; and now, and by his
act, that piece of life had been arrested, as the horol-
ogist, with interjected finger, arrests the beating of the
clock. So he reasoned in vain; he could rise to no
more remorseful consciousness; the same heart which
had shuddered before the painted effigies of crime,
looked on its reality unmoved. At best, he felt a gleam
of pity for one who had been endowed in vain with all
those faculties that can make the world a garden of
enchantment, one who had never lived and who was
now dead. But of penitence, no, not a tremor.

With that, shaking himself clear of these considerations, he found the keys and advanced towards the
open door of the shop. Outside, it had begun to rain
smartly, and the sound of the shower upon the roof
had banished silence. Like some dripping cavern, the
chambers of the house were haunted by an incessant
echoing, which filled the ear and mingled with the
ticking of the clocks. And, as Markheim approached
the door, he seemed to hear, in answer to his own
cautious tread, the steps of another foot withdrawing
up the stair. The shadow still palpitated loosely on
the threshold. He threw a ton's weight of resolve upon
his muscles, and drew back the door.

The faint, foggy daylight glimmered dimly on the
bare floor and stairs; on the bright suit of armour
posted, halbert in hand, upon the landing; and on the
dark wood-carvings, and framed pictures that hung
against the yellow panels of the wainscot. So loud was
the beating of the rain through all the house that, in
Markheim's ears, it began to be distinguished into
many different sounds. Footsteps and sighs, the tread
of regiments marching in the distance, the chink of
money in the counting, and the creaking of doors
held stealthily ajar, appeared to mingle with the patter
of the drops upon the cupola and the gushing of the
water in the pipes. The sense that he was not alone
grew upon him to the verge of madness. On every
side he was haunted and begirt by presences. He
heard them moving in the upper chambers; from the
shop, he heard the dead man getting to his legs; and
as he began with a great effort to mount the stairs,
feet fled quietly before him and followed stealthily
behind. If he were but deaf, he thought, how tran-
quilly he would possess his soul! And then again, and

hearkening with ever fresh attention, he blessed himself for that unresting sense which held the outposts and stood a trusty sentinel upon his life. His head turned continually on his neck; his eyes, which seemed starting from their orbits, scouted on every side, and on every side were half rewarded as with the tail of something nameless vanishing. The four and twenty steps to the first floor were four and twenty agonies.

On that first storey, the doors stood ajar – three of them, like three ambushes, shaking his nerves like the throats of cannon. He could never again, he felt, be sufficiently immured and fortified from men's observing eyes; he longed to be home, girt in by walls, buried among bedclothes, and invisible to all but God. And at that thought he wondered a little, recollecting tales of other murderers and the fear they were said to entertain of heavenly avengers. It was not so, at least, with him. He feared the laws of nature, lest, in their callous and immutable procedure, they should preserve some damning evidence of his crime. He feared tenfold more, with a slavish, superstitious terror, some scission in the continuity of man's experience, some wilful illegality of nature. He played a game of skill, depending on the rules, calculating consequence from cause; and what if nature, as the defeated tyrant overthrew the chessboard, should break the mould of their succession? The like had befallen Napoleon (so writers said) when the winter changed the time of its appearance. The like might befall Markheim: the solid walls might become transparent and reveal his doings like those of bees in a glass hive; the stout planks might yield under his foot like quicksands and detain him in their clutch. Ay, and there were soberer accidents that might destroy him; if, for instance, the house should fall and imprison him beside the body of his victim, or the house next door should fly on fire, and the firemen invade him from all sides. These things he feared; and, in a sense, these things might be called the hands of God reached forth against sin. But about God himself he was at ease; his act was doubtless exceptional, but so were his excuses, which God knew; it was there, and not among men, that he felt sure of justice.

When he had got safe into the drawing-room, and shut the door behind him, he was aware of a respite from alarms. The room was quite dismantled, uncarpeted besides, and strewn with packing-cases and incongruous furniture; several great pier-glasses, in which he beheld himself at various angles, like an actor on a stage; many pictures, framed and unframed, standing, with their faces to the wall; a fine Sheraton sideboard, a cabinet of marquetry, and a great old bed, with tapestry hangings. The windows opened to the floor; but by great good fortune the lower part of the shutters had been closed, and this concealed him from the neighbours. Here, then, Markheim drew in a packing-case before the cabinet, and began to search among the keys. It was a long business, for there were many; and it was irksome, besides; for, after all, there might be nothing in the cabinet, and time was on the wing. But the closeness of the occupation sobered him. With the tail of his eye he saw the door – even glanced at it from time to time directly, like a besieged commander pleased to verify the good estate of his defences. But in truth he was at peace. The rain falling in the street sounded natural and pleasant. Presently, on the other side, the notes of a piano were wakened to the music of a hymn, and the voices of many children took up the air and words. How stately, how comfortable was the melody! How fresh the youthful voices! Markheim gave ear to it smilingly, as he sorted out the keys; and his mind was thronged with answerable ideas and images: church-going children, and the pealing of the high organ; children afield, bathers by the brookside, ramblers on the brambly common, kite-flyers in the windy and cloud-navigated sky; and then, at another cadence of the hymn, back again to church, and the somnolence of summer Sundays, and the high genteel voice of the parson (which he smiled a little to recall) and the painted Jacobean tombs, and the dim lettering of the Ten Commandments in the chancel.

And as he sat thus, at once busy and absent, he was startled to his feet. A flash of ice, a flash of fire, a bursting gush of blood, went over him, and then he stood transfixed and thrilling. A step mounted the stair slowly and steadily, and presently a hand was laid upon the knob, and the lock clicked, and the door opened.

Fear held Markheim in a vice. What to expect he knew not – whether the dead man walking, or the official ministers of human justice, or some chance witness blindly stumbling in to consign him to the gallows. But when a face was thrust into the aperture, glanced round the room, looked at him, nodded and smiled as if in friendly recognition, and then withdrew again, and the door closed behind it, his fear broke loose from his control in a hoarse cry. At the sound of this the visitant returned.

'Did you call me?' he asked, pleasantly, and with that he entered the room and closed the door behind him.

Markheim stood and gazed at him with all his eyes. Perhaps there was a film upon his sight, but the out-lines of the newcomer seemed to change and waver like those of the idols in the wavering candlelight of the shop; and at times he thought he knew him; and at times he thought he bore a likeness to himself; and always, like a lump of living terror, there lay in his bosom the conviction that this thing was not of the earth and not of God.

And yet the creature had a strange air of the commonplace, as he stood looking on Markheim with a smile; and when he added, 'You are looking for the money, I believe?' it was in the tones of everyday politeness.

Markheim made no answer.

'I should warn you,' resumed the other, 'that the maid has left her sweetheart earlier than usual and will soon be here. If Mr Markheim be found in this house, I need not describe to him the consequences.'

'You know me?' cried the murderer.

The visitor smiled. 'You have long been a favourite of mine,' he said; 'and I have long observed and often sought to help you.'

'What are you?' cried Markheim: 'the devil?'

'What I may be,' returned the other, 'cannot affect the service I propose to render you.'

'It can,' cried Markheim; 'it does! Be helped by you? No, never; not by you! You do not know me yet; thank God, you do not know me!'

'I know you,' replied the visitant, with a sort of kind severity or rather firmness. 'I know you to the soul.'

'Know me!' cried Markheim. 'Who can do so? My life is but a travesty and slander on myself. I have lived to belie my nature. All men do; all men are better than this disguise that grows about and stifles them. You see each dragged away by life, like one whom braves have seized and muffled in a cloak. If they had their own control – if you could see their faces, they would be altogether different, they would shine out for heroes and saints! I am worse than most; my self is more overlaid; my excuse is known to me and God. But, had I the time, I could disclose myself.'

'To me?' enquired the visitant.

'To you before all,' returned the murderer. 'I supposed you were intelligent. I thought – since you exist – you would prove a reader of the heart. And yet you would propose to judge me by my acts! Think of it – my acts! I was born and I have lived in a land of giants; giants have dragged me by the wrists since I was born out of my mother – the giants of circumstance. And you would judge me by my acts! But can you not look within? Can you not understand that evil is hateful to me? Can you not see within me the clear writing of conscience, never blurred by any wilful sophistry, although too often disregarded? Can you not read me for a thing that surely must be common as humanity – the unwilling sinner?'

'All this is very feelingly expressed,' was the reply, 'but it regards me not. These points of consistency are beyond my province, and I care not in the least by what compulsion you may have been dragged away, so as you are but carried in the right direction. But time flies; the servant delays, looking in the faces of the crowd and at the pictures on the hoardings, but still she keeps moving nearer; and remember, it is as if the gallows itself was striding towards you through the Christmas streets! Shall I help you – I, who know all? Shall I tell you where to find the money?'

'For what price?' asked Markheim.

'I offer you the service for a Christmas gift,' returned the other.

Markheim could not refrain from smiling with a kind of bitter triumph. 'No,' said he, 'I will take nothing at your hands; if I were dying of thirst, and it was your hand that put the pitcher to my lips, I should find the courage to refuse. It may be credulous, but I will do nothing to commit myself to evil.'

'I have no objection to a deathbed repentance,' observed the visitant.

'Because you disbelieve their efficacy!' Markheim cried.

'I do not say so,' returned the other; 'but I look on these things from a different side, and when the life is done my interest falls. The man has lived to serve me, to spread black looks under colour of religion, or to sow tares in the wheat-field, as you do, in a course of weak compliance with desire. Now that he draws so near to his deliverance, he can add but one act of service: to repent, to die smiling, and thus to build up in confidence and hope the more timorous of my surviving followers. I am not so hard a master. Try me; accept my help. Please yourself in life as you have done hitherto; please yourself more amply, spread your elbows at the board; and when the night begins to fall and the curtains to be drawn, I tell you, for your greater comfort, that you will find it even easy to compound your quarrel with your conscience, and to make a truckling peace with God. I came but now from such a deathbed, and the room was full of sincere mourners, listening to the man's last words; and when

I looked into that face, which had been set as a flint against mercy, I found it smiling with hope.'

'And do you, then, suppose me such a creature?' asked Markheim. 'Do you think I have no more generous aspirations than to sin, and sin, and sin, and at last sneak into heaven? My heart rises at the thought. Is this, then, your experience of mankind? or is it because you find me with red hands that you presume such baseness? And is this crime of murder indeed so impious as to dry up the very springs of good?'

'Murder is to me no special category,' replied the other. 'All sins are murder, even as all life is war. I behold your race, like starving mariners on a raft, plucking crusts out of the hands of famine and feeding on each other's lives. I follow sins beyond the moment of their acting; I find in all that the last consequence is death, and to my eyes, the pretty maid who thwarts her mother with such taking graces on a question of a ball, drips no less visibly with human gore than such a murderer as yourself. Do I say that I follow sins? I follow virtues also. They differ not by the thickness of a nail; they are both scythes for the reaping angel of Death. Evil, for which I live, consists not in action but in character. The bad man is dear to me, not the bad act, whose fruits, if we could follow them far enough down the hurtling cataract of the ages, might yet be found more blessed than those of the rarest virtues. And it is not because you have killed a dealer, but because you are Markheim, that I offer to forward your escape.'

'I will lay my heart open to you,' answered Markheim. 'This crime on which you find me is my last. On my way to it I have learned many lessons; itself is a lesson – a momentous lesson. Hitherto I have been driven with revolt to what I would not; I was a bond-slave to poverty, driven and scourged. There are robust virtues that can stand in these temptations; mine was not so; I had a thirst of pleasure. But today, and out of this deed, I pluck both warning and riches – both the power and a fresh resolve to be myself. I become in all things a free actor in the world; I begin to see myself all changed, these hands the agents of good, this heart at peace. Something comes over me out of the past – something of what I have dreamed on Sabbath evenings to the sound of the church organ, of what I forecast when I shed tears over noble books, or talked, an innocent child, with my mother. There lies my life; I have wandered a few years, but now I see once more my city of destination.'

'You are to use this money on the Stock Exchange, I think?' remarked the visitor; 'and there, if I mistake not, you have already lost some thousands?'

'Ah,' said Markheim, 'but this time I have a sure thing.'

'This time, again, you will lose,' replied the visitor quietly.

'Ah, but I keep back the half!' cried Markheim.

'That also you will lose,' said the other.

The sweat started upon Markheim's brow. 'Well then, what matter?' he exclaimed. 'Say it be lost, say I am plunged again in poverty, shall one part of me, and that the worse, continue until the end to override the better? Evil and good run strong in me, haling me both ways. I do not love the one thing; I love all. I can conceive great deeds, renunciations, martyrdoms; and though I be fallen to such a crime as murder, pity is no stranger to my thoughts. I pity the poor; who knows their trials better than myself? I pity and help them. I prize love; I love honest laughter; there is no good thing nor true thing on earth but I love it from my heart. And are my vices only to direct my life, and my virtues to lie without effect, like some passive lumber of the mind? Not so; good, also, is a spring of acts.'

But the visitant raised his finger. 'For six and thirty years that you have been in this world,' said he, 'through many changes of fortune and varieties of humour, I have watched you steadily fall. Fifteen years ago you would have started at a theft. Three years back you would have blenched at the name of murder. Is there any crime, is there any cruelty or meanness, from which you still recoil? Five years from now I shall detect you in the fact! Downward, downward, lies your way; nor can anything but death avail to stop you.'

'It is true,' Markheim said huskily, 'I have in some degree complied with evil. But it is so with all; the very saints, in the mere exercise of living, grow less dainty, and take on the tone of their surroundings.'

'I will propound to you one simple question,' said the other; 'and as you answer I shall read to you your moral horoscope. You have grown in many things more lax; possibly you do right to be so; and at any account, it is the same with all men. But granting that, are you in any one particular, however trifling, more difficult to please with your own conduct, or do you go in all things with a looser rein?'

'In any one?' repeated Markheim, with an anguish of consideration. 'No,' he added, with despair; 'in none! I have gone down in all.'

'Then,' said the visitor, 'content yourself with what

you are, for you will never change; and the words of your part on this stage are irrevocably written down.'

Markheim stood for a long while silent, and, indeed, it was the visitor who first broke the silence. 'That being so,' he said, 'shall I show you the money?'

'And grace?' cried Markheim.

'Have you not tried it?' returned the other. 'Two or three years ago did I not see you on the platform of revival meetings, and was not your voice the loudest in the hymn?'

'It is true,' said Markheim; 'and I see clearly what remains for me by way of duty. I thank you for these lessons from my soul; my eyes are opened, and I behold myself at last for what I am.'

At this moment, the sharp note of the doorbell rang through the house; and the visitant, as though this were some concerted signal for which he had been waiting, changed at once in his demeanour.

'The maid!' he cried. 'She has returned, as I fore-warned you, and there is now before you one more difficult passage. Her master, you must say, is ill; you must let her in, with an assured but rather serious countenance; no smiles, no overacting, and I promise you success! Once the girl is within, and the door closed, the same dexterity that has already rid you of the dealer will relieve you of this last danger in your path. Thenceforward you have the whole evening – the whole night, if needful – to ransack the treasures of the house and to make good your safety. This is help that comes to you with the mask of danger. Up!' he cried; 'up, friend. Your life hangs trembling in the scales; up, and act!'

Markheim steadily regarded his counsellor. 'If I be condemned to evil acts,' he said, 'there is still one door of freedom open: I can cease from action. If my life be an ill thing, I can lay it down. Though I be, as you say truly, at the beck of every small temptation, I can yet, by one decisive gesture, place myself beyond the reach of all. My love of good is damned to barrenness; it may, and let it be! But I have still my hatred of evil; and from that, to your galling disappointment, you shall see that I can draw both energy and courage.'

The features of the visitor began to undergo a wonderful and lovely change: they brightened and softened with a tender triumph, and, even as they brightened, faded and dislimned. But Markheim did not pause to watch or understand the transformation. He opened the door and went downstairs very slowly, thinking to himself. His past went soberly before him; he beheld it as it was, ugly and strenuous like a dream, random as chance-medley – a scene of defeat. Life, as he thus reviewed it, tempted him no longer; but on the farther side he perceived a quiet haven for his bark. He paused in the passage, and looked into the shop, where the candle still burned by the dead body. It was strangely silent. Thoughts of the dealer swarmed into his mind, as he stood gazing. And then the bell once more broke out into impatient clamour.

He confronted the maid upon the threshold with something like a smile.

'You had better go for the police,' said he; 'I have killed your master.'

CAPTAIN FREDERICK MARRYAT

The White Wolf of the Hartz Mountains

Before noon Philip and Krantz had embarked, and
made sail in the peroqua.

They had no difficulty in steering their course; the
islands by day, and the clear stars by night, were
their compass. It is true that they did not follow the
more direct track, but they followed the more secure,
working up through the smooth waters, and gaining
to the northward more than to the west. Many times
were they chased by the Malay proas, which infested
the islands, but the swiftness of their little peroqua
was their security; indeed the chase was, generally
speaking, abandoned, as soon as the smallness of the
vessel was made out by the pirates, who expected
that little or no booty was to be gained.

One morning, as they were sailing between the
isles, with less wind than usual, Philip observed:
'Krantz, you said that there were events in your own
life, or connected with it, which would corroborate
the mysterious tale I confided to you. Will you now
tell me to what you referred?'

'Certainly,' replied Krantz; 'I have often thought of
doing so, but one circumstance or another has hitherto
prevented me; this is, however, a fitting opportunity.
Prepare therefore to listen to a strange story, quite as
strange, perhaps, as your own.

'I take it for granted, that you have heard people
speak of the Hartz Mountains,' observed Krantz.

'I have never heard people speak of them that I can

recollect,' replied Philip; 'but I have read of them in some book, and of the strange things which have occurred there.'

'It is indeed a wild region,' rejoined Krantz, 'and many strange tales are told of it; but, strange as they are, I have good reason for believing them to be true. I have told you, Philip, that I fully believe in your communion with the other world – that I credit the history of your father, and the lawfulness of your mission; for that we are surrounded, impelled, and worked upon by beings different in their nature from ourselves, I have had full evidence, as you will acknowledge, when I state what has occurred in my own family. Why such malevolent beings as I am about to speak of should be permitted to interfere with us, and punish, I may say, comparatively un-offending mortals, is beyond my comprehension; but that they are so permitted is most certain.'

'The great principle of all evil fulfils his work of evil; why, then, not the other minor spirits of the same class?' enquired Philip. 'What matters it to us, whether we are tried by, and have to suffer from, the enmity of our fellow-mortals, or whether we are per-secuted by beings more powerful and more malevol-ent than ourselves? We know that we have to work out our salvation, and that we shall be judged according to our strength; if then there be evil spirits who delight to oppress man, there surely must be, as Amine asserts, good spirits, whose delight is to do him service. Whether, then, we have to struggle against our passions only, or whether we have to struggle not only against our passions, but also the dire influence of unseen enemies, we ever struggle with the same odds in our favour, as the good are stronger than the evil which we combat. In either case we are on the 'vantage ground, whether, as in the first, we fight the good cause single-handed, or as in the second, although opposed, we have the host of Heaven ranged on our side. Thus are the scales of Divine Justice evenly balanced, and man is still a free agent, as his own virtuous or vicious propensities must ever decide whether he shall gain or lose the victory.'

'Most true,' replied Krantz, 'and now to my history.

'My father was not born, or originally a resident, in the Hartz Mountains; he was the serf of an Hungarian nobleman, of great possessions, in Transylvania; but, although a serf, he was not by any means a poor or illiterate man. In fact, he was rich, and his intelligence and respectability were such, that he had been raised by his lord to the stewardship; but, whoever may happen to be born a serf, a serf must he remain, even though he become a wealthy man; such was the condition of my father. My father had been married for about five years; and, by his marriage, had three children – my eldest brother Caesar, myself (Hermann), and a sister named Marcella. You know, Philip, that Latin is still the language spoken in that country; and that will account for our high-sounding names. My mother was a very beautiful woman, unfortunately more beautiful than virtuous: she was seen and admired by the lord of the soil; my father was sent away upon some mission; and, during his absence, my mother, flattered by the attentions, and won by the assiduities, of this nobleman, yielded to his wishes. It so happened that my father returned very unexpectedly, and discovered the intrigue. The evidence of my mother's shame was positive: he surprised her in the company of her seducer! Carried away by the impetuosity of his feelings, he watched the opportunity of a meeting taking place between them, and murdered both his wife and her seducer. Conscious that, as a serf, not even the provocation which he had received would be allowed as a justification of his conduct, he hastily collected together what money he could lay his hands upon, and, as we were then in the depth of winter, he put his horses to the sleigh, and taking his children with him, he set off in the middle of the night, and was far away before the tragical circumstance had transpired. Aware that he would be pursued, and that he had no chance of escape if he remained in any portion of his native country (in which the authorities could lay hold of him), he continued his flight without intermission until he had buried himself in the intricacies and seclusion of the Hartz Mountains. Of course, all that I have now told you I learned afterwards. My oldest recollections are knit to a rude, yet comfortable cottage, in which I lived with my father, brother, and sister. It was on the confines of one of those vast forests which cover the northern part of Germany; around it were a few acres of ground, which, during the summer months, my father cultivated, and which, though they yielded a doubtful harvest, were sufficient for our support. In the winter we remained much indoors, for, as my father followed the chase, we were left alone, and the wolves, during that season, incessantly prowled about. My father had purchased the cottage, and land about it, of one of the rude foresters, who gain their livelihood partly by hunting, and partly by burning charcoal, for the purpose of smelting the ore from the neighbouring mines; it was distant about two miles from any other habitation. I can call to mind the whole landscape now: the tall pines which rose up on the mountain above us, and the wide expanse of forest beneath, on the topmost boughs and heads of whose trees we looked down from our cottage, as the mountain below us rapidly descended into the distant valley. In summertime the prospect was beautiful; but during the severe winter, a more desolate scene could not well be imagined.

'I said that, in the winter, my father occupied himself with the chase; every day he left us, and often would he lock the door, that we might not leave the cottage. He had no one to assist him, or to take care of us – indeed, it was not easy to find a female servant who would live in such a solitude; but, could he have found one, my father would not have received her, for he had imbibed a horror of the sex, as the difference of his conduct towards us, his two boys, and my poor little sister, Marcella, evidently proved. You may suppose we were sadly neglected; indeed, we suffered much, for my father, fearful that we might come to some harm, would not allow us fuel, when he left the cottage; and we were obliged, therefore, to creep under the heaps of bears'-skins, and there to keep ourselves as warm as we could until he returned in the evening, when a blazing fire was our delight. That my father chose this restless sort of life may appear strange, but the fact was that he could not remain quiet; whether from remorse for having committed murder, or from the misery consequent on his change of situation, or from both combined, he was never happy unless he was in a state of activity. Children, however, when left much to themselves, acquire a thoughtfulness not common to their age. So it was with us; and during the short cold days of winter we would sit silent, longing for the happy hours when the snow would melt, and the leaves burst out, and the birds begin their songs, and when we should again be set at liberty.

'Such was our peculiar and savage sort of life until my brother Caesar was nine, myself seven, and my sister five, years old, when the circumstances occurred on which is based the extraordinary narrative which I am about to relate.

'One evening my father returned home rather later than usual; he had been unsuccessful, and, as the weather was very severe, and many feet of snow were upon the ground, he was not only very cold, but in a very bad humour. He had brought in wood, and we were all three of us gladly assisting each other in blowing on the embers to create the blaze, when he caught poor little Marcella by the arm and threw her aside; the child fell, struck her mouth, and bled very much. My brother ran to raise her up. Accustomed to ill-usage, and afraid of my father, she did not dare to cry, but looked up in his face very piteously. My father drew his stool nearer to the hearth, muttered something in abuse of women, and busied himself with the fire, which both my brother and I had deserted when our sister was so unkindly treated. A cheerful blaze was soon the result of his exertions; but we did not, as usual, crowd round it. Marcella, still bleeding, retired to a corner, and my brother and I took our seats beside her, while my father hung over the fire gloomily and alone. Such had been our position for about half an hour, when the howl of a wolf, close under the window of the cottage, fell on our ears. My father started up, and seized his gun: the howl was repeated, he examined the priming, and then hastily left the cottage, shutting the door after him. We all waited (anxiously listening), for we thought that if he succeeded in shooting the wolf, he would return in a better humour; and although he was harsh to all of us, and particularly so to our little sister, still we loved our father, and loved to see him cheerful and happy, for what else had we to look up to? And I may here observe, that perhaps there never were three children who were fonder of each other; we did not, like other children, fight and dispute together; and if, by chance, any disagreement did arise between my elder brother and me, little Marcella would run to us, and kissing us both, seal, through her entreaties, the peace between us. Marcella was a lovely, amiable child; I can recall her beautiful features even now – Alas! poor little Marcella.'

'She is dead then?' observed Philip.

'Dead! Yes, dead! – and how did she die? – But I must not anticipate, Philip; let me tell my story.

'We waited for some time, but the report of the gun did not reach us, and my elder brother then said, "Our father has followed the wolf, and will not be back for some time. Marcella, let us wash the blood from your mouth, and then we will leave this corner, and go to the fire and warm ourselves."

'We did so, and remained there until near midnight, every minute wondering, as it grew later, why our father did not return. We had no idea that he was in any danger, but we thought that he must have chased the wolf for a very long time. "I will look out and see if father is coming," said my brother Caesar, going to the door.

' "Take care," said Marcella, "the wolves must be about now, and we cannot kill them, brother."

73

'My brother opened the door very cautiously, and but a few inches; he peeped out. – "I see nothing," said he, after a time, and once more he joined us at the fire.

' "We have had no supper," said I, for my father usually cooked the meat as soon as he came home; and during his absence we had nothing but the fragments of the preceding day.

' "And if our father comes home after his hunt, Caesar," said Marcella, "he will be pleased to have some supper; let us cook it for him and for ourselves."

'Caesar climbed upon the stool, and reached down some meat – I forget now whether it was venison or bear's meat; but we cut off the usual quantity, and proceeded to dress it, as we used to do under our father's superintendence. We were all busied putting it into the platters before the fire, to await his coming, when we heard the sound of a horn. We listened – there was a noise outside, and a minute afterwards my father entered, ushering in a young female, and a large dark man in a hunter's dress.

'Perhaps I had better now relate, what was only known to me many years afterwards. When my father had left the cottage, he perceived a large white wolf about thirty yards from him; as soon as the animal saw my father, it retreated slowly, growling and snarling. My father followed; the animal did not run, but always kept at some distance; and my father did not like to fire until he was pretty certain that his ball would take effect: thus they went on for some time, the wolf now leaving my father far behind, and then stopping and snarling defiance at him, and then again, on his approach, setting off at speed.

'Anxious to shoot the animal (for the white wolf is

74

very rare), my father continued the pursuit for several hours, during which he continually ascended the mountain.

'You must know, Philip, that there are peculiar spots on those mountains which are supposed, and, as my story will prove, truly supposed, to be inhabited by the evil influences; they are well known to the huntsmen, who invariably avoid them. Now, one of these spots, an open space in the pine forests above us, had been pointed out to my father as dangerous on that account. But, whether he disbelieved these wild stories, or whether, in his eager pursuit of the chase, he disregarded them, I know not; certain, however, it is, that he was decoyed by the white wolf to this open space, when the animal appeared to slacken her speed. My father approached, came close up to her, raised his gun to his shoulder, and was about to fire; when the wolf suddenly disappeared. He thought that the snow on the ground must have dazzled his sight, and he let down his gun to look for the beast – but she was gone; how she could have escaped over the clearance, without his seeing her, was beyond his comprehension. Mortified at the ill success of his chase, he was about to retrace his steps, when he heard the distant sound of a horn. Astonishment at such a sound – at such an hour – in such a wilderness, made him forget for the moment his disappointment, and he remained riveted to the spot. In a minute the horn was blown a second time, and at no great distance; my father stood still, and listened: a third time it was blown. I forget the term used to express it, but it was the signal which, my father well knew, implied that the party was lost in the woods. In a few minutes more my father beheld a man on horseback, with a female seated on the crupper, enter the cleared space, and ride up to him. At first, my father called to mind the strange stories which he had heard of the supernatural beings who were said to frequent these mountains; but the nearer approach of the parties satisfied him that they were mortals like himself.

'As soon as they came up to him, the man who guided the horse accosted him. "Friend Hunter, you are out late, the better fortune for us: we have ridden far, and are in fear of our lives, which are eagerly sought after. These mountains have enabled us to elude our pursuers; but if we find not shelter and refreshment, that will avail us little, as we must perish from hunger and the inclemency of the night. My daughter, who rides behind me, is now more dead than alive, – say, can you assist us in our difficulty?"

' "My cottage is some few miles distant," replied my father, "but I have little to offer you besides a shelter from the weather; to the little I have you are welcome. May I ask whence you come?"

' "Yes, friend, it is no secret now; we have escaped from Transylvania, where my daughter's honour and my life were equally in jeopardy!"

'This information was quite enough to raise an interest in my father's heart. He remembered his own escape: he remembered the loss of his wife's honour, and the tragedy by which it was wound up. He immediately, and warmly, offered all the assistance which he could afford them.

' "There is no time to be lost, then, good sir," observed the horseman; "my daughter is chilled with the frost, and cannot hold out much longer against the severity of the weather."

' "Follow me," replied my father, leading the way

towards his home. "I was lured away in pursuit of a large white wolf," observed my father; "it came to the very window of my hut, or I should not have been out at this time of night."

' "The creature passed by us just as we came out of the wood," said the female in a silvery tone.

' "I was nearly discharging my piece at it," observed the hunter; "but since it did us such good service, I am glad that I allowed it to escape."

'In about an hour and a half, during which my father walked at a rapid pace, the party arrived at the cottage, and, as I said before, came in.

' "We are in good time, apparently," observed the dark hunter, catching the smell of the roasted meat, as he walked to the fire and surveyed my brother and sister, and myself. "You have young cooks here, mynheer."

' "I am glad that we shall not have to wait," replied my father. "Come, mistress, seat yourself by the fire; you require warmth after your cold ride."

' "And where can I put up my horse, mynheer?" enquired the huntsman.

' "I will take care of him," replied my father, going out of the cottage door.

'The female must, however, be particularly described. She was young, it seemed about twenty years of age. She was dressed in a travelling dress, deeply bordered with white fur, and wore a cap of white ermine on her head. Her features were very beautiful, at least I thought so, and so my father has since declared. Her hair was flaxen, glossy and shining, and bright as a mirror; and her mouth, although somewhat large when it was open, showed the most brilliant teeth I have ever beheld. But there was something about her eyes, bright as they were, which made us children afraid; they were so restless, so furtive; I could not at that time tell why, but I felt as if there was cruelty in her eye; and when she beckoned us to come to her, we approached her with fear and trembling. Still she was beautiful, very beautiful. She spoke kindly to my brother and myself, patted our heads, and caressed us; but Marcella would not come near her; on the contrary, she slunk away, and hid herself in the bed, and would not wait for the supper, which half an hour before she had been so anxious for.

'My father, having put the horse into a close shed, soon returned, and supper was placed upon the table. When it was over, my father requested that the young lady would take possession of his bed, and he would remain at the fire, and sit up with her father. After some hesitation on her part, this arrangement was agreed to, and I and my brother crept into the other bed with Marcella, for we had as yet always slept together.

'But we could not sleep; there was something so unusual, not only in seeing strange people, but in having those people sleep at the cottage, that we were bewildered. As for poor little Marcella, she was quiet, but I perceived that she trembled during the whole night, and sometimes I thought that she was checking a sob. My father had brought out some spirits, which he rarely used, and he and the strange hunter remained drinking and talking before the fire. Our ears were ready to catch the slightest whisper – so much was our curiosity excited.

' "You said you came from Transylvania?" observed my father.

' "Even so, mynheer," replied the hunter. "I was a

serf to the noble house of —; my master would insist upon my surrendering up my fair girl to his wishes; it ended in my giving him a few inches of my hunting-knife."

' "We are countrymen, and brothers in misfortune," replied my father, taking the huntsman's hand, and pressing it warmly.

' "Indeed! Are you, then, from that country?"

' "Yes; and I too have fled for my life. But mine is a melancholy tale."

' "Your name?" enquired the hunter.

' "Krantz."

' "What! Krantz of — ! I have heard your tale; you need not renew your grief by repeating it now. Welcome, most welcome, mynheer, and, I may say, my worthy kinsman. I am your second cousin, Wilfred of Barnsdorf," cried the hunter, rising up and embracing my father.

'They filled their horn mugs to the brim, and drank to one another, after the German fashion. The conversation was then carried on in a low tone; all that we could collect from it was that our new relative and his daughter were to take up their abode in our cottage, at least for the present. In about an hour they both fell back in their chairs, and appeared to sleep.

' "Marcella, dear, did you hear?" said my brother in a low tone.

' "Yes," replied Marcella, in a whisper; "I heard all. Oh! brother, I cannot bear to look upon that woman – I feel so frightened."

'My brother made no reply, and shortly afterwards we were all three fast asleep.

'When we awoke the next morning, we found that the hunter's daughter had risen before us. I thought

79

she looked more beautiful than ever. She came up to little Marcella and caressed her; the child burst into tears, and sobbed as if her heart would break.

'But, not to detain you with too long a story, the huntsman and his daughter were accommodated in the cottage. My father and he went out hunting daily, leaving Christina with us. She performed all the household duties; was very kind to us children; and, gradually, the dislike even of little Marcella wore away. But a great change took place in my father; he appeared to have conquered his aversion to the sex, and was most attentive to Christina. Often, after her father and we were in bed, would he sit up with her, conversing in a low tone by the fire. I ought to have mentioned, that my father and the huntsman Wilfred, slept in another portion of the cottage, and that the bed which he formerly occupied, and which was in the same room as ours, had been given up to the use of Christina. These visitors had been about three weeks at the cottage, when, one night, after we children had been sent to bed, a consultation was held. My father had asked Christina in marriage, and had obtained both her own consent and that of Wilfred; after this a conversation took place, which was, as nearly as I can recollect, as follows:

' "You may take my child, Mynheer Krantz, and my blessing with her, and I shall then leave you and seek some other habitation – it matters little where."

' "Why not remain here, Wilfred?"

' "No, no, I am called elsewhere; let that suffice, and ask no more questions. You have my child."

' "I thank you for her, and will duly value her; but there is one difficulty."

' "I know what you would say; there is no priest

80

here in this wild country: true; neither is there any law to bind; still must some ceremony pass between you, to satisfy a father. Will you consent to marry her after my fashion? if so, I will marry you directly."

' "I will," replied my father.

' "Then take her by the hand. Now, mynheer, swear."

' "I swear," repeated my father.

' "By all the spirits of the Hartz Mountains – "

' "Nay, why not by Heaven?" interrupted my father.

' "Because it is not my humour," rejoined Wilfred; "if I prefer that oath, less binding perhaps, than another, surely you will not thwart me."

' "Well, be it so then; have your humour. Will you make me swear by that in which I do not believe?"

' "Yet many do so, who in outward appearance are Christians," rejoined Wilfred; "say, will you be married, or shall I take my daughter away with me?"

' "Proceed," replied my father, impatiently.

' "I swear by all the spirits of the Hartz Mountains, by all their power for good or for evil, that I take Christina for my wedded wife; that I will ever protect her, cherish her, and love her; that my hand shall never be raised against her to harm her."

'My father repeated the words after Wilfred.

' "And if I fail in this my vow, may all the vengeance of the spirits fall upon me and upon my children; may they perish by the vulture, by the wolf, or other beasts of the forest; may their flesh be torn from their limbs, and their bones blanch in the wilderness; all this I swear."

'My father hesitated, as he repeated the last words; little Marcella could not restrain herself, and as my father repeated the last sentence, she burst into tears.

This sudden interruption appeared to discompose the party, particularly my father; he spoke harshly to the child, who controlled her sobs, burying her face under the bedclothes.

'Such was the second marriage of my father. The next morning, the hunter Wilfred mounted his horse, and rode away.

'My father resumed his bed, which was in the same room as ours; and things went on much as before the marriage, except that our new mother-in-law did not show any kindness towards us; indeed, during my father's absence, she would often beat us, particularly little Marcella, and her eyes would flash fire, as she looked eagerly upon the fair and lovely child.

'One night, my sister awoke me and my brother.

' "What is the matter?" said Caesar.

' "She has gone out," whispered Marcella.

' "Gone out!"

' "Yes, gone out at the door, in her nightclothes," replied the child; "I saw her get out of bed, look at my father to see if he slept, and then she went out at the door."

'What could induce her to leave her bed, and all undressed to go out, in such bitter wintry weather, with the snow deep on the ground, was to us incomprehensible; we lay awake, and in about an hour we heard the growl of a wolf, close under the window.

' "There is a wolf," said Caesar; "she will be torn to pieces."

' "Oh, no!" cried Marcella.

'In a few minutes afterwards our mother-in-law appeared; she was in her nightdress, as Marcella had stated. She let down the latch of the door, so as to make no noise, went to a pail of water, and washed her face and hands, and then slipped into the bed where my father lay.

'We all three trembled, we hardly knew why, but we resolved to watch the next night: we did so – and not only on the ensuing night, but on many others, and always at about the same hour, would our mother-in-law rise from her bed, and leave the cottage – and after she was gone, we invariably heard the growl of a wolf under our window, and always saw her, on her return, wash herself before she retired to bed. We observed, also, that she seldom sat down to meals, and that when she did, she appeared to eat with dislike; but when the meat was taken down, to be prepared for dinner, she would often furtively put a raw piece into her mouth.

'My brother Caesar was a courageous boy; he did not like to speak to my father until he knew more. He resolved that he would follow her out, and ascertain what she did. Marcella and I endeavoured to dissuade him from this project; but he would not be controlled, and the very next night he lay down in his clothes, and as soon as our mother-in-law had left the cottage, he jumped up, took down my father's gun, and followed her.

'You may imagine in what a state of suspense Marcella and I remained, during his absence. After a few minutes, we heard the report of a gun. It did not awaken my father, and we lay trembling with anxiety. In a minute afterwards we saw our mother-in-law enter the cottage – her dress was bloody. I put my hand to Marcella's mouth to prevent her crying out, although I was myself in great alarm.

Our mother-in-law approached my father's bed, looked to see if he was asleep, and then went to the chimney, and blew up the embers into a blaze.

' "Who is there?" said my father, waking up.

' "Lie still, dearest," replied my mother-in-law, "it is only me; I have lighted the fire to warm some water; I am not quite well."

'My father turned round and was soon asleep; but we watched our mother-in-law. She changed her linen, and threw the garments she had worn into the fire; and we then perceived that her right leg was bleeding profusely, as if from a gunshot wound. She bandaged it up, and then dressing herself, remained before the fire until the break of day.

'Poor little Marcella, her heart beat quick as she pressed me to her side – so indeed did mine. Where was our brother, Caesar? How did my mother-in-law receive the wound unless from his gun? At last my father rose, and then, for the first time I spoke, saying, "Father, where is my brother, Caesar?"

' "Your brother!" exclaimed he, "why, where can he be?"

' "Merciful Heaven! I thought as I lay very restless last night," observed our mother-in-law, "that I heard somebody open the latch of the door; and, dear me, husband, what has become of your gun?"

'My father cast his eyes up above the chimney, and perceived that his gun was missing. For a moment he looked perplexed, then seizing a broad axe, he went out of the cottage without saying another word.

'He did not remain away from us long: in a few minutes he returned, bearing in his arms the mangled body of my poor brother; he laid it down, and covered up his face.

'My mother-in-law rose up, and looked at the body, while Marcella and I threw ourselves by its side wailing and sobbing bitterly.

' "Go to bed again, children," said she sharply. "Husband," continued she, "your boy must have taken the gun down to shoot a wolf, and the animal has been too powerful for him. Poor boy! he has paid dearly for his rashness."

'My father made no reply; I wished to speak – to tell all – but Marcella, who perceived my intention, held me by the arm, and looked at me so imploringly, that I desisted.

'My father, therefore, was left in his error; but Marcella and I, although we could not comprehend it, were conscious that our mother-in-law was in some way connected with my brother's death.

'That day my father went out and dug a grave, and when he laid the body in the earth, he piled up stones over it, so that the wolves should not be able to dig it up. The shock of this catastrophe was to my poor father very severe; for several days he never went to the chase, although at times he would utter bitter anathemas and vengeance against the wolves.

'But during this time of mourning on his part, my mother-in-law's nocturnal wanderings continued with the same regularity as before.

'At last, my father took down his gun, to repair to the forest; but he soon returned, and appeared much annoyed.

' "Would you believe it, Christina, that the wolves – perdition to the whole race – have actually contrived to dig up the body of my poor boy, and now there is nothing left of him but his bones?"

' "Indeed!" replied my mother-in-law. Marcella

85

looked at me, and I saw in her intelligent eye all she would have uttered.

' "A wolf growls under our window every night, father," said I.

' "Aye, indeed? – Why did you not tell me, boy? – Wake me the next time you hear it."

'I saw my mother-in-law turn away; her eyes flashed fire, and she gnashed her teeth.

'My father went out again, and covered up with a larger pile of stones the little remnants of my poor brother which the wolves had spared. Such was the first act of the tragedy.

'The spring now came on: the snow disappeared, and we were permitted to leave the cottage; but never would I quit, for one moment, my dear little sister, to whom, since the death of my brother, I was more ardently attached than ever; indeed I was afraid to leave her alone with my mother-in-law, who appeared to have a particular pleasure in ill-treating the child. My father was now employed upon his little farm, and I was able to render him some assistance.

'Marcella used to sit by us while we were at work, leaving my mother-in-law alone in the cottage. I ought to observe that, as the spring advanced, so did my mother-in-law decrease her nocturnal rambles, and that we never heard the growl of the wolf under the window after I had spoken of it to my father.

'One day, when my father and I were in the field, Marcella being with us, my mother-in-law came out, saying that she was going into the forest to collect some herbs my father wanted, and that Marcella must go to the cottage and watch the dinner. Marcella went, and my mother-in-law soon disappeared in the forest, taking a direction quite contrary to that in which the cottage stood, and leaving my father and I, as it were, between her and Marcella.

'About an hour afterwards we were startled by shrieks from the cottage, evidently the shrieks of little Marcella. "Marcella has burnt herself, father," said I, throwing down my spade. My father threw down his, and we both hastened to the cottage. Before we could gain the door, out darted a large white wolf, which fled with the utmost celerity. My father had no weapon; he rushed into the cottage, and there saw poor little Marcella expiring: her body was dreadfully mangled, and the blood pouring from it had formed a large pool on the cottage floor. My father's first intention had been to seize his gun and pursue, but he was checked by this horrid spectacle; he knelt down by his dying child, and burst into tears: Marcella could just look kindly on us for a few seconds, and then her eyes were closed in death.

'My father and I were still hanging over my poor sister's body, when my mother-in-law came in. At the dreadful sight she expressed much concern, but she did not appear to recoil from the sight of blood, as most women do.

' "Poor child!" said she, "it must have been that great white wolf which passed me just now, and frightened me so – she's quite dead, Krantz."

' "I know it – I know it!" cried my father in agony.

'I thought my father would never recover from the effects of this second tragedy: he mourned bitterly over the body of his sweet child, and for several days would not consign it to its grave, although frequently requested by my mother-in-law to do so. At last he yielded, and dug a grave for her close by that of my poor brother, and took every precaution that the wolves should not violate her remains.

'I was now really miserable, as I lay alone in the bed which I had formerly shared with my brother and sister. I could not help thinking that my mother-in-law was implicated in both their deaths, although I could not account for the manner; but I no longer felt afraid of her: my little heart was full of hatred and revenge.

'The night after my sister had been buried, as I lay awake, I perceived my mother-in-law get up and go out of the cottage. I waited some time, then dressed myself, and looked out through the door, which I half opened. The moon shone bright, and I could see the spot where my brother and my sister had been buried; and what was my horror, when I perceived my mother-in-law busily removing the stones from Marcella's grave.

'She was in her white nightdress, and the moon shone full upon her. She was digging with her hands, and throwing away the stones behind her with all the ferocity of a wild beast. It was some time before I could collect my senses and decide what I should do. At last, I perceived that she had arrived at the body, and raised it up to the side of the grave. I could bear it no longer; I ran to my father and awoke him.

' "Father! father!" cried I, "dress yourself, and get your gun."

' "What!" cried my father, "the wolves are there, are they?"

'He jumped out of bed, threw on his clothes, and in his anxiety did not appear to perceive the absence of his wife. As soon as he was ready, I opened the door, he went out, and I followed him.

'Imagine his horror, when (unprepared as he was for such a sight) he beheld, as he advanced towards the grave, not a wolf, but his wife, in her nightdress, on her hands and knees, crouching by the body of my sister, and tearing off large pieces of the flesh, and devouring them with all the avidity of a wolf. She was too busy to be aware of our approach. My father dropped his gun, his hair stood on end; so did mine; he breathed heavily, and then his breath for a time stopped. I picked up the gun and put it into his hand. Suddenly he appeared as if concentrated rage had restored him to double vigour; he levelled his piece, fired, and with a loud shriek, down fell the wretch whom he had fostered in his bosom.

' "God of Heaven!" cried my father, sinking down upon the earth in a swoon, as soon as he had discharged his gun.

'I remained some time by his side before he recovered. "Where am I?" said he. "What has happened? – Oh! – yes, yes! I recollect now. Heaven forgive me!"

'He rose and we walked up to the grave; what again was our astonishment and horror to find that instead of the dead body of my mother-in-law, as we expected, there was lying over the remains of my poor sister, a large, white she-wolf.

' "The white wolf!" exclaimed my father, "the white wolf which decoyed me into the forest – I see it all now – I have dealt with the spirits of the Hartz Mountains."

'For some time my father remained in silence and deep thought. He then carefully lifted up the body of my sister, replaced it in the grave, and covered it over as before, having struck the head of the dead animal with the heel of his boot, and raving like a madman. He walked back to the cottage, shut the door, and threw himself on the bed; I did the same, for I was in a stupor of amazement.

'Early in the morning we were both roused by a loud knocking at the door, and in rushed the hunter Wilfred.

' "My daughter! – Man – my daughter! – where is my daughter!" cried he in a rage.

' "Where the wretch, the fiend, should be, I trust," replied my father, starting up and displaying equal choler; "where she should be – in hell! – Leave this cottage or you may fare worse."

' "Ha – ha!" replied the hunter, "would you harm a potent spirit of the Hartz Mountains. Poor mortal, who must needs wed a weir wolf."

' "Out demon! I defy thee and thy power."

' "Yet shall you feel it; remember your oath – your solemn oath – never to raise your hand against her to harm her."

' "I made no compact with evil spirits."

' "You did; and if you failed in your vow, you were to meet the vengeance of the spirits. Your children were to perish by the vulture, the wolf – "

' "Out, out, demon!"

' "And their bones blanch in the wilderness. Ha! – ha!"

'My father, frantic with rage, seized his axe, and raised it over Wilfred's head to strike.

' "All this I swear," continued the huntsman, mockingly.

'The axe descended; but it passed through the form of the hunter, and my father lost his balance, and fell heavily on the floor.

' "Mortal!" said the hunter, striding over my father's body, "we have power over those only who have committed murder. You have been guilty of a double murder – you shall pay the penalty attached to your marriage vow. Two of your children are gone; the third is yet to follow – and follow them he will, for your oath is registered. Go – it were kindness to kill thee – your punishment is – that you live!"

'With these words the spirit disappeared. My father rose from the floor, embraced me tenderly, and knelt down in prayer.

'The next morning he quitted the cottage for ever. He took me with him and bent his steps to Holland, where we safely arrived. He had some little money with him; but he had not been many days in Amsterdam before he was seized with a brain fever, and died raving mad. I was put into the Asylum, and afterwards was sent to sea before the mast. You now know all my history. The question is, whether I am to pay the penalty of my father's oath? I am myself perfectly convinced that, in some way or another, I shall.'

On the twenty-second day the high land of the south of Sumatra was in view; as there were no vessels in sight, they resolved to keep their course through the Straits, and run for Pulo Penang, which they expected, as their vessel laid so close to the wind, to reach in seven or eight days. By constant exposure, Philip and Krantz were now so bronzed, that with their long beards and Mussulman dresses, they might easily have passed off for natives. They had steered during the whole of the days exposed to a burning sun; they had lain down and slept in the dew of night, but their health had not suffered. But for several days, since he had confided the history of his family to Philip, Krantz had become silent and melancholy; his usual flow of spirits had vanished, and Philip had often questioned him as to the cause. As they entered the Straits, Philip talked of what they should do upon their arrival at Goa, when Krantz gravely replied, 'For some days, Philip, I have had a presentiment that I shall never see that city.'

'You are out of health, Krantz,' replied Philip.

'No; I am in sound health, body and mind. I have endeavoured to shake off the presentiment, but in vain; there is a warning voice that continually tells me that I shall not be long with you. Philip, will you oblige me by making me content on one point: I have gold about my person which may be useful to you; oblige me by taking it, and securing it on your own.'

'What nonsense, Krantz.'

'It is no nonsense, Philip. Have you not had your warnings? Why should I not have mine? You know that I have little fear in my composition, and that I care not about death; but I feel the presentiment which I speak of more strongly every hour. It is some kind spirit who would warn me to prepare for another world. Be it so. I have lived long enough in this world to leave it without regret; although to part with you and Amine, the only two now dear to me, is painful, I acknowledge.'

'May not this arise from over-exertion and fatigue, Krantz? Consider how much excitement you have laboured under within these last four months. Is not that enough to create a corresponding depression? Depend upon it, my dear friend, such is the fact.'

'I wish it were – but I feel otherwise, and there is a feeling of gladness connected with the idea that I am

92

to leave this world, arising from another presentiment, which equally occupies my mind.'

'Which is?'

'I hardly can tell you; but Amine and you are connected with it. In my dreams I have seen you meet again; but it has appeared to me, as if a portion of your trial was purposely shut from my sight in dark clouds; and I have asked, "May not I see what is there concealed?" – and an invisible has answered, "No! 'twould make you wretched. Before these trials take place, you will be summoned away" – and then I have thanked Heaven, and felt resigned.'

'These are the imaginings of a disturbed brain, Krantz; that I am destined to suffering may be true; but why Amine should suffer, or why you, young, in full health and vigour, should not pass your days in peace, and live to a good old age, there is no cause for believing. You will be better tomorrow.'

'Perhaps so,' replied Krantz; – 'but still you must yield to my whim, and take the gold. If I am wrong, and we do arrive safe, you know, Philip, you can let me have it back,' observed Krantz, with a faint smile – 'but you forget, our water is nearly out, and we must look out for a rill on the coast to obtain a fresh supply.'

'I was thinking of that when you commenced this unwelcome topic. We had better look out for the water before dark, and as soon as we have replenished our jars, we will make sail again.'

At the time that this conversation took place, they were on the eastern side of the Strait, about forty miles to the northward. The interior of the coast was rocky and mountainous, but it slowly descended to

93

low land of alternate forest and jungles, which continued to the beach: the country appeared to be uninhabited. Keeping close in to the shore, they discovered, after two hours' run, a fresh stream which burst in a cascade from the mountains, and swept its devious course through the jungle, until it poured its tribute into the waters of the Strait.

They ran close in to the mouth of the stream, lowered the sails, and pulled the peroqua against the current, until they had advanced far enough to assure them that the water was quite fresh. The jars were soon filled, and they were again thinking of pushing off; when, enticed by the beauty of the spot, the coolness of the fresh water, and wearied with their long confinement on board of the peroqua, they proposed to bathe – a luxury hardly to be appreciated by those who have not been in a similar situation. They threw off their Mussulman dresses, and plunged into the stream, where they remained for some time. Krantz was the first to get out; he complained of feeling chilled, and he walked on to the banks where their clothes had been laid. Philip also approached nearer to the beach, intending to follow him.

'And now, Philip,' said Krantz, 'this will be a good opportunity for me to give you the money. I will open my sash, and pour it out, and you can put it into your own before you put it on.'

Philip was standing in the water, which was about level with his waist.

'Well, Krantz,' said he, 'I suppose if it must be so, it must; but it appears to me an idea so ridiculous – however, you shall have your own way.'

Philip quitted the run, and sat down by Krantz, who was already busy in shaking the doubloons out of the folds of his sash; at last he said – 'I believe, Philip, you have got them all, now? – I feel satisfied.'

'What danger there can be to you, which I am not equally exposed to, I cannot conceive,' replied Philip; 'however –'

Hardly had he said these words, when there was a tremendous roar – a rush like a mighty wind through the air – a blow which threw him on his back – a loud cry – and a contention. Philip recovered himself, and perceived the naked form of Krantz carried off with the speed of an arrow by an enormous tiger through the jungle. He watched with distended eyeballs; in a few seconds the animal and Krantz had disappeared!

'God of Heaven! Would that Thou hadst spared me this,' cried Philip, throwing himself down in agony on his face. 'Oh! Krantz, my friend – my brother – too sure was your presentiment. Merciful God! have pity – but Thy will be done;' and Philip burst into a flood of tears.

For more than an hour did he remain fixed upon the spot, careless and indifferent to the danger by which he was surrounded. At last, somewhat recovered, he rose, dressed himself, and then again sat down – his eyes fixed upon the clothes of Krantz, and the gold which still lay on the sand.

'He would give me that gold. He foretold his doom. Yes! yes! it was his destiny, and it has been fulfilled. *His bones will bleach in the wilderness*, and the spirit-hunter and his wolfish daughter are avenged.'

The Vengeance of the Dead

It is a bad thing for a man to die with an unsatisfied thirst for revenge parching his soul. David Allen died, cursing Bernard Heaton and lawyer Grey; hating the lawyer who had won the case even more than the man who was to gain by the winning. Yet if cursing were to be done, David should rather have cursed his own stubbornness and stupidity.

To go back for some years, this is what had happened. Squire Heaton's only son went wrong. The Squire raged, as was natural. He was one of a long line of hard-drinking, hard-riding, hard-swearing squires, and it was maddening to think that his only son should deliberately take to books and cold water, when there was manly sport in the countryside and old wine in the cellar. Yet before now such blows have descended upon deserving men, and they have to be borne as best they may. Squire Heaton bore it badly, and when his son went off on a government scientific expedition around the world the Squire drank harder, and swore harder than ever, but never mentioned the boy's name.

Two years after, young Heaton returned, but the doors of the Hall were closed against him. He had no mother to plead for him, although it was not likely that would have made any difference, for the Squire was not a man to be appealed to and swayed this way or that. He took his hedges, his drinks, and his course in life straight. The young man went to India, where he was drowned. As there is no mystery in this matter, it may as well be stated here that young Heaton ultimately returned to England, as drowned men have ever been in the habit of doing, when their return will mightily inconvenience innocent persons who have taken their places. It is a disputed question whether the sudden disappearance of a man, or his reappearance after a lapse of years, is the more annoying.

If the old Squire felt remorse at the supposed death of his only son he did not show it. The hatred which had been directed against his unnatural offspring redoubled itself and was bestowed on his nephew David Allen, who was now the legal heir to the estate and its income. Allen was the impecunious son of the Squire's sister who had married badly. It is hard to starve when one is heir to a fine property, but that is what David did, and it soured him. The Jews would not lend on the security – the son might return – so David Allen waited for a dead man's shoes, impoverished and embittered.

At last the shoes were ready for him to step into. The old Squire died as a gentleman should, of apoplexy, in his armchair, with a decanter at his elbow. David Allen entered into his belated inheritance, and his first act was to discharge every servant, male and female, about the place and engage others who owed their situations to him alone. Then were the Jews sorry they had not trusted him.

He was now rich but broken in health, with bent shoulders, without a friend on the earth. He was a man suspicious of all the world, and he had a furtive look over his shoulder as if he expected fate to deal him a sudden blow – as indeed it did.

It was a beautiful June day, when there passed the porter's lodge and walked up the avenue to the main entrance of the Hall a man whose face was bronzed by a torrid sun. He requested speech with the master and was asked into a room to wait.

At length David Allen shuffled in, with his bent shoulders, glaring at the intruder from under his bushy eyebrows. The stranger rose as he entered and extended his hand.

'You don't know me, of course. I believe we have never met before. I am your cousin.'

Allen ignored the outstretched hand.

'I have no cousin,' he said.

'I am Bernard Heaton, the son of your uncle.'

'Bernard Heaton is dead.'

'I beg your pardon, he is not. I ought to know, for I tell you I am he.'

'You lie!'

Heaton, who had been standing since his cousin's entrance, now sat down again, Allen remaining on his feet.

'Look here,' said the newcomer. 'Civility costs nothing and –'

'I cannot be civil to an impostor.'

'Quite so. It *is* difficult. Still, if I am an impostor, civility can do no harm, while if it should turn out that I am not an impostor, then your present tone may make after arrangements all the harder upon you. Now will you oblige me by sitting down? I dislike, while sitting myself, talking to a standing man.'

'Will you oblige me by stating what you want before I order my servants to turn you out?'

'I see you are going to be hard on yourself. I will endeavour to keep my temper, and if I succeed it will be a triumph for a member of our family. I am to state what I want? I will. I want as my own the three rooms on the first floor of the south wing – the rooms communicating with each other. You perceive I at least know the house. I want my meals served there, and I wish to be undisturbed at all hours. Next I desire that you settle upon me say five hundred a year – or six hundred – out of the revenues of the estate. I am engaged in scientific research of a peculiar kind. I can make money, of course, but I wish my mind left entirely free from financial worry. I shall not interfere with your enjoyment of the estate in the least.'

'I'll wager you will not. So you think I am fool enough to harbour and feed the first idle vagabond that comes along and claims to be my dead cousin. Go to the courts with your story and be imprisoned as similar perjurers have been.'

'Of course I don't expect you to take my word for it. If you were any judge of human nature you would see I am not a vagabond. Still that's neither here nor there. Choose three of your own friends. I will lay my proofs before them and abide by their decision. Come, nothing could be fairer than that, now could it?'

'Go to the courts, I tell you.'

'Oh, certainly. But only as a last resort. No wise man goes to law if there is another course open. But what is the use of taking such an absurd position? You *know* I'm your cousin. I'll take you blindfold into every room in the place.'

'Any discharged servant could do that. I have had enough of you. I am not a man to be blackmailed. Will you leave the house yourself, or shall I call the servants to put you out?'

'I should be sorry to trouble you,' said Heaton, rising. 'That is your last word, I take it?'

'Absolutely.'

'Then goodbye. We shall meet at Philippi.'

Allen watched him disappear down the avenue, and it dimly occurred to him that he had not acted diplomatically.

Heaton went directly to lawyer Grey, and laid the case before him. He told the lawyer what his modest demands were, and gave instructions that if, at any time before the suit came off, his cousin would compromise, an arrangement avoiding publicity should be arrived at.

'Excuse me for saying that looks like weakness,' remarked the lawyer.

'I know it does,' answered Heaton. 'But my case is so strong that I can afford to have it appear weak.'

The lawyer shook his head. He knew how uncertain the law was. But he soon discovered that no compromise was possible.

The case came to trial, and the verdict was entirely in favour of Bernard Heaton.

The pallor of death spread over the sallow face of David Allen, as he realised that he was once again a man without a penny or a foot of land. He left the court with bowed head, speaking no word to those who had defended him. Heaton hurried after him, overtaking him on the pavement.

'I knew this had to be the result,' he said to the defeated man. 'No other outcome was possible. I have no desire to cast you penniless into the street. What you refused to me I shall be glad to offer you. I will make the annuity a thousand pounds.'

Allen, trembling, darted one look of malignant hate at his cousin.

'You successful scoundrel!' he cried. 'You and your villainous confederate Grey. I tell you – '

The blood rushed to his mouth; he fell upon the pavement and died. One and the same day had robbed him of his land and his life.

Bernard Heaton deeply regretted the tragic issue, but went on with his researches at the Hall, keeping much to himself. Lawyer Grey, who had won renown by his conduct of the celebrated case, was almost his only friend. To him Heaton partially disclosed his hopes, told what he had learned during those years he had been lost to the world in India, and claimed that if he succeeded in combining the occultism of the East with the science of the West, he would make for himself a name of imperishable renown.

The lawyer, a practical man of the world, tried to persuade Heaton to abandon his particular line of research, but without success.

'No good can come of it,' said Grey. 'India has spoiled you. Men who dabble too much in that sort of thing go mad. The brain is a delicate instrument. Do not trifle with it.'

'Nevertheless,' persisted Heaton, 'the great discoveries of the twentieth century are going to be in that line, just as the great discoveries of the nineteenth century have been in the direction of electricity.'

'The cases are not parallel. Electricity is a tangible substance.'

'Is it? Then tell me what it is composed of? We all know how it is generated, and we know partly what it will do, but what *is* it?'

'I shall have to charge you six-and-eightpence for answering that question,' the lawyer had said with a laugh. 'At any rate there is a good deal to be discovered about electricity yet. Turn your attention to that and leave this Indian nonsense alone.'

Yet, astonishing as it may seem, Bernard Heaton, to his undoing, succeeded, after many futile attempts, several times narrowly escaping death. Inventors and discoverers have to risk their lives as often as soldiers, with less chance of worldly glory.

First his invisible excursions were confined to the house and his own grounds, then he went farther afield, and to his intense astonishment one day he met the spirit of the man who hated him.

'Ah,' said David Allen, 'you did not live long to enjoy your ill-gotten gains.'

'You are as wrong in this sphere of existence as you were in the other. I am not dead.'

'Then why are you here and in this shape?'

'I suppose there is no harm in telling *you*. What I wanted to discover, at the time you would not give me a hearing, was how to separate the spirit from its servant, the body – that is, temporarily and not finally. My body is at this moment lying apparently asleep in a locked room in my house – one of the rooms I begged from you. In an hour or two I shall return and take possession of it.'

'And how do you take possession of it and quit it?'

Heaton, pleased to notice the absence of that rancour which had formerly been Allen's most prominent characteristic, and feeling that any information given to a disembodied spirit was safe as far as the world was concerned, launched out on the subject that possessed his whole mind.

'It is very interesting,' said Allen, when he had finished.

And so they parted.

David Allen at once proceeded to the Hall, which he had not seen since the day he left it to attend the trial. He passed quickly through the familiar apartments until he entered the locked room on the first floor of the south wing. There on the bed lay the body of Heaton, most of the colour gone from the face, but breathing regularly, if almost imperceptibly, like a mechanical wax figure.

If a watcher had been in the room, he would have seen the colour slowly return to the face and the sleeper gradually awaken, at last rising from the bed.

Allen, in the body of Heaton, at first felt very uncomfortable, as a man does who puts on an ill-fitting suit of clothes. The limitations caused by the wearing of a body also discommoded him. He looked carefully around the room. It was plainly furnished. A desk in the corner he found contained the manuscript of a book prepared for the printer, all executed with the neat accuracy of a scientific man. Above the desk, pasted against the wall, was a sheet of paper headed: 'What to do if I am found here apparently dead.' Underneath were plainly written instructions. It was evident that Heaton had taken no one into his confidence.

It is well if you go in for revenge to make it as complete as possible. Allen gathered up the manuscript, placed it in the grate, and set a match to it. Thus he at once destroyed his enemy's chances of posthumous renown, and also removed evidence that might, in certain contingencies, prove Heaton's insanity.

Unlocking the door, he proceeded down the stairs, where he met a servant who told him luncheon was ready. He noticed that the servant was one whom he had discharged, so he came to the conclusion that Heaton had taken back all the old retainers who had applied to him when the result of the trial became public. Before lunch was over he saw that some of his own servants were also there still.

'Send the gamekeeper to me,' said Allen to the servant.

Brown came in, who had been on the estate for twenty years continuously, with the exception of the few months after Allen had packed him off.

'What pistols have I, Brown?'

'Well, sir, there's the old Squire's duelling pistols, rather out of date, sir; then your own pair and that American revolver.'

'Is the revolver in working order?'

'Oh yes, sir.'

'Then bring it to me and some cartridges.'

When Brown returned with the revolver his master took it and examined it.

'Be careful, sir,' said Brown, anxiously. 'You know it's a self-cocker, sir.'

'A what?'

'A self-cocking revolver, sir' – trying to repress his astonishment at the question his master asked about a weapon with which he should have been familiar.

'Show me what you mean,' said Allen, handing back the revolver.

Brown explained that the mere pulling of the trigger fired the weapon.

'Now shoot at the end window – never mind the glass. Don't stand gaping at me, do as I tell you.'

Brown fired the revolver, and a diamond pane snapped out of the window.

'How many times will that shoot without reloading?'

'Seven times, sir.'

'Very good. Put in a cartridge for the one you fired

and leave the revolver with me. Find out when there is a train to town, and let me know.'

It will be remembered that the dining-room incident was used at the trial, but without effect, as going to show that Bernard Heaton was insane. Brown also testified that there was something queer about his master that day.

David Allen found all the money he needed in the pockets of Bernard Heaton. He caught his train, and took a cab from the station directly to the law offices of Messrs Grey, Leason and Grey, anxious to catch the lawyer before he left for the day.

The clerk sent up word that Mr Heaton wished to see the senior Mr Grey for a few moments. Allen was asked to walk up.

'You know the way, sir,' said the clerk.

Allen hesitated.

'Announce me, if you please.'

The clerk, being well trained, showed no surprise, but led the visitor to Mr Grey's door.

'How are you, Heaton?' said the lawyer, cordially. 'Take a chair. Where have you been keeping yourself this long time? How are the Indian experiments coming on?'

'Admirably, admirably,' answered Allen.

At the sound of his voice the lawyer looked up quickly, then apparently reassured he said –

'You're not looking quite the same. Been keeping yourself too much indoors, I imagine. You ought to quit research and do some shooting this autumn.'

'I intend to, and I hope then to have your company.'

'I shall be pleased to run down, although I am no great hand at a gun.'

'I want to speak with you a few moments in private.

Would you mind locking the door so that we may not be interrupted?'

'We are quite safe from interruption here,' said the lawyer, as he turned the key in the lock; then resuming his seat he added, 'Nothing serious, I hope?'

'It is rather serious. Do you mind my sitting here?' asked Allen, as he drew up his chair so that he was between Grey and the door, with the table separating them. The lawyer was watching him with anxious face, but without, as yet, serious apprehension.

'Now,' said Allen, 'will you answer me a simple question? To whom are you talking?'

'To whom – ?' The lawyer in his amazement could get no further.

'Yes. To whom are you talking? Name him.'

'Heaton, what is the matter with you? Are you ill?'

'Well, you have mentioned a name, but, being a villain and a lawyer, you cannot give a direct answer to a very simple question. You think you are talking to that poor fool Bernard Heaton. It is true that the body you are staring at is Heaton's body, but the man you are talking to is – David Allen – the man you swindled and then murdered. Sit down. If you move you are a dead man. Don't try to edge to the door. There are seven deaths in this revolver and the whole seven can be let loose in less than that many seconds, for this is a self-cocking instrument. Now it will take you at least ten seconds to get to the door, so remain exactly where you are. That advice will strike you as wise, even if, as you think, you have to do with a madman. You asked me a minute ago how the Indian experiments were coming on, and I answered admirably. Bernard Heaton left his body this morning, and I, David Allen, am now in possession

of it. Do you understand? I admit it is a little difficult
for the legal mind to grasp such a situation.'

'Ah, not at all,' said Grey, airily. 'I comprehend it
perfectly. The man I see before me is the spirit, life,
soul, whatever you like to call it – of David Allen in
the body of my friend Bernard Heaton. The – ah –
essence of my friend is at this moment fruitlessly
searching for his missing body. Perhaps he is in this
room now, not knowing how to get out a spiritual
writ of ejectment against you.'

'You show more quickness than I expected of you,'
said Allen.

'Thanks,' rejoined Grey, although he said to himself, 'Heaton has gone mad! stark staring mad, as I
expected he would. He is armed. The situation is
becoming dangerous. I must humour him.'

'Thanks. And now may I ask what you propose to
do? You have not come here for legal advice. You
never, unluckily for me, were a client of mine.'

'No. I did not come either to give or take advice. I
am here, alone with you – you gave orders that we
were not to be disturbed, remember – for the sole
purpose of revenging myself on you and on Heaton.
Now listen, for the scheme will commend itself to
your ingenious mind. I shall murder you in this room.
I shall then give myself up. I shall vacate this body in
Newgate prison and your friend may then resume his
tenancy or not as he chooses. He may allow the
unoccupied body to die in the cell or he may take
possession of it and be hanged for murder. Do you
appreciate the completeness of my vengeance on you
both? Do you think your friend will care to put on his
body again?'

'It is a nice question,' said the lawyer, as he edged

his chair imperceptibly along and tried to grope behind himself, unperceived by his visitor, for the electric button, placed against the wall. 'It is a nice question, and I would like to have time to consider it in all its bearings before I gave an answer.'

'You shall have all the time you care to allow yourself. I am in no hurry, and I wish you to realise your situation as completely as possible. Allow me to say that the electric button is a little to the left and slightly above where you are feeling for it. I merely mention this because I must add, in fairness to you, that the moment you touch it, time ends as far as you are concerned. When you press the ivory button, I fire.'

The lawyer rested his arms on the table before him, and for the first time a hunted look of alarm came into his eyes, which died out of them when, after a moment or two of intense fear, he regained possession of himself.

'I would like to ask you a question or two,' he said at last.

'As many as you choose. I am in no hurry, as I said before.'

'I am thankful for your reiteration of that. The first question is then: has a temporary residence in another sphere interfered in any way with your reasoning powers?'

'I think not.'

'Ah, I had hoped that your appreciation of logic might have improved during your – well, let us say absence; you were not very logical – not very amenable to reason, formerly.'

'I know you thought so.'

'I did; so did your own legal adviser, by the way. Well, now let me ask why you are so bitter against me? Why not murder the judge who charged against you, or the jury that unanimously gave a verdict in our favour? I was merely an instrument, as were they.'

'It was your devilish trickiness that won the case.'

'That statement is flattering but untrue. The case was its own best advocate. But you haven't answered the question. Why not murder judge and jury?'

'I would gladly do so if I had them in my power. You see, I am perfectly logical.'

'Quite, quite,' said the lawyer. 'I am encouraged to proceed. Now of what did my devilish trickiness rob you?'

'Of my property, and then of my life.'

'I deny both allegations, but will for the sake of the argument admit them for the moment. First, as to your property. It was a possession that might at any moment be jeopardised by the return of Bernard Heaton.'

'By the *real* Bernard Heaton – yes.'

'Very well then. As you are now repossessed of the property, and as you have the outward semblance of Heaton, your rights cannot be questioned. As far as property is concerned you are now in an unassailable position where formerly you were in an assailable one. Do you follow me?'

'Perfectly.'

'We come (second) to the question of life. You then occupied a body frail, bent, and diseased, a body which, as events showed, gave way under exceptional excitement. You are now in a body strong and healthy, with apparently a long life before it. You admit the truth of all I have said on these two points?'

'I quite admit it.'

'Then to sum up, you are now in a better position –

infinitely – both as regards life and property, than the one from which my malignity – ingenuity I think was your word – ah, yes – trickiness – thanks – removed you. Now why cut your career short? Why murder *me*? Why not live out your life, under better conditions, in luxury and health, and thus be completely revenged on Bernard Heaton? If you are logical, now is the time to show it.'

Allen rose slowly, holding the pistol in his right hand.

'You miserable scoundrel!' he cried. 'You pettifogging lawyer – tricky to the last! How gladly you would throw over your friend to prolong your own wretched existence! Do you think you are now talking to a biased judge and a susceptible, brainless jury? Revenged on Heaton? I *am* revenged on him already. But part of my vengeance involves your death. Are you ready for it?'

Allen pointed the revolver at Grey, who had now also risen, his face ashen. He kept his eyes fastened on the man he believed to be mad. His hand crept along the wall. There was intense silence between them. Allen did not fire. Slowly the lawyer's hand moved towards the electric button. At last he felt the ebony rim and his fingers quickly covered it. In the stillness, the vibrating ring of an electric bell somewhere below was audible. Then the sharp crack of the revolver suddenly split the silence. The lawyer dropped on one knee, holding his arm in the air as if to ward off attack. Again the revolver rang out, and Grey plunged forward on his face. The other five shots struck a lifeless body.

A stratum of blue smoke hung breast high in the room as if it were the departing soul of the man who lay motionless on the floor. Outside were excited voices, and someone flung himself ineffectually against the stout locked door.

Allen crossed the room and, turning the key, flung open the door. 'I have murdered your master,' he said, handing the revolver butt forward to the nearest man. 'I give myself up. Go and get an officer.'

EDITH WHARTON

A Bottle of Perrier

1

A two days' struggle over the treacherous trails in a well-intentioned but short-winded 'flivver', and a ride of two more on a hired mount of unamiable temper, had disposed young Medford, of the American School of Archaeology at Athens, to wonder why his queer English friend, Henry Almodham, had chosen to live in the desert.

Now he understood.

He was leaning against the roof parapet of the old building, half Christian fortress, half Arab palace, which had been Almodham's pretext; or one of them. Below, in an inner court, a little wind, rising as the sun sank, sent through a knot of palms the rain-like rattle so cooling to the pilgrims of the desert. An ancient fig tree, enormous, exuberant, writhed over a white-washed well-head, sucking life from what appeared to be the only source of moisture within the walls. Beyond these, on every side, stretched away the mystery of the sands, all golden with promise, all livid with menace, as the sun alternately touched or abandoned them.

Young Medford, somewhat weary after his journey from the coast, and awed by his first intimate sense of the omnipresence of the desert, shivered and drew back. Undoubtedly, for a scholar and a misogynist, it was a wonderful refuge; but one would have to be, incurably, both.

'Let's take a look at the house,' Medford said to himself, as if speedy contact with man's handiwork were necessary to his reassurance.

The house, he already knew, was empty save for the quick cosmopolitan manservant, who spoke a sort of palimpsest Cockney lined with Mediterranean tongues and desert dialects – English, Italian or Greek, which was he? – and two or three burnoused underlings who, having carried Medford's bags to his room, had relieved the palace of their gliding presences. Mr Almodham, the servant told him, was away; suddenly summoned by a friendly chief to visit some unexplored ruins to the south, he had ridden off at dawn, too hurriedly to write, but leaving messages of excuse and regret. That evening late he might be back, or next morning. Meanwhile Mr Medford was to make himself at home.

Almodham, as young Medford knew, was always making these archaeological explorations; they had been his ostensible reason for settling in that remote place, and his desultory search had already resulted in the discovery of several early Christian ruins of great interest.

Medford was glad that his host had not stood on ceremony, and rather relieved, on the whole, to have the next few hours to himself. He had had a malarial fever the previous summer, and in spite of his cork helmet he had probably caught a touch of the sun; he felt curiously, helplessly tired, yet deeply content.

And what a place it was to rest in! The silence, the remoteness, the illimitable air! And in the heart of the wilderness green leafage, water, comfort – he had already caught a glimpse of wide wicker chairs under the palms – a humane and welcoming habitation.

Yes, he began to understand Almodham. To anyone sick of the Western fret and fever the very walls of this desert fortress exuded peace.

As his foot was on the ladder-like stair leading down from the roof, Medford saw the manservant's head rising towards him. It rose slowly and Medford had time to remark that it was sallow, bald on the top, diagonally dented with a long white scar, and ringed with thick ash-blond hair. Hitherto Medford had noticed only the man's face – youngish, but sallow also – and been chiefly struck by its wearing an odd expression which could best be defined as surprise.

The servant, moving aside, looked up, and Medford perceived that his air of surprise was produced by the fact that his intensely blue eyes were rather wider open than most eyes, and fringed with thick ash-blond lashes; otherwise there was nothing noticeable about him.

'Just to ask – what wine for dinner, sir? Champagne, or – '

'No wine, thanks.'

The man's disciplined lips were played over by a faint flicker of deprecation or irony, or both.

'Not any at all, sir?'

Medford smiled back. 'Well, no; I've been rather seedy, and wine's forbidden.'

The servant remained incredulous. 'Just a little light Moselle, though, to colour the water, sir?'

'No wine at all,' said Medford, growing bored. He was still in the stage of convalescence when it is irritating to be argued with about one's dietary.

'Oh – what's your name, by the way?' he added, to soften the curtness of his refusal.

'Gosling,' said the other unexpectedly, though Medford didn't in the least know what he had expected him to be called.

'You're English, then?'

'Oh, yes, sir.'

'You've been in these parts a good many years, though?'

Yes, he had, Gosling said; rather too long for his own liking; and added that he had been born in Malta. 'But I know England well too.' His deprecating look returned. 'I will confess, sir, I'd like to have 'ad a look at Wembley.* Mr Almodham 'ad promised me – but there – ' As if to minimise the *abandon* of this confidence, he followed it up by a ceremonious request for Medford's keys, and an enquiry as to when he would like to dine. Having received a reply, he still lingered, looking more surprised than ever.

'Just a mineral water, then, sir?'

'Oh, yes – anything.'

'Shall we say a bottle of Perrier?'

Perrier in the desert! Medford smiled assentingly, surrendered his keys and strolled away.

The house turned out to be smaller than he had imagined, or at least the habitable part of it; for above this towered mighty dilapidated walls of yellow stone, and in their crevices clung plaster chambers, one above the other, cedar-beamed, crimson-shuttered but crumbling. Out of this jumble of masonry and stucco, Christian and Muslim, the latest tenant of the fortress had chosen a cluster of rooms tucked into an angle of the ancient keep. These apartments

---

* The famous exhibition at Wembley, near London, took place in 1924.

opened on the uppermost court, where the palms chattered and the fig tree coiled above the well. On the broken marble pavement, chairs and a low table were grouped, and a few geraniums and blue morning-glories had been coaxed to grow between the slabs.

A white-skirted boy with watchful eyes was watering the plants; but at Medford's approach he vanished like a wisp of vapour.

There was something vaporous and insubstantial about the whole scene; even the long arcaded room opening on the court, furnished with saddlebag cushions, divans with gazelle skins and rough indigenous rugs; even the table piled with the old copies of *The Times* and ultra-modern French and English reviews – all seemed, in that clear mocking air, born of the delusion of some desert wayfarer.

A seat under the fig tree invited Medford to doze, and when he woke the hard blue dome above him was gemmed with stars and the night breeze gossiped with the palms.

Rest – beauty – peace. Wise Almodham!

2

Wise Almodham! Having carried out – with somewhat disappointing results – the excavation with which an archaeological society had charged him twenty-five years ago, he had lingered on, taken possession of the Crusaders' stronghold, and turned his attention from ancient to medieval remains. But even these investigations, Medford suspected, he prosecuted only at intervals, when the enchantment of his leisure did not lie on him too heavily.

The young American had met Henry Almodham at Luxor the previous winter; had dined with him at old Colonel Swordsley's, on that perfumed starlit terrace above the Nile; and, having somehow awakened the archaeologist's interest, had been invited to look him up in the desert the following year.

They had spent only that one evening together, with old Swordsley blinking at them under memory-laden lids, and two or three charming women from the Winter Palace chattering and exclaiming; but the two men had ridden back to Luxor together in the moonlight, and during that ride Medford fancied he had puzzled out the essential lines of Henry Almodham's character. A nature saturnine yet sentimental; chronic indolence alternating with spurts of highly intelligent activity; gnawing self-distrust soothed by intimate self-appreciation; a craving for complete solitude coupled with the inability to tolerate it for long.

There was more, too, Medford suspected; a dash of Victorian romance, gratified by the setting, the remoteness, the inaccessibility of his retreat, and by being known as *the* Henry Almodham – 'the one who lives in a Crusaders' castle, you know' – the gradual imprisonment in a pose assumed in youth, and into which middle age had slowly stiffened; and something deeper, darker, too, perhaps, though the young man doubted that; probably just the fact that living in that particular way had brought healing to an old wound, an old mortification, something which years ago had touched a vital part and left him writhing. Above all, in Almodham's hesitating movements and the dreaming look of his long well-featured brown face with its shock of grey hair, Medford detected an inertia, mental and moral, which life in this castle of romance must have fostered and excused.

'Once here, how easy not to leave!' he mused.

'Dinner, sir,' Gosling announced.

The table stood in an open arch of the living-room; shaded candles made a rosy pool in the dusk. Each time he emerged into their light the servant, white-jacketed, velvet-footed, looked more competent and more surprised than ever. Such dishes, too – the cook also a Maltese? Ah, they were geniuses, these Maltese! Gosling bridled, smiled his acknowledgement, and started to fill the guest's glass with Chablis.

'No wine,' said Medford patiently.

'Sorry, sir. But the fact is – '

'You said there was Perrier?'

'Yes, sir; but I find there's none left. It's been awfully hot, and Mr Almodham has been and drank it all up. The new supply isn't due till next week. We 'ave to depend on the caravans going south.'

'No matter. Water, then. I really prefer it.'

Gosling's surprise widened to amazement. 'Not water, sir? Water – in these parts?'

Medford's irritability stirred again. 'Something wrong with your water? Boil it then, can't you? I won't – ' He pushed away the half-filled wineglass.

'Oh – boiled? Certainly, sir.' The man's voice dropped almost to a whisper. He placed on the table a succulent mess of rice and mutton, and vanished.

Medford leaned back, surrendering himself to the night, the coolness, the ripple of wind in the palms.

One agreeable dish succeeded another. As the last appeared, the diner began to feel the pangs of thirst, and at the same moment a beaker of water was placed at his elbow. 'Boiled, sir, and I squeezed a lemon into it.'

'Right. I suppose at the end of the summer your water gets a bit muddy?'

'That's it, sir. But you'll find this all right, sir.'

Medford tasted. 'Better than Perrier.' He emptied the glass, leaned back and groped in his pocket. A tray was instantly at his hand with cigars and cigarettes.

'You don't – smoke sir?'

Medford, for answer, held up his cigar to the man's light. 'What do you call this?'

'Oh, just so. I meant the other style.' Gosling glanced discreetly at the opium pipes of jade and amber laid out on the low table.

Medford shrugged away the invitation – and wondered. Was that perhaps Almodham's other secret – or one of them? For he began to think there might be many; and all, he was sure, safely stored away behind Gosling's vigilant brow.

'No news yet of Mr Almodham?'

Gosling was gathering up the dishes with dexterous gestures. For a moment he seemed not to hear. Then – from beyond the candle gleam – 'News, sir? There couldn't 'ardly be, could there? There's no wireless in the desert, sir; not like London.' His respectful tone tempered the slight irony. 'But tomorrow evening ought to see him riding in.' Gosling paused, drew nearer, swept one of his swift hands across the table in pursuit of the last crumbs, and added tentatively: 'You'll surely be able, sir, to stay till then?'

Medford laughed. The night was too rich in healing; it sank on his spirit like wings. Time vanished, fret and trouble were no more. 'Stay, I'll stay a year if I have to!'

'Oh – a year?' Gosling echoed it playfully, gathered up the dessert dishes and was gone.

3

Medford had said that he would wait for Almodham a year; but the next morning he found that such arbitrary terms had lost their meaning. There were no time measures in a place like this. The silly face of his watch told its daily tale to emptiness. The wheeling of the constellations over those ruined walls marked only the revolutions of the earth; the spasmodic motions of man meant nothing.

The very fact of being hungry, that stroke of the inward clock, was minimised by the slightness of the sensation – just the ghost of a pang, that might have been quieted by dried fruit and honey. Life had the light monotonous smoothness of eternity.

Towards sunset Medford shook off this queer sense of other-whereness and climbed to the roof. Across the desert he spied for Almodham. Southward the Mountains of Alabaster hung like a blue veil lined with light. In the west a great column of fire shot up, spraying into plumy cloudlets which turned the sky to a fountain of rose-leaves, the sands beneath to gold.

No riders specked them; Medford watched in vain for his absent host till night fell, and the punctual Gosling invited him once more to table.

In the evening Medford absently fingered the ultra-modern reviews – three months old, and already so stale to the touch – then tossed them aside, flung himself on a divan and dreamed. Almodham must spend a lot of time dreaming; that was it. Then, just as he felt himself sinking down into torpor, he would be off on one of these dashes across the desert in quest of unknown ruins. Not such a bad life.

Gosling appeared with Turkish coffee in a cup cased in filigree.

'Are there any horses in the stable?' Medford suddenly asked.

'Horses? Only what you might call packhorses, sir. Mr Almodham has the two best saddle-horses with him.'

'I was thinking I might ride out to meet him.'

Gosling considered. 'So you might, sir.'

'Do you know which way he went?'

'Not rightly, sir. The *caid*'s man was to guide them.'

'Them? Who went with him?'

'Just one of our men, sir. They've got the two thoroughbreds. There's a third, but he's lame.' Gosling paused. 'Do you know the trails, sir? Excuse me, but I don't think I ever saw you here before.'

'No,' Medford acquiesced, 'I've never been here before.'

'Oh, then' – Gosling's gesture added: 'in that case, even the best thoroughbred wouldn't help you.'

'I suppose he may still turn up tonight?'

'Oh, easily, sir. I expect to see you both breakfasting here tomorrow morning,' said Gosling cheerfully.

Medford sipped his coffee. 'You said you'd never seen me here before. How long have you been here yourself?'

Gosling answered instantly, as though the figures were never long out of his memory: 'Eleven years and seven months altogether, sir.'

'Nearly twelve years! That's a longish time.'

'Yes, it is.'

'And I don't suppose you often get away?'

Gosling was moving off with the tray. He halted, turned back, and said with sudden emphasis: 'I've never once been away. Not since Mr Almodham first brought me here.'

'Good Lord! Not a single holiday?'

'Not one, sir.'

'But Mr Almodham goes off occasionally. I met him at Luxor last year.'

'Just so, sir. But when he's here he needs me for himself; and when he's away he needs me to watch over the others. So you see – '

'Yes, I see. But it must seem to you devilish long.'

'It seems long, sir.'

'But the others? You mean they're not – wholly trustworthy?'

'Well, sir, they're just Arabs,' said Gosling with careless contempt.

'I see. And not a single old reliable among them?'

'The term isn't in their language, sir.'

Medford was busy lighting his cigar. When he looked up he found that Gosling still stood a few feet off.

'It wasn't as if it 'adn't been a promise, you know, sir,' he said, almost passionately.

'A promise?'

'To let me 'ave my holiday, sir. A promise – agine and agine.'

'And the time never came?'

'No, sir, the days just drifted by – '

'Ah. They would, here. Don't sit up for me,' Medford added. 'I think I shall wait up – wait for Mr Almodham.'

Gosling's stare widened. 'Here, sir? Here in the court?'

The young man nodded, and the servant stood still regarding him, turned by the moonlight to a white spectral figure, the unquiet ghost of a patient butler who might have died without his holiday.

'Down here in the court all night, sir? It's a lonely spot. I couldn't 'ear you if you was to call. You're best in bed, sir. The air's bad. You might bring your fever on again.'

Medford laughed and stretched himself in his long chair. 'Decidedly,' he thought, 'the fellow needs a change.' Aloud he remarked: 'Oh, I'm all right. It's you who are nervous, Gosling. When Mr Almodham comes back I mean to put in a word for you. You shall have your holiday.'

Gosling still stood motionless. For a minute he did not speak. 'You would, sir, you would?' He gasped it out on a high cracked note, and the last word ran into a laugh – a brief shrill cackle, the laugh of one long unused to such indulgences.

'Thank you, sir. Good-night, sir.' He was gone.

4

'You do boil my drinking water, always?' Medford questioned, his hand clasping the glass without lifting it.

The tone was amicable, almost confidential; Medford felt that since his rash promise to secure a holiday for Gosling he and Gosling were on terms of real friendship.

'Boil it? Always, sir. Naturally.' Gosling spoke with a slight note of reproach, as though Medford's question implied a slur – unconscious, he hoped – on their newly established relation. He scrutinised

Medford with his astonished eyes, in which a genuine concern showed itself through the glaze of professional indifference.

'Because, you know, my bath this morning – '

Gosling was in the act of receiving from the hands of a gliding Arab a fragrant dish of *kuskus*. Under his breath he hissed to the native: 'You damned aboriginy, you, can't you even 'old a dish steady? Ugh!' The Arab vanished before the imprecation, and Gosling, with a calm deliberate hand, set the dish before Medford. 'All alike, they are.' Fastidiously he wiped a trail of grease from his linen sleeve.

'Because, you know, my bath this morning simply stank,' said Medford, plunging fork and spoon into the dish.

'Your bath, sir?' Gosling stressed the word. Astonishment, to the exclusion of all other emotion, again filled his eyes as he rested them on Medford. 'Now, I wouldn't 'ave 'ad that 'appen for the world,' he said self-reproachfully.

'There's only the one well here, eh? The one in the court?'

Gosling aroused himself from absorbed consideration of the visitor's complaint. 'Yes, sir; only the one.'

'What sort of well is it? Where does the water come from?'

'Oh, it's just a cistern, sir. Rain water. There's never been any other here. Not that I ever knew it to fail; but at this season sometimes it does turn queer. Ask any o' them Arabs, sir; they'll tell you. Liars as they are, they won't trouble to lie about that.'

Medford was cautiously tasting the water in his glass. 'This seems all right,' he pronounced.

Sincere satisfaction was depicted on Gosling's countenance. 'I seen to its being boiled myself, sir. I always do. I 'ope that Perrier'll turn up tomorrow, sir.'

'Oh, tomorrow' – Medford shrugged, taking a second helping. 'Tomorrow I may not be here to drink it.'

'What – going away, sir?'

Medford, wheeling round abruptly, caught a new and incomprehensible look in Gosling's eyes. The man had seemed to feel a sort of dog-like affection for him; had wanted, Medford could have sworn, to keep him on, persuade him to patience and delay; yet now, Medford could equally have sworn, there was relief in his look, satisfaction, almost, in his voice.

'So soon, sir?'

'Well, this is the fifth day since my arrival. And as there's no news yet of Mr Almodham, and you say he may very well have forgotten all about my coming – '

'Oh, I don't say that, sir; not forgotten! Only, when one of those old piles of stones takes 'old of him, he does forget about the time, sir. That's what I meant. The days drift by – 'e's in a dream. Very likely he thinks you're just due now, sir.' A small thin smile sharpened the lustreless gravity of Gosling's features. It was the first time that Medford had seen him smile.

'Oh, I understand. But still – ' Medford paused. Through the spell of inertia laid on him by the drowsy place and its easeful comforts his instinct of alertness was struggling back. 'It's odd – '

'What's odd?' Gosling echoed unexpectedly, setting the dried dates and figs on the table.

'Everything,' said Medford.

He leaned back in his chair and glanced up through

the arch at the lofty sky from which noon was pouring down in cataracts of blue and gold. Almodham was out there somewhere under that canopy of fire, perhaps, as the servant said, absorbed in his dream. The land was full of spells.

'Coffee, sir?' Gosling reminded him. Medford took it.

'It's odd that you say you don't trust any of these fellows – these Arabs – and yet that you don't seem to feel worried at Mr Almodham's being off God knows where, all alone with them.'

Gosling received this attentively, impartially; he saw the point. 'Well, sir, no – you wouldn't understand. It's the very thing that can't be taught, when to trust 'em and when not. It's 'ow their interests lie, of course, sir; and their religion, as they call it.' His contempt was unlimited. 'But even to begin to understand why I'm not worried about Mr Almodham, you'd 'ave to 'ave lived among them, sir, and you'd 'ave to speak their language.'

'But I – ' Medford began. He pulled himself up short and bent above his coffee.

'Yes, sir.'

'But I've travelled among them more or less.'

'Oh, travelled!' Even Gosling's intonation could hardly conciliate respect with derision in his reception of this boast.

'This makes the fifth day, though,' Medford continued argumentatively. The midday heat lay heavy even on the shaded side of the court, and the sinews of his will were weakening.

'I can understand, sir, a gentleman like you 'aving other engagements – being pressed for time, as it were,' Gosling reasonably conceded.

He cleared the table, committed its freight to a pair of Arab arms that just showed and vanished, and finally took himself off while Medford sank into the divan. A land of dreams . . .

The afternoon hung over the place like a great *velarium* of cloth-of-gold stretched across the battlements and drooping down in ever slacker folds upon the heavy-headed palms. When at length the gold turned to violet, and the west to a bow of crystal clasping the desert sands, Medford shook off his sleep and wandered out. But this time, instead of mounting to the roof, he took another direction.

He was surprised to find how little he knew of the place after five days of loitering and waiting. Perhaps this was to be his last evening alone in it. He passed out of the court by a vaulted stone passage which led to another walled enclosure. At his approach two or three Arabs who had been squatting there rose and melted out of sight. It was as if the solid masonry had received them.

Beyond, Medford heard a stamping of hoofs, the stir of a stable at nightfall. He went under another archway and found himself among horses and mules. In the fading light an Arab was rubbing down one of the horses, a powerful young chestnut. He too seemed about to vanish; but Medford caught him by the sleeve.

'Go on with your work,' he said in Arabic.

The man, who was young and muscular, with a lean Bedouin face, stopped and looked at him.

'I didn't know your Excellency spoke our language.'

'Oh, yes,' said Medford.

The man was silent, one hand on the horse's restless neck, the other thrust into his woollen girdle.

He and Medford examined each other in the faint light.

'Is that the horse that's lame?' Medford asked.

'Lame?' The Arab's eyes ran down the animal's legs. 'Oh, yes; lame,' he answered vaguely.

Medford stooped and felt the horse's knees and fetlocks. 'He seems pretty fit. Couldn't he carry me for a canter this evening if I felt like it?'

The Arab considered; he was evidently perplexed by the weight of responsibility which the question placed on him.

'Your Excellency would like to go for a ride this evening?'

'Oh, just a fancy. I might or I might not.' Medford lit a cigarette and offered one to the groom, whose white teeth flashed his gratification. Over the shared match they drew nearer and the Arab's diffidence seemed to lessen.

'Is this one of Mr Almodham's own mounts?' Medford asked.

'Yes, sir; it's his favourite,' said the groom, his hand passing proudly down the horse's bright shoulder.

'His favourite? Yet he didn't take him on this long expedition?'

The Arab fell silent and stared at the ground.

'Weren't you surprised at that?' Medford queried.

The man's gesture declared that it was not his business to be surprised.

The two remained without speaking while the quick blue night descended.

At length Medford said carelessly: 'Where do you suppose your master is at this moment?'

The moon, unperceived in the radiant fall of day, had now suddenly possessed the world, and a broad white beam lay full on the Arab's white smock, his brown face and the turban of camel's hair knotted above it. His agitated eyeballs glistened like jewels.

'If Allah would vouchsafe to let us know!'

'But you suppose he's safe enough, don't you? You don't think it's necessary yet for a party to go out in search of him?'

The Arab appeared to ponder this deeply. The question must have taken him by surprise. He flung a brown arm about the horse's neck and continued to scrutinise the stones of the court.

'When the master is away, Mr Gosling is our master.'

'And he doesn't think it necessary?'

The Arab sighed: 'Not yet.'

'But if Mr Almodham were away much longer – '

The man was again silent, and Medford continued: 'You're the head groom, I suppose?'

'Yes, Excellency.'

There was another pause. Medford half turned away; then over his shoulder: 'I suppose you know the direction Mr Almodham took? The place he's gone to?'

'Oh, assuredly, Excellency.'

'Then you and I are going to ride after him. Be ready an hour before daylight. Say nothing to anyone – Mr Gosling or anybody else. We two ought to be able to find him without other help.'

The Arab's face was all a responsive flash of eyes and teeth. 'Oh, sir, I undertake that you and my master shall meet before tomorrow night. And none shall know of it.'

'He's as anxious about Almodham as I am,' Medford thought; and a faint shiver ran down his back.

'All right. Be ready,' he repeated.

He strolled back and found the court empty of life, but fantastically peopled by palms of beaten silver and a white marble fig tree.

'After all,' he thought irrelevantly, 'I'm glad I didn't tell Gosling that I speak Arabic.'

He sat down and waited till Gosling, approaching from the living-room, ceremoniously announced for the fifth time that dinner was served.

5

Medford sat up in bed with the jerk which resembles no other. Someone was in his room. The fact reached him not by sight or sound – for the moon had set, and the silence of the night was complete – but by a peculiar faint disturbance of the invisible currents that enclose us.

He was awake in an instant, caught up his electric hand-lamp and flashed it into two astonished eyes. Gosling stood above the bed.

'Mr Almodham – he's back?' Medford exclaimed.

'No, sir; he's not back.' Gosling spoke in low controlled tones. His extreme self-possession gave Medford a sense of danger – he couldn't say why, or of what nature. He sat upright, looking hard at the man.

'Then what's the matter?'

'Well, sir, you might have told me you talk Arabic' – Gosling's tone was now wistfully reproachful – 'before you got 'obnobbing with that Selim. Making randy-voos with 'im by night in the desert.'

Medford reached for his matches and lit the candle by the bed. He did not know whether to kick Gosling out of the room or to listen to what the man had to say; but a quick movement of curiosity made him determine on the latter course.

'Such folly! First I thought I'd lock you in. I might 'ave.' Gosling drew a key from his pocket and held it up. 'Or again I might 'ave let you go. Easier than not. But there was Wembley.'

'Wembley?' Medford echoed. He began to think that the man was going mad. One might, so conceivably, in that place of postponements and enchantments! He wondered whether Almodham himself were not a little mad.

'Wembley. You promised to get Mr Almodham to give me an 'oliday – to let me go back to England in time for a look at Wembley. Every man 'as 'is fancies, 'asn't 'e, sir? And that's mine. I've told Mr Almodham so, agine and agine. He'd never listen, or only make believe to; say: "We'll see, now, Gosling, we'll see"; and no more 'eard of it. But you was different, sir. You said it, and I knew you meant it – about my 'oliday. So I'm going to lock you in.'

Gosling spoke composedly, but with an underthrill of emotion in his queer Mediterranean-Cockney voice.

'Lock me in?'

'Prevent you somehow from going off with that murderer. You don't suppose you'd ever 'ave come back alive from that ride, do you?'

A shiver ran over Medford, as it had the evening before when he had said to himself that the Arab was as anxious as he was about Almodham. He gave a slight laugh.

'I don't know what you're talking about. But you're not going to lock me in.'

The effect of this was unexpected. Gosling's face

was drawn up into a convulsive grimace and two tears rose to his pale eyelashes and ran down his cheeks.

'You don't trust me, after all,' he said plaintively.

Medford leaned on his pillow and considered. Nothing as queer had ever before happened to him. The fellow looked almost ridiculous enough to laugh at; yet his tears were certainly not simulated. Was he weeping for Almodham, already dead, or for Medford, about to be committed to the same grave?

'I should trust you at once,' said Medford, 'if you'd tell me where your master is.'

Gosling's face resumed its usual guarded expression, though the trace of the tears still glittered on it.

'I can't do that, sir.'

'Ah, I thought so!'

'Because – 'ow do I know?'

Medford thrust a leg out of bed. One hand, under the blanket, lay on his revolver.

'Well, you may go now. Put that key down on the table first. And don't try to do anything to interfere with my plans. If you do I'll shoot you,' he added concisely.

'Oh, no, you wouldn't shoot a British subject; it makes such a fuss. Not that I'd care – I've often thought of doing it myself. Sometimes in the sirocco season. That don't scare me. And you shan't go.'

Medford was on his feet now, the revolver visible. Gosling eyed it with indifference.

'Then you do know where Mr Almodham is? And you're determined that I shan't find out?' Medford challenged him.

'Selim's determined,' said Gosling, 'and all the others are. They all want you out of the way. That's why I've kept 'em to their quarters – done all the waiting on you myself. Now will you stay here? For God's sake, sir! The return caravan is going through to the coast the day after tomorrow. Join it, sir – it's the only safe way! I darsn't let you go with one of our men, not even if you was to swear you'd ride straight for the coast and let this business be.'

'This business? What business?'

'This worrying about where Mr Almodham is, sir. Not that there's anything to worry about. The men all know that. But the plain fact is they've stolen some money from his box, since he's been gone, and if I hadn't winked at it they'd 'ave killed me; and all they want is to get you to ride out after 'im, and put you safe away under a 'eap of sand somewhere off the caravan trails. Easy job. There; that's all, sir. My word it is.'

There was a long silence. In the weak candlelight the two men stood considering each other.

Medford's wits began to clear as the sense of peril closed in on him. His mind reached out on all sides into the enfolding mystery, but it was everywhere impenetrable. The odd thing was that, though he did not believe half of what Gosling had told him, the man yet inspired him with a queer sense of confidence as far as their mutual relation was concerned.

Medford laid his revolver on the table. 'Very well,' he said. 'I won't ride out to look for Mr Almodham, since you advise me not to. But I won't leave by the caravan; I'll wait here till he comes back.'

He saw Gosling whiten under his sallowness. 'Oh, don't do that, sir; I couldn't answer for them if you was to wait. The caravan'll take you to the coast the day after tomorrow as easy as if you was riding in Rotten Row.'

'Ah, then you know that Mr Almodham won't be back by the day after tomorrow?' Medford caught him up.

'I don't know anything, sir.'

'Not even where he is now?'

Gosling reflected. 'He's been gone too long, sir, for me to know that,' he said from the threshold.

The door closed on him.

Medford found sleep unrecoverable. He leaned in his window and watched the stars fade and the dawn break in all its holiness. As the stir of life rose among the ancient walls he marvelled at the contrast between that fountain of purity welling up into the heavens and the evil secrets clinging bat-like to the nest of masonry below.

He no longer knew what to believe or whom. Had some enemy of Almodham's lured him into the desert and bought the connivance of his people? Or had the servants had some reason of their own for spiriting him away, and was Gosling possibly telling the truth when he said that the same fate would befall Medford?

Medford, as the light brightened, felt his energy return. The very impenetrableness of the mystery stimulated him. He would stay, and he would find out the truth.

6

It was always Gosling himself who brought up the water for Medford's bath; but this morning he failed to appear with it, and when he came it was to bring the breakfast tray. Medford noticed that his face was of a pasty pallor, and that his lids were reddened as if with weeping. The contrast was unpleasant, and a dislike for Gosling began to shape itself in the young man's breast.

'My bath?' he queried.

'Well, sir, you complained yesterday of the water – '

'Can't you boil it?'

'I 'ave, sir.'

'Well, then – '

Gosling went out sullenly and presently returned with a brass jug. 'It's the time of year – we're dying for rain,' he grumbled, pouring a scant measure of water into the tub.

Yes, the well must be pretty low, Medford thought. Even boiled, the water had the disagreeable smell that he had noticed the day before, though of course in a slighter degree. But a bath was a necessity in that climate.

He spent the day in rather fruitlessly considering his situation. He had hoped the morning would bring counsel, but it brought only courage and resolution, and these were of small use without enlightenment. Suddenly he remembered that the caravan going south from the coast would pass near the castle that afternoon. Gosling had dwelt on the date often enough, for it was the caravan which was to bring the box of Perrier water.

'Well, I'm not sorry for that,' Medford reflected, with a slight shrinking of the flesh. Something sick and viscous, half smell, half substance, seemed to have clung to his skin since his morning bath, and the idea of having to drink that water again was nauseating.

But his chief reason for welcoming the caravan was the hope of finding in it some European, or at any rate some native official from the coast, to whom he might confide his anxiety. He hung about, listening and waiting, and then mounted to the roof to gaze northward along the trail. But in the afternoon glow he saw only three Bedouins guiding laden packmules towards the castle.

As they mounted the steep path he recognised some of Almodham's men, and guessed at once that the southward caravan trail did not actually pass under the walls and that the men had been out to meet it, probably at a small oasis behind some fold of the sandhills. Vexed at his own thoughtlessness in not foreseeing such a possibility, Medford dashed down to the court, hoping the men might have brought back some news of Almodham.

Gosling, master of all the desert dialects, was cursing his subordinates in a half-dozen.

'And you didn't bring it – and you tell me it wasn't there, and I tell you it was, and that you know it, and that you either left it on a sand-heap while you were jawing with some of those slimy fellows from the coast, or else fastened it on to the horse so carelessly that it fell off on the way – and all of you too sleepy to notice. Oh, you sons of females I wouldn't soil my lips by naming! Well, back you go to hunt it up, that's all.'

'By Allah and the tomb of his Prophet, you wrong us unpardonably. There was nothing left at the oasis, nor yet dropped off on the way back. It was not there, and that is the truth in its purity.'

'Truth! Purity! You miserable lot of shirks and liars, you – and the gentleman here not touching a drop of anything but water – as you profess to do, you liquor-swilling humbugs!'

Medford drew back from the parapet with a smile of relief. It was nothing but a case of Perrier – the missing case – which had raised the passions of these grown men to the pitch of frenzy! The anticlimax lifted a load from his breast. If Gosling, the calm and self-controlled, could waste his wrath on so slight a hitch in the working of the commissariat, he at least must have a free mind. How absurd this homely incident made Medford's speculations seem!

He was at once touched by Gosling's solicitude, and annoyed that he should have been so duped by the hallucinating fancies of the East.

Almodham was off on his own business; very likely the men knew where and what the business was; and even if they had robbed him in his absence, and quarrelled over the spoils, Medford did not see what he could do. It might even be that his eccentric host – with whom, after all, he had had but one evening's acquaintance – repenting an invitation too rashly given, had ridden away to escape the boredom of entertaining him. As this alternative occurred to Medford it seemed so plausible that he began to wonder if Almodham had not simply withdrawn to some secret suite of that intricate dwelling, and were waiting there for his guest's departure.

So well would this explain Gosling's solicitude to see the visitor off – so completely account for the man's nervous and contradictory behaviour – that Medford, smiling at his own obtuseness, hastily resolved to leave on the morrow. Tranquillised by this decision, he lingered about the court till dusk fell, and then, as usual, went up to the roof. But today his eyes, instead of raking the horizon, fastened on the clustering edifice of which, after six days' residence, he knew so little.

Aerial chambers, jutting out at capricious angles, baffled him with closely shuttered windows, or here and there with the enigma of painted panes. Behind which window was his host concealed, spying, it might be, at this very moment on the movements of his lingering guest?

The idea that that strange moody man, with his long brown face and shock of white hair, his half-guessed selfishness and tyranny, and his morbid self-absorption, might be actually within a stone's throw, gave Medford, for the first time, a sharp sense of isolation. He felt himself shut out, unwanted – the place, now that he imagined someone might be living in it unknown to him, became lonely, inhospitable, dangerous.

'Fool that I am – he probably expected me to pack up and go as soon as I found he was away!' the young man reflected. Yes; decidedly he would leave the next morning.

Gosling had not shown himself all the afternoon. When at length, belatedly, he came to set the table, he wore a look of sullen, almost surly, reserve which Medford had not yet seen on his face. He hardly returned the young man's friendly, 'Hello – dinner?' and when Medford was seated handed him the first dish in silence. Medford's glass remained unfilled till he touched its brim.

'Oh, there's nothing to drink, sir. The men lost the case of Perrier – or dropped it and smashed the bottles. They say it never came. 'Ow do I know, when they never open their 'eathen lips but to lie?' Gosling burst out with sudden violence.

He set down the dish he was handing, and Medford

saw that he had been obliged to do so because his whole body was shaking as if with fever.

'My dear man, what does it matter? You're going to be ill,' Medford exclaimed, laying his hand on the servant's arm. But the latter, muttering: 'Oh, God, if I'd only 'a' gone for it myself,' jerked away and vanished from the room.

Medford sat pondering; it certainly looked as if poor Gosling were on the edge of a breakdown. No wonder, when Medford himself was so oppressed by the uncanniness of the place. Gosling reappeared after an interval, correct, close-lipped, with the dessert and a bottle of white wine. 'Sorry, sir.'

To pacify him, Medford sipped the wine and then pushed his chair away and returned to the court. He was making for the fig tree by the well when Gosling, slipping ahead, transferred his chair and wicker table to the other end of the court.

'You'll be better here – there'll be a breeze presently,' he said. 'I'll fetch your coffee.'

He disappeared again, and Medford sat gazing up at the pile of masonry and plaster, and wondering whether he had not been moved away from his favourite corner to get him out of – or into? – the angle of vision of the invisible watcher. Gosling, having brought the coffee, went away and Medford sat on.

At length he rose and began to pace up and down as he smoked. The moon was not up yet, and darkness fell solemnly on the ancient walls. Presently the breeze arose and began its secret commerce with the palms.

Medford went back to his seat; but as soon as he had resumed it he fancied that the gaze of his hidden watcher was jealously fixed on the red spark of his cigar. The sensation became increasingly distasteful; he could almost feel Almodham reaching out long ghostly arms from somewhere above him in the darkness. He moved back into the living-room, where a shaded light hung from the ceiling; but the room was airless, and finally he went out again and dragged his seat to its old place under the fig tree. From there the windows which he suspected could not command him, and he felt easier, though the corner was out of the breeze and the heavy air seemed tainted with the exhalation of the adjoining well.

'The water must be very low,' Medford mused. The smell, though faint, was unpleasant; it smirched the purity of the night. But he felt safer there, somehow, farther from those unseen eyes which seemed mysteriously to have become his enemies.

'If one of the men had knifed me in the desert, I shouldn't wonder if it would have been at Almodham's orders,' Medford thought. He drowsed.

When he woke the moon was pushing up its ponderous orange disk above the walls, and the darkness in the court was less dense. He must have slept for an hour or more. The night was delicious, or would have been anywhere but there. Medford felt a shiver of his old fever and remembered that Gosling had warned him that the court was unhealthy at night.

'On account of the well, I suppose. I've been sitting too close to it,' he reflected. His head ached, and he fancied that the sweetish foulish smell clung to his face as it had after his bath. He stood up and approached the well to see how much water was left in it. But the moon was not yet high enough to light those depths, and he peered down into blackness.

Suddenly he felt both shoulders gripped from behind and forcibly pressed forward, as if by someone seeking to push him over the edge. An instant later, almost coinciding with his own swift resistance, the push became a strong tug backwards, and he swung round to confront Gosling, whose hands immediately dropped from his shoulders.

'I thought you had the fever, sir – I seemed to see you pitching over,' the man stammered.

Medford's wits returned. 'We must both have it, for I fancied you were pitching me,' he said with a laugh.

'Me, sir?' Gosling gasped. 'I pulled you back as 'ard as ever – '

'Of course. I know.'

Gosling was silent. At length he asked: 'Aren't you going up to bed, sir?'

'No,' said Medford, 'I prefer to stay here.'

Gosling's face took on an expression of dogged anger. 'Well, then, I prefer that you shouldn't.'

Medford laughed again. 'Why? Because it's the hour when Mr Almodham comes out to take the air?'

The effect of this question was unexpected. Gosling dropped back a step or two and flung up his hands, pressing them to his lips as if to stifle a low outcry.

'Come! Own up that he's here and have done with it!' cried Medford.

'Here? What do you mean by "here"? You 'aven't seen 'im, 'ave you?' Before the words were out of the man's lips he flung up his arms again, stumbled forward and fell in a heap at Medford's feet.

Medford, still leaning against the well-head, smiled down contemptuously at the stricken wretch. His conjecture had been the right one, then.

'Get up, man. Don't be a fool! It's not your fault if I guessed that Mr Almodham walks here at night – '

'Walks here!' wailed the other, still cowering.

'Well, doesn't he? He won't kill you for owning up will he?'

'Kill me? Kill me? I wish I'd killed *you*!' Gosling half got to his feet, his head thrown back in ashen terror. 'And I might 'ave, too, so easy! You felt me pushing of you over, didn't you? Coming 'ere spying and sniffing – '

Medford had not changed his position. The very abjectness of the creature at his feet gave him an easy sense of power. But Gosling's last cry had suddenly deflected the course of his speculations. Almodham was here, then; that was certain; but just where was he, and in what shape? A new fear scuttled down Medford's spine.

'So you did want to push me over?' he said. 'Why? As the quickest way of joining your master?'

The effect was more immediate than he had foreseen.

Gosling, getting to his feet, stood there bowed and shrunken in the accusing moonlight.

'Oh, God – and I 'ad you 'arf over! You know I did! And then – it was what you said about Wembley. So help me, sir, I felt you meant it, and it 'eld me back.' The man's face was again wet with tears, but this time Medford recoiled from them as if they had been drops splashed up by a falling body from the foul waters below.

Medford was silent.

Gosling continued to ramble on.

'And if only that Perrier 'ad of come. I don't believe it'd ever 'ave crossed your mind, if only you'd 'ave had your Perrier regular, now would it? But you say 'e walks – and I knew he would! Only – what was I to do with him, with you turning up like that the very day?'

Still Medford did not move.

'And 'im driving me to madness, sir, sheer madness, that same morning. Will you believe it? The very week before you come, I was to sail for England and 'ave my 'oliday, a 'ole month, sir – and I was entitled to six, if there was any justice – a 'ole month in 'Ammersmith, sir, in a cousin's 'ouse, and the chance to see Wembley thoroughly; and then 'e 'eard you was coming, sir, and 'e was bored and lonely 'ere, you understand – 'e 'ad to have new excitements provided for 'im or 'e'd go off 'is bat – and when 'e 'eard you was coming, 'e come out of his black mood in a flash and was 'arf crazy with pleasure, and said: "I'll keep 'im 'ere all winter – a remarkable young man, Gosling – just my kind." And when I says to him: "And 'ow about my 'oliday?" he stares at me with those stony eyes of 'is and says: " 'Oliday? Oh, to be sure; why, next year – we'll see what can be done about it next year." Next year, sir, as if 'e was doing me a favour! And that's the way it 'ad been for nigh on twelve years.

'But this time, if you 'adn't 'ave come I do believe I'd 'ave got away, for he was getting used to 'aving Selim about 'im and his 'ealth was never better – and, well, I told 'im as much, and 'ow a man 'ad his rights after all, and my youth was going, and me that 'ad served him so well chained up 'ere like 'is watchdog, and always next year and next year – and, well, sir, 'e just laughed, sneering-like, and lit 'is cigarette. "Oh, Gosling, cut it out," 'e says.

'He was standing on the very spot where you are now, sir; and he turned to walk into the 'ouse. And it was then I 'it 'im. He was a heavy man, and he fell against the well kerb. And just when you were expected any minute – oh, my God!'

Gosling's voice died out in a strangled murmur.

Medford, at his last words, had unvoluntarily shrunk back a few feet. The two men stood in the middle of the court and stared at each other without speaking. The moon, swinging high above the battlements, sent a searching spear of light down into the guilty darkness of the well.

BERNARD CAPES

The Mask

Le masque tombe, l'homme reste.

There are mental modes as there are sartorial, and,
commercially, the successful publisher is like the
successful tailor, a man who knows how timely to
exploit the fashion. Is it for the moment realism,
romance, the psychic, the analytic, the homely – he
makes, with Rabelais, his soup according to his bread,
and feeds the multitude, as it asks, either on turtle or
pease-porridge.

It was on the crest of a big psychic wave that Hands
and Cumberbatch launched their *Haunted Houses* – a
commonplace but quite effective title. It was all projected and floated within the compass of a few months,
and it proved a first success. The idea was, of course,
authentic possessions, or manifestations, and the thing
was to be done in convincing style, with photogravure
illustrations. The letterpress was entrusted to Penn-
Howard, and the camera business to an old college
friend of his selection, J. B. Lamont. The two worked
in double harness, and collected between them more
material than could be used. But the cream of it was
in the book, though not that particular skimming I am
here to present, and for whose suppression at the time
there were reasons.

I knew Penn-Howard pretty intimately, and should
not have thought him an ideal hand for the task. He

was a younger son of Lord Staveley, and carried an Honourable to his name. A brilliant fellow, cool, practical, modern, with infinite humour and aplomb, he would yet to my mind have lacked the first essential of an evangelist, a faith in the gospel he preached. He did not, in short, believe in spooks, and his dealings with the supernatural must all have been in the nature of an urbane pyrrhonism. But he was a fine, imaginative writer, who could raise terrors he did not feel; and that, no doubt, explained in part his publishers' choice. What chiefly influenced them, however, was unquestionably his social popularity; he was known and liked everywhere, and could count most countable people among his friends, actual or potential. Where he wanted to go he went, and where he went he was welcome – an invaluable factor in this somewhat delicate business of ghost-hunting. But fashion affects even spirits, and, when the supernatural is *en vogue*, doors long jealously shut upon family secrets will be found to open themselves in a quite wonderful way. Hence, the time and the man agreeing, the success of the book.

I met Penn-Howard at Lady Caroon's during the time he was collecting his material. There were a few other guests at Hawkesbury, among them, just arrived, a tall, serious young fellow called Howick. Mr Howick, I understood, had lately succeeded, from a collateral branch, to the Howick estates in Hampshire. His sister was to have come with him, but had excused herself at the last moment – or rather, had been excused by him. She was indefinitely 'ailing', it appeared, and unfit for society. He used the word, in my hearing, with a certain hard decisiveness, in which there seemed a hint of something painful. Others may have felt it too, for the subject of the absentee was at once and discreetly waived.

Hawkesbury has its ghost – a nebulous radiance with a face that floats before one in the gloom of corridors – and naturally at some time during the evening the talk turned upon visitations. Penn-Howard was very picturesque, but, to me, unconvincing on the subject. There was no feeling behind his imagination; and, when put to it, he admitted as much. Someone had complimented him on the gruesome originality of a story of his which had recently appeared in one of the sixpenny magazines, and, quite good-humouredly, he had repudiated the term.

'No mortal being,' he said, 'may claim originality for his productions. There are the three primary colours, blue, red and yellow, and the three dimensions, length, breadth and thickness. They are original; it would be original to make a fourth; only *we* can't do it. We can only exploit creation ready-made as we find it. Everything for us is comprised within those limits – even Lady Caroon's ghost. It is a question of selection and chemical affinities, that is all. There is no such thing here as a supernature.'

He was cried out on for his heresy to his own art – for his confession of its soullessness.

'Soul,' he contended at that, 'is not wanted in art, nor is religion; but only the five unperturbed and explorative senses. Pan, I think, would have made the ideal artist.'

I saw Howick, who was sitting silently apart, suddenly hug himself at these words, bending forward and stiffening his lips, as a man does who mutely traverses a sentiment he is too shy or too superior to discuss. I did not know which it was with him; but inclined to the latter. There was something bonily professorial in his aspect.

While we were talking Lamont came in. He had not appeared at dinner, and I had not yet seen him. He was a compact, stubby man, in astigmatic glasses, and very dark, with a cleft chin, and a resolute mouth under a moustache in keeping with his strong, thick eyebrows. He gave me somehow in the connection a feeling of much greater fitness than did Penn-Howard. There was no suggestion of the *esprit-fort* about *him*, and I got an idea that, though only the technical collaborator, the right atmosphere of the book, if and when it appeared, would be due more to him than to the other. He spoke little, but authoritatively; and I remember he told us that night some queer things about photography – such, for instance, as its mysterious relation to *something* in light-rays, which was not heat and was not light, and yet like light could reveal the hidden, as a mirror reveals to one the objects out of sight behind one's back. Thence, touching upon astral charts and composite portraits by the way, he came to his illustration, which was creepy enough. He had once for some reason, it appeared, taken a post-mortem photograph. The man, the subject, had cut in life a considerable figure in the parliamentary world as an advanced advocate of social and moral reform, and had died in the odour of political sanctity. In securing the negative, circumstances had necessitated a long exposure; but accident had contrived a longer and a deadlier, in the double sense. The searchlight of the lens, being left concentrated an undue time on the lifeless face, had discovered things hitherto impenetrable and unguessed-at. The nature of the real horror had been drawn through the super-imposing veil, and the revelation of what had been existing all the time under the surface was not pleasant. The photograph had not appeared in the illustrated paper for which it was intended, and Lamont had destroyed the negative.

So he told us, in a forcible, economic way which was more effective than much verbal adornment; and again my attention was caught by Howick, who seemed dwelling upon the speaker's words with an expression quite arresting in its ungainly intensity. Later on I saw the two in earnest conversation together.

That was in October, and I left Hawkesbury on the following day. Full ten months passed before I saw Penn-Howard again; and then one hot evening towards dusk he walked into my chambers in Brick Court and asked for a cigarette.

He seemed distraught, withdrawn, like a man who, having something on his mind, was pondering an uncompromising way of relief from it. Quite undesignedly and inevitably I gave him his cue by asking how the book progressed. He heaved out a great, smoke-laden sigh at once, stirred, drew up and dropped his shoulders, and looked at the fiery point of his cigarette before replacing the butt between his lips.

'Oh, the book!' he said. 'It's ready for the press, so far as I'm concerned.'

'And Lamont?'

'Yes, and J. B.'

He got up, paced the width of the room and back, and stood before me, alternately drawing at and with-drawing his cigarette.

'There's one thing that won't go into it,' he said,

his eyes suggesting a rather forced evasion of mine.

'Oh! What's that?'

Again, as if doubtful of himself, he turned to tramp out his restlessness or agitation; thought better of it, and sat resolutely down in a chair against the dark end of the bookcase.

'Would you care to know?' he said. 'Truth is, I came to tell you – if I could; to ask your opinion on the thing. There's the comfort of the judicial brain about you: I can imagine, like a client, that simply to confide one's case to such is to feel relieved of a load of responsibility. It won't go into the book, I say; but I want it to go out of me. I'm too full of it for comfort.'

'Of *it*? Of what?'

'What?' he said, as if in a sudden spasm of violence. 'I wish to God you'd tell me.'

He sat moodily silent for some minutes, and I did nothing to help him out. A hot, sour air came in by the open window, and the heavy red curtains shrank and dilated languidly in it, as if they were the lungs of the stifling room. Outside the dusty roar of the traffic went on unceasingly, with a noise like that of overhead machinery. I was feeling stale and tired, and wished, in the Rooseveltian phrase, that Penn-Howard would either get on or get out.

'It's a queer thing, isn't it,' he said suddenly, with an obvious effort, 'that of all the stuff collected for that book you were speaking of, the only authentic instance for which I can personally vouch is the only instance to be excluded? All the rest was on hearsay.'

'Well, you surprise me,' I said, quietly, after a pause. 'Not because any authentic instance, about which I know nothing, is excluded, but because, by your own confession, there is one to exclude.'

'I know what you mean, of course,' he answered; and quoted: ' "But, spite of all the criticising elves, those who would make us feel must feel themselves." Quite right. I never really believed in supernatural influences. Do I now? That is what I want you to decide for me.'

He laughed slightly; sighed again, and seemed rather to shrink into his dusky corner.

'I'm going to tell you at a run,' he said. 'Bear with me, like an angelic fellow. You remember that man Howick at Lady Caroon's?'

'Yes, quite well.'

'It seemed, when he learnt our business, Lamont's and mine, that there was something he wished to tell us. He pitched upon J. B. as the more responsible partner; and I'm not sure he wasn't right.'

'Nor am I.'

'Oh! you aren't, are you? Well, Jemmy was my choice, anyhow, and for the sake of the qualities you think I lack. He has a way of getting behind things – always had, even at Oxford. Some men seem to know the trick by instinct. He is a very queer sort, and the featest with the camera of any one I've ever seen or heard of. It was for that reason I asked him to come – to get the ghostliest possible out of ghostly buildings and haunted rooms. You remember what he told us that night? I've seen some of his spirit photographs, though without feeling convinced. But his description of that dead face! My God! I thought at the time he was just improvising to suit the occasion; but – '

He stopped abruptly. There was something odd here. It was evident that, for an unknown reason, the thought of *that* time was not the thought of this. I detected an obvious emotion, quite strange to it, in

Penn-Howard's voice. His face, from our positions and the dusk, was almost hidden from me. I made no comment; and thenceforth he spoke on uninterruptedly, while the room slowly darkened about us as we sat.

'Howick wanted us, at the end of our visit, to go with him to his house. Something was happening there, he said, for which he was unable to account. We could not, however, consent, owing to our engagements; but we undertook to include him sooner or later in our ghostly itinerary. He was obliged; but, being so put off, would give us no clue to the nature of the mystery which was disturbing him. As it turned out, we had no choice but to take "Haggarts" the very last on our list.'

'That is the name of his place?'

'Yes. It sounds a bit thin and eerie, doesn't it? but in point of fact, I believe, Haggart is a local word for hawthorn. We went there last of all, and we went there intending to stay a night, and we stayed seven. It was a queer business; and I come to you fresh from it.

'The estate lies slap in the middle of Hampshire. To reach it you alight at a country station which might serve roughly on the map for the hub of the county wheel. The train slides from a tunnel into a ravine of chalk, deep and dazzling, and you have to get on a level with the top of that ravine; and there at once you find immeasurable silence and loneliness. Nothing in my home peregrinations has struck me more forcibly than the real insignificance of urban expansion in its relation to the country as a whole. Towns, however they grow and multiply, remain but inconsiderable freckles on that vast open countenance. Outside the City man's possible radius, and excepting the great manufacturing centres, two miles, one mile beyond the boundary of ninety-nine towns out of a hundred will find you in pastoral solitudes apparently limitless. Here, with Winchester lying but eight miles southward, it was so. From the top of the tunnel we had just penetrated came into view, first a wilderness of thorn-scattered downs, dipping steeply and ruggedly into the railway cutting, then an endlessly extended panorama of wood and waste and field, seemingly houseless and hamletless, and broken only by the white scars of roads, mounting few and far like the crests of waves on a desert sea. Howick had sent a car to meet us, and we switchbacked on monotonously, by unrailed pastures, by woody bottoms, by old hedges grey with dust and draggled with straw. We saw the house long before we headed for it – a strange, ill-designed structure standing out by itself in the fields. It was an antique moat-house, disproportionately tall for its area, and its front flanked by a couple of brick towers, one squat, one lofty. One wound about the lanes to reach it, having it now at this side, now at that, now fairly at one's back, until suddenly it came into close view, a building far more grandiose and imposing than one had surmised. There was the ancient moat surrounding it, and much water channelling the flats about. But there was evidence too, at close quarters, of what one had not guessed – rich, quiet gardens, substantial outbuildings, and a general atmosphere of prosperity.

'An odd, remote place, but in itself distinctly attractive. And Howick did us well. You remember him? A tall stick of a fellow, without a laugh to his whole anatomy, and the hair gone from his temples at thirty; but with the grand manner in entertaining.

We had some '47 port that night – a treat – one of a few remaining bottles laid down by his grand-uncle, Roger Howick, of whom more in a little. And everything was in mellow keeping – pictures, furniture, old crusted anecdote. Only our host was, for all his gracious unbending, somehow out of tone with his environments – in that connection of fruitiness, like the dry nodule on a juicy apple. Constitutionally reserved, I should think, circumstance at that time had drained him of the last capacity for spontaneity. The little fits of abstraction and the wincing starts from them; the forced conversation; the atmosphere of brooding trouble felt through his most hospitable efforts – all pointed to a state of mind which he could neither conceal nor as yet indulge. Often I detected him looking furtively at J. B., often, still more secretively, at his sister, who was the only other one present at the dinner-table.'

For a moment Penn-Howard ceased speaking; and I heard him shift his position, as if suddenly cramped, and slightly clear his throat.

'I mention her now for the first time,' he went on presently. 'She came in after we were seated, and there was the briefest formal introduction, of which she took no notice. She was a slender, unprepossessing woman – her brother's senior by some ten years, I judged – with a strange, unnatural complexion, rather long, pale eyes in red rims, and a sullen manner. Responding only after the curtest fashion to any commonplaces addressed to her, she left us, much to my relief, before dessert, and we saw her no more that evening.

' "Unfit for society"? Most assuredly she was. I remembered her brother's words spoken ten months before, and concluded that nothing had occurred since then to qualify his verdict. A most disagreeable person; unless, perhaps –

'It came to me all at once: was she connected with the mystery, or the mystery with her? A ghost seer, perhaps – neurotic – a victim to hallucinations? Well, Howick had not spoken so far, and it was no good speculating. I turned to the pious discussion of the '47.

'After dinner we went into the gardens where, the night being hot and still, we lingered until the stars came out. During the whole time Howick spoke no word of our mission; but, about the hour the household turned in, he took us back to the hall – a spacious, panelled lounge between the towers – where we settled for a pipe and nightcap. And there silence, like a ghostly overture to the impending, entered our brains and we sat, as it were, listening to it.

'Presently Howick got up. The strained look on his face was succeeded all at once by a sort of sombre light, odd and revealing. All sound in the house had long since ceased.

' "I want you to come with me," he said quietly.

'We rose at once; and he went before, but a few paces, and opened a door.

' "Yes, here," he said, in answer to a look of J. B.'s, "quite close, quite domestic; no bogey of rat-infested corridors or tumble-down attics – no bogey at all, perhaps. It lies under the east tower, this room. When we first came here I *thought* to make it my study."

'He seemed to me then, and always, like a man whose strait concepts of decency had suffered some startling offence, as it might be with one into whose perfectly planned tenement had crept the insidious poison of sewer-gas. Sliding his hand along the wall, he switched on the electric light ("Haggarts" had its own power station), and the room leapt into being. We entered, I leading a little. You must remember I was by then a hardened witchfinder, and inured to atmospheres concocted of the imagination.

'It was not a large room, and it was quite comfortable. There was a heavily clothed table in the middle, a few brass-nailed, leather-backed and seated Jacobean chairs, a high white Adams mantelpiece surmounted by a portrait, a full Chippendale bookcase to either side of it, and on the walls three or four pictures, including a second portrait, of a woman, half-length in an oval frame, which hung opposite the other.

' "Miss Howick, I see," I murmured, turning with a nod to our host. He heard me, as his eyes denoted: but he gave no answer. And then the portrait over the mantelpiece drew my attention. It was in a very poor style of art; yet somehow, one felt, crudely truthful in an amateurish way. There is a class of peripatetic painters, a sort of pedlars in portraiture among country folk, which, having a gift for likenesses, often succeeds photographically in delineating what a higher art inclines to idealise – the obvious in character. Such a one, I concluded, had worked here, painting just what he saw, and only too faithfully. For the obvious was not pleasant – a dark, pitiless face, with a brutal underlip and challenging green eyes, that seemed for ever fixed on the face on the wall opposite. It was that of a middle-aged man, lean and thin-haired, and must have dated, by the cut of its black, brass-buttoned coat, from the late Georgian era.

'I turned again questioningly to Howick. This time

he enlightened me. "Roger Howick," he said, "my great-uncle. It is said he painted that himself, looking in the glass. He had a small gift. Most of the pictures in this room are by him."

'Instinctively I glanced once more towards the oval frame, and thought: "Most – but not that one." Unmistakably it was a portrait of our host's sister – the odd complexion, the sullen, fixed expression, the very dress and coiffure, they were all the same. I wondered how the living subject could endure the thought of that day-long, night-long stare focused for ever on her painted presentment.

'And then silence ensued. We were all in the room, and not a word was spoken. I don't know how long it lasted; but suddenly Lamont addressed me, in a quick, sharp voice: "What's the matter, Penn-Howard?"

'The shock of the question took me like a blow out of sleep. I answered at once: "Something's shut up here. Why don't you let it out?"

'Howick pushed us from the room, and closed the door. "That's it," he said, and that was all. I felt dazed and amazed. I wanted to explain, to protest. A most extraordinary sensation like suppressed tears kept me dumb. I felt humiliated to a degree, and inclined to ease all my conflict of emotions in hysterical laughter. Curse the thing now! It makes me go hot to think of it.

'Howick showed me up to my bedroom. "We'll talk of it tomorrow," he said, and he left me. I was glad to be alone, to get, after a few moments, resolute command of myself. I had a good night after all, and awoke, refreshed and sane, in the clear morning.

'I learned, when I came downstairs, that J. B. and our host were gone out together for an early stroll in the cool. Pending their return, I came to a resolution. I would go and face the room alone, in the bright daylight. Both my pride and my principles were at stake, and I owed the effort to myself. There was nothing to prevent me. I found the door unlocked, and I went in.

'There was some sunlight in the room, penetrating through a thickish shrubbery outside the two windows. I thought the place peculiarly quiet, with an atmosphere of suspense in it which suggested the inaudible whisperings of some infernal inquisition. Nothing was watching me: the green eyes of the man were fixed eternally on the face opposite; and yet I was being watched by everything. It was indescribable, maddening. Determined not to succumb to what I still insisted to myself was a mere trick of the nerves, I walked manfully up to the oval portrait to examine it at close hand. A name and date near the lower margin caught my eye – *T. Lawrence, 1828.* I fairly gasped, reading it. A "Lawrence", and of that remoteness? Then it was not our host's sister! I turned sharply, hearing light breathing – and there she was behind me.

' "What are you doing here?" she said, in a small, cold voice. "Don't you know it is my room?"

'How can I convey the impression she made upon me by daylight? I can think only of one fantastic image to describe her complexion – the hands of a young laundress, puffed and mottled and mealily wrinkled after many hours' work at the tub. So in this face was somehow spoilt and slandered youth, subdued, like the dyer's hand, to "what it worked in". And yet it was the face of the portrait, even to the dusty gold of the hair.

'I made some lame apology. She stamped her foot to end it and dismiss me. But as I passed her to go, she spoke again: "*You* will never find it. It is only faith that can move such mountains."

'I encountered J. B. in the morning-room, and we breakfasted alone together. Howick did not appear – purposely, I think. I felt somehow depressed and uneasy, but resolved to hold fast to myself without too many words. Once I enlightened Lamont: "That portrait," I said, "is not Howick's sister." J. B. lifted his eyebrows. "Oh!" said he, "you have been paying it a morning visit, have you? No, it is a portrait of Maud Howick, daughter to Roger, the man who hangs opposite her." It was my turn to stare. "Howick has been giving you his family history?" I asked. J. B. did not answer for a minute; then he said: "I hope you won't take it in bad part, Penn-Howard; but – yes, he has been talking to me. I know, I think, all there is to know." I had some right to be offended; and he admitted it. "Howick *would* put it to me," he said. "He was struck, it seemed, by something I said that night at Lady Caroon's; and he thinks you at heart a polite sceptic." "Well," I said, "have *you* solved the mystery, whatever it is?" He answered no, but that he had a theory; and asked me if I had formed any. "Not a ghost of one," I replied; "and so Howick was certainly right in confiding first in you – first and last, indeed, if I am to be kept in the dark." "On the contrary," said J. B.; "I am going to repeat every word of Howick's story to you – only in a quiet place."

'We found one presently, out in the fields in the shadow of a ruined byre. It stood up bare and lonely, like a tattered baldachin, and far away under the stoop of its roof we could see the walls of the moat-house rising lean and brown into a cloudless sky. Lamont began his narration with a question: "How old would you suppose this Miss Ruth Howick, the sister, to be?" I was about to answer promptly, recalled my perplexity, and hesitated. "Tell me, without more ado," I responded. "Nineteen," he said, and shut his lips like a trap. Something caught at me, and I at myself. "Go on," I said; "anything after that." And J. B. responded, speaking in his abrupt, incisive way: "This James Howick came into his own here some year and a half ago. There were only himself and his sister – to whom he was and is devoted – the sole survivors of a once considerable family. Their father, Gilbert Howick – son of Paul, who was younger brother to the Roger of the portrait – married one Margaret (a beautiful ward of Paul's, and brought up by him as a member of his own family) about whose origin attached some mystery, which was only made clear to her husband on the occasion of their marriage. Margaret, in brief, was then revealed to Gilbert for his own first cousin once removed, being the natural daughter of his cousin Maud, one of the two children of Roger. I know nothing about the liaison which necessitated this explanation, nor do we need to know. Its results are what concern us. Roger, it is certain, took his daughter's dereliction in a truly devilish spirit. He was an evil, dark man, it was said, pledged to the world and its pride, and once a notorious liver. There is none so extreme in fanaticism as a convert from irreligion; none so damnably righteous as a rake reformed. Having committed the fruits of her sin to the merciful custody of his younger brother – a very different soul, of a humane and pious disposition – Roger turned his attention to the moral and physical ruin of the sinner. He swore that she should forfeit the youth she had abused; and he was as good as his word. No one knows how it happened; no one knows what passed in that dark and haunted house. But Maud grew old in youth. She had been spoiled and petted for her beauty; now the spirit broke in her, and she seemed to shrink and disappear behind the wrinkled, crumbling veil of what had been – like a snake, Penn-Howard, that struggles and cannot cast its dead skin. She grew old in youth. That portrait of her was painted when she was nineteen."

'I cried out. "It was impossible!" "It would seem so," said Lamont. "By what infernal arts he held her to his will – holds her now – it is sickening to conjecture." I turned to look at him. "Holds her now!" I repeated. "Then you mean – " "Yes," he said; "it is imprisoned youth that is for ever trying to escape, to emerge, like the snake, from its dead self. That is the secret of the room. At least, such is my theory."

'I sat as in a dream, awed by, yet struggling to reject, a conclusion so fantastic. "Well, grant your theory," I said at length, with a deep breath; "how does it affect this woman – or girl – this Ruth?"

' "Think," said Lamont. "She is actually that erring child's granddaughter. It seems wonderfully pitiful to me. Her own mother died in that house, during a visit, in giving birth to her. At the time, the son, Roger's son, was master of Haggarts. He was a poor-witted creature, Howick tells me; but he lived, as the imbecile often will, to a ripe old age. Ruth was born prematurely. Her mother, it was said, fell under the cursed influence of the place, and withered in her prime. Maud herself, according to the story, had already died in that very room – was found dead there, little more than a child still in years, a poor, worn ghost of womanhood in seeming. Since then, the room has always had an evil reputation – with what justice Howick never knew or regarded, until the death of his uncle put him, a year and a half ago, in possession of the place."

' "But this Ruth – "

' "It came upon her, it seems, gradually at first, then more rapidly. She lost her health and vivacity; she was for ever haunting the room. When we first met Howick, she was already horribly changed. Ten months have passed since then. He has tried to hide it from the world; has made practically a hermit of himself. The servants of that date have been changed for others, and changed again. She feels, it must be supposed, what we felt – a ceaseless anguish to release something – nothing – a mere pent shadow of horror. And more than that: the sin of the mother is being visited on the child of the child – and through the same diabolical agency." Lamont paused a moment, staring before him, and knotting his fingers together till they cracked. "Penn-Howard," he said, "I believe – I do believe, on my soul, that the secret, whatever it is, lies at the hands of that devil portrait."

' "Then why, in God's name, not remove and burn the thing?"

' "He has offered to. It had a dreadful effect upon her. She cried that so the clue would be lost for ever. And so it affects her to be excluded from the room. He has had to give it all up as hopeless."

'He rose, and I rose with him, not in truth convinced, but oddly agitated.

' "Well," I said, "what do you propose doing?"

'He seemed deep in thought, and did not answer

me. At the door we parted. Entering alone, I met Howick in the hall. He looked at me searchingly in his lank, haggard way, then suddenly took my hand. "You know?" he said. "He has told you? Mr Penn-Howard, she was such a bright and pretty child." I saw tears in his eyes, and understood him better from that moment.

'Lamont was absent all day, and returned late from a prolonged tramp over the hills. The poignant subject was tacitly shelved that night, and we went to bed early.

'The next morning, after breakfast, J. B. turned upon our host. "I want," he said, "that room to myself, possibly for the whole morning, possibly for longer. Can you secure it to me?" Howick nodded. I could detect in his eyes some faint reflection of the strong spirit which faced him. Somehow one never despairs in J. B.'s presence. "I will say you are looking for it," he said. "She will not disturb you then." "There is a closet," said Lamont, "in my bedroom which will do very well for a darkroom."

'He disappeared soon after with his camera. It was his business, and I seldom disturbed him at it. We left him alone, and tried to forget him, though I could see all the morning that Howick was in a state of painful nervous tension. Not till after lunch did we hear or see anything of my colleague, and then he came in, descending from his improvised darkroom. He held a negative in his hand, and he shut the door behind him like a man who had something to reveal. "Mr Howick," he said, straight out and at once, "I am going to ask you to let me destroy that portrait of your great-uncle."

'The words took us like a smack; and, as we stood

163

gaping, J. B. held out his negative. "Look at this," he said, and beckoning us to the window, let the light slant upon the thing so as to disclose its subject. "The secret stands revealed, does it not?" said he, quiet and low. "A long, a very long exposure, and the devil is betrayed. Oh, a wonderful detective is the camera."

'I heard Howick breathing fast over my shoulder. For myself, I was as much perplexed as astonished. "It is the portrait," I muttered, "and yet it is not. There is the ghost of something revealing itself through it." "Exactly," said J. B. drily – and went and put the negative behind the clock on the mantelpiece. "Well, shall we do it?" he asked, turning to our host. Howick's face was ghastly. He could hardly get out the words, "In God's name, do what you will! Better to dare and end it all than live on like this." J. B. stood looking at him earnestly. "No," he said. "You go to *her*. Penn-Howard and I will manage the business."

'We left him, and went to the room and locked ourselves in. I confess my blood was tingling. So shut in with it, the unspeakable atmosphere of that place seemed to intensify to a degree quite infernal. I seemed to realise in it a battle of two wills, Lamont's and another's. My friend's face was a little pale; but the set of its every feature spoke of an inexorable purpose. As we handled the portrait to lower it, it fell heavily and unaccountably forward, an edge of the massive frame just missing J. B.'s skull by an inch. "That miscarriage does for *you*, my friend," he said, showing his teeth a little, like a dog. Portrait and frame lay apart on the floor; the shock had disunited them. Lamont knelt, and went over the former unflinchingly. The green eyes, caught from their age-long inquisition of the face on the wall opposite, seemed to glare up into his in hate and fury. "Get out your knife," I cried irresistibly, "and slash the cursed thing to pieces." "No," he answered; "that is not at all my purpose."

'What was his purpose? I knew in a moment. He fetched out his knife indeed, and, hunting over the surface of the thing, found a blister in the paint, cut into it, seized an edge between thumb and finger, and, flaying away a long strip, uttered a loud, jubilant exclamation. "Look at this, Penn-Howard." I bent over – and then I understood in a flash. It was but a strip exposed; but it was like a chink of dazzling daylight let through. There was another portrait underneath.

'Artists tell me that when one oil painting is superimposed on another within a few years of the production of the first, only exceptional circumstances can render their successful separation possible. I know nothing about the technical difficulties; I know only that in this case we were able to remove the overlying skin, strip by strip, almost without a hitch, until the whole of the upper portrait lay in flakes of rubbish upon the floor – to be delivered within a few minutes to consuming fire. And the thing revealed! I cannot describe the beauty of that vision, bursting into flower out of its age-long cimmerian darkness. It was the personification of youth – a young girl (she might have been sixteen), laughing and lovely, the most wilful, bewitching face you could imagine – Maud Howick.'

Once more Penn-Howard fell silent. The room by now was dark; his figure was indistinguishable, and his voice, when he spoke again, seemed a shadow borne out of the shadows: 'While we gazed, fascinated, there came a knock on the door. It was Howick. His face was transfigured – his eyes glowed. "She has fallen asleep," he said; "and that is not all. My God, what has happened?" We took him in and showed him the portrait. He broke down before it. "The little grand-mother!" he said, "the poor, erring child! And it was of that, and by that damnable method, that that fiend incarnate robbed her! To imprison her youth within his wicked soul, drawn by him out of the mirror to stand for ever at sentry over her lest she escape. And she pined and withered in that hideous bondage, until he could show her, in that other, what his hate had wrought of her. But she is free at last – her soul is free to fly for ever this dark house of its captivity."

'J. B. looked at him searchingly. "And your sister?" he said. Howick did not answer; but he beckoned us to follow him, and he led us into the drawing-room where she lay. Fast in dreamless slumber as the sleeping beauty. But the change! God in heaven; she was already a child again!'

The speaker halted for the last time. It was minutes before he took up the tale, in a constrained and hesitating way: 'I saw all this, I tell you – saw it with these eyes. We stayed there yet a week longer; and I left her in the end a radiant, laughing child, a joyous, captivating little soul, who remembered, or seemed to remember, nothing of the fearful months pre-ceding. And yet, now I am away, I doubt. It is the curse of my disposition. What, for instance, if one were to yield her one's soul and discover, too late, that one had succumbed to some unreal glamour, to the arts of a veritable and most feminine Lamia. I believe it is not so; I know it is not so – and yet, the incredible – '

His voice died out. I saw how it was, and answered, I am afraid, brutally: 'You aren't really in love with her, of course. That is as clear as print.'

He rose at once. 'That decides it,' he said. 'I shall go back and ask her to be my wife.'

But he did not do so. Two days later I met him in the street. His manner was quite breezy and insouciant. 'Oh, by the by!' he said, in a break of our conversation, 'did I tell you that I had heard from J. B.? He and Miss Howick are engaged.'

ELIZABETH GASKELL

The Grey Woman

1

There is a mill by the Neckar-side, to which many
people resort for coffee, according to the fashion
which is almost national in Germany. There is
nothing particularly attractive in the situation of this
mill; it is on the Mannheim (the flat and unromantic)
side of Heidelberg. The river turns the mill-wheel
with a plenteous gushing sound; the out-buildings
and the dwelling-house of the miller form a well-kept
dusty quadrangle. Again, farther from the river, there
is a garden full of willows, and arbours, and flower-
beds not well kept, but very profuse in flowers and
luxuriant creepers, knotting and looping the arbours
together. In each of these arbours is a stationary table
of white painted wood, and light moveable chairs of
the same colour and material.

I went to drink coffee there with some friends in
184—. The stately old miller came out to greet us, as
some of the party were known to him of old. He was
of a grand build of a man, and his loud musical voice,
with its tone friendly and familiar, his rolling laugh of
welcome, went well with the keen bright eye, the fine
cloth of his coat, and the general look of substance
about the place. Poultry of all kinds abounded in the
mill-yard, where there were ample means of livelihood
for them strewed on the ground; but not content with
this, the miller took out handfuls of corn from the

sacks, and threw liberally to the cocks and hens that ran almost under his feet in their eagerness. And all the time he was doing this, as it were habitually, he was talking to us, and ever and anon calling to his daughter and the serving-maids, to bid them hasten the coffee we had ordered. He followed us to an arbour, and saw us served to his satisfaction with the best of everything we could ask for; and then left us to go round to the different arbours and see that each party was properly attended to; and, as he went, this great, prosperous, happy-looking man whistled softly one of the most plaintive airs I ever heard.

'His family have held this mill ever since the old Palatinate days; or rather, I should say, have possessed the ground ever since then, for two successive mills of theirs have been burnt down by the French. If you want to see Scherer in a passion, just talk to him of the possibility of a French invasion.'

But at this moment, still whistling that mournful air, we saw the miller going down the steps that led from the somewhat raised garden into the mill-yard; and so I seemed to have lost my chance of putting him in a passion.

We had nearly finished our coffee and our *kucken* and our cinnamon cake, when heavy splashes fell on our thick leafy covering; quicker and quicker they came, coming through the tender leaves as if they were tearing them asunder; all the people in the garden were hurrying under shelter, or seeking for their carriages standing outside. Up the steps the miller came hastening, with a crimson umbrella, fit to cover everyone left in the garden, and followed by his daughter, and one or two maidens, each bearing an umbrella.

'Come into the house – come in, I say. It is a summer-storm, and will flood the place for an hour or two, till the river carries it away. Here, here.'

And we followed him back into his own house. We went into the kitchen first. Such an array of bright copper and tin vessels I never saw; and all the wooden things were as thoroughly scoured. The red tile floor was spotless when we went in, but in two minutes it was all over slop and dirt with the tread of many feet; for the kitchen was filled, and still the worthy miller kept bringing in more people under his great crimson umbrella. He even called the dogs in, and made them lie down under the tables.

His daughter said something to him in German, and he shook his head merrily at her. Everybody laughed.

'What did she say?' I asked.

'She told him to bring the ducks in next; but indeed if more people come we shall be suffocated. What with the thundery weather, and the stove, and all these steaming clothes, I really think we must ask leave to pass on. Perhaps we might go in and see Frau Scherer.'

My friend asked the daughter of the house for permission to go into an inner chamber and see her mother. It was granted, and we went into a sort of saloon, overlooking the Neckar; very small, very bright, and very close. The floor was slippery with polish; long narrow pieces of looking-glass against the walls reflected the perpetual motion of the river opposite; a white porcelain stove, with some old-fashioned ornaments of brass about it; a sofa, covered with Utrecht velvet, a table before it, and a piece of worsted-worked carpet under it; a vase of artificial flowers; and, lastly, an alcove with a bed in it, on which lay the paralysed wife of the good miller, knitting busily, formed the furniture. I spoke as if this was all that was to be seen in the room; but, sitting quietly, while my friend kept up a brisk conversation in a language which I but half understood, my eye was caught by a picture in a dark corner of the room, and I got up to examine it more nearly.

It was that of a young girl of extreme beauty; evidently of middle rank. There was a sensitive refinement in her face, as if she almost shrank from the gaze which, of necessity, the painter must have fixed upon her. It was not over-well painted, but I felt that it must have been a good likeness, from this strong impress of peculiar character which I have tried to describe. From the dress, I should guess it to have been painted in the latter half of the last century. And I afterwards heard that I was right.

There was a little pause in the conversation.

'Will you ask Frau Scherer who this is?'

My friend repeated my question, and received a long reply in German. Then she turned round and translated it to me.

'It is the likeness of a great-aunt of her husband's.' (My friend was standing by me, and looking at the picture with sympathetic curiosity.) 'See! here is the name on the open page of this Bible, "Anna Scherer, 1778". Frau Scherer says there is a tradition in the family that this pretty girl, with her complexion of lilies and roses, lost her colour so entirely through fright, that she was known by the name of the Grey Woman. She speaks as if this Anna Scherer lived in some state of life-long terror. But she does not know details; refers me to her husband for them. She thinks he has some papers which were written by the original of that picture for her daughter, who died in this very house not long after our friend there was married. We can ask Herr Scherer for the whole story if you like.'

'Oh yes, pray do!' said I. And, as our host came in at this moment to ask how we were faring, and to tell us that he had sent to Heidelberg for carriages to convey us home, seeing no chance of the heavy rain abating, my friend, after thanking him, passed on to my request.

'Ah!' said he, his face changing, 'the aunt Anna had a sad history. It was all owing to one of those hellish Frenchmen; and her daughter suffered for it – the cousin Ursula, as we all called her when I was a child. To be sure, the good cousin Ursula was his child as well. The sins of the fathers are visited on their children. The lady would like to know all about it, would she? Well, there are papers – a kind of apology the aunt Anna wrote for putting an end to her daughter's engagement – or rather facts which she revealed, that prevented cousin Ursula from marrying the man she loved; and so she would never have any other good fellow, else I have heard say my father would have been thankful to have made her his wife.' All this time he was rummaging in the drawer of an old-fashioned bureau, and now he turned round, with a bundle of yellow manuscript in his hand, which he gave to my friend, saying, 'Take it home, take it home, and if you care to make out our crabbed German writing, you may keep it as long as you like, and read it at your leisure. Only I must have it back again when you have done with it, that's all.'

And so we became possessed of the manuscript of the following letter, which it was our employment, during many a long evening that ensuing winter, to translate, and in some parts to abbreviate. The letter began with some reference to the pain which she had already inflicted upon her daughter by some unexplained opposition to a project of marriage; but I doubt if, without the clue with which the good miller had furnished us, we could have made out even this much from the passionate, broken sentences that made us fancy that some scene between the mother and daughter – and possibly a third person – had occurred just before the mother had begun to write.

'Thou dost not love thy child, mother! Thou dost not care if her heart is broken!' Ah, God! and these words of my heart-beloved Ursula ring in my ears as if the sound of them would fill them when I lie a-dying. And her poor tear-stained face comes between me and everything else. Child! hearts do not break; life is very tough as well as very terrible. But I will not decide for thee. I will tell thee all; and thou shalt bear the burden of choice. I may be wrong; I have little wit left, and never had much, I think; but an instinct serves me in place of judgement, and that instinct tells me that thou and thy Henri must never be married. Yet I may be in error. I would fain make my child happy. Lay this paper before the good priest Schriesheim if, after reading it, thou hast doubts which make thee uncertain. Only I will tell thee all now, on condition that no spoken word ever passes between us on the subject. It would kill me to be questioned. I should have to see all present again.

My father held, as thou knowest, the mill on the Neckar, where thy new-found uncle, Scherer, now lives. Thou rememberest the surprise with which we were received there last vintage twelvemonth. How thy uncle disbelieved me when I said that I was his sister Anna, whom he had long believed to be dead, and how I had to lead thee underneath the picture, painted of me long ago, and point out, feature by feature, the likeness between it and thee; and how, as I spoke, I recalled first to my own mind, and then by speech to his, the details of the time when it was painted; the merry words that passed between us then, a happy boy and girl; the position of the articles of furniture in the room; our father's habits; the cherry tree, now cut down, that shaded the window of my bedroom, through which my brother was wont to squeeze himself, in order to spring on to the topmost bough that would bear his weight; and thence would pass me back his cap laden with fruit to where I sat on the window-sill, too sick with fright for him to care much for eating the cherries.

And at length Fritz gave way, and believed me to be his sister Anna, even as though I were risen from the dead. And thou rememberest how he fetched in his wife, and told her that I was not dead, but was come back to the old home once more, changed as I was. And she would scarce believe him, and scanned me with a cold, distrustful eye, till at length – for I knew her of old as Babette Müller – I said that I was well-to-do, and needed not to seek out friends for what they had to give. And then she asked – not me, but her husband – why I had kept silent so long, leading all – father, brother, everyone that loved me in my own dear home – to esteem me dead. And then thine uncle (thou rememberest?) said he cared not to know more than I cared to tell; that I was his Anna, found again, to be a blessing to him in his old age, as I had been in his boyhood. I thanked him in my heart for his trust; for were the need for telling all less than it seems to me now I could not speak of my past life. But she, who was my sister-in-law still, held back her welcome, and, for want of that, I did not go to live in Heidelberg as I had planned beforehand, in order to be near my brother Fritz, but contented myself with his promise to be a father to my Ursula when I should die and leave this weary world.

That Babette Müller was, as I may say, the cause of all my life's suffering. She was a baker's daughter in Heidelberg – a great beauty, as people said, and, indeed, as I could see for myself. I, too – thou sawest my picture – was reckoned a beauty, and I believe I was so. Babette Müller looked upon me as a rival. She liked to be admired, and had no one much to love her. I had several people to love me – thy grandfather, Fritz, the old servant Kätchen, Karl, the head apprentice at the mill – and I feared admiration and notice, and being stared at as the 'Schöne Müllerin', whenever I went to make my purchases in Heidelberg.

Those were happy, peaceful days. I had Kätchen to help me in the housework, and whatever we did pleased my brave old father, who was always gentle and indulgent towards us women, though he was stern enough with the apprentices in the mill. Karl, the oldest of these, was his favourite; and I can see now that my father wished him to marry me, and that Karl himself was desirous to do so. But Karl was rough-spoken, and passionate – not with me, but with the others – and I shrank from him in a way which, I fear, gave him pain. And then came thy uncle Fritz's marriage; and Babette was brought to the mill to be its mistress. Not that I cared much for giving up my post, for, in spite of my father's great kindness, I always feared that I did not manage well for so large a family (with the men, and a girl under Kätchen, we sat down eleven each night to supper). But when Babette began to find fault with Kätchen, I was unhappy at the blame that fell on faithful servants; and by and by I began to see that Babette was egging on Karl to make more open love to me, and, as she once said, to get done with it, and take me off to a home of my own. My father was growing old, and did not perceive all my daily discomfort. The more Karl advanced, the more I disliked him. He was good in the main, but I had no notion of being married, and could not bear anyone who talked to me about it.

Things were in this way when I had an invitation to go to Carlsruhe to visit a schoolfellow, of whom I had been very fond. Babette was all for my going; I don't think I wanted to leave home, and yet I had been very fond of Sophie Rupprecht. But I was always shy among strangers. Somehow the affair was settled for me, but not until both Fritz and my father had made enquiries as to the character and position of the Rupprechts. They learned that the father had held some kind of inferior position about the Grand-duke's court, and was now dead, leaving a widow, a noble lady, and two daughters, the elder of whom was Sophie, my friend. Madame Rupprecht was not rich, but more than respectable – genteel. When this was ascertained, my father made no opposition to my going; Babette forwarded it by all the means in her power, and even my dear Fritz had his word to say in its favour. Only Kätchen was against it – Kätchen and Karl. The opposition of Karl did more to send me to Carlsruhe than anything. For I could have objected to go; but when he took upon himself to ask what was the good of going a-gadding, visiting strangers of whom no one knew anything, I yielded to circumstances – to the pulling of Sophie and the pushing of Babette. I was silently vexed, I remember, at Babette's inspection of my clothes; at the way in which she settled that this gown was too old-fashioned, or that too common, to go with me on my visit to a noble lady; and at the way in which she took upon herself to spend the money my father had given me to buy what was requisite for the occasion. And yet I blamed myself, for everyone else thought her so kind for doing all this; and she herself meant kindly, too.

At last I quitted the mill by the Neckar-side. It was a long day's journey, and Fritz went with me to Carlsruhe. The Rupprechts lived on the third floor of a house a little behind one of the principal streets, in a cramped-up court, to which we gained admittance through a doorway in the street. I remember how pinched their rooms looked after the large space we had at the mill, and yet they had an air of grandeur about them which was new to me, and which gave me pleasure, faded as some of it was. Madame Rupprecht was too formal a lady for me; I was never at my ease with her; but Sophie was all that I had recollected her at school: kind, affectionate, and only rather too ready with her expressions of admiration and regard. The little sister kept out of our way; and that was all we needed, in the first enthusiastic renewal of our early friendship. The one great object of Madame Rupprecht's life was to retain her position in society; and as her means were much diminished since her husband's death, there was not much comfort, though there was a great deal of show, in their way of living; just the opposite of what it was at my father's house. I believe that my coming was not too much desired by Madame Rupprecht, as I brought with me another mouth to be fed; but Sophie had spent a year or more in entreating for permission to invite me, and her mother, having once consented, was too well bred not to give me a stately welcome.

The life in Carlsruhe was very different from what it was at home. The hours were later, the coffee was weaker in the morning, the pottage was weaker, the boiled beef less relieved by other diet, the dresses finer, the evening engagements constant. I did not find these visits pleasant. We might not knit, which would have relieved the tedium a little; but we sat in a circle, talking together, only interrupted occasionally by a gentleman, who, breaking out of the knot of men who stood near the door, talking eagerly together, stole across the room on tiptoe, his hat under his arm, and, bringing his feet together in the position we called the first at the dancing-school, made a low bow to the lady he was going to address. The first time I saw these manners I could not help smiling; but Madame Rupprecht saw me, and spoke to me next morning rather severely, telling me that, of course, in my country breeding I could have seen nothing of court manners, or French fashions, but that that was no reason for my laughing at them. Of course I tried never to smile again in company. This visit to Carlsruhe took place in '89, just when everyone was full of the events taking place at Paris; and yet at Carlsruhe French fashions were more talked of than French politics. Madame Rupprecht, especially, thought a great deal of all French people. And this again was quite different to us at home. Fritz could hardly bear the name of a Frenchman; and it had nearly been an obstacle to my visit to Sophie that her mother preferred being called Madame to her proper title of Frau.

One night I was sitting next to Sophie, and longing for the time when we might have supper and go home, so as to be able to speak together, a thing forbidden by Madame Rupprecht's rules of etiquette, which strictly prohibited any but the most necessary conversation passing between members of the same family when in society. I was sitting, I say, scarcely keeping back my inclination to yawn, when two gentlemen came in, one of whom was evidently a stranger to the whole party, from the formal manner in which the host led him up, and presented him to the hostess. I thought I had never seen anyone so handsome or so elegant. His hair was powdered, of course, but one could see from his complexion that it was fair in its natural state. His features were as delicate as a girl's, and set off by two little 'mouches', as we called patches in those days, one at the left corner of his mouth, the other prolonging, as it were, the right eye. His dress was blue and silver. I was so lost in admiration of this beautiful young man, that I was as much surprised as if the angel Gabriel had spoken to me, when the lady of the house brought him forward to present him to me. She called him Monsieur de la Tourelle, and he began to speak to me in French; but though I understood him perfectly, I dared not trust myself to reply to him in that language. Then he tried German, speaking it with a kind of soft lisp that I thought charming. But, before the end of the evening, I became a little tired of the affected softness and effeminacy of his manners, and the exaggerated compliments he paid me, which had the effect of making all the company turn round and look at me. Madame Rupprecht was, however, pleased with the precise thing that displeased me. She liked either Sophie or me to create a sensation; of course she would have preferred that it should have been her daughter, but her daughter's friend was next best. As we went away, I heard Madame Rupprecht and Monsieur de la Tourelle reciprocating civil speeches with might and main, from which I found out that the French gentleman was coming to call on us the next day. I do not know whether I was more glad or frightened, for I had been kept upon stilts of good manners all the evening. But still I was flattered when Madame Rupprecht spoke as if she had invited him, because he had shown pleasure in my society, and even more gratified by Sophie's ungrudging delight at the evident interest I had excited in so fine and agreeable a gentleman. Yet, with all this, they had hard work to keep me from running out of the salon the next day, when we heard his voice enquiring at the gate on the stairs for Madame Rupprecht. They had made me put on my Sunday gown, and they themselves were dressed as for a reception.

When he was gone away, Madame Rupprecht congratulated me on the conquest I had made; for, indeed, he had scarcely spoken to anyone else, beyond what mere civility required, and had almost invited himself to come in the evening to bring some new song, which was all the fashion in Paris, he said. Madame Rupprecht had been out all morning, as she told me, to glean information about Monsieur

de la Tourelle. He was a *propriétaire*, had a small
château on the Vosges mountains; he owned land
there, but had a large income from some sources
quite independent of this property. Altogether, he
was a good match, as she emphatically observed.
She never seemed to think that I could refuse him
after this account of his wealth, nor do I believe she
would have allowed Sophie a choice, even had he
been as old and ugly as he was young and handsome.
I do not quite know – so many events have come to
pass since then, and blurred the clearness of my
recollections – if I loved him or not. He was very
much devoted to me; he almost frightened me by
the excess of his demonstrations of love. And he was
very charming to everybody around me, who all
spoke of him as the most fascinating of men, and of
me as the most fortunate of girls. And yet I never felt
quite at my ease with him. I was always relieved
when his visits were over, although I missed his
presence when he did not come. He prolonged his
visit to the friend with whom he was staying at Carlsruhe, on purpose to woo me. He loaded me with
presents, which I was unwilling to take, only Madame
Rupprecht seemed to consider me an affected prude
if I refused them. Many of these presents consisted of
articles of valuable old jewellery, evidently belonging
to his family; by accepting these I doubled the ties
which were formed around me by circumstances even
more than by my own consent. In those days we did
not write letters to absent friends as frequently as is
done now, and I had been unwilling to name him in
the few letters that I wrote home. At length, however,
I learned from Madame Rupprecht that she had
written to my father to announce the splendid

conquest I had made, and to request his presence at my betrothal. I started with astonishment. I had not realised that affairs had gone so far as this. But when she asked me, in a stern, offended manner, what I had meant by my conduct if I did not intend to marry Monsieur de la Tourelle – I had received his visits, his presents, all his various advances without showing any unwillingness or repugnance – (and it was all true; I had shown no repugnance, though I did not wish to be married to him – at least, not so soon) – what could I do but hang my head, and silently consent to the rapid enunciation of the only course which now remained for me if I would not be esteemed a heartless coquette all the rest of my days?

There was some difficulty, which I afterwards learnt that my sister-in-law had obviated, about my betrothal taking place from home. My father, and Fritz especially, were for having me return to the mill, and there be betrothed, and from thence be married. But the Rupprechts and Monsieur de la Tourelle were equally urgent on the other side; and Babette was unwilling to have the trouble of the commotion at the mill; and also, I think, a little disliked the idea of the contrast of my grander marriage with her own.

So my father and Fritz came over to the betrothal. They were to stay at an inn in Carlsruhe for a fortnight, at the end of which time the marriage was to take place. Monsieur de la Tourelle told me he had business at home, which would oblige him to be absent during the interval between the two events; and I was very glad of it, for I did not think that he valued my father and my brother as I could have wished him to do. He was very polite to them; put on all the soft, grand manner, which he had rather dropped with me; and complimented us all round, beginning with my father and Madame Rupprecht, and ending with little Alwina. But he a little scoffed at the old-fashioned church ceremonies which my father insisted on; and I fancy Fritz must have taken some of his compliments as satire, for I saw certain signs of manner by which I knew that my future husband, for all his civil words, had irritated and annoyed my brother. But all the money arrangements were liberal in the extreme, and more than satisfied, almost surprised, my father. Even Fritz lifted up his eyebrows and whistled. I alone did not care about anything. I was bewitched – in a dream – a kind of despair. I had got into a net through my own timidity and weakness, and I did not see how to get out of it. I clung to my own home-people that fortnight as I had never done before. Their voices, their ways were all so pleasant and familiar to me, after the constraint in which I had been living. I might speak and do as I liked without being corrected by Madame Rupprecht, or reproved in a delicate, complimentary way by Monsieur de la Tourelle. One day I said to my father that I did not want to be married, that I would rather go back to the dear old mill; but he seemed to feel this speech of mine as a dereliction of duty as great as if I had committed perjury; as if, after the ceremony of betrothal, no one had any right over me but my future husband. And yet he asked me some solemn questions; but my answers were not such as to do me any good.

'Dost thou know any fault or crime in this man that should prevent God's blessing from resting on thy marriage with him? Dost thou feel aversion or repugnance to him in any way?'

And to all this what could I say? I could only

stammer out that I did not think I loved him enough; and my poor old father saw in this reluctance only the fancy of a silly girl who did not know her own mind, but who had now gone too far to recede.

So we were married, in the Court chapel, a privilege which Madame Rupprecht had used no end of efforts to obtain for us, and which she must have thought was to secure us all possible happiness, both at the time and in recollection afterwards.

We were married; and after two days spent in festivity at Carlsruhe, among all our new fashionable friends there, I bade goodbye for ever to my dear old father. I had begged my husband to take me by way of Heidelberg to his old castle in the Vosges; but I found an amount of determination, under that effeminate appearance and manner, for which I was not prepared, and he refused my first request so decidedly that I dared not urge it. 'Henceforth, Anna,' said he, 'you will move in a different sphere of life; and though it is possible that you may have the power of showing favour to your relations from time to time, yet much or familiar intercourse will be undesirable, and is what I cannot allow.' I felt almost afraid, after this formal speech, of asking my father and Fritz to come and see me; but, when the agony of bidding them farewell overcame all my prudence, I did beg them to pay me a visit ere long. But they shook their heads, and spoke of business at home, of different kinds of life, of my being a Frenchwoman now. Only my father broke out at last with a blessing, and said, 'If my child is unhappy – which God forbid – let her remember that her father's house is ever open to her.' I was on the point of crying out, 'Oh! take me back then now, my father! oh, my father!' when I felt, rather than saw, my husband present near me. He looked on with a slightly contemptuous air; and, taking my hand in his, he led me weeping away, saying that short farewells were always the best when they were inevitable.

It took us two days to reach his château in the Vosges, for the roads were bad and the way difficult to ascertain. Nothing could be more devoted than he was all the time of the journey. It seemed as if he were trying in every way to make up for the separation which every hour made me feel the more complete between my present and my former life. I seemed as if I were only now wakening up to a full sense of what marriage was, and I dare say I was not a cheerful companion on the tedious journey. At length, jealousy of my regret for my father and brother got the better of M. de la Tourelle, and he became so much displeased with me that I thought my heart would break with the sense of desolation. So it was in no cheerful frame of mind that we approached Les Rochers, and I thought that perhaps it was because I was so unhappy that the place looked so dreary. On one side, the château looked like a raw new building, hastily run up for some immediate purpose, without any growth of trees or underwood near it, only the remains of the stone used for building, not yet cleared away from the immediate neighbourhood, although weeds and lichens had been suffered to grow near and over the heaps of rubbish; on the other, were the great rocks from which the place took its name, and rising close against them, as if almost a natural formation, was the old castle, whose building dated many centuries back.

It was not large nor grand, but it was strong and picturesque, and I used to wish that we lived in it rather than in the smart, half-furnished apartment in the new edifice, which had been hastily got ready for my reception. Incongruous as the two parts were, they were joined into a whole by means of intricate passages and unexpected doors, the exact positions of which I never fully understood. M. de la Tourelle led me to a suite of rooms set apart for me, and formally installed me in them, as in a domain of which I was sovereign. He apologised for the hasty preparation which was all he had been able to make for me, but promised, before I asked, or even thought of complaining, that they should be made as luxurious as heart could wish before many weeks had elapsed. But when, in the gloom of an autumnal evening, I caught my own face and figure reflected in all the mirrors, which showed only a mysterious background in the dim light of the many candles which failed to illuminate the great proportions of the half-furnished salon, I clung to M. de la Tourelle, and begged to be taken to the rooms he had occupied before his marriage, he seemed angry with me, although he affected to laugh, and so decidedly put aside the notion of my having any other rooms but these, that I trembled in silence at the fantastic figures and shapes which my imagination called up as peopling the background of those gloomy mirrors. There was my boudoir, a little less dreary – my bedroom, with its grand and tarnished furniture, which I commonly made into my sitting-room, locking up the various doors which led into the boudoir, the salon, the passages – all but one, through which M. de la Tourelle always entered from his own apartments in the older part of the castle. But this preference of mine for occupying my bedroom annoyed M. de la

Tourelle, I am sure, though he did not care to express his displeasure. He would always allure me back into the salon, which I disliked more and more from its complete separation from the rest of the building by the long passage into which all the doors of my apartment opened. This passage was closed by heavy doors and *portières*, through which I could not hear a sound from the other parts of the house, and, of course, the servants could not hear any movement or cry of mine unless expressly summoned. To a girl brought up as I had been in a household where every individual lived all day in the sight of every other member of the family, never wanted either cheerful words or the sense of silent companionship, this grand isolation of mine was very formidable; and the more so, because M. de la Tourelle, as landed proprietor, sportsman, and what not, was generally out of doors the greater part of every day, and sometimes for two or three days at a time. I had no pride to keep me from associating with the domestics; it would have been natural to me in many ways to have sought them out for a word of sympathy in those dreary days when I was left so entirely to myself, had they been like our kindly German servants. But I disliked them, one and all; I could not tell why. Some were civil, but there was a familiarity in their civility which repelled me; others were rude, and treated me more as if I were an intruder than their master's chosen wife; and yet of the two sets I liked these last the best.

The principal male servant belonged to this latter class. I was very much afraid of him, he had such an air of suspicious surliness about him in all he did for me; and yet M. de la Tourelle spoke of him as most valuable and faithful. Indeed, it sometimes struck

me that Lefebvre ruled his master in some things;
and this I could not make out. For, while M. de la
Tourelle behaved towards me as if I were some
precious toy or idol, to be cherished, and fostered,
and petted, and indulged, I soon found out how
little I, or, apparently, anyone else, could bend the
terrible will of the man who had on first acquaintance
appeared to me too effeminate and languid to exert
his will in the slightest particular. I had learnt to
know his face better now; and to see that some
vehement depth of feeling, the cause of which I could
not fathom, made his grey eye glitter with pale light,
and his lips contract, and his delicate cheek whiten
on certain occasions. But all had been so open and
above board at home, that I had no experience to
help me to unravel any mysteries among those who
lived under the same roof. I understood that I had
made what Madame Rupprecht and her set would
have called a great marriage, because I lived in a
château with many servants, bound ostensibly to
obey me as a mistress. I understood that M. de la
Tourelle was fond enough of me in his way – proud
of my beauty, I dare say (for he often enough spoke
about it to me) – but he was also jealous, and
suspicious, and uninfluenced by my wishes, unless
they tallied with his own. I felt at this time as if I
could have been fond of him too, if he would have
let me; but I was timid from my childhood, and before
long my dread of his displeasure (coming down like
thunder into the midst of his love, for such slight
causes as a hesitation in reply, a wrong word, or
a sigh for my father), conquered my humorous
inclination to love one who was so handsome, so
accomplished, so indulgent and devoted. But if I

could not please him when indeed I loved him, you may imagine how often I did wrong when I was so much afraid of him as to quietly avoid his company for fear of his outbursts of passion. One thing I remember noticing, that the more M. de la Tourelle was displeased with me, the more Lefebvre seemed to chuckle; and when I was restored to favour, sometimes on as sudden an impulse as that which occasioned my disgrace, Lefebvre would look askance at me with his cold, malicious eyes, and once or twice at such times he spoke most disrespectfully to M. de la Tourelle.

I have almost forgotten to say that, in the early days of my life at Les Rochers, M. de la Tourelle, in contemptuous indulgent pity at my weakness in disliking the dreary grandeur of the salon, wrote up to the milliner in Paris from whom my *corbeille de marriage* had come, to desire her to look out for me a maid of middle age, experienced in the toilette, and with so much refinement that she might on occasion serve as companion to me.

2

A Norman woman, Amante by name, was sent to Les Rochers by the Paris milliner, to become my maid. She was tall and handsome, though upwards of forty, and somewhat gaunt. But, on first seeing her, I liked her; she was neither rude nor familiar in her manners, and had a pleasant look of straightforwardness about her that I had missed in all the inhabitants of the château, and had foolishly set down in my own mind as a national want. Amante was directed by M. de la Tourelle to sit in my boudoir, and to be always within call. He also gave her many instructions as to her duties in matters which, perhaps, strictly belonged to my department of management. But I was young and inexperienced, and thankful to be spared any responsibility.

I dare say it was true what M. de la Tourelle said – before many weeks had elapsed – that, for a great lady, a lady of a castle, I became sadly too familiar with my Norman waiting-maid. But you know that by birth we were not very far apart in rank: Amante was the daughter of a Norman farmer, I of a German miller; and besides that, my life was so lonely! It almost seemed as if I could not please my husband. He had written for someone capable of being my companion at times, and now he was jealous of my free regard for her – angry because I could sometimes laugh at her original tunes and amusing proverbs, while when with him I was too much frightened to smile.

From time to time families from a distance of some leagues drove through the bad roads in their heavy carriages to pay us a visit, and there was an occasional talk of our going to Paris when public affairs should be a little more settled. These little events and plans were the only variations in my life for the first twelve months, if I except the alternations in M. de la Tourelle's temper, his unreasonable anger, and his passionate fondness.

Perhaps one of the reasons that made me take pleasure and comfort in Amante's society was, that whereas I was afraid of everybody (I do not think I was half as much afraid of things as of persons), Amante feared no one. She would quietly beard Lefebvre, and he respected her all the more for it; she had a knack of putting questions to M. de la Tourelle, which respectfully informed him that she had detected the weak point, but forebore to press him too closely upon it out of deference to his position as her master. And with all her shrewdness to others, she had quite tender ways with me; all the more so at this time because she knew, what I had not yet ventured to tell M. de la Tourelle, that by and by I might become a mother – that wonderful object of mysterious interest to single women, who no longer hope to enjoy such blessedness themselves.

It was once more autumn; late in October. But I was reconciled to my habitation; the walls of the new part of the building no longer looked bare and desolate; the débris had been so far cleared away by M. de la Tourelle's desire as to make me a little flower-garden, in which I tried to cultivate those plants that I remembered as growing at home. Amante and I had moved the furniture in the rooms, and adjusted it to our liking; my husband had ordered many an article from time to time that he thought would give me pleasure, and I was becoming tame to my apparent imprisonment in a certain part of the great building, the whole of which I had never yet explored. It was October, as I say, once more. The days were lovely, though short in duration, and M. de la Tourelle had occasion, so he said, to go to that distant estate the superintendence of which so frequently took him away from home. He took Lefebvre with him, and possibly some more of the lacqueys; he often did. And my spirits rose a little at the thought of his absence; and then the new sensation that he was the father of my unborn babe came over me, and I tried to invest him with this fresh character. I tried to believe that it was his passionate love for me that made him so jealous and tyrannical, imposing, as he did, restrictions on my very intercourse with my dear father, from whom I was so entirely separated, as far as personal intercourse was concerned.

I had, it is true, let myself go into a sorrowful review of all the troubles which lay hidden beneath the seeming luxury of my life. I knew that no one cared for me except my husband and Amante; for it was clear enough to see that I, as his wife, and also as a parvenue, was not popular among the few neighbours who surrounded us; and as for the servants, the women were all hard and impudent-looking, treating me with a semblance of respect that had more of mockery than reality in it; while the men had a lurking kind of fierceness about them, sometimes displayed even to M. de la Tourelle, who on his part, it must be confessed, was often severe even to cruelty in his management of them. My husband loved me, I said to myself, but I said it almost in the form of a question. His love was shown fitfully, and more in ways calculated to please himself than to please me. I felt that for no wish of mine would he deviate one tittle from any predetermined course of action. I had learnt the inflexibility of those thin, delicate lips; I knew how anger would turn his fair complexion to deadly white, and bring the cruel light into his pale blue eyes. The love I bore to anyone seemed to be a reason for his hating them, and so I went on pitying myself one long dreary afternoon during that absence of his of which I have spoken, only sometimes remembering to check myself in my murmurings by thinking of the new unseen link between us, and then crying afresh to think how wicked I was. Oh, how well I remember that long October evening! Amante came in from time to time, talking away to cheer me – talking about dress and Paris, and I hardly know what, but from time to time looking at me keenly with her friendly dark eyes, and with serious interest, too, though all her words were about frivolity. At length she heaped the fire with wood, drew the heavy silken curtains close; for I had been anxious hitherto to keep them open, so that I might see the pale moon mounting the skies, as I used to see her – the same moon – rise from behind the Kaiser Stuhl at Heidelberg; but the sight made me cry, so Amante shut it out. She dictated to me as a nurse does to a child.

'Now, madame must have the little kitten to keep her company,' she said, 'while I go and ask Marthon for a cup of coffee.' I remember that speech, and the way it roused me, for I did not like Amante to think I wanted amusing by a kitten. It might be my petulance, but this speech – such as she might have made to a child – annoyed me, and I said that I had reason for my lowness of spirits – meaning that they were not of so imaginary a nature that I could be diverted from them by the gambols of a kitten. So, though I did not choose to tell her all, I told her a part; and as I spoke, I began to suspect that the good creature knew much of what I withheld, and that the little speech about the kitten was more thoughtfully kind than it had seemed at first. I said that it was so long since I had heard from my father; that he was an old man, and so many things might happen – I might never see him again – and I so seldom heard from him or my brother. It was a more complete and total separation than I had ever anticipated when I married, and something of my home and of my life previous to my marriage I told the good Amante; for I had not been brought up as a great lady, and the sympathy of any human being was precious to me.

Amante listened with interest, and in return told me some of the events and sorrows of her own life. Then, remembering her purpose, she set out in search of the coffee, which ought to have been brought to me an hour before; but, in my husband's absence, my wishes were but seldom attended to, and I never dared to give orders.

Presently she returned, bringing the coffee and a great large cake.

'See!' said she, setting it down. 'Look at my plunder. Madame must eat. Those who eat always laugh. And, besides, I have a little news that will please madame.' Then she told me that, lying on a table in the great kitchen, was a bundle of letters, come by the courier from Strasburg that very afternoon: then, fresh from her conversation with me, she had hastily untied the string that bound them, but had only just traced out one that she thought was from Germany, when a servant-man came in, and, with the start he gave her, she dropped the letters, which he picked up, swearing at her for having untied and disarranged them. She told him that she believed there was a letter there for her mistress; but he only swore the more, saying, that if there was it was no business of hers, or of his either, for that he had the strictest orders always to take all letters that arrived during his master's absence into the private sitting-room of the latter – a room into which I had never entered, although it opened out of my husband's dressing-room.

I asked Amante if she had not conquered and brought me this letter. No, indeed, she replied, it was almost as much as her life was worth to live among such a set of servants: it was only a month ago that Jacques had stabbed Valentin for some jesting talk. Had I never missed Valentin – that handsome young lad who carried up the wood into my salon? Poor fellow! he lies dead and cold now, and they said in the village he had put an end to himself, but those of the household knew better. Oh! I need not be afraid; Jacques was gone, no one knew where; but with such people it was not safe to upbraid or insist. Monsieur would be at home the next day, and it would not be long to wait.

But I felt as if I could not exist till the next day, without the letter. It might be to say that my father was ill, dying – he might cry for his daughter from his deathbed! In short, there was no end to the thoughts and fancies that haunted me. It was of no use for Amante to say that, after all, she might be mistaken – that she did not read writing well – that she had but a glimpse of the address; I let my coffee cool, my food all became distasteful, and I wrung my hands with impatience to get at the letter, and have some news of my dear ones at home. All the time, Amante kept her imperturbable good temper, first reasoning, then scolding. At last she said, as if wearied out, that if I would consent to make a good supper, she would see what could be done as to our going to monsieur's room in search of the letter, after the servants were all gone to bed. We agreed to go together when all was still, and look over the letters; there could be no harm in that; and yet, somehow, we were such cowards we dared not do it openly and in the face of the household.

Presently my supper came up – partridges, bread, fruits, and cream. How well I remember that supper!

We put the untouched cake away in a sort of buffet, and poured the cold coffee out of the window, in order that the servants might not take offence at the apparent fancifulness of sending down for food I could not eat. I was so anxious for all to be in bed, that I told the footman who served that he need not wait to take away the plates and dishes, but might go to bed. Long after I thought the house was quiet, Amante, in her caution, made me wait. It was past eleven before we set out, with cat-like steps and veiled light, along the passages, to go to my husband's room and steal my own letter, if it was indeed there; a fact about which Amante had become very uncertain in the progress of our discussion.

To make you understand my story, I must now try to explain to you the plan of the château. It had been at one time a fortified place of some strength, perched on the summit of a rock, which projected from the side of the mountain. But additions had been made to the old building (which must have borne a strong resemblance to the castles overhanging the Rhine), and these new buildings were placed so as to command a magnificent view, being on the steepest side of the rock, from which the mountain fell away, as it were, leaving the great plain of France in full survey. The ground-plan was something of the shape of three sides of an oblong; my apartments in the modern edifice occupied the narrow end, and had this grand prospect. The front of the castle was old, and ran parallel to the road far below. In this were contained the offices and public rooms of various descriptions, into which I never penetrated. The back wing (considering the new building, in which my apartments were, as the centre) consisted of many rooms, of a dark and gloomy character, as the mountain-side shut out much of the sun, and heavy pine woods came down within a few yards of the windows. Yet on this side – on a projecting plateau of the rock – my husband had formed the flower-garden of which I have spoken; for he was a great cultivator of flowers in his leisure moments.

Now my bedroom was the corner room of the new buildings on the part next to the mountain. Hence I could have let myself down into the flower-garden by my hands on the window-sill on one side, without danger of hurting myself; while the windows at right angles with these looked sheer down a descent of a hundred feet at least. Going still farther along this wing, you came to the old building; in fact, these two fragments of the ancient castle had formerly been attached by some such connecting apartments as my husband had rebuilt. These rooms belonged to M. de la Tourelle. His bedroom opened into mine, his dressing-room lay beyond; and that was pretty nearly all I knew, for the servants, as well as he himself, had a knack of turning me back, under some pretence, if ever they found me walking about alone, as I was inclined to do, when first I came, from a sort of curiosity to see the whole of the place of which I found myself mistress. M. de la Tourelle never encouraged me to go out alone, either in a carriage or for a walk, saying always that the roads were unsafe in those disturbed times; indeed, I have sometimes fancied since that the flower-garden, to which the only access from the castle was through his rooms, was designed in order to give me exercise and employment under his own eye.

But to return to that night. I knew, as I have said,

that M. de la Tourelle's private room opened out of his dressing-room, and this out of his bedroom, which again opened into mine, the corner-room. But there were other doors into all these rooms, and these doors led into a long gallery, lighted by windows, looking into the inner court. I do not remember our consulting much about it; we went through my room into my husband's apartment through the dressing-room, but the door of communication into his study was locked, so there was nothing for it but to turn back and go by the gallery to the other door. I recollect noticing one or two things in these rooms, then seen by me for the first time. I remember the sweet perfume that hung in the air, the scent bottles of silver that decked his toilet-table, and the whole apparatus for bathing and dressing, more luxurious even than those which he had provided for me. But the room itself was less splendid in its proportions than mine. In truth, the new buildings ended at the entrance to my husband's dressing-room. There were deep window recesses in walls eight or nine feet thick, and even the partitions between the chambers were three feet deep; but over all these doors or windows there fell thick, heavy draperies, so that I should think no one could have heard in one room what passed in another. We went back into my room, and out into the gallery. We had to shade our candle, from a fear that possessed us, I don't know why, lest some of the servants in the opposite wing might trace our progress towards the part of the castle unused by anyone except my husband. Somehow, I had always the feeling that all the domestics, except Amante, were spies upon me, and that I was trammelled in a web of observation and unspoken limitation extending over all my actions.

There was a light in the upper room; we paused, and Amante would have again retreated, but I was chafing under the delays. What was the harm of my seeking my father's unopened letter to me in my husband's study? I, generally the coward, now blamed Amante for her unusual timidity. But the truth was, she had far more reason for suspicion as to the proceedings of that terrible household than I had ever known of. I urged her on, I pressed on myself; we came to the door, locked, but with the key in it; we turned it, we entered; the letters lay on the table, their white oblongs catching the light in an instant, and revealing themselves to my eager eyes, hungering after the words of love from my peaceful, distant home. But just as I pressed forward to examine the letters, the candle which Amante held, caught in some draught, went out, and we were in darkness. Amante proposed that we should carry the letters back to my salon, collecting them as well as we could in the dark, and returning all but the expected one for me; but I begged her to return to my room, where I kept tinder and flint, and to strike a fresh light; and so she went, and I remained alone in the room, of which I could only just distinguish the size, and the principal articles of furniture: a large table, with a deep, over-hanging cloth, in the middle, escritoires and other heavy articles against the walls; all this I could see as I stood there, my hand on the table close by the letters, my face towards the window, which, both from the darkness of the wood growing high up the mountain-side and the faint light of the declining moon, seemed only like an oblong of paler purpler black than the shadowy room. How much I remembered from my one instantaneous glance before the candle went out, how much I saw as my eyes became accustomed to the darkness, I do not know, but even now, in my dreams, comes up that room of horror, distinct in its profound shadow. Amante could hardly have been gone a minute before I felt an additional gloom before the window, and heard soft movements outside – soft, but resolute, and continued until the end was accomplished, and the window raised.

In mortal terror of people forcing an entrance at such an hour, and in such a manner as to leave no doubt of their purpose, I would have turned to fly when first I heard the noise, only that I feared by any quick motion to catch their attention, as I also ran the danger of doing by opening the door, which was all but closed, and to whose handlings I was un-accustomed. Again, quick as lightning, I bethought me of the hiding-place between the locked door to my husband's dressing-room and the *portière* which covered it; but I gave that up, I felt as if I could not reach it without screaming or fainting. So I sank down softly, and crept under the table, hidden, as I hoped, by the great, deep table-cover, with its heavy fringe. I had not recovered my swooning senses fully, and was trying to reassure myself as to my being in a place of comparative safety, for, above all things, I dreaded the betrayal of fainting, and struggled hard for such courage as I might attain by deadening myself to the danger I was in by inflicting intense pain on myself. You have often asked me the reason of that mark on my hand; it was where, in my agony, I bit out a piece of flesh with my relentless teeth, thankful for the pain, which helped to numb my terror. I say, I was but just concealed when I heard the window lifted, and one after another stepped over the sill, and stood by me so close that I could have touched their feet. Then they laughed and whispered; my brain swam so that I could not tell the meaning of their words, but I heard my husband's laughter among the rest – low, hissing, scornful – as he kicked something heavy that they had dragged in over the floor, and which lay near me; so near, that my husband's kick, in touching it, touched me too. I don't know why – I can't tell how – but some feeling, and not curiosity, prompted me to put out my hand, ever so softly, ever so little, and feel in the darkness for what lay spurned beside me. I stole my groping palm upon the clenched and chilly hand of a corpse!

Strange to say, this roused me to instant vividness of thought. Till this moment I had almost forgotten Amante; now I planned with feverish rapidity how I could give her a warning not to return; or rather, I should say, I tried to plan, for all my projects were utterly futile, as I might have seen from the first. I could only hope she would hear the voices of those who were now busy in trying to kindle a light, swearing awful oaths at the mislaid articles which would have enabled them to strike fire. I heard her step outside coming nearer and nearer; I saw from my hiding-place the line of light beneath the door more and more distinctly; close to it her footstep paused; the men inside – at the time I thought they had been only two, but I found out afterwards there were three – paused in their endeavours, and were quite still, as breathless as myself, I suppose. Then she slowly pushed the door open with gentle motion, to save her flickering candle from being again extinguished. For a moment all was still. Then I heard my husband say, as he advanced towards her (he wore riding-boots, the shape of which I knew well, as I could see them in the light): 'Amante, may I ask what brings you here into my private room?'

He stood between her and the dead body of a man, from which ghastly heap I shrank away as it almost touched me, so close were we all together. I could not tell whether she saw it or not; I could give her no warning, nor make any dumb utterance of signs to bid her what to say – if, indeed, I knew myself what would be best for her to say.

Her voice was quite changed when she spoke; quite hoarse, and very low; yet it was steady enough as she said, what was the truth, that she had come to look for a letter which she believed had arrived for me from Germany. Good, brave Amante! Not a word about me. M. de la Tourelle answered with a grim blasphemy and a fearful threat. He would have no one prying into his premises; madame should have her letters, if there were any, when he chose to give them to her, if, indeed, he thought it well to give them to her at all. As for Amante, this was her first warning, but it was also her last; and, taking the candle out of her hand, he turned her out of the room, his companions discreetly making a screen, so as to throw the corpse into deep shadow. I heard the key turn in the door after her – if I had ever had any thought of escape it was gone now. I only hoped that whatever was to befall me might soon be over, for the tension of nerve was growing more than I could bear. The instant she could be supposed to be out of hearing, two voices began speaking in the most angry terms to my husband, upbraiding him for not having detained her, gagged her – nay, one was for killing her, saying he had seen her eye fall on the face of the dead man, whom he now kicked in his passion. Though the form of their speech was as if they were speaking to equals, yet in their tone there was something of fear. I am sure my husband was their superior, or captain, or somewhat. He replied to them almost as if he were scoffing at them, saying it was such an expenditure of labour having to do with fools; that, ten to one, the woman was only telling the simple truth, and that she was frightened enough by discovering her master in his room to be thankful to escape and return to her mistress, to whom he could easily explain on the morrow how he happened to return in the dead of night. But his companions fell to cursing me, and saying that since M. de la Tourelle had been married he was fit for nothing but to dress himself fine and scent himself with perfume; that, as for me, they could have got him twenty girls prettier, and with far more spirit in them. He quietly answered that I suited him, and that was enough. All this time they were doing something – I could not see what – to the corpse; sometimes they were too busy rifling the dead body, I believe, to talk; again they let it fall with a heavy, resistless thud, and took to quarrelling. They taunted my husband with angry vehemence, enraged at his scoffing and scornful replies, his mocking laughter. Yes, holding up his poor dead victim, the better to strip him of whatever he wore that was valuable, I heard my husband laugh just as he had done when exchanging repartees in the little salon of the Rupprechts at Carlsruhe. I hated and dreaded him from that moment. At length, as if to make an end of the subject, he said, with cool determination in his voice: 'Now, my good friends, what is the use of all this talking, when you know in your hearts that, if

I suspected my wife of knowing more than I chose of my affairs, she would not outlive the day? Remember Victorine. Because she merely joked about my affairs in an imprudent manner, and rejected my advice to keep a prudent tongue – to see what she liked, but ask nothing and say nothing – she has gone a long journey – longer than to Paris.'

'But this one is different to her; we knew all that Madame Victorine knew, she was such a chatterbox; but this one may find out a vast deal, and never breathe a word about it, she is so sly. Some fine day we may have the country raised, and the gendarmes down upon us from Strasburg, and all owing to your pretty doll, with her cunning ways of coming over you.'

I think this roused M. de la Tourelle a little from his contemptuous indifference, for he ground an oath through his teeth, and said, 'Feel! this dagger is sharp, Henri. If my wife breathes a word, and I am such a fool as not to have stopped her mouth effectually before she can bring down gendarmes upon us, just let that good steel find its way to my heart. Let her guess but one tittle, let her have but one slight sus- picion that I am not a *grand propriétaire*, much less imagine that I am a chief of *Chauffeurs*, and she follows Victorine on the long journey beyond Paris that very day.'

'She'll outwit you yet; or I never judged women well. Those still silent ones are the devil. She'll be off during some of your absences, having picked out some secret that will break us all on the wheel.'

'Bah!' said his voice; and then in a minute he added, 'Let her go if she will. But, where she goes, I will follow; so don't cry before you're hurt.'

By this time, they had nearly stripped the body; and the conversation turned on what they should do with it. I learnt that the dead man was the Sieur de Poissy, a neighbouring gentleman, whom I had often heard of as hunting with my husband. I had never seen him, but they spoke as if he had come upon them while they were robbing some Cologne merchant, torturing him after the cruel practice of the *Chauffeurs*, by roasting the feet of their victims in order to compel them to reveal any hidden circumstances connected with their wealth, of which the *Chauffeurs* afterwards made use; and this Sieur de Poissy coming down upon them, and recognising M. de la Tourelle, they had killed him, and brought him thither after nightfall. I heard him whom I called my husband, laugh his little light laugh as he spoke of the way in which the dead body had been strapped before one of the riders, in such a way that it appeared to any passer-by as if, in truth, the murderer were tenderly supporting some sick person. He repeated some mocking reply of double meaning, which he himself had given to someone who made enquiry. He enjoyed the play upon words, softly applauding his own wit. And all the time the poor helpless outstretched arms of the dead lay close to his dainty boot! Then another stooped (my heart stopped beating), and picked up a letter lying on the ground – a letter that had dropped out of M. de Poissy's pocket – a letter from his wife, full of tender words of endearment and pretty babblings of love. This was read aloud, with coarse ribald comments on every sentence, each trying to outdo the previous speaker. When they came to some pretty words about a sweet Maurice, their little child away with its mother on some visit, they laughed at M. de la Tourelle, and told him that he would be hearing such woman's drivelling some day. Up to that moment, I think, I had only feared him, but his unnatural, half-ferocious reply made me hate even more than I dreaded him. But now they grew weary of their savage merriment; the jewels and watch had been apprised, the money and papers examined; and apparently there was some necessity for the body being interred quietly and before daybreak. They had not dared to leave him where he was slain for fear lest people should come and recognise him, and raise the hue and cry upon them. For they all along spoke as if it was their constant endeavour to keep the immediate neighbourhood of Les Rochers in the most orderly and tranquil condition, so as never to give cause for visits from the gendarmes. They disputed a little as to whether they should make their way into the castle larder through the gallery, and satisfy their hunger before the hasty interment, or afterwards. I listened with eager feverish interest as soon as this meaning of their speeches reached my hot and troubled brain, for at the time the words they uttered seemed only to stamp themselves with terrible force on my memory, so that I could hardly keep from repeating them aloud like a dull, miserable, unconscious echo; but my brain was numb to the sense of what they said, unless I myself were named, and then, I suppose, some instinct of self-preservation stirred within me, and quickened my sense. And how I strained my ears, and nerved my hands and limbs, beginning to twitch with convulsive movements, which I feared might betray me! I gathered every word they spoke, not knowing which proposal to wish for, but feeling that whatever was finally decided upon, my only chance of escape was drawing near. I once feared lest my husband should go to his bedroom before I had had that one chance, in which case he would most likely have perceived my absence. He said that his hands were soiled (I shuddered, for it might be with life-blood), and he would go and cleanse them; but some bitter jest turned his purpose, and he left the room with the other two – left it by the gallery door. Left me alone in the dark with the stiffening corpse!

Now, now was my time, if ever; and yet I could not move. It was not my cramped and stiffened joints that crippled me, it was the sensation of that dead man's close presence. I almost fancied – I almost fancy still – I heard the arm nearest to me move; lift itself up, as if once more imploring, and fall in dead despair. At that fancy – if fancy it were – I screamed aloud in mad terror, and the sound of my own strange voice broke the spell. I drew myself to the side of the table farthest from the corpse, with as much slow caution as if I really could have feared the clutch of that poor dead arm, powerless for evermore. I softly raised myself up, and stood sick and trembling, holding by the table, too dizzy to know what to do next. I nearly fainted, when a low voice spoke – when Amante, from the outside of the door, whispered, 'Madame!' The faithful creature had been on the watch, had heard my scream, and having seen the three ruffians troop along the gallery down the stairs, and across the court to the offices in the other wing of the castle, she had stolen to the door of the room in which I was. The sound of her voice gave me strength; I walked straight towards it, as one benighted on a dreary moor, suddenly perceiving the small steady light which tells of human dwellings, takes heart, and steers straight onward. Where I was, where that voice was, I knew not; but go to it I must, or die. The door once opened – I know not by which of us – I fell upon her neck, grasping her tight, till my hands ached with the tension of their hold. Yet she never uttered a word. Only she took me up in her vigorous arms, and bore me to my room, and laid me on my bed. I do not know more; as soon as I was placed there I lost sense; I came to myself with a horrible dread lest my husband was by me, with a belief that he was in the room, in hiding, waiting to hear my first words, watching for the least sign of the terrible knowledge I possessed to murder me. I dared not breathe quicker, I measured and timed each heavy inspiration; I did not speak, nor move, nor even open my eyes, for long after I was in my full, my miserable senses. I heard someone treading softly about the room, as if with a purpose, not as if for curiosity, or merely to beguile the time; someone passed in and out of the salon; and I still lay quiet, feeling as if death were inevitable, but wishing that the agony of death were past. Again faintness stole over me; but just as I was sinking into the horrible feeling of nothingness, I heard Amante's voice close to me, saying: 'Drink this, madame, and let us begone. All is ready.'

I let her put her arm under my head and raise me, and pour something down my throat. All the time she kept talking in a quiet, measured voice, unlike her own, so dry and authoritative; she told me that a suit of her clothes lay ready for me, that she herself was as much disguised as the circumstances permitted her to be, that what provisions I had left from my supper were stowed away in her pockets, and so she went on, dwelling on little details of the most commonplace description, but never alluding for an instant to the fearful cause why flight was necessary. I made no enquiry as to how she knew, or what she knew. I never asked her either then or afterwards, I could not bear it – we kept our dreadful secret close. But I suppose she must have been in the dressing-room adjoining, and heard all.

In fact, I dared not speak even to her, as if there were anything beyond the most common event in life in our preparing thus to leave the house of blood by stealth in the dead of night. She gave me directions – short condensed directions, without reasons – just as you do to a child; and like a child I obeyed her. She went often to the door and listened; and often, too, she went to the window, and looked anxiously out. For me, I saw nothing but her, and I dared not let my eyes wander from her for a minute; and I heard nothing in the deep midnight silence but her soft movements, and the heavy beating of my own heart. At last she took my hand, and led me in the dark, through the salon, once more into the terrible gallery, where across the black darkness the windows admitted pale sheeted ghosts of light upon the floor. Clinging to her I went; unquestioning – for she was human sympathy to me after the isolation of my unspeakable terror. On we went, turning to the left instead of to the right, past my suite of sitting-rooms where the gilding was red with blood, into that unknown wing of the castle that fronted the main road lying parallel far below. She guided me along the basement passages to which we had now descended, until we came to a little open door, through which the air blew chill and cold, bringing for the first time a sensation of life to me. The door led into a kind of cellar, through which we groped our way to an opening like a window, but which, instead of being glazed, was only fenced with iron bars, two of which were loose, as Amante evidently knew, for she took them out with the ease of one who had performed the action often before, and then helped me to follow her out into the free, open air.

We stole round the end of the building, and on turning the corner – she first – I felt her hold on me tighten for an instant, and the next step I, too, heard distant voices, and the blows of a spade upon the heavy soil, for the night was very warm and still.

We had not spoken a word; we did not speak now. Touch was safer and as expressive. She turned down towards the high road; I followed. I did not know the path; we stumbled again and again, and I was much bruised; so doubtless was she; but bodily pain did me good. At last, we were on the plainer path of the high road.

I had such faith in her that I did not venture to speak, even when she paused, as wondering to which hand she should turn. But now, for the first time, she spoke: 'Which way did you come when he brought you here first?'

I pointed, I could not speak.

We turned in the opposite direction; still going along the high road. In about an hour, we struck up to the mountainside, scrambling far up before we even dared to rest; far up and away again before day had fully dawned. Then we looked about for some place of rest and concealment: and now we dared to speak in whispers. Amante told me that she had locked the door of communication between his bedroom and mine, and, as in a dream, I was aware that she had also locked and brought away the key of the door between the latter and the salon.

'He will have been too busy this night to think much about you – he will suppose you are asleep – I shall be the first to be missed; but they will only just now be discovering our loss.'

I remember those last words of hers made me pray to go on; I felt as if we were losing precious time in thinking either of rest or concealment; but she hardly replied to me, so busy was she in seeking out some hiding-place. At length, giving it up in despair, we proceeded onwards a little way; the mountainside sloped downwards rapidly, and in the full morning light we saw ourselves in a narrow valley, made by a stream which forced its way along it. About a mile lower down there rose the pale blue smoke of a village, a mill-wheel was lashing up the water close at hand, though out of sight. Keeping under the cover of every sheltering tree or bush, we worked our way down past the mill, down to a one-arched bridge, which doubtless formed part of the road between the village and the mill.

'This will do,' said she; and we crept under the space, and climbing a little way up the rough stone-work, we seated ourselves on a projecting ledge, and crouched in the deep damp shadow. Amante sat a little above me, and made me lay my head on her lap. Then she fed me, and took some food herself; and opening out her great dark cloak, she covered up every light-coloured speck about us; and thus we sat, shivering and shuddering, yet feeling a kind of rest through it all, simply from the fact that motion was no longer imperative, and that during the daylight our only chance of safety was to be still. But the damp shadow in which we were sitting was blighting, from the circumstance of the sunlight never penetrating there; and I dreaded lest, before night and the time for exertion again came on, I should feel illness creeping all over me. To add to our discomfort, it had rained the whole day long, and the stream, fed by a thousand little mountain brooklets, began to swell into a torrent, rushing over the stones with a perpetual and dizzying noise.

Every now and then I was wakened from the painful doze into which I continually fell, by a sound of horses' feet over our head: sometimes lumbering heavily as if dragging a burden, sometimes rattling and galloping, and with the sharper cry of men's voices coming cutting through the roar of the waters. At length, day fell. We had to drop into the stream, which came above our knees as we waded to the bank. There we stood, stiff and shivering. Even Amante's courage seemed to fail.

'We must pass this night in shelter, somehow,' said she. For indeed the rain was coming down pitilessly. I said nothing. I thought that surely the end must be death in some shape; and I only hoped that to death might not be added the terror of the cruelty of men. In a minute or so she had resolved on her course of action. We went up the stream to the mill. The familiar sounds, the scent of the wheat, the flour whitening the walls – all reminded me of home, and it seemed to me as if I must struggle out of this nightmare and waken, and find myself once more a happy girl by the Neckar-side. They were long in unbarring the door at which Amante had knocked: at length, an old feeble voice enquired who was there, and what was sought? Amante answered shelter from the storm for two women; but the old woman replied, with suspicious hesitation, that she was sure it was a man who was asking for shelter, and that she could not let us in. But at length she satisfied herself, and unbarred the heavy door, and admitted us. She was not an unkindly woman; but her thoughts all travelled in one circle, and that was, that her master, the miller, had told her on no account to let any man into the place during his absence, and that she did not know if he would not think two women as bad; and yet that as we were not men, no one could say she had disobeyed him, for it was a shame to let a dog be out such a night as this. Amante, with ready wit, told her to let no one know that we had taken shelter there that night, and that then her master could not blame her; and while she was thus enjoining secrecy as the wisest course, with a view to far other people than the miller, she was hastily helping me to take off my wet clothes, and spreading them, as well as the brown mantle that had covered us both, before the great stove which warmed the room with the effectual heat that the old woman's failing vitality required. All this time the poor creature was discussing with herself as to whether she had disobeyed orders, in a kind of garrulous way that made me fear much for her capability of retaining anything secret if she was questioned. By and by, she wandered away to an unnecessary revelation of her master's whereabouts: gone to help in the search for his landlord, the Sieur de Poissy, who lived at the château just above, and who had not returned from his chase the day before; so the intendant imagined he might have met with some accident, and had summoned the neighbours to beat the forest and the hillside. She told us much besides, giving us to understand that she would fain meet with a place as housekeeper where there were more servants and less to do, as her life here was very lonely and dull, especially since her master's son had gone away – gone to the wars. She then took her supper, which was evidently apportioned out to her with a sparing hand, as, even if the idea had come into her head, she had not enough to offer us any. Fortunately, warmth was all that we required, and that, thanks to Amante's cares, was returning to our chilled bodies. After supper, the old woman grew drowsy; but she seemed uncomfortable at the idea of going to sleep and leaving us still in the house. Indeed, she gave us pretty broad hints as to the propriety of our going once more out into the bleak and stormy night; but we begged to be allowed to stay under shelter of some kind; and, at last, a bright idea came over her, and she bade us mount by a ladder to a kind of loft, which went half over the lofty mill-kitchen in which we were sitting. We obeyed her – what else could we do? – and found ourselves in a spacious floor, without any safeguard or wall, boarding, or railing, to keep us from falling over into the kitchen in case we went too near the edge. It was, in fact, the storeroom or garret for the household. There was bedding piled up, boxes and chests, mill sacks, the winter store of apples and nuts, bundles of old clothes, broken furniture, and many other things. No sooner were we up there, than the old woman dragged the ladder, by which we had ascended, away with a chuckle, as if she was now secure that we could do no mischief, and sat herself down again once more, to doze and await her master's return. We pulled out some bedding, and gladly laid ourselves down in our dried clothes and in some warmth, hoping to have the sleep we so much needed to refresh us and prepare us for the next day. But I could not sleep, and I was aware, from her breathing, that Amante was equally wakeful. We could both see through the crevices between the boards that formed the flooring into the kitchen below, very partially lighted by the common lamp that hung against the wall near the stove on the opposite side to that on which we were.

3

Far on in the night there were voices outside which reached us in our hiding-place; an angry knocking at the door, and we saw through the chinks the old woman rouse herself up to go and open it for her master, who came in, evidently half drunk. To my sick horror, he was followed by Lefebvre, apparently as sober and wily as ever. They were talking together as they came in, disputing about something; but the miller stopped the conversation to swear at the old woman for having fallen asleep, and, with tipsy anger, and even with blows, drove the poor old creature out of the kitchen to bed. Then he and Lefebvre went on talking – about the Sieur de Poissy's disappearance. It seemed that Lefebvre had been out all day, along with other of my husband's men, ostensibly assisting in the search; in all probability trying to blind the Sieur de Poissy's followers by putting them on a wrong scent, and also, I fancied, from one or two of Lefebvre's sly questions, combining the hidden purpose of discovering us.

Although the miller was tenant and vassal to the Sieur de Poissy, he seemed to me to be much more in league with the people of M. de la Tourelle. He was evidently aware, in part, of the life which Lefebvre and the others led; although, again, I do not suppose he knew or imagined one-half of their crimes; and also, I think, he was seriously interested in discovering the fate of his master, little suspecting Lefebvre of murder or violence. He kept talking himself, and letting out all sorts of thoughts and opinions; watched by the keen eyes of Lefebvre gleaming out below his shaggy eyebrows. It was evidently not the cue of the latter to let out that his master's wife had escaped from that vile and terrible den; but though he never breathed a word relating to us, not the less was I certain he was thirsting for our blood, and lying in wait for us at every turn of events. Presently he got up and took his leave; and the miller bolted him out, and stumbled off to bed. Then we fell asleep, and slept sound and long.

The next morning, when I awoke, I saw Amante, half raised, resting on one hand, and eagerly gazing, with straining eyes, into the kitchen below. I looked too, and both heard and saw the miller and two of his men eagerly and loudly talking about the old woman, who had not appeared as usual to make the fire in the stove, and prepare her master's breakfast, and who now, late on in the morning, had been found dead in her bed; whether from the effect of her master's blows the night before, or from natural causes, who can tell? The miller's conscience upbraided him a little, I should say, for he was eagerly declaring his value for his housekeeper, and repeating how often she had spoken of the happy life she led with him. The men might have their doubts, but they did not wish to offend the miller, and all agreed that the necessary steps should be taken for a speedy funeral. And so they went out, leaving us in our loft, but so much alone, that, for the first time almost, we ventured to speak freely, though still in a hushed voice, pausing to listen continually. Amante took a more cheerful view of the whole occurrence than I did. She said that, had the old woman lived, we should have had to depart that morning, and that this quiet departure would have been the best thing we could have had to hope for, as, in all probability, the housekeeper would have told her master of us and of our resting-place, and this fact would, sooner or later, have been brought to the knowledge of those from whom we most desired to keep it concealed; but that now we had time to rest, and a shelter to rest in, during the first hot pursuit, which we knew to a fatal certainty was being carried on. The remnants of our food, and the stored-up fruit, would supply us with provision; the only thing to be feared was, that something might be required from the loft, and the miller or someone else mount up in search of it. But even then, with a little arrangement of boxes and chests, one part might be so kept in shadow that we might yet escape observation. All this comforted me a little; but, I asked, how were we ever to escape? The ladder was taken away, which was our only means of descent. But Amante replied that she could make a sufficient ladder of the rope lying coiled among other things, to drop us down the ten feet or so – with the advantage of its being portable, so that we might carry it away, and thus avoid all betrayal of the fact that anyone had ever been hidden in the loft.

During the two days that intervened before we did escape, Amante made good use of her time. She looked into every box and chest during the man's absence at his mill; and finding in one box an old suit of man's clothes, which had probably belonged to the miller's absent son, she put them on to see if they would fit her; and, when she found that they did, she cut her own hair to the shortness of a man's, made me clip her black eyebrows as close as though they had been shaved, and by cutting up old corks into pieces such as would go into her cheeks, she altered both the shape of her face and her voice to a degree which I should not have believed possible.

All this time I lay like one stunned; my body resting, and renewing its strength, but I myself in an almost idiotic state – else surely I could not have taken the stupid interest which I remember I did in all Amante's energetic preparations for disguise. I absolutely recollect once the feeling of a smile coming over my stiff face as some new exercise of her cleverness proved a success.

But towards the second day, she required me, too, to exert myself; and then all my heavy despair returned. I let her dye my fair hair and complexion with the decaying shells of the stored-up walnuts, I let her blacken my teeth, and even voluntarily broke a front tooth the better to effect my disguise. But through it all I had no hope of evading my terrible husband. The third night the funeral was over, the drinking ended, the guests gone; the miller put to bed by his men, being too drunk to help himself. They stopped a little while in the kitchen, talking and laughing about the new housekeeper likely to come; and they, too, went off, shutting, but not locking the door. Everything favoured us. Amante had tried her ladder on one of the two previous nights, and could, by a dexterous throw from beneath, unfasten it from the hook to which it was fixed, when it had served its office; she made up a bundle of worthless old clothes in order that we might the better preserve our characters of a travelling pedlar and his wife; she stuffed a hump on her back, she thickened my figure, she left her own clothes deep down beneath a heap of others in the chest from which she had taken the man's dress which she wore; and with a few francs in her pocket – the sole money we had either of us had about us when we escaped – we let ourselves down the ladder, unhooked it, and passed into the cold darkness of night again.

We had discussed the route which it would be well for us to take while we lay *perdues* in our loft. Amante had told me then that her reason for enquiring, when we first left Les Rochers, by which way I had first been brought to it, was to avoid the pursuit which she was sure would first be made in the direction of Germany; but that now she thought we might return to that district of country where my German fashion of speaking French would excite least observation. I thought that Amante herself had something peculiar in her accent, which I had heard M. de la Tourelle sneer at as Norman *patois*; but I said not a word beyond agreeing to her proposal that we should bend our steps towards Germany. Once there, we should, I thought, be safe. Alas! I forgot the unruly time that was overspreading all Europe, overturning all law, and all the protection which law gives.

How we wandered – not daring to ask our way – how we lived, how we struggled through many a danger and still more terrors of danger, I shall not tell you now. I will only relate two of our adventures before we reached Frankfort. The first, although fatal to an innocent lady, was yet, I believe, the cause of my safety; the second I shall tell you, that you may understand why I did not return to my former home, as I had hoped to do when we lay in the miller's loft, and I first became capable of groping after an idea of what my future life might be. I cannot tell you how much in these doubtings and wanderings I became attached to Amante. I have sometimes feared since, lest I cared for her only because she was so necessary to my own safety; but, no! it was not so; or not so only, or principally. She said once that she was flying for her own life as well as for mine; but we dared not speak much on our danger, or on the horrors that had gone before. We planned a little what was to be our future course; but even for that we did not look forward long; how could we, when every day we scarcely knew if we should see the sun go down? For Amante knew or conjectured far more than I did of the atrocity of the gang to which M. de la Tourelle belonged; and every now and then, just as we seemed to be sinking into the calm of security, we fell upon traces of a pursuit after us in all directions. Once I remember – we must have been nearly three weeks wearily walking through unfrequented ways, day after day, not daring to make enquiry as to our whereabouts, nor yet to seem purposeless in our wanderings – we came to a kind of lonely roadside farrier's and blacksmith's. I was so tired, that Amante declared that, come what might, we would stay there all night; and accordingly she entered the house, and boldly announced herself as a travelling tailor, ready to do any odd jobs of work that might be required, for a night's lodging and food for herself and wife. She had adopted this plan once or twice before, and with good success; for her father had been a tailor in Rouen, and as a girl she had often helped him with his work, and knew the tailors' slang and habits, down to the particular whistle and cry which in France tells so much to those of a trade. At this blacksmith's, as at most other solitary houses far away from a town, there was not only a store of men's clothes laid by as wanting mending when the housewife could afford time, but there was a natural craving after news from a distance, such news as a wandering tailor is bound to furnish. The early November afternoon was closing into evening, as we sat down, she cross-legged on the great table in the blacksmith's kitchen, drawn close to the window, I close behind her, sewing at another part of the same garment, and from time to time well scolded by my seeming husband. All at once she turned round to speak to me. It was only one word, 'Courage!' I had seen nothing; I sat out of the light; but I turned sick for an instant, and then I braced myself up into a strange strength of endurance to go through I knew not what.

The blacksmith's forge was in a shed beside the house, and fronting the road. I heard the hammers stop plying their continual rhythmical beat. She had seen why they ceased. A rider had come up to the forge and dismounted, leading his horse in to be re-shod. The broad red light of the forge-fire had revealed the face of the rider to Amante, and she apprehended the consequence that really ensued.

The rider, after some words with the blacksmith, was ushered in by him into the house-place where we sat.

'Here, good wife, a cup of wine and some galette for this gentleman.'

'Anything, anything, madame, that I can eat and drink in my hand while my horse is being shod. I am in haste, and must get on to Forbach tonight.'

The blacksmith's wife lighted her lamp; Amante had asked her for it five minutes before. How thankful we were that she had not more speedily complied with our request! As it was, we sat in dusk shadow, pretending to stitch away, but scarcely able to see. The lamp was placed on the stove, near which my husband, for it was he, stood and warmed himself. By and by he turned round, and looked all over the room, taking us in with about the same degree of interest as the inanimate furniture. Amante, cross-legged, fronting him, stooped over her work, whistling softly all the while. He turned again to the stove, impatiently rubbing his hands. He had finished his wine and galette, and wanted to be off.

'I am in haste, my good woman. Ask thy husband to get on more quickly. I will pay him double if he makes haste.'

The woman went out to do his bidding; and he once more turned round to face us. Amante went on to the second part of the tune. He took it up, whistled a second for an instant or so, and then the black-smith's wife re-entering, he moved towards her, as if to receive her answer the more speedily.

'One moment, monsieur – only one moment. There was a nail out of the off-foreshoe which my husband is replacing; it would delay monsieur again if that shoe also came off.'

'Madame is right,' said he, 'but my haste is urgent. If madame knew my reasons, she would pardon my impatience. Once a happy husband, now a deserted and betrayed man, I pursue a wife on whom I lavished all my love, but who has abused my confidence, and fled from my house, doubtless to some paramour, carrying off with her all the jewels and money on which she could lay her hands. It is possible madame may have heard or seen something of her; she was accompanied in her flight by a base, profligate woman from Paris, whom I, unhappy man, had myself engaged for my wife's waiting-maid, little dreaming what corruption I was bringing into my house!'

'Is it possible?' said the good woman, throwing up her hands.

Amante went on whistling a little lower, out of respect to the conversation.

'However, I am tracing the wicked fugitives; I am on their track' (and the handsome, effeminate face looked as ferocious as any demon's). 'They will not escape me; but every minute is a minute of misery to me, till I meet my wife. Madame has sympathy, has she not?'

He drew his face into a hard, unnatural smile, and then both went out to the forge, as if once more to hasten the blacksmith over his work.

Amante stopped her whistling for one instant.

'Go on as you are, without change of an eyelid even; in a few minutes he will be gone, and it will be over!'

It was a necessary caution, for I was on the point of giving way, and throwing myself weakly upon her neck. We went on; she whistling and stitching, I making semblance to sew. And it was well we did so; for almost directly he came back for his whip, which he had laid down and forgotten; and again I felt one of those sharp, quick-scanning glances, sent all round the room, and taking in all.

Then we heard him ride away; and then, it had been long too dark to see well, I dropped my work, and gave way to my trembling and shuddering. The blacksmith's wife returned. She was a good creature. Amante told her I was cold and weary, and she insisted on my stopping my work, and going to sit near the stove; hastening, at the same time, her preparations for supper, which, in honour of us, and of monsieur's liberal payment, was to be a little less frugal than ordinary. It was well for me that she made me taste a little of the cider-soup she was preparing, or I could not have held up, in spite of Amante's warning look, and the remembrance of her frequent exhortations to act resolutely up to the characters we had assumed, whatever befell. To cover my agitation, Amante stopped her whistling, and began to talk; and, by the time the blacksmith came in, she and the good woman of the house were in full flow. He began at once upon the handsome gentleman, who had paid him so well; all his sympathy was with him, and both he and his wife only wished he might overtake his wicked wife, and punish her as she deserved. And then the conversation took a turn, not uncommon to those whose lives are quiet and monotonous; everyone seemed to vie with each other in telling about some horror; and the savage and mysterious band of robbers called the *Chauffeurs*, who infested all the roads leading to the Rhine, with Schinderhannes at their head, furnished many a tale which made the very marrow of my bones run cold, and quenched even Amante's power of talking. Her eyes grew large and wild, her cheeks blanched, and for once she sought by her looks help from me. The new call upon me roused me. I rose and said, with their permission my husband and I would seek our bed, for that we had travelled far and were early risers. I added that we would get up betimes, and finish our piece of work. The blacksmith said we should be early birds if we rose before him; and the good wife seconded my proposal with kindly bustle. One other such story as those they had been relating, and I do believe Amante would have fainted.

As it was, a night's rest set her up; we arose and finished our work betimes, and shared the plentiful breakfast of the family. Then we had to set forth again; only knowing that to Forbach we must not go, yet believing, as was indeed the case, that Forbach lay between us and that Germany to which we were directing our course. Two days more we wandered on, making a round, I suspect, and returning upon the road to Forbach, a league or two nearer to that town than the blacksmith's house. But as we never made enquiries I hardly knew where we were, when we came one night to a small town, with a good large rambling inn in the very centre of the principal street. We had begun to feel as if there were more safety in towns than in the loneliness of the country. As we had parted with a ring of mine not many days before to a travelling jeweller, who was too glad to purchase it far below its real value to make many enquiries as to how it came into the possession of a poor working tailor, such as Amante seemed to be, we resolved to stay at this inn all night, and gather such particulars and information as we could by which to direct our onward course.

We took our supper in the darkest corner of the *salle-à-manger*, having previously bargained for a small bedroom across the court, and over the stables. We needed food sorely; but we hurried on our meal from dread of any one entering that public room who might recognise us. Just in the middle of our meal, the public diligence drove lumbering up under the *porte-cochère*, and disgorged its passengers. Most of them turned into the room where we sat, cowering and fearful, for the door was opposite to the porter's lodge, and both opened on to the wide-covered entrance from the street. Among the passengers came in a young, fair-haired lady, attended by an elderly French maid. The poor young creature tossed her head, and shrank away from the common room, full of evil smells and promiscuous company, and demanded, in German French, to be taken to some private apartment. We heard that she and her maid had come in the *coupé*, and, probably from pride, poor young lady! she had avoided all association with her fellow-passengers, thereby exciting their dislike and ridicule. All these little pieces of hearsay had a significance to us after-wards, though, at the time, the only remark made that bore upon the future was Amante's whisper to me that the young lady's hair was exactly the colour of mine, which she had cut off and burnt in the stove in the miller's kitchen in one of her descents from our hiding-place in the loft.

As soon as we could, we struck round in the shadow, leaving the boisterous and merry fellow-passengers to their supper. We crossed the court, borrowed a lantern from the ostler, and scrambled up the rude steps to our chamber above the stable. There was no door into it; the entrance was the hole into which the ladder fitted. The window looked into the court. We were tired and soon fell asleep. I was wakened by a noise in the stable below. One instant of listening, and I wakened Amante, placing my hand on her mouth, to prevent any exclamation in her half-roused state. We heard my husband speaking about his horse to the ostler. It was his voice. I am sure of it. Amante said so too. We durst not move to rise and satisfy ourselves. For five minutes or so he went on giving directions. Then he left the stable, and, softly stealing to our window, we saw him cross the court and re-enter the inn. We consulted as to what we should do. We feared to excite remark or suspicion by descending and leaving our chamber, or else immediate escape was our strongest idea. Then the ostler left the stable, locking the door on the outside.

'We must try and drop through the window – if, indeed, it is well to go at all,' said Amante.

With reflection came wisdom. We should excite suspicion by leaving without paying our bill. We were on foot, and might easily be pursued. So we sat on our bed's edge, talking and shivering, while from across the court the laughter rang merrily, and the company slowly dispersed one by one, their lights flitting past the windows as they went upstairs and settled each one to his rest.

We crept into our bed, holding each other tight, and listening to every sound, as if we thought we were tracked, and might meet our death at any moment. In the dead of night, just at the profound stillness preceding the turn into another day, we heard a soft, cautious step crossing the yard. The key into the stable was turned – someone came into the stable – we felt rather than heard him there. A horse started a little, and made a restless movement with his feet, then whinnied recognition. He who had entered made two or three low sounds to the animal, and then led him into the court. Amante sprang to the window with the noiseless activity of a cat. She looked out, but dared not speak a word. We heard the great door into the street open – a pause for mounting, and the horse's footsteps were lost in distance.

Then Amante came back to me. 'It was he! he is gone!' said she, and once more we lay down, trembling and shaking.

This time we fell sound asleep. We slept long and late. We were wakened by many hurrying feet, and many confused voices; all the world seemed awake and astir. We rose and dressed ourselves, and coming down we looked around among the crowd collected in the courtyard, in order to assure ourselves *he* was not there before we left the shelter of the stable.

The instant we were seen, two or three people rushed to us.

'Have you heard? – Do you know? – That poor young lady – oh, come and see!' and so we were hurried, almost in spite of ourselves, across the court, and up the great open stairs of the main building of the inn, into a bedchamber, where lay the beautiful young German lady, so full of graceful pride the night before, now white and still in death. By her stood the French maid, crying and gesticulating.

'Oh, madame! if you had but suffered me to stay with you! Oh! the baron, what will he say?' and so she went on. Her state had but just been discovered; it had been supposed that she was fatigued, and was sleeping late, until a few minutes before. The surgeon of the town had been sent for, and the landlord of the inn was trying vainly to enforce order until he came, and, from time to time, drinking little cups of brandy, and offering them to the guests, who were all assembled there, pretty much as the servants were doing in the courtyard.

At last the surgeon came. All fell back, and hung on the words that were to fall from his lips.

'See!' said the landlord. 'This lady came last night by the diligence with her maid. Doubtless a great lady, for she must have a private sitting-room – '

'She was Madame the Baroness de Roeder,' said the French maid.

' – And was difficult to please in the matter of supper, and a sleeping-room. She went to bed well, though fatigued. Her maid left her – '

'I begged to be allowed to sleep in her room, as we were in a strange inn, of the character of which we knew nothing; but she would not let me, my mistress was such a great lady.'

' – And slept with my servants,' continued the landlord. 'This morning we thought madame was still slumbering; but when eight, nine, ten, and near eleven o'clock came, I bade her maid use my passkey, and enter her room – '

'The door was not locked, only closed. And here she was found – dead is she not, monsieur? – with her face down on her pillow, and her beautiful hair all scattered wild; she never would let me tie it up, saying it made her head ache. Such hair!' said the waiting-maid, lifting up a long golden tress, and letting it fall again.

I remembered Amante's words the night before, and crept close up to her.

Meanwhile, the doctor was examining the body underneath the bedclothes, which the landlord, until now, had not allowed to be disarranged. The surgeon drew out his hand, all bathed and stained with blood;

and holding up a short, sharp knife, with a piece of paper fastened round it.

'Here has been foul play,' he said. 'The deceased lady has been murdered. This dagger was aimed straight at her heart.' Then, putting on his spectacles, he read the writing on the bloody paper, dimmed and horribly obscured as it was:

Numéro Un
Ainsi les Chauffeurs se vengent

'Let us go!' said I to Amante. 'Oh, let us leave this horrible place!'

'Wait a little,' said she. 'Only a few minutes more. It will be better.'

Immediately the voices of all proclaimed their suspicions of the cavalier who had arrived last the night before. He had, they said, made so many enquiries about the young lady, whose supercilious conduct all in the *salle-à-manger* had been discussing on his entrance. They were talking about her as we left the room; he must have come in directly afterwards, and not until he had learnt all about her, had he spoken of the business which necessitated his departure at dawn of day, and made his arrangements with both landlord and ostler for the possession of the keys of the stable and *porte-cochère*. In short, there was no doubt as to the murderer, even before the arrival of the legal functionary who had been sent for by the surgeon; but the word on the paper chilled everyone with terror. *Les Chauffeurs*, who were they? No one knew, some of the gang might even then be in the room overhearing, and noting down fresh objects for vengeance. In Germany, I had heard little of this terrible gang, and I had paid no greater heed to the stories related once or twice about them in Carlsruhe than one does to tales about ogres. But here in their very haunts, I learnt the full amount of the terror they inspired. No one would be legally responsible for any evidence criminating the murderer. The public prosecutor shrank from the duties of his office. What do I say? Neither Amante nor I, knowing far more of the actual guilt of the man who had killed that poor sleeping young lady, durst breathe a word. We appeared to be wholly ignorant of everything: we, who might have told so much. But how could we? we were broken down with terrific anxiety and fatigue, with the knowledge that we, above all, were doomed victims; and that the blood, heavily dripping from the bedclothes on to the floor, was dripping thus out of the poor dead body, because, when living, she had been mistaken for me.

At length Amante went up to the landlord, and asked permission to leave his inn, doing all openly and humbly, so as to excite neither ill-will nor suspicion. Indeed, suspicion was otherwise directed, and he willingly gave us leave to depart. A few days afterwards we were across the Rhine, in Germany, making our way towards Frankfort, but still keeping our disguises, and Amante still working at her trade.

On the way, we met a young man, a wandering journeyman from Heidelberg. I knew him, although I did not choose that he should know me. I asked him, as carelessly as I could, how the old miller was now? He told me he was dead. This realisation of the worst apprehensions caused by his long silence shocked me inexpressibly. It seemed as though every prop gave way from under me. I had been talking to Amante only that very day of the safety and comfort of the home that awaited her in my father's house; of the gratitude which the old man would feel towards her; and how there, in that peaceful dwelling, far away from the terrible land of France, she should find ease and security for all the rest of her life. All this I thought I had to promise, and even yet more had I looked for, for myself. I looked to the unburdening of my heart and conscience by telling all I knew to my best and wisest friend. I looked to his love as a sure guidance as well as a comforting stay, and, behold, he was gone away from me for ever!

I had left the room hastily on hearing of this sad news from the Heidelberger. Presently, Amante followed: 'Poor madame,' said she, consoling me to the best of her ability. And then she told me by degrees what more she had learned respecting my home, about which she knew almost as much as I did, from my frequent talks on the subject both at Les Rochers and on the dreary, doleful road we had come along. She had continued the conversation after I left, by asking about my brother and his wife. Of course, they lived on at the mill, but the man said (with what truth I know not, but I believed it firmly at the time) that Babette had completely got the upper hand of my brother, who only saw through her eyes and heard with her ears. That there had been much Heidelberg gossip of late days about her sudden intimacy with a grand French gentleman who had appeared at the mill – a relation, by marriage – married, in fact, to the miller's sister, who, by all accounts, had behaved abominably and ungratefully. But that was no reason for Babette's extreme and sudden intimacy with him, going about everywhere with the French gentleman; and since he left (as the

Heidelberger said he knew for a fact) corresponding with him constantly. Yet her husband saw no harm in it all, seemingly; though, to be sure, he was so out of spirits, what with his father's death and the news of his sister's infamy, that he hardly knew how to hold up his head.

'Now,' said Amante, 'all this proves that M. de la Tourelle has suspected that you would go back to the nest in which you were reared, and that he has been there, and found that you have not yet returned; but probably he still imagines that you will do so, and has accordingly engaged your sister-in-law as a kind of informant. Madame has said that her sister-in-law bore her no extreme good will; and the defamatory story he has got the start of us in spreading, will not tend to increase the favour in which your sister-in-law holds you. No doubt the assassin was retracing his steps when we met him near Forbach, and having heard of the poor German lady, with her French maid, and her pretty blonde complexion, he followed her. If madame will still be guided by me – and, my child, I beg of you still to trust me,' said Amante, breaking out of her respectful formality into the way of talking more natural to those who had shared and escaped from common dangers – more natural, too, where the speaker was conscious of a power of protection which the other did not possess – 'we will go on to Frankfort, and lose ourselves, for a time, at least, in the numbers of people who throng a great town; and you have told me that Frankfort is a great town. We will still be husband and wife; we will take a small lodging, and you shall housekeep and live indoors. I, as the rougher and the more alert, will continue my father's trade, and seek work at the tailors' shops.'

I could think of no better plan, so we followed this out. In a back street at Frankfort we found two furnished rooms to let on a sixth storey. The one we entered had no light from day; a dingy lamp swung perpetually from the ceiling, and from that, or from the open door leading into the bedroom beyond, came our only light. The bedroom was more cheerful, but very small. Such as it was, it almost exceeded our possible means. The money from the sale of my ring was almost exhausted, and Amante was a stranger in the place, speaking only French, moreover, and the good Germans were hating the French people right heartily. However, we succeeded better than our hopes, and even laid by a little against the time of my confinement. I never stirred abroad, and saw no one, and Amante's want of knowledge of German kept her in a state of comparative isolation.

At length my child was born – my poor worse than fatherless child. It was a girl, as I had prayed for. I had feared lest a boy might have something of the tiger nature of its father, but a girl seemed all my own. And yet not all my own, for the faithful Amante's delight and glory in the babe almost exceeded mine; in out-ward show it certainly did.

We had not been able to afford any attendance beyond what a neighbouring *sage-femme* could give, and she came frequently, bringing in with her a little store of gossip, and wonderful tales culled out of her own experience, every time. One day she began to tell me about a great lady in whose service her daughter had lived as scullion, or some such thing. Such a beautiful lady! with such a handsome husband. But grief comes to the palace as well as to the garret, and why or wherefore no one knew, but somehow the

Baron de Roeder must have incurred the vengeance of the terrible *Chauffeurs*; for not many months ago, as madame was going to see her relations in Alsace, she was stabbed dead as she lay in bed at some hotel on the road. Had I not seen it in the *Gazette*? Had I not heard? Why, she had been told that as far off as Lyons there were placards offering a heavy reward on the part of the Baron de Roeder for information respecting the murderer of his wife. But no one could help him, for all who could bear evidence were in such terror of the *Chauffeurs*; there were hundreds of them she had been told, rich and poor, great gentlemen and peasants, all leagued together by most frightful oaths to hunt to the death anyone who bore witness against them; so that even they who survived the tortures to which the *Chauffeurs* subjected many of the people whom they plundered, dared not to recognise them again, would not dare, even did they see them at the bar of a court of justice; for, if one were condemned, were there not hundreds sworn to avenge his death?

I told all this to Amante, and we began to fear that if M. de la Tourelle, or Lefebvre, or any of the gang at Les Rochers, had seen these placards, they would know that the poor lady stabbed by the former was the Baroness de Roeder, and that they would set forth again in search of me.

This fresh apprehension told on my health and impeded my recovery. We had so little money we could not call in a physician, at least, not one in established practice. But Amante found out a young doctor for whom, indeed, she had sometimes worked; and offering to pay him in kind, she brought him to see me, her sick wife. He was very gentle and thoughtful, though, like ourselves, very poor. But he gave much time and consideration to the case, saying once to Amante that he saw my constitution had experienced some severe shock from which it was probable that my nerves would never entirely recover. By and by I shall name this doctor, and then you will know, better than I can describe, his character.

I grew strong in time – stronger, at least. I was able to work a little at home, and to sun myself and my baby at the garret-window in the roof. It was all the air I dared to take. I constantly wore the disguise I had first set out with; as constantly had I renewed the disfiguring dye which changed my hair and complexion. But the perpetual state of terror in which I had been during the whole months succeeding my escape from Les Rochers made me loathe the idea of ever again walking in the open daylight, exposed to the sight and recognition of every passer-by. In vain Amante reasoned – in vain the doctor urged. Docile in every other thing, in this I was obstinate. I would not stir out. One day Amante returned from her work, full of news – some of it good, some such as to cause us apprehension. The good news was this; the master for whom she worked as journeyman was going to send her with some others to a great house at the other side of Frankfort, where there were to be private theatricals, and where many new dresses and much alteration of old ones would be required. The tailors employed were all to stay at this house until the day of representation was over, as it was at some distance from the town, and no one could tell when their work would be ended. But the pay was to be proportionately good.

The other thing she had to say was this: she had

that day met the travelling jeweller to whom she and I had sold my ring. It was rather a peculiar one, given to me by my husband; we had felt at the time that it might be the means of tracing us, but we were penniless and starving, and what else could we do? She had seen that this Frenchman had recognised her at the same instant that she did him, and she thought at the same time that there was a gleam of more than common intelligence on his face as he did so. This idea had been confirmed by his following her for some way on the other side of the street; but she had evaded him with her better knowledge of the town, and the increasing darkness of the night. Still it was well that she was going to such a distance from our dwelling on the next day; and she had brought me in a stock of provisions, begging me to keep within doors, with a strange kind of fearful oblivion of the fact that I had never set foot beyond the threshold of the house since I had first entered it – scarce ever ventured down the stairs. But, although my poor, my dear, very faithful Amante was like one possessed that last night, she spoke continually of the dead, which is a bad sign for the living. She kissed you – yes! it was you, my daughter, my darling, whom I bore beneath my bosom away from the fearful castle of your father – I call him so for the first time, I must call him so once again before I have done – Amante kissed you, sweet baby, blessed little comforter, as if she never could leave off. And then she went away, alive.

Two days, three days passed away. That third evening I was sitting within my bolted doors – you asleep on your pillow by my side – when a step came up the stair, and I knew it must be for me; for ours were the topmost rooms. Someone knocked; I held my very breath. But someone spoke, and I knew it was the good Doctor Voss. Then I crept to the door, and answered.

'Are you alone?' asked I.

'Yes,' said he, in a still lower voice. 'Let me in.' I let him in, and he was as alert as I in bolting and barring the door. Then he came and whispered to me his doleful tale. He had come from the hospital in the opposite quarter of the town, the hospital which he visited; he should have been with me sooner, but he had feared lest he should be watched. He had come from Amante's deathbed. Her fears of the jeweller were too well founded. She had left the house where she was employed that morning, to transact some errand connected with her work in the town; she must have been followed, and dogged on her way back through solitary wood-paths, for some of the wood-rangers belonging to the great house had found her lying there, stabbed to death, but not dead; with the poniard again plunged through the fatal writing, once more; but this time with the word 'un' underlined, so as to show that the assassin was aware of his previous mistake.

Numero Un. Ainsi les Chauffeurs se vengent.

They had carried her to the house, and given her restoratives till she had recovered the feeble use of her speech. But, oh, faithful, dear friend and sister! even then she remembered me, and refused to tell (what no one else among her fellow-workmen knew) where she lived or with whom. Life was ebbing away fast, and they had no resource but to carry her to the nearest hospital, where, of course, the fact of her sex was made known. Fortunately both for her and for me, the doctor in attendance was the very Doctor Voss whom we already knew. To him, while awaiting her confessor, she told enough to enable him to understand the position in which I was left; before the priest had heard half her tale Amante was dead.

Doctor Voss told me he had made all sorts of *détours*, and waited thus, late at night, for fear of being watched and followed. But I do not think he was. At any rate, as I afterwards learnt from him, the Baron Roeder, on hearing of the similitude of this murder with that of his wife in every particular, made such a search after the assassins, that, although they were not discovered, they were compelled to take to flight for the time.

I can hardly tell you now by what arguments Dr Voss, at first merely my benefactor, sparing me a portion of his small modicum, at length persuaded me to become his wife. His wife he called it, I called it; for we went through the religious ceremony too much slighted at the time, and as we were both Lutherans, and M. de la Tourelle had pretended to be of the reformed religion, a divorce from the latter would have been easily procurable by German law both ecclesiastical and legal, could we have summoned so fearful a man into any court.

The good doctor took me and my child by stealth to his modest dwelling; and there I lived in the same deep retirement, never seeing the full light of day, although when the dye had once passed away from my face my husband did not wish me to renew it. There was no need; my yellow hair was grey, my complexion was ashen-coloured, no creature could have recognised the fresh-coloured, bright-haired young woman of eighteen months before. The few people whom I saw knew me only as Madame Voss; a widow much older than himself, whom Dr Voss had secretly married. They called me the Grey Woman.

He made me give you his surname. Till now you have known no other father – while he lived you needed no father's love. Once only, only once more, did the old terror come upon me. For some reason which I forget, I broke through my usual custom, and went to the window of my room for some purpose, either to shut or to open it. Looking out into the street for an instant, I was fascinated by the sight of M. de la Tourelle, gay, young, elegant as ever, walking along on the opposite side of the street. The noise I had made with the window caused him to look up; he saw me, an old grey woman, and he did not recognise me! Yet it was not three years since we had parted, and his eyes were keen and dreadful like those of the lynx.

I told M. Voss, on his return home, and he tried to cheer me, but the shock of seeing M. de la Tourelle had been too terrible for me. I was ill for long months afterwards.

Once again I saw him. Dead. He and Lefebvre were at last caught; hunted down by the Baron de Roeder in some of their crimes. Dr Voss had heard of their arrest; their condemnation, their death; but he never said a word to me, until one day he bade me show him that I loved him by my obedience and my trust. He took me a long carriage journey, where to I know not, for we never spoke of that day again; I was led through a prison, into a closed courtyard, where, decently draped in the last robes of death, concealing the marks of decapitation, lay M. de la Tourelle, and two or three others, whom I had known at Les Rochers.

After that conviction Dr Voss tried to persuade me to return to a more natural mode of life, and to go out more. But although I sometimes complied with his wish, yet the old terror was ever strong upon me, and he, seeing what an effort it was, gave up urging me at last.

You know all the rest. How we both mourned bitterly the loss of that dear husband and father – for such I will call him ever – and as such you must consider him, my child, after this one revelation is over.

Why has it been made, you ask. For this reason, my child. The lover, whom you have only known as M. Lebrun, a French artist, told me but yesterday his real name, dropped because the bloodthirsty republicans might consider it as too aristocratic. It is Maurice de Poissy.

F. MARION CRAWFORD

For the Blood is the Life

We had dined at sunset on the broad roof of the old
tower, because it was cooler there during the great
heat of summer. Besides, the little kitchen was built
at one corner of the great square platform, which
made it more convenient than if the dishes had to be
carried down the steep stone steps, broken in places
and everywhere worn with age. The tower was one of
those built all down the west coast of Calabria by the
Emperor Charles V early in the sixteenth century, to
keep off the Barbary pirates, when the unbelievers
were allied with Francis I against the Emperor and
the Church. They have gone to ruin, a few still stand
intact, and mine is one of the largest. How it came
into my possession ten years ago, and why I spend a
part of each year in it, are matters which do not
concern this tale. The tower stands in one of the
loneliest spots in southern Italy, at the extremity of a
curving, rocky promontory, which forms a small but
safe natural harbour at the southern extremity of the
Gulf of Policastro, and just north of Cape Scalea, the
birthplace of Judas Iscariot, according to the old local
legend. The tower stands alone on this hooked spur
of the rock, and there is not a house to be seen within
three miles of it. When I go there I take a couple of
sailors, one of whom is a fair cook, and when I am
away it is in charge of a gnome-like little being who
was once a miner and who attached himself to me
long ago.

My friend, who sometimes visits me in my summer solitude, is an artist by profession, a Scandinavian by birth, and a cosmopolitan by force of circumstances. We had dined at sunset; the sunset glow had reddened and faded again, and the evening purple steeped the vast chain of the mountains that embrace the deep gulf to eastward and rear themselves higher and higher towards the south. It was hot, and we sat at the landward corner of the platform, waiting for the night breeze to come down from the lower hills. The colour sank out of the air, there was a little interval of deep-grey twilight, and a lamp sent a yellow streak from the open door of the kitchen, where the men were getting their supper.

Then the moon rose suddenly above the crest of the promontory, flooding the platform and lighting up every little spur of rock and knoll of grass below us, down to the edge of the motionless water. My friend lighted his pipe and sat looking at a spot on the hillside. I knew that he was looking at it, and for a long time past I had wondered whether he would ever see anything there that would fix his attention. I knew that spot well. It was clear that he was interested at last, though it was a long time before he spoke. Like most painters, he trusts to his own eyesight, as a lion trusts his strength and a stag his speed, and he is always disturbed when he cannot reconcile what he sees with what he believes that he ought to see.

'It's strange,' he said. 'Do you see that little mound just on this side of the boulder?'

'Yes,' I said, and I guessed what was coming.

'It looks like a grave,' observed Holger.

'Very true. It does look like a grave.'

'Yes,' continued my friend, his eyes still fixed on

the spot. 'But the strange thing is that I see the body lying on the top of it. Of course,' continued Holger, turning his head on one side as artists do, 'it must be an effect of light. In the first place, it is not a grave at all. Secondly, if it were, the body would be inside and not outside. Therefore, it's an effect of the moonlight. Don't you see it?'

'Perfectly; I always see it on moonlight nights.'

'It doesn't seem to interest you much,' said Holger.

'On the contrary, it does interest me, though I am used to it. You're not so far wrong, either. The mound is really a grave.'

'Nonsense!' cried Holger incredulously. 'I suppose you'll tell me that what I see lying on it is really a corpse!'

'No,' I answered, 'it's not. I know, because I have taken the trouble to go down and see.'

'Then what is it?' asked Holger.

'It's nothing.'

'You mean that it's an effect of light, I suppose?'

'Perhaps it is. But the inexplicable part of the matter is that it makes no difference whether the moon is rising or setting, or waxing or waning. If there's any moonlight at all, from east or west or overhead, so long as it shines on the grave you can see the outline of the body on top.'

Holger stirred up his pipe with the point of his knife, and then used his finger for a stopper. When the tobacco burned well, he rose from his chair.

'If you don't mind,' he said, 'I'll go down and take a look at it.'

He left me, crossed the roof, and disappeared down the dark steps. I did not move, but sat looking down until he came out of the tower below. I heard

him humming an old Danish song as he crossed the
open space in the bright moonlight, going straight to
the mysterious mound. When he was ten paces from
it, Holger stopped short, made two steps forward,
and then three or four backward, and then stopped
again. I knew what that meant. He had reached the
spot where the Thing ceased to be visible – where, as
he would have said, the effect of light changed.

Then he went on till he reached the mound and
stood upon it. I could see the Thing still, but it was no
longer lying down; it was on its knees now, winding
its white arms round Holger's body and looking up
into his face. A cool breeze stirred my hair at that
moment, as the night wind began to come down from
the hills, but it felt like a breath from another world.

The Thing seemed to be trying to climb to its feet,
helping itself up by Holger's body while he stood
upright, quite unconscious of it and apparently looking
towards the tower, which is very picturesque when the
moonlight falls upon it on that side.

'Come along!' I shouted. 'Don't stay there all night!'

It seemed to me that he moved reluctantly as he
stepped from the mound, or else with difficulty. That
was it. The Thing's arms were still round his waist,
but its feet could not leave the grave. As he came
slowly forward it was drawn and lengthened like a
wreath of mist, thin and white, till I saw distinctly that
Holger shook himself, as a man does who feels a chill.
At the same instant a little wail of pain came to me on
the breeze – it might have been the cry of the small owl
that lives among the rocks – and the misty presence
floated swiftly back from Holger's advancing figure
and lay once more at its length upon the mound.

Again I felt the cool breeze in my hair, and this

time an icy thrill of dread ran down my spine. I remembered very well that I had once gone down there alone in the moonlight; that presently, being near, I had seen nothing; that, like Holger, I had gone and had stood upon the mound; and I remembered how when I came back, sure that there was nothing there, I had felt the sudden conviction that there was something after all if I would only look back, a temptation I had resisted as unworthy of a man of sense, until, to get rid of it, I had shaken myself just as Holger did.

And now I knew that those white, misty arms had been round me, too; I knew it in a flash, and I shuddered as I remembered that I had heard the night owl then, too. But it had not been the night owl. It was the cry of the Thing.

I refilled my pipe and poured out a cup of strong southern wine; in less than a minute Holger was seated beside me again.

'Of course there's nothing there,' he said, 'but it's creepy, all the same. Do you know, when I was coming back I was so sure that there was something behind me that I wanted to turn around and look? It was an effort not to.'

He laughed a little, knocked the ashes out of his pipe, and poured himself out some wine. For a while neither of us spoke, and the moon rose higher and we both looked at the Thing that lay on the mound.

'You might make a story about that,' said Holger after a long time.

'There is one,' I answered. 'If you're not sleepy, I'll tell it to you.'

'Go ahead,' said Holger, who likes stories.

*

Old Alario was dying up there in the village beyond the hill. You remember him, I have no doubt. They say that he made his money by selling sham jewellery in South America, and escaped with his gains when he was found out. Like all those fellows, if they bring anything back with them, he at once set to work to enlarge his house, and as there are no masons here, he sent all the way to Paola for two workmen. They were a rough-looking pair of scoundrels – a Neapolitan who had lost one eye and a Sicilian with an old scar half an inch deep across his left cheek. I often saw them, for on Sundays they used to come down here and fish off the rocks. When Alario caught the fever that killed him the masons were still at work. As he had agreed that part of their pay should be their board and lodging, he made them sleep in the house. His wife was dead, and he had an only son called Angelo, who was a much better sort than himself. Angelo was to marry the daughter of the richest man in the village, and, strange to say, though the marriage was arranged by their parents, the young people were said to be in love with each other.

For that matter, the whole village was in love with Angelo, and among the rest a wild, good-looking creature called Cristina, who was more like a gypsy than any girl I ever saw about here. She had very red lips and very black eyes, she was built like a greyhound, and had the tongue of the devil. But Angelo did not care a straw for her. He was rather a simple-minded fellow, quite different from his old scoundrel of a father, and under what I should call normal circumstances I really believe that he would never have looked at any girl except the nice plump little creature, with a fat dowry, whom his father meant him to marry. But things turned up which were neither normal nor natural.

On the other hand, a very handsome young shepherd from the hills above Maratea was in love with Cristina, who seems to have been quite indifferent to him. Cristina had no regular means of subsistence, but she was a good girl and willing to do any work or go on errands to any distance for the sake of a loaf of bread or a mess of beans, and permission to sleep under cover. She was especially glad when she could get something to do about the house of Angelo's father. There is no doctor in the village, and when the neighbours saw that old Alario was dying they sent Cristina to Scalea to fetch one. That was late in the afternoon, and if they had waited so long it was because the dying miser refused to allow any such extravagance while he was able to speak. But while Cristina was gone matters grew rapidly worse, the priest was brought to the bedside, and when he had done what he could he gave it as his opinion to the bystanders that the old man was dead, and left the house.

You know these people. They have a physical horror of death. Until the priest spoke, the room had been full of people. The words were hardly out of his mouth before it was empty. It was night now. They hurried down the dark steps and out into the street.

Angelo, as I have said, was away. Cristina had not come back – the simple woman-servant who had nursed the sick man fled with the rest, and the body was left alone in the flickering light of the earthen oil lamp.

Five minutes later two men looked in cautiously and crept forward towards the bed. They were the

one-eyed Neapolitan mason and his Sicilian companion. They knew what they wanted. In a moment
they had dragged from under the bed a small
but heavy iron-bound box, and long before anyone
thought of coming back to the dead man they had
left the house and the village under cover of darkness.
It was easy enough, for Alario's house is the last
towards the gorge which leads down here, and the
thieves merely went out by the back door, got over
the stone wall, and had nothing to risk after that except
the possibility of meeting some belated countryman,
which was very small indeed, since few of the people
use that path. They had a mattock and shovel, and
they made their way without accident.

I am telling you this story as it must have happened,
for, of course, there were no witnesses to this part of
it. The men brought the box down by the gorge,
intending to bury it until they should be able to come
back and take it away in a boat. They must have been
clever enough to guess that some of the money would
be in paper notes, for they would otherwise have
buried it on the beach in the wet sand, where it would
have been much safer. But the paper would have
rotted if they had been obliged to leave it there long,
so they dug their hole down there, close to that
boulder. Yes, just where the mound is now.

Cristina did not find the doctor in Scalea, for he
had been sent for from a place up the valley, halfway
to San Domenico. If she had found him, he would
have come on his mule by the upper road, which is
smoother but much longer. But Cristina took the
short cut by the rocks, which passes about fifty feet
above the mound, and goes round that corner. The
men were digging when she passed, and she heard

them at work. It would not have been like her to go by without finding out what the noise was, for she was never afraid of anything in her life, and, besides, the fishermen sometimes come ashore here at night to get a stone for an anchor or to gather sticks to make a little fire. The night was dark, and Cristina probably came close to the two men before she could see what they were doing. She knew them, of course, and they knew her, and understood instantly that they were in her power. There was only one thing to be done for their safety, and they did it. They knocked her on the head, they dug the hole deep, and they buried her quickly with the iron-bound chest. They must have understood that their only chance of escaping suspicion lay in getting back to the village before their absence was noticed, for they returned immediately, and were found half an hour later gossiping quietly with the man who was making Alario's coffin. He was a crony of theirs, and had been working at the repairs in the old man's house. So far as I have been able to make out, the only persons who were supposed to know where Alario kept his treasure were Angelo and the one woman-servant I have mentioned. Angelo was away; it was the woman who discovered the theft.

It is easy enough to understand why no one else knew where the money was. The old man kept his door locked and the key in his pocket when he was out, and did not let the woman enter to clean the place unless he was there himself. The whole village knew that he had money somewhere, however, and the masons had probably discovered the whereabouts of the chest by climbing in at the window in his absence. If the old man had not been delirious until he lost consciousness, he would have been in frightful agony of mind for his riches. The faithful woman-servant forgot their existence only for a few moments when she fled with the rest, overcome by the horror of death. Twenty minutes had not passed before she returned with the two hideous old hags who are always called in to prepare the dead for burial. Even then she had not at first the courage to go near the bed with them, but she made a pretence of dropping something, went down on her knees as if to find it, and looked under the bedstead. The walls of the room were newly whitewashed down to the floor, and she saw at a glance that the chest was gone. It had been there in the afternoon, it had therefore been stolen in the short interval since she had left the room.

There are no carabineers stationed in the village; there is not so much as a municipal watchman, for there is no municipality. There never was such a place, I believe. Scalea is supposed to look after it in some mysterious way, and it takes a couple of hours to get anybody from there. As the old woman had lived in the village all her life, it did not even occur to her to apply to any civil authority for help. She simply set up a howl and ran through the village in the dark, screaming out that her dead master's house had been robbed. Many of the people looked out, but at first no one seemed inclined to help her. Most of them, judging her by themselves, whispered to each other that she had probably stolen the money herself. The first man to move was the father of the girl whom Angelo was to marry; having collected his household, all of whom felt a personal interest in the wealth which was to have come into the family, he declared it to be his opinion that the chest had been stolen by the two journeymen masons who lodged in the house. He headed a search for them, which naturally began in Alario's house and ended in the carpenter's workshop, where the thieves were found discussing a measure of wine with the carpenter over the half-finished coffin, by the light of one earthen lamp filled with oil and tallow. The search-party at once accused the delinquents of the crime, and threatened to lock them up in the cellar till the carabineers could be fetched from Scalea. The two men looked at each other for one moment, and then without the slightest hesitation they put out the single light, seized the unfinished coffin between them, and using it as a sort of battering ram, dashed upon their assailants in the dark. In a few moments they were beyond pursuit.

That is the end of the first part of the story. The treasure had disappeared, and as no trace of it could be found the people naturally supposed that the thieves had succeeded in carrying it off. The old man was buried, and when Angelo came back at last he had to borrow money to pay for the miserable funeral, and had some difficulty in doing so. He hardly needed to be told that in losing his inheritance he had lost his bride. In this part of the world marriages are made on strictly business principles, and if the promised cash is not forthcoming on the appointed day, the bride or the bridegroom whose parents have failed to produce it may as well take themselves off, for there will be no wedding. Poor Angelo knew that well enough. His father had been possessed of hardly any land, and now that the hard cash which he had brought from South America was gone, there was nothing left but debts for the building materials that were to have been used for enlarging and improving the old house.

Angelo was beggared, and the nice plump little creature who was to have been his turned up her nose at him in the most approved fashion. As for Cristina, it was several days before she was missed, for no one remembered that she had been sent to Scalea for the doctor, who had never come. She often disappeared in the same way for days together, when she could find a little work here and there at the distant farms among the hills. But when she did not come back at all, people began to wonder, and at last made up their minds that she had connived with the masons and had escaped with them.

I paused and emptied my glass.

'That sort of thing could not happen anywhere else,' observed Holger, filling his everlasting pipe again. 'It is wonderful what a natural charm there is about murder and sudden death in a romantic country like this. Deeds that would be simply brutal and disgusting anywhere else become dramatic and mysterious because this is Italy and we are living in a genuine tower of Charles V built against Barbary pirates.'

'There's something in that,' I admitted. Holger is the most romantic man in the world inside of himself, but he always thinks it necessary to explain why he feels anything.

'I suppose they found the poor girl's body with the box,' he said presently.

'As it seems to interest you,' I answered, 'I'll tell you the rest of the story.'

The moon had risen by this time; the outline of the Thing on the mound was clearer to our eyes than before.

*

The village very soon settled down to its small, dull life. No one missed old Alario, who had been away so much on his voyages to South America that he had never been a familiar figure in his native place. Angelo lived in the half-finished house, and because he had no money to pay the old woman-servant, she would not stay with him, but once in a long time she would come and wash a shirt for him for old acquaintance' sake. Besides the house, he had inherited a small patch of ground at some distance from the village; he tried to cultivate it, but he had no heart in the work, for he knew he could never pay the taxes on it and on the house, which would certainly be confiscated by the Government, or seized for the debt of the building material, which the man who had supplied it refused to take back.

Angelo was very unhappy. So long as his father had been alive and rich, every girl in the village had been in love with him; but that was all changed now. It had been pleasant to be admired and courted, and invited to drink wine by fathers who had girls to marry. It was hard to be stared at coldly, and sometimes laughed at because he had been robbed of his inheritance. He cooked his miserable meals for himself, and from being sad became melancholy and morose.

At twilight, when the day's work was done, instead of hanging about in the open space before the church with young fellows of his own age, he took to wandering in lonely places on the outskirts of the village till it was quite dark. Then he slunk home and went to bed to save the expense of a light. But in those lonely twilight hours he began to have strange waking dreams. He was not always alone, for often when he sat on the stump of a tree, where the narrow path turns down the gorge, he was sure that a woman came up noiselessly over the rough stones, as if her feet were bare; and she stood under a clump of chestnut trees only half a dozen yards down the path, and beckoned to him without speaking. Though she was in the shadow he knew that her lips were red, and that when they parted a little and smiled at him she showed two small sharp teeth. He knew this at first rather than saw it, and he knew that it was Cristina, and that she was dead. Yet he was not afraid; he only wondered whether it was a dream, for he thought that if he had been awake he should have been frightened.

Besides, the dead woman had red lips, and that could only happen in a dream. Whenever he went near the gorge after sunset she was already there waiting for him, or else she very soon appeared, and he began to be sure that she came a little nearer to him every day. At first he had only been sure of her blood-red mouth, but now each feature grew distinct, and the pale face looked at him with deep and hungry eyes.

It was the eyes that grew dim. Little by little he came to know that some day the dream would not end when he turned away to go home, but would lead him down the gorge out of which the vision rose. She was nearer now when she beckoned to him. Her cheeks were not livid like those of the dead, but pale with starvation, with the furious and unappeased physical hunger of her eyes that devoured him. They feasted on his soul and cast a spell over him, and at last they were close to his own and held him. He could not tell whether her breath was as hot as fire, or as cold as ice; he could not tell whether her red lips burned his or froze them, or whether her five fingers on his wrists seared scorching scars or bit his flesh like frost; he could not tell whether he was awake or asleep, whether she was alive or dead, but he knew that she loved him, she alone of all creatures, earthly or unearthly, and her spell had power over him.

When the moon rose high that night the shadow of that Thing was not alone down there upon the mound.

Angelo awoke in the cool dawn, drenched with dew and chilled through flesh, and blood, and bone. He opened his eyes to the faint grey light, and saw the stars were still shining overhead. He was very weak, and his heart was beating so slowly that he was almost like a man fainting. Slowly he turned his head on the mound, as on a pillow, but the other face was not there. Fear seized him suddenly, a fear unspeakable and unknown; he sprang to his feet and fled up the gorge, and he never looked behind him until he reached the door of the house on the outskirts of the village. Drearily he went to his work that day, and wearily the hours dragged themselves after the sun, till at last it touched the sea and sank, and the great sharp hills above Maratea turned purple against the dove-coloured eastern sky.

Angelo shouldered his heavy hoe and left the field. He felt less tired now than in the morning when he had begun to work, but he promised himself that he would go home without lingering by the gorge, and eat the best supper he could get himself, and sleep all night in his bed like a Christian man. Not again would he be tempted down the narrow way by a shadow with red lips and icy breath; not again would he dream that dream of terror and delight. He was near the village now; it was half an hour since the sun had set, and the cracked church bell sent little discordant echoes across the rocks and ravines to tell all good people that the day was done. Angelo stood still a moment where the path forked, where it led towards the village on the left, and down to the gorge on the right, where a clump of chestnut trees overhung the narrow way. He stood still a minute, lifting his battered hat from his head and gazing at the fast-fading sea westward, and his lips moved as he silently repeated the familiar evening prayer. His lips moved, but the words that followed them in his brain lost their meaning and turned into others, and ended in a name that he spoke aloud – 'Cristina!' With the name, the tension of his will relaxed suddenly, reality went out and the dream took him again, and bore him on swiftly and surely like a man walking in his sleep, down, down, by the steep path in the gathering darkness. And as she glided beside him, Cristina whispered strange, sweet things in his ear, which somehow, if he had been awake, he knew that he could not quite have understood; but now they were the most wonderful words he had ever heard in his life. And she kissed him also, but not upon his mouth. He felt her sharp kisses upon his white throat, and he knew that her lips were red. So the wild dream sped on through twilight and darkness and moonrise, and all the glory of the summer's night. But in the chilly dawn he lay as one half dead upon the mound down there, recalling and not recalling, drained of his blood, yet strangely longing to give those red lips more. Then came the fear, the awful nameless panic, the mortal horror that guards the confines of the world we see not, neither know of as we know of other things, but which we feel when its icy chill freezes our bones and stirs our hair with the touch of a ghostly hand. Once more Angelo sprang from the mound and fled up the gorge in the breaking day, but his step was less sure this time, and he panted for breath as he ran; and when he came to the bright spring of water that rises halfway up the hillside, he dropped upon his knees and hands and plunged his whole face in and drank as he had never drunk before – for it was the thirst of the wounded man who has lain bleeding all night upon the battlefield.

She had him fast now, and he could not escape her, but would come to her every evening at dusk until she had drained him of his last drop of blood. It was in vain that when the day was done he tried to take another turning and to go home by a path that did not lead near the gorge. It was in vain that he made promises to himself each morning at dawn when he climbed the lonely way up from the shore to the village. It was all in vain, for when the sun sank burning into the sea, and the coolness of the evening stole out as from a hiding-place to delight the weary world, his feet turned towards the old way, and she was waiting for him in the shadow under the chestnut trees; and then all happened as before, and she fell to kissing his white throat even as she flitted lightly down the way, winding one arm about him. And as his blood failed, she grew more hungry and more thirsty every day, and every day when he awoke in the early dawn it was harder to rouse himself to the effort of climbing the steep path to the village; and when he went to his work his feet dragged painfully, and there was hardly strength in his arms to wield the heavy hoe. He scarcely spoke to anyone now, but the people

said he was 'consuming himself' for love of the girl he
was to have married when he lost his inheritance; and
they laughed heartily at the thought, for this is not a
very romantic country. At this time Antonio, the man
who stays here to look after the tower, returned from
a visit to his people, who live near Salerno. He had
been away all the time since before Alario's death and
knew nothing of what had happened. He has told me
that he came back late in the afternoon and shut
himself up in the tower to eat and sleep, for he was
very tired. It was past midnight when he awoke, and
when he looked out the waning moon was rising over
the shoulder of the hill. He looked out towards the
mound, and he saw something, and he did not sleep
again that night. When he went out again in the
morning it was broad daylight, and there was nothing
to be seen on the mound but loose stones and driven
sand. Yet he did not go very near it; he went straight
up the path to the village and directly to the house of
the old priest.

'I have seen an evil thing this night,' he said; 'I have
seen how the dead drink the blood of the living. And
the blood is the life.'

'Tell me what you have seen,' said the priest in
reply.

Antonio told him everything he had seen.

'You must bring your book and your holy water
tonight,' he added. 'I will be here before sunset to go
down with you, and if it pleases your reverence to sup
with me while we wait, I will make ready.'

'I will come,' the priest answered, 'for I have read
in old books of these strange beings which are neither
quick nor dead, and which lie ever fresh in their
graves, stealing out in the dusk to taste life and blood.'

Antonio cannot read, but he was glad to see that the priest understood the business; for, of course, the books must have instructed him as to the best means of quieting the half-living Thing for ever.

So Antonio went away to his work, which consists largely in sitting on the shady side of the tower, when he is not perched upon a rock with a fishing-line catching nothing. But on that day he went twice to look at the mound in the bright sunlight, and he searched round and round it for some hole through which the being might get in and out; but he found none. When the sun began to sink and the air was cooler in the shadows, he went up to fetch the old priest, carrying a little wicker basket with him; and in this they placed a bottle of holy water, and the basin, and sprinkler, and the stole which the priest would need; and they came down and waited in the door of the tower till it should be dark. But while the light still lingered very grey and faint, they saw something moving, just there, two figures, a man's that walked, and a woman's that flitted beside him, and while her head lay on his shoulder she kissed his throat. The priest has told me that, too, and that his teeth chattered and he grasped Antonio's arm. The vision passed and disappeared into the shadow. Then Antonio got the leathern flask of strong liquor, which he kept for great occasions, and poured such a draught as made the old man feel almost young again; and gave the priest his stole to put on and the holy water to carry, and they went out together towards the spot where the work was to be done. Antonio says that in spite of the rum his own knees shook together, and the priest stumbled over his Latin. For when they were yet a few yards from the mound the flickering light of the lantern fell upon Angelo's white face, unconscious as if in sleep, and on his upturned throat, over which a very thin red line of blood trickled down into his collar; and the flickering light of the lantern played upon another face that looked up from the feast – upon two deep, dead eyes that saw in spite of death – upon parted lips redder than life itself – upon two gleaming teeth on which glistened a rosy drop. Then the priest, good old man, shut his eyes tight and showered holy water before him, and his cracked voice rose almost to a scream; and then Antonio, who is no coward after all, raised his pick in one hand and the lantern in the other, as he sprang forward, not knowing what the end should be; and then he swears that he heard a woman's cry, and the Thing was gone, and Angelo lay alone on the mound unconscious, with the red line on his throat and the beads of deathly sweat on his cold forehead. They lifted him, half-dead as he was, and laid him on the ground close by; then Antonio went to work, and the priest helped him, though he was old and could not do much; and they dug deep, and at last Antonio, standing in the grave, stooped down with his lantern to see what he might see.

His hair used to be dark brown, with grizzled streaks about the temples; in less than a month from that day he was as grey as a badger. He was a miner when he was young, and most of these fellows have seen ugly sights now and then, when accidents have happened, but he had never seen what he saw that night – that Thing which is neither alive nor dead, that Thing that will abide neither above ground nor in the grave. Antonio had brought something with him which the priest had not noticed – a sharp stake shaped from a piece of tough old driftwood. He had it with him now, and he had his heavy pick, and he had taken the lantern down into the grave. I don't think any power on earth could make him speak of what happened then, and the old priest was too frightened to look in. He says he heard Antonio breathing like a wild beast, and moving as if he were fighting with something almost as strong as himself; and he heard an evil sound also, with blows, as of something violently driven through flesh and bone; and then, the most awful sound of all – a woman's shriek, the unearthly scream of a woman neither dead nor alive, but buried deep for many days. And he, the poor old priest, could only rock himself as he knelt there in the sand, crying aloud his prayers and exorcisms to drown these dreadful sounds. Then suddenly a small iron-bound chest was thrown up and rolled over against the old man's knee, and in a moment more Antonio was beside him, his face as white as tallow in the flickering light of the lantern, shovelling the sand and pebbles into the grave with furious haste, and looking over the edge till the pit was half full; and the priest said that there was much fresh blood on Antonio's hands and on his clothes.

I had come to the end of my story. Holger finished his wine and leaned back in his chair.

'So Angelo got his own again,' he said. 'Did he marry the prim and plump young person to whom he had been betrothed?'

'No; he had been badly frightened. He went to South America, and has not been heard of since.'

'And that poor thing's body is there still, I suppose,' said Holger. 'Is it quite dead yet, I wonder?'

I wonder, too. But whether it be dead or alive, I should hardly care to see it, even in broad daylight.

Antonio is as grey as a badger, and he has never been quite the same man since that night.

AMYAS NORTHCOTE

Brickett Bottom

The Reverend Arthur Maydew was the hard-working incumbent of a large parish in one of our manufacturing towns. He was also a student and a man of no strong physique, so that when an opportunity was presented to him to take an annual holiday by exchanging parsonages with an elderly clergyman, Mr Roberts, the parson of the Parish of Overbury, and an acquaintance of his own, he was glad to avail himself of it.

Overbury is a small and very remote village in one of our most lovely and rural counties, and Mr Roberts had long held the living of it.

Without further delay we can transport Mr Maydew and his family, which consisted only of two daughters, to their temporary home. The two young ladies, Alice and Maggie, the heroines of this narrative, were at that time aged twenty-six and twenty-four years respectively. Both of them were attractive girls, fond of such society as they could find in their own parish and, the former especially, always pleased to extend the circle of their acquaintance. Although the elder in years, Alice in many ways yielded place to her sister, who was the more energetic and practical and upon whose shoulders the bulk of the family cares and responsibilities rested. Alice was inclined to be absent-minded and emotional and to devote more of her thoughts and time to speculations of an abstract nature than her sister.

264

Both of the girls, however, rejoiced at the prospect of a period of quiet and rest in a pleasant country neighbourhood, and both were gratified at knowing that their father would find in Mr Roberts's library much that would entertain his mind, and in Mr Roberts's garden an opportunity to indulge freely in his favourite game of croquet. They would have, no doubt, preferred some cheerful neighbours, but Mr Roberts was positive in his assurances that there was no one in the neighbourhood whose acquaintance would be of interest to them.

The first few weeks of their new life passed pleasantly for the Maydew family. Mr Maydew quickly gained renewed vigour in his quiet and congenial surroundings, and in the delightful air, while his daughters spent much of their time in long walks about the country and in exploring its beauties.

One evening late in August the two girls were returning from a long walk along one of their favourite paths, which led along the side of the Downs. On their right, as they walked, the ground fell away sharply to a narrow glen, named Brickett Bottom, about three-quarters of a mile in length, along the bottom of which ran a little-used country road leading to a farm, known as Blaise's Farm, and then onward and upward to lose itself as a sheep track on the higher Downs. On their side of the slope some scattered trees and bushes grew, but beyond the lane and running up over the farther slope of the glen was a thick wood, which extended away to Carew Court, the seat of a neighbouring magnate, Lord Carew. On their left the open Down rose above them and beyond its crest lay Overbury.

The girls were walking hastily, as they were later

than they had intended to be and were anxious to reach home. At a certain point at which they had now arrived the path forked, the right hand branch leading down into Brickett Bottom and the left hand turning up over the Down to Overbury.

Just as they were about to turn into the left hand path Alice suddenly stopped and pointing downwards exclaimed: 'How very curious, Maggie! Look, there is a house down there in the Bottom, which we have, or at least I have, never noticed before, often as we have walked up the Bottom.'

Maggie followed with her eyes her sister's pointing finger. 'I don't see any house,' she said.

'Why, Maggie,' said her sister, 'can't you see it! A quaint-looking, old-fashioned red-brick house, there just where the road bends to the right. It seems to be standing in a nice, well-kept garden too.'

Maggie looked again, but the light was beginning to fade in the glen and she was short-sighted to boot.

'I certainly don't see anything,' she said, 'but then I am so blind and the light is getting bad; yes, perhaps I do see a house,' she added, straining her eyes.

'Well, it is there,' replied her sister, 'and tomorrow we will come and explore it.'

Maggie agreed readily enough, and the sisters went home, still speculating on how they had happened not to notice the house before and resolving firmly on an expedition thither the next day. However, the expedition did not come off as planned, for that evening Maggie slipped on the stairs and fell, spraining her ankle in such a fashion as to preclude walking for some time.

Notwithstanding the accident to her sister, Alice remained possessed by the idea of making further investigations into the house she had looked down upon from the hill the evening before; and the next day, having seen Maggie carefully settled for the afternoon, she started off for Brickett Bottom. She returned in triumph and much intrigued over her discoveries, which she eagerly narrated to her sister.

Yes. There was a nice, old-fashioned red-brick house, not very large and set in a charming, old-world garden in the Bottom. It stood on a tongue of land jutting out from the woods, just at the point where the lane, after a fairly straight course from its junction with the main road half a mile away, turned sharply to the right in the direction of Blaise's Farm. More than that, Alice had seen the people of the house, whom she described as an old gentleman and a lady, presumably his wife. She had not clearly made out the gentleman, who was sitting in the porch, but the old lady, who had been in the garden busy with her flowers, had looked up and smiled pleasantly at her as she passed. She was sure, she said, that they were nice people and that it would be pleasant to make their acquaintance.

Maggie was not quite satisfied with Alice's story. She was of a more prudent and retiring nature than her sister; she had an uneasy feeling that, if the old couple had been desirable or attractive neighbours, Mr Roberts would have mentioned them, and knowing Alice's nature she said what she could to discourage her vague idea of endeavouring to make acquaintance with the owners of the red-brick house.

On the following morning, when Alice came to her sister's room to enquire how she did, Maggie noticed that she looked pale and rather absent-minded, and, after a few commonplace remarks had passed, she

267

asked: 'What is the matter, Alice? You don't look yourself this morning.'

Her sister gave a slightly embarrassed laugh.

'Oh, I am all right,' she replied, 'only I did not sleep very well. I kept on dreaming about the house. It was such an odd dream too; the house seemed to be home, and yet to be different.'

'What, that house in Brickett Bottom?' said Maggie. 'Why, what is the matter with you? You seem to be quite crazy about the place.'

'Well, it is curious, isn't it, Maggie, that we should have only just discovered it, and that it looks to be lived in by nice people? I wish we could get to know them.'

Maggie did not care to resume the argument of the night before and the subject dropped, nor did Alice again refer to the house or its inhabitants for some little time. In fact, for some days the weather was wet and Alice was forced to abandon her walks, but when the weather once more became fine she resumed them, and Maggie suspected that Brickett Bottom formed one of her sister's favourite expeditions. Maggie became anxious over her sister, who seemed to grow daily more absent-minded and silent, but she refused to be drawn into any confidential talk, and Maggie was nonplussed.

One day, however, Alice returned from her afternoon walk in an unusually excited state of mind, of which Maggie sought an explanation. It came with a rush. Alice said that, that afternoon, as she approached the house in Brickett Bottom, the old lady, who as usual was busy in her garden, had walked down to the gate as she passed and had wished her good-day.

Alice had replied and, pausing, a short conversation

had followed. Alice could not remember the exact tenor of it, but, after she had paid a compliment to the old lady's flowers, the latter had rather diffidently asked her to enter the garden for a closer view. Alice had hesitated, and the old lady had said, 'Don't be afraid of me, my dear, I like to see young ladies about me and my husband finds their society quite necessary to him.' After a pause she went on: 'Of course nobody has told you about us. My husband is Colonel Paxton, late of the Indian Army, and we have been here for many, many years. It's rather lonely, for so few people ever see us. Do come in and meet the Colonel.'

'I hope you didn't go in,' said Maggie rather sharply.

'Why not?' replied Alice.

'Well, I don't like Mrs Paxton asking you in that way,' answered Maggie.

'I don't see what harm there was in the invitation,' said Alice. 'I didn't go in because it was getting late and I was anxious to get home; but – '

'But what?' asked Maggie.

Alice shrugged her shoulders.

'Well,' she said, 'I have accepted Mrs Paxton's invitation to pay her a little visit tomorrow.' And she gazed defiantly at Maggie.

Maggie became distinctly uneasy on hearing of this resolution. She did not like the idea of her impulsive sister visiting people on such slight acquaintance, especially as they had never heard them mentioned before. She endeavoured by all means, short of appealing to Mr Maydew, to dissuade her sister from going, at any rate until there had been time to make some enquiries as to the Paxtons. Alice, however, was obdurate.

What harm could happen to her? she asked. Mrs

Paxton was a charming old lady. She was going early in the afternoon for a short visit. She would be back for tea and croquet with her father and, anyway, now that Maggie was laid up, long solitary walks were unendurable and she was not going to let slip the chance of following up what promised to be a pleasant acquaintance.

Maggie could do nothing more. Her ankle was better and she was able to get down to the garden and sit in a long chair near her father, but walking was still quite out of the question, and it was with some misgivings that on the following day she watched Alice depart gaily for her visit, promising to be back by half-past four at the very latest.

The afternoon passed quietly till nearly five, when Mr Maydew, looking up from his book, noticed Maggie's uneasy expression and asked: 'Where is Alice?'

'Out for a walk,' replied Maggie; and then after a short pause she went on: 'And she has also gone to pay a call on some neighbours whom she has recently discovered.'

'Neighbours,' ejaculated Mr Maydew, 'what neighbours? Mr Roberts never spoke of any neighbours to me.'

'Well, I don't know much about them,' answered Maggie. 'Only Alice and I were out walking the day of my accident and saw – or at least she saw, for I am so blind I could not quite make it out – a house in Brickett Bottom. The next day she went to look at it closer, and yesterday she told me that she had made the acquaintance of the people living in it. She says that they are a retired Indian officer and his wife, a Colonel and Mrs Paxton, and Alice describes Mrs Paxton as a charming old lady, who pressed her to come and see them. So she has gone this afternoon, but she promised me she would be back long before this.'

Mr Maydew was silent for a moment and then said: 'I am not well pleased about this. Alice should not be so impulsive and scrape acquaintance with absolutely unknown people. Had there been nice neighbours in Brickett Bottom, I am certain Mr Roberts would have told us.'

The conversation dropped; but both father and daughter were disturbed and uneasy and, tea having been finished and the clock striking half-past five, Mr Maydew asked Maggie: 'When did you say Alice would be back?'

'Before half-past four at the latest, father.'

'Well, what can she be doing? What can have delayed her? You say you did not see the house,' he went on.

'No,' said Maggie, 'I cannot say I did. It was getting dark and you know how short-sighted I am.'

'But surely you must have seen it at some other time,' said her father.

'That is the strangest part of the whole affair,' answered Maggie. 'We have often walked up the Bottom, but I never noticed the house, nor had Alice till that evening. I wonder,' she went on after a short pause, 'if it would not be well to ask Smith to harness the pony and drive over to bring her back. I am not happy about her – I am afraid – '

'Afraid of what?' said her father in the irritated voice of a man who is growing frightened. 'What can have gone wrong in this quiet place? Still, I'll send Smith over for her.'

So saying he rose from his chair and sought out

Smith, the rather dull-witted gardener-groom attached to Mr Roberts's service.

'Smith,' he said, 'I want you to harness the pony at once and go over to Colonel Paxton's in Brickett Bottom and bring Miss Maydew home.'

The man stared at him. 'Go where, sir?' he said.

Mr Maydew repeated the order and the man, still staring stupidly, answered: 'I never heard of Colonel Paxton, sir. I don't know what house you mean.'

Mr Maydew was now growing really anxious. 'Well, harness the pony at once,' he said; and going back to Maggie he told her of what he called Smith's stupidity, and asked her if she felt that her ankle would be strong enough to permit her to go with him and Smith to the Bottom to point out the house.

Maggie agreed readily and in a few minutes the party started off. Brickett Bottom, although not more than three-quarters of a mile away over the Downs, was at least three miles by road; and as it was nearly six o'clock before Mr Maydew left the Vicarage, and the pony was old and slow, it was getting late before the entrance to Brickett Bottom was reached. Turning into the lane the cart proceeded slowly up the Bottom, Mr Maydew and Maggie looking anxiously from side to side, while Smith drove stolidly on looking neither to the right nor left.

'Where is the house?' said Mr Maydew presently.

'At the bend of the road,' answered Maggie, her heart sickening as she looked out through the failing light to see the trees stretching their ranks in unbroken formation along it. The cart reached the bend. 'It should be here,' whispered Maggie.

They pulled up. Just in front of them the road bent to the right round a tongue of land, which, unlike the rest of the right hand side of the road, was free from trees and was covered only by rough grass and stray bushes. A closer inspection disclosed evident signs of terraces having once been formed on it, but of a house there was no trace.

'Is this the place?' said Mr Maydew in a low voice.

Maggie nodded.

'But there is no house here,' said her father. 'What does it all mean? Are you sure of yourself, Maggie? Where is Alice?'

Before Maggie could answer a voice was heard calling 'Father! Maggie!' The sound of the voice was thin and high and, paradoxically, it sounded both very near and yet as if it came from some infinite distance. The cry was thrice repeated and then silence fell. Mr Maydew and Maggie stared at each other.

'That was Alice's voice,' said Mr Maydew huskily, 'she is near and in trouble, and is calling us. Which way did you think it came from, Smith?' he added, turning to the gardener.

'I didn't hear anybody calling,' said the man.

'Nonsense!' answered Mr Maydew.

And then he and Maggie both began to call, 'Alice. Alice. Where are you?'

There was no reply and Mr Maydew sprang from the cart, at the same time bidding Smith to hand the reins to Maggie and come and search for the missing girl. Smith obeyed him and both men, scrambling up the turfy bit of ground, began to search and call through the neighbouring wood. They heard and saw nothing, however, and after an agonised search Mr Maydew ran down to the cart and begged Maggie to drive on to Blaise's Farm for help, leaving himself and Smith to continue the search. Maggie followed her father's instructions and was fortunate enough to find Mr Rumbold, the farmer, his two sons and a couple of labourers just returning from the harvest field. She explained what had happened, and the farmer and his men promptly volunteered to form a search party, though Maggie, in spite of her anxiety, noticed a queer expression on Mr Rumbold's face as she told him her tale.

The party, provided with lanterns, now went down the Bottom, joined Mr Maydew and Smith and made an exhaustive but absolutely fruitless search of the woods near the bend of the road. No trace of the missing girl was to be found, and after a long and anxious time the search was abandoned, one of the young Rumbolds volunteering to ride into the nearest town and notify the police.

Maggie, though with little hope in her own heart, endeavoured to cheer her father on their homeward way with the idea that Alice might have returned to Overbury over the Downs whilst they were going by road to the Bottom, and that she had seen them and called to them in jest when they were opposite the tongue of land.

However, when they reached home there was no Alice and, though the next day the search was resumed and full enquiries were instituted by the police, all was to no purpose. No trace of Alice was ever found, the last human being that saw her having been an old woman, who had met her going down the path into the Bottom on the afternoon of her disappearance, and who described her as smiling but looking 'queerlike'.

*

This is the end of the story, but the following may throw some light upon it.

The history of Alice's mysterious disappearance became widely known through the medium of the press, and Mr Roberts, distressed beyond measure at what had taken place, returned in all haste to Overbury to offer what comfort and help he could give to his afflicted friend and tenant. He called upon the Maydews and, having heard their tale, sat for a short time in silence. Then he said: 'Have you ever heard any local gossip concerning this Colonel and Mrs Paxton?'

'No,' replied Mr Maydew, 'I never heard their names until the day of my poor daughter's fatal visit.'

'Well,' said Mr Roberts, 'I will tell you all I can about them, which is not very much, I fear.' He paused and then went on: 'I am now nearly seventy-five years old, and for nearly seventy years no house has stood in Brickett Bottom. But when I was a child of about five there was an old-fashioned, red-brick house standing in a garden at the bend of the road, such as you have described. It was owned and lived in by a retired Indian soldier and his wife, a Colonel and Mrs Paxton. At the time I speak of, certain events having taken place at the house and the old couple having died, it was sold by their heirs to Lord Carew, who shortly after pulled it down on the ground that it interfered with his shooting. Colonel and Mrs Paxton were well known to my father, who was the clergyman here before me, and to the neighbourhood in general. They lived quietly and were not unpopular, but the Colonel was supposed to possess a violent and vindictive temper. Their family consisted only of themselves, their daughter and a couple of servants, the Colonel's old army servant and his Eurasian wife. Well, I cannot tell you details of what happened, I was only a child; my father never liked gossip and in later years, when he talked to me on the subject, he always avoided any appearance of exaggeration or sensationalism. However, it is known that Miss Paxton fell in love with and became engaged to a young man to whom her parents took a strong dislike. They used every possible means to break off the match, and many rumours were set on foot as to their conduct – undue influence, even cruelty were charged against them. I do not know the truth, all I can say is that Miss Paxton died and a very bitter feeling against her parents sprang up. My father, however, continued to call, but was rarely admitted. In fact, he never saw Colonel Paxton after his daughter's death and only saw Mrs Paxton once or twice. He described her as an utterly broken woman, and was not surprised at her following her daughter to the grave in about three months' time. Colonel Paxton became, if possible, more of a recluse than ever after his wife's death and himself died not more than a month after her under circumstances which pointed to suicide. Again a crop of rumours sprang up, but there was no one in particular to take action, the doctor certified Death from Natural Causes, and Colonel Paxton, like his wife and daughter, was buried in this churchyard. The property passed to a distant relative, who came to it for one night shortly afterwards; he never came again, having apparently conceived a violent dislike of the place, but arranged to pension off the servants and then sold the house to Lord Carew, who was glad to purchase this little island in the middle of his property. He pulled it down soon after he had bought it, and the garden was left to relapse into a wilderness.'

Mr Roberts paused. 'Those are all the facts,' he added.

'But there is something more,' said Maggie.

Mr Roberts hesitated for a while. 'You have a right to know all,' he said almost to himself; then louder he continued: 'What I am now going to tell you is really rumour, vague and uncertain; I cannot fathom its truth or its meaning. About five years after the house had been pulled down a young maidservant at Carew Court was out walking one afternoon. She was a stranger to the village and a newcomer to the Court. On returning home to tea she told her fellow-servants that as she walked down Brickett Bottom, which place she described clearly, she passed a red-brick house at the bend of the road and that a kind-faced old lady had asked her to step in for a while. She did not go in, not because she had any suspicions of there being anything uncanny, but simply because she feared to be late for tea.

'I do not think she ever visited the Bottom again and she had no other similar experience, so far as I am aware.

'Two or three years later, shortly after my father's death, a travelling tinker with his wife and daughter camped for the night at the foot of the Bottom. The girl strolled away up the glen to gather blackberries and was never seen or heard of again. She was searched for in vain – of course, one does not know the truth – and she may have run away voluntarily from her parents, although there was no known cause for her doing so.

'That,' concluded Mr Roberts, 'is all I can tell you of either facts or rumours; all that I can now do is to pray for you and for her.'

W. F. HARVEY

August Heat

Penistone Road, Clapham
20th August 190—

I have had what I believe to be the most remarkable
day in my life, and while the events are still fresh in
my mind, I wish to put them down on paper as clearly
as possible.

Let me say at the outset that my name is James
Clarence Withencroft.

I am forty years old, in perfect health, never having
known a day's illness.

By profession I am an artist, not a very successful
one, but I earn enough money by my black-and-white
work to satisfy my necessary wants.

My only near relative, a sister, died five years ago,
so that I am independent.

I breakfasted this morning at nine, and after
glancing through the morning paper I lighted my pipe
and proceeded to let my mind wander in the hope
that I might chance upon some subject for my pencil.

The room, though door and windows were open,
was oppressively hot, and I had just made up my
mind that the coolest and most comfortable place in
the neighbourhood would be the deep end of the
public swimming-bath, when the idea came.

I began to draw. So intent was I on my work that I
left my lunch untouched, only stopping work when
the clock of St Jude's struck four.

The final result, for a hurried sketch, was, I felt sure, the best thing I had done.

It showed a criminal in the dock immediately after the judge had pronounced sentence. The man was fat – enormously fat. The flesh hung in rolls about his chin; it creased his huge, stumpy neck. He was clean-shaven (perhaps I should say a few days before he must have been clean shaven) and almost bald. He stood in the dock, his short, clumsy fingers clasping the rail, looking straight in front of him. The feeling that his expression conveyed was not so much one of horror as of utter, absolute collapse.

There seemed nothing in the man strong enough to sustain that mountain of flesh.

I rolled up the sketch, and without quite knowing why, placed it in my pocket. Then with the rare sense of happiness which the knowledge of a good thing well done gives, I left the house.

I believe that I set out with the idea of calling upon Trenton, for I remember walking along Lytton Street and turning to the right along Gilchrist Road at the bottom of the hill where the men were at work on the new tram lines.

From there onwards I have only the vaguest recollection of where I went. The one thing of which I was fully conscious was the awful heat, that came up from the dusty asphalt pavement as an almost palpable wave. I longed for the thunder promised by the great banks of copper-coloured cloud that hung low over the western sky.

I must have walked five or six miles, when a small boy roused me from my reverie by asking the time.

It was twenty minutes to seven.

When he left me I began to take stock of my

bearings. I found myself standing before a gate that led into a yard bordered by a strip of thirsty earth, where there were flowers, purple stock and scarlet geranium. Above the entrance was a board with the inscription:

CHAS. ATKINSON
MONUMENTAL MASON
WORKER IN ENGLISH AND ITALIAN MARBLES

From the yard itself came a cheery whistle, the noise of hammer blows, and the cold sound of steel meeting stone.

A sudden impulse made me enter.

A man was sitting with his back towards me, busy at work on a slab of curiously veined marble. He turned round as he heard my steps and I stopped short.

It was the man I had been drawing, whose portrait lay in my pocket.

He sat there, huge and elephantine, the sweat pouring from his scalp, which he wiped with a red silk handkerchief. But though the face was the same, the expression was absolutely different.

He greeted me smiling, as if we were old friends, and shook my hand.

I apologised for my intrusion.

'Everything is hot and glary outside,' I said. 'This seems an oasis in the wilderness.'

'I don't know about the oasis,' he replied, 'but it certainly is hot, as hot as hell. Take a seat, sir!'

He pointed to the end of the gravestone on which he was at work, and I sat down.

'That's a beautiful piece of stone you've got hold of,' I said.

He shook his head. 'In a way it is,' he answered; 'the surface here is as fine as anything you could wish, but there's a big flaw at the back, though I don't expect you'd ever notice it. I could never make a really good job of a bit of marble like that. It would be all right in a summer like this; it wouldn't mind the blasted heat. But wait till the winter comes. There's nothing quite like frost to find out the weak points in stone.'

'Then what's it for?' I asked.

The man burst out laughing.

'You'd hardly believe me if I was to tell you it's for an exhibition, but it's the truth. Artists have exhibitions: so do grocers and butchers; we have them too. All the latest little things in headstones, you know.'

He went on to talk of marbles, which sort best withstood wind and rain, and which were easiest to work; then of his garden and a new sort of carnation he had bought. At the end of every other minute he would drop his tools, wipe his shining head, and curse the heat.

I said little, for I felt uneasy. There was something unnatural, uncanny, in meeting this man.

I tried at first to persuade myself that I had seen him before, that his face, unknown to me, had found a place in some out-of-the-way corner of my memory, but I knew that I was practising little more than a plausible piece of self-deception.

Mr Atkinson finished his work, spat on the ground, and got up with a sigh of relief.

'There! what do you think of that?' he said, with an air of evident pride.

The inscription which I read for the first time was this:

𝔖𝔞𝔠𝔯𝔢𝔡 𝔱𝔬 𝔱𝔥𝔢 𝔐𝔢𝔪𝔬𝔯𝔶 𝔬𝔣

JAMES CLARENCE WITHENCROFT

BORN JAN. 18TH, 1860
HE PASSED AWAY VERY SUDDENLY
ON AUGUST 20TH, 190—
'In the midst of life we are in death'

For some time I sat in silence. Then a cold shudder ran down my spine. I asked him where he had seen the name.

'Oh, I didn't see it anywhere,' replied Mr Atkinson. 'I wanted some name, and I put down the first that came into my head. Why do you want to know?'

'It's a strange coincidence, but it happens to be mine.'

He gave a long, low whistle.

'And the dates?'

'I can only answer for one of them, and that's correct.'

'It's a rum go!' he said.

But he knew less than I did. I told him of my morning's work. I took the sketch from my pocket and showed it to him. As he looked, the expression of his face altered until it became more and more like that of the man I had drawn.

'And it was only the day before yesterday,' he said, 'that I told Maria there were no such things as ghosts!'

Neither of us had seen a ghost, but I knew what he meant.

'You probably heard my name,' I said.

'And you must have seen me somewhere and have forgotten it! Were you at Clacton-on-Sea last July?'

I had never been to Clacton in my life. We were silent for some time. We were both looking at the same thing, the two dates on the gravestone, and one was right.

'Come inside and have some supper,' said Mr Atkinson.

His wife is a cheerful little woman, with the flaky red cheeks of the country-bred. Her husband introduced me as a friend of his who was an artist. The result was unfortunate, for after the sardines and watercress had been removed, she brought out a Doré Bible, and I had to sit and express my admiration for nearly half an hour.

I went outside, and found Atkinson sitting on the gravestone smoking.

We resumed the conversation at the point we had left off.

'You must excuse my asking,' I said, 'but do you know of anything you've done for which you could be put on trial?'

He shook his head.

'I'm not a bankrupt, the business is prosperous enough. Three years ago I gave turkeys to some of the guardians at Christmas, but that's all I can think of. And they were small ones, too,' he added as an afterthought.

He got up, fetched a can from the porch, and began to water the flowers. 'Twice a day regular in the hot weather,' he said, 'and then the heat sometimes gets the better of the delicate ones. And ferns, good Lord! they could never stand it. Where do you live?'

I told him my address. It would take an hour's quick walk to get back home.

'It's like this,' he said. 'We'll look at the matter

straight. If you go back home tonight, you take your chance of accidents. A cart may run over you, and there's always banana skins and orange peel, to say nothing of falling ladders.'

He spoke of the improbable with an intense seriousness that would have been laughable six hours before. But I did not laugh.

'The best thing we can do,' he continued, 'is for you to stay here till twelve o'clock. We'll go upstairs and smoke; it may be cooler inside.'

To my surprise I agreed.

We are sitting now in a long, low room beneath the eaves. Atkinson has sent his wife to bed. He himself is busy sharpening some tools at a little oilstone, smoking one of my cigars the while.

The air seems charged with thunder. I am writing this at a shaky table before the open window. The leg is cracked, and Atkinson, who seems a handy man with his tools, is going to mend it as soon as he has finished putting an edge on his chisel.

It is after eleven now. I shall be gone in less than an hour.

But the heat is stifling.

It is enough to send a man mad.

E. G. SWAIN

Bone to His Bone

William Whitehead, Fellow of Emmanuel College, in the University of Cambridge, became Vicar of Stoneground in the year 1731. The annals of his incumbency were doubtless short and simple: they have not survived. In his day were no newspapers to collect gossip, no parish magazines to record the simple events of parochial life. One event, however, of greater moment then than now, is recorded in two places. Vicar Whitehead failed in health after twenty-three years of work, and journeyed to Bath in what his monument calls 'the vain hope of being restored'. The duration of his visit is unknown; it is reasonable to suppose that he made his journey in the summer, it is certain that by the month of November his physician told him to lay aside all hope of recovery.

Then it was that the thoughts of the patient turned to the comfortable straggling vicarage he had left at Stoneground, in which he had hoped to end his days. He prayed that his successor might be as happy there as he had been himself. Setting his affairs in order, as became one who had but a short time to live, he executed a will, bequeathing to the vicars of Stoneground, for ever, the close of ground he had recently purchased because it lay next to the vicarage garden. And by a codicil, he added to the bequest his library of books. Within a few days, William Whitehead was gathered to his fathers.

A mural tablet in the north aisle of the church

records, in Latin, his services and his bequests, his two marriages, and his fruitless journey to Bath. The house he loved, but never again saw, was taken down forty years later, and rebuilt by vicar James Devie. The garden, with vicar Whitehead's 'close of ground' and other adjacent lands, was opened out and planted, somewhat before 1850, by vicar Robert Towerson. The aspect of everything has changed. But in a convenient chamber on the first floor of the present vicarage the library of vicar Whitehead stands very much as he used it and loved it, and as he bequeathed it to his successors 'for ever'.

The books there are arranged as he arranged and ticketed them. Little slips of paper, sometimes bearing interesting fragments of writing, still mark his places. His marginal comments still give life to pages from which all other interest has faded, and he would have but a dull imagination who could sit in the chamber amidst these books without ever being carried back 180 years into the past, to the time when the newest of them left the printer's hands.

Of those into whose possession the books have come, some have doubtless loved them more, and some less; some, perhaps, have left them severely alone. But neither those who loved them, nor those who loved them not, have lost them, and they passed, some century and a half after William Whitehead's death, into the hands of Mr Batchel, who loved them as a father loves his children. He lived alone, and had few domestic cares to distract his mind. He was able, therefore, to enjoy to the full what vicar Whitehead had enjoyed so long before him. During many a long summer evening would he sit poring over long-forgotten books; and since the chamber, otherwise called the library, faced the south, he could also spend sunny winter mornings there without discomfort. Writing at a small table, or reading as he stood at a tall desk, he would browse among the books like an ox in a pleasant pasture.

There were other times also, at which Mr Batchel would use the books. Not being a sound sleeper (for book-loving men seldom are), he elected to use as a bedroom one of the two chambers which opened at either side into the library. The arrangement enabled him to beguile many a sleepless hour among the books, and in view of these nocturnal visits he kept a candle standing in a sconce above the desk, and matches always ready to his hand.

There was one disadvantage in this close proximity of his bed to the library. Owing, apparently, to some defect in the fittings of the room, which, having no mechanical tastes, Mr Batchel had never investigated, there could be heard, in the stillness of the night, exactly such sounds as might arise from a person moving about among the books. Visitors using the other adjacent room would often remark at breakfast, that they had heard their host in the library at one or two o'clock in the morning, when, in fact, he had not left his bed. Invariably Mr Batchel allowed them to suppose that he had been where they thought him. He disliked idle controversy, and was unwilling to afford an opening for supernatural talk. Knowing well enough the sounds by which his guests had been deceived, he wanted no other explanation of them than his own, though it was of too vague a character to count as an explanation. He conjectured that the window-sashes, or the doors, or 'something', were defective, and was too phlegmatic and too unpractical to make any investigation. The matter gave him no concern.

Persons whose sleep is uncertain are apt to have their worst nights when they would like their best. The consciousness of a special need for rest seems to bring enough mental disturbance to forbid it. So on Christmas Eve, in the year 1907, Mr Batchel, who would have liked to sleep well, in view of the labours of Christmas Day, lay hopelessly wide awake. He exhausted all the known devices for courting sleep, and, at the end, found himself wider awake than ever. A brilliant moon shone into his room, for he hated window-blinds. There was a light wind blowing, and the sounds in the library were more than usually suggestive of a person moving about. He almost determined to have the sashes 'seen to', although he could seldom be induced to have anything 'seen to'. He disliked changes, even for the better, and would submit to great inconvenience rather than have things altered with which he had become familiar.

As he revolved these matters in his mind, he heard the clocks strike the hour of midnight, and having now lost all hope of falling asleep, he rose from his bed, got into a large dressing gown which hung in readiness for such occasions, and passed into the library, with the intention of reading himself sleepy, if he could.

The moon, by this time, had passed out of the south, and the library seemed all the darker by contrast with the moonlit chamber he had left. He could see nothing but two blue-grey rectangles formed by the windows against the sky, the furniture of the room being altogether invisible. Groping along to where the table stood, Mr Batchel felt over its surface for the matches which usually lay there; he found, however, that the table was cleared of everything. He raised his right hand, therefore, in order to feel his way to a shelf where the matches were sometimes mislaid, and at that moment, whilst his hand was in mid-air, the matchbox was gently put into it!

Such an incident could hardly fail to disturb even a phlegmatic person, and Mr Batchel cried, 'Who's this?' somewhat nervously. There was no answer. He struck a match, looked hastily round the room, and found it empty, as usual. There was everything, that is to say, that he was accustomed to see, but no other person than himself.

It is not quite accurate, however, to say that everything was in its usual state. Upon the tall desk lay a quarto volume that he had certainly not placed there. It was his quite invariable practice to replace his books upon the shelves after using them, and what we may call his library habits were precise and methodical. A book out of place like this, was not only an offence against good order, but a sign that his privacy had been intruded upon. With some surprise, therefore, he lit the candle standing ready in the sconce, and proceeded to examine the book, not sorry, in the disturbed condition in which he was, to have an occupation found for him.

The book proved to be one with which he was unfamiliar, and this made it certain that some other hand than his had removed it from its place. Its title was *The Compleat Gard'ner* of M. de la Quintinye made English by John Evelyn Esquire. It was not a work in which Mr Batchel felt any great interest. It consisted of diverse reflections on various parts of husbandry, doubtless entertaining enough, but too deliberate and discursive for practical purposes. He had certainly never used the book, and growing restless now in mind, said to himself that some boy having the freedom of the house, had taken it down from its place in the hope of finding pictures.

But even whilst he made this explanation he felt its weakness. To begin with, the desk was too high for a boy. The improbability that any boy would place a book there was equalled by the improbability that he would leave it there. To discover its uninviting character would be the work only of a moment, and no boy would have brought it so far from its shelf.

Mr Batchel had, however, come to read, and habit was too strong with him to be wholly set aside. Leaving *The Compleat Gard'ner* on the desk, he turned round to the shelves to find some more congenial reading.

Hardly had he done this when he was startled by a sharp rap upon the desk behind him, followed by a rustling of paper. He turned quickly about and saw the quarto lying open. In obedience to the instinct of the moment, he at once sought a natural cause for what he saw. Only a wind, and that of the strongest, could have opened the book, and laid back its heavy cover; and though he accepted, for a brief moment, that explanation, he was too candid to retain it longer. The wind out of doors was very light. The window sash was closed and latched, and, to decide the matter finally, the book had its back, and not its edges, turned towards the only quarter from which a wind could strike.

Mr Batchel approached the desk again and stood over the book. With increasing perturbation of mind (for he still thought of the matchbox) he looked upon the open page. Without much reason beyond that he felt constrained to do something, he read the words of the half completed sentence at the turn of the page: 'at dead of night he left the house and passed into the solitude of the garden'.

But he read no more, nor did he give himself the trouble of discovering whose midnight wandering was being described, although the habit was singularly like one of his own. He was in no condition for reading, and turning his back upon the volume he slowly paced the length of the chamber, 'wondering at that which had come to pass'.

He reached the opposite end of the chamber and was in the act of turning, when again he heard the rustling of paper, and by the time he had faced round, saw the leaves of the book again turning over. In a moment the volume lay at rest, open in another place, and there was no further movement as he approached it. To make sure that he had not been deceived, he read again the words as they entered the page. The author was following a not uncommon practice of the time, and throwing common speech into forms suggested by Holy Writ: 'So dig,' it said, 'that ye may obtain.'

This passage, which to Mr Batchel seemed reprehensible in its levity, excited at once his interest and his disapproval. He was prepared to read more, but this time was not allowed. Before his eye could pass beyond the passage already cited, the leaves of the book slowly turned again, and presented but a termination of five words and a colophon.

The words were, 'to the North, an Ilex'. These three passages, in which he saw no meaning and no connection, began to entangle themselves together in Mr Batchel's mind. He found himself repeating them in different orders, now beginning with one, and now with another. Any further attempt at reading he felt to be impossible, and he was in no mind for any more experiences of the unaccountable. Sleep was, of course, further from him than ever, if that were conceivable. What he did, therefore, was to blow out the candle, to return to his moonlit bedroom, and put on more clothing, and then to pass downstairs with the object of going out of doors.

It was not unusual with Mr Batchel to walk about his garden at night-time. This form of exercise had often, after a wakeful hour, sent him back to his bed refreshed and ready for sleep. The convenient access to the garden at such times lay through his study, whose French windows opened on to a short flight of steps, and upon these he now paused for a moment to admire the snow-like appearance of the lawns, bathed as they were in the moonlight. As he paused, he heard the city clocks strike the half-hour after midnight, and he could not forbear repeating aloud: 'At dead of night he left the house, and passed into the solitude of the garden.'

It was solitary enough. At intervals the screech of an owl, and now and then the noise of a train, seemed to emphasise the solitude by drawing attention to it and then leaving it in possession of the night. Mr Batchel found himself wondering and conjecturing what Vicar Whitehead, who had acquired the close of land to secure quiet and privacy for a garden, would have thought of the railways to the west and north. He turned his face northwards, whence a whistle had just sounded, and saw a tree beautifully outlined against the sky. His breath caught at the sight. Not because the tree was unfamiliar. Mr Batchel knew all his trees. But what he had seen was 'to the North, an Ilex'.

Mr Batchel knew not what to make of it all. He had walked into the garden hundreds of times and as often seen the Ilex, but the words out of *The Compleat Gard'ner* seemed to be pursuing him in a way that made him almost afraid. His temperament, however, as has been said already, was phlegmatic. It was commonly said, and Mr Batchel approved the verdict, whilst he condemned its inexactness, that 'his nerves were made of fiddle-string', so he braced himself afresh and set upon his walk round the silent garden, which he was accustomed to begin in a northerly direction, and was now too proud to change. He usually passed the Ilex at the beginning of his perambulation, and so would pass it now.

He did not pass it. A small discovery, as he reached it, annoyed and disturbed him. His gardener, as careful and punctilious as himself, never failed to house all his tools at the end of a day's work. Yet there, under the Ilex, standing upright in moonlight brilliant enough to cast a shadow of it, was a spade.

Mr Batchel's second thought was one of relief. After his extraordinary experiences in the library (he hardly knew now whether they had been real or not) something quite commonplace would act sedatively, and he determined to carry the spade to the tool-house.

The soil was quite dry, and the surface even a little frozen, so Mr Batchel left the path, walked up to the spade, and would have drawn it towards him. But it was as if he had made the attempt upon the trunk of the Ilex itself. The spade would not be moved. Then, first with one hand, and then with both, he tried to raise it, and still it stood firm. Mr Batchel, of course, attributed this to the frost, slight as it was. Wondering at the spade's being there, and annoyed at its being frozen, he was about to leave it and continue his walk, when the remaining words of *The Compleat Gard'ner* seemed rather to utter themselves, than to await his will: 'So dig, that ye may obtain.'

Mr Batchel's power of independent action now deserted him. He took the spade, which no longer resisted, and began to dig. 'Five spadefuls and no more,' he said aloud. 'This is all foolishness.'

Four spadefuls of earth he then raised and spread out before him in the moonlight. There was nothing unusual to be seen. Nor did Mr Batchel decide what he would look for, whether coins, jewels, documents in canisters, or weapons. In point of fact, he dug against what he deemed his better judgement, and expected nothing. He spread before him the fifth and last spadeful of earth, not quite without result, but with no result that was at all sensational. The earth contained a bone. Mr Batchel's knowledge of anatomy was sufficient to show him that it was a human bone. He identified it, even by moonlight, as the radius, a bone of the forearm, as he removed the earth from it, with his thumb.

Such a discovery might be thought worthy of more than the very ordinary interest Mr Batchel showed. As a matter of fact, the presence of a human bone was easily to be accounted for. Recent excavations within the church had caused the up turning of numberless bones, which had been collected and reverently buried. But an earth-stained bone is also easily overlooked, and this radius had obviously found its way into the garden with some of the earth brought out of the church.

Mr Batchel was glad, rather than regretful at this termination to his adventure. He was once more provided with something to do. The re-interment of such bones as this had been his constant care, and he decided at once to restore the bone to consecrated earth. The time seemed opportune. The eyes of the curious were closed in sleep, he himself was still alert and wakeful. The spade remained by his side and the bone in his hand. So he betook himself, there and then, to the churchyard. By the still generous light of the moon, he found a place where the earth yielded to his spade, and within a few minutes the bone was laid decently to earth, some eighteen inches deep.

The city clocks struck one as he finished. The whole world seemed asleep, and Mr Batchel slowly returned to the garden with his spade. As he hung it in its accustomed place he felt stealing over him the welcome desire to sleep. He walked quietly on to the house and ascended to his room. It was now dark: the moon had passed on and left the room in shadow. He lit a candle, and before undressing passed into the library. He had an irresistible curiosity to see the passages in John Evelyn's book which had so strangely adapted themselves to the events of the past hour.

In the library a last surprise awaited him. The desk upon which the book had lain was empty. *The Compleat Gard'ner* stood in its place on the shelf. And then Mr Batchel knew that he had handled a bone of William Whitehead, and that in response to his own entreaty.

MARY E. BRADDON

The Cold Embrace

He was an artist – such things as happened to him happen sometimes to artists.

He was a German – such things as happened to him happen sometimes to Germans.

He was young, handsome, studious, enthusiastic, metaphysical, reckless, unbelieving, heartless.

And being young, handsome and eloquent, he was beloved.

He was an orphan, under the guardianship of his dead father's brother, his uncle Wilhelm, in whose house he had been brought up from a little child; and she who loved him was his cousin – his cousin Gertrude, whom he swore he loved in return.

Did he love her? Yes, when he first swore it. It soon wore out, this passionate love; how threadbare and wretched a sentiment it became at last in the selfish heart of the student! But in its golden dawn, when he was only nineteen, and had just returned from his apprenticeship to a great painter at Antwerp, and they wandered together in the most romantic outskirts of the city at rosy sunset, by holy moonlight, or bright and joyous morning, how beautiful a dream!

They keep it a secret from Wilhelm, as he has the father's ambition of a wealthy suitor for his only child – a cold and dreary vision beside the lover's dream.

So they are betrothed; and standing side by side when the dying sun and the pale rising moon divide the heavens, he puts the betrothal ring upon her finger, the white and taper finger whose slender shape he knows so well. This ring is a peculiar one, a massive golden serpent, its tail in its mouth, the symbol of eternity; it had been his mother's, and he would know it among a thousand. If he were to become blind tomorrow, he could select it from among a thousand by the touch alone.

He places it on her finger, and they swear to be true to each other for ever and ever – through trouble and danger – sorrow and change – in wealth or poverty. Her father must needs be won to consent to their union by and by, for they were now betrothed, and death alone could part them.

But the young student, the scoffer at revelation, yet the enthusiastic adorer of the mystical, asks: 'Can death part us? I would return to you from the grave, Gertrude. My soul would come back to be near my love. And you – you, if you died before me – the cold earth would not hold you from me; if you loved me, you would return, and again these fair arms would be clasped round my neck as they are now.'

But she told him, with a holier light in her deep-blue eyes than had ever shone in his – she told him that the dead who die at peace with God are happy in heaven, and cannot return to the troubled earth; and that it is only the suicide – the lost wretch on whom sorrowful angels shut the door of Paradise – whose unholy spirit haunts the footsteps of the living.

The first year of their betrothal is passed, and she is alone, for he has gone to Italy, on a commission for some rich man, to copy Raphaels, Titians, Guidos, in a gallery at Florence. He has gone to win fame, perhaps; but it is not the less bitter – he is gone!

Of course her father misses his young nephew, who has been as a son to him; and he thinks his daughter's sadness no more than a cousin should feel for a cousin's absence.

In the meantime, the weeks and months pass. The lover writes – often at first, then seldom – at last, not at all.

How many excuses she invents for him! How many times she goes to the distant little post-office, to which he is to address his letters! How many times she hopes, only to be disappointed! How many times she despairs, only to hope again!

But real despair comes at last, and will not be put off any more. The rich suitor appears on the scene, and her father is determined. She is to marry at once. The wedding-day is fixed – the fifteenth of June.

The date seems burnt into her brain.

The date, written in fire, dances for ever before her eyes.

The date, shrieked by the Furies, sounds continually in her ears.

But there is time yet – it is the middle of May – there is time for a letter to reach him at Florence; there is time for him to come to Brunswick, to take her away and marry her, in spite of her father – in spite of the whole world.

But the days and the weeks fly by, and he does not write – he does not come. This is indeed despair which usurps her heart, and will not be put away.

It is the fourteenth of June. For the last time she goes to the little post-office; for the last time she asks the old question, and they give her for the last time the dreary answer, 'No; no letter.'

For the last time – for tomorrow is the day appointed for her bridal. Her father will hear no entreaties; her rich suitor will not listen to her prayers. They will not be put off a day – an hour; tonight alone is hers – this night, which she may employ as she will.

She takes another path than that which leads home; she hurries through some by-streets of the city, out on to a lonely bridge, where he and she had stood so often in the sunset, watching the rose-coloured light glow, fade and die upon the river.

He returns from Florence. He had received her letter. That letter, blotted with tears, entreating, despairing – he had received it, but he loved her no longer. A young Florentine, who has sat to him for a model, had bewitched his fancy – that fancy which with him stood in place of a heart – and Gertrude had been half-forgotten. If she had a rich suitor, good; let her marry him; better for her, better far for himself. He had no wish to fetter himself with a wife. Had he not his art always? – his eternal bride, his unchanging mistress.

Thus he thought it wiser to delay his journey to Brunswick, so that he should arrive when the wedding was over – arrive in time to salute the bride.

And the vows – the mystical fancies – the belief in his return, even after death, to the embrace of his beloved? Oh, gone out of his life; melted away for ever, those foolish dreams of his boyhood.

So on the fifteenth of June he enters Brunswick, by that very bridge on which she stood, the stars looking down on her, the night before. He strolls across the bridge and down by the water's edge, a great rough dog at his heels, and the smoke from his short meerschaum-pipe curling in blue wreaths fantastically in the pure morning air. He has his sketchbook under his arm, and attracted now and then by some object that catches his artist's eye, stops to draw: a few weeds and pebbles on the river's brink – a crag on the opposite shore – a group of pollard willows in the distance. When he has done, he admires his drawing, shuts his sketchbook, empties the ashes from his pipe, refills from his tobacco-pouch, sings the refrain of a gay drinking-song, calls to his dog, smokes again, and walks on. Suddenly he opens his sketchbook again; this time that which attracts him is a group of figures: but what is it?

It is not a funeral, for there are no mourners.

It is not a funeral, but a corpse lying on a rude bier, covered with an old sail, carried between two bearers.

It is not a funeral, for the bearers are fishermen – fishermen in their everyday garb.

About a hundred yards from him they rest their burden on a bank – one stands at the head of the bier, the other throws himself down at the foot of it.

And thus they form the perfect group; he walks back two or three paces, selects his point of sight, and begins to sketch a hurried outline. He has finished it before they move; he hears their voices, though he cannot hear their words, and wonders what they can be talking of. Presently he walks on and joins them.

'You have a corpse there, my friends?' he says.

'Yes; a corpse washed ashore an hour ago.'

'Drowned?'

'Yes, drowned. A young girl, very handsome.'

'Suicides are always handsome,' says the painter;

and then he stands for a little while idly smoking and meditating, looking at the sharp outline of the corpse and the stiff folds of the rough canvas covering.

Life is such a golden holiday for him – young, ambitious, clever – that it seems as though sorrow and death could have no part in his destiny.

At last he says that, as this poor suicide is so handsome, he should like to make a sketch of her.

He gives the fishermen some money, and they offer to remove the sailcloth that covers her features.

No; he will do it himself. He lifts the rough, coarse, wet canvas from her face. What face?

The face that shone on the dreams of his foolish boyhood; the face which once was the light of his uncle's home. His cousin Gertrude – his betrothed!

He sees, as in one glance, while he draws one breath, the rigid features – the marble arms – the hands crossed on the cold bosom; and, on the third finger of the left hand, the ring which had been his mother's – the golden serpent; the ring which, if he were to become blind, he could select from a thousand others by the touch alone.

But he is a genius and a metaphysician – grief, true grief, is not for such as he. His first thought is flight – flight anywhere out of that accursed city – anywhere far from the brink of that hideous river – anywhere away from remorse – anywhere to forget.

He is miles on the road that leads away from Brunswick before he knows that he has walked a step.

It is only when his dog lies down panting at his feet that he feels how exhausted he is himself, and sits down upon a bank to rest. How the landscape spins round and round before his dazzled eyes, while his morning's sketch of the two fishermen and the canvas-covered bier glares redly at him out of the twilight!

At last, after sitting a long time by the roadside, idly playing with his dog, idly smoking, idly lounging, looking as any idle, light-hearted travelling student might look, yet all the while acting over that morning's scene in his burning brain a hundred times a minute; at last he grows a little more composed, and tries presently to think of himself as he is, apart from his cousin's suicide. Apart from that, he was no worse off than he was yesterday. His genius was not gone; the money he had earned at Florence still lined his pocketbook; he was his own master, free to go whither he would.

And while he sits on the roadside, trying to separate himself from the scene of that morning – trying to put away the image of the corpse covered with the damp canvas sail – trying to think of what he should do next, where he should go, to be farthest away from Brunswick and remorse, the old diligence comes rumbling and jingling along. He remembers it; it goes from Brunswick to Aix-la-Chapelle.

He whistles to the dog, shouts to the postillion to stop, and springs into the *coupé*.

During the whole evening, through the long night, though he does not once close his eyes, he never speaks a word; but when morning dawns, and the other passengers awake and begin to talk to each other, he joins in the conversation. He tells them that he is an artist, that he is going to Cologne and to Antwerp to copy Rubenses, and the great picture by Quentin Matsys, in the museum. He remembered afterwards that he talked and laughed boisterously, and that when he was talking and laughing loudest, a passenger, older and graver than the rest, opened the window near him, and told him to put his head out. He remembered the fresh air blowing in his face, the singing of the birds in his ears, and the flat fields and roadside reeling before his eyes. He remembered this, and then falling in a lifeless heap on the floor of the diligence.

It is a fever that keeps him for six long weeks on a bed at a hotel in Aix-la-Chapelle.

He gets well, and, accompanied by his dog, starts on foot for Cologne. By this time he is his former self once more. Again the blue smoke from his short meer-schaum curls upwards in the morning air – again he sings some old university drinking song – again stops here and there, meditating and sketching.

He is happy, and has forgotten his cousin – and so on to Cologne.

It is by the great cathedral he is standing, with his dog at his side. It is night, the bells have just chimed the hour, and the clocks are striking eleven; the moon-light shines full upon the magnificent pile, over which the artist's eye wanders, absorbed in the beauty of form.

He is not thinking of his drowned cousin, for he has forgotten her and is happy.

Suddenly someone, something from behind him, puts two cold arms round his neck, and clasps its hands on his breast.

And yet there is no one behind him, for on the flags bathed in the broad moonlight there are only two shadows, his own and his dog's. He turns quickly round – there is no one – nothing to be seen in the broad square but himself and his dog; and though he feels, he cannot see the cold arms clasped round his neck.

It is not ghostly, this embrace, for it is palpable to the touch – it cannot be real, for it is invisible.

He tries to throw off the cold caress. He clasps the hands in his own to tear them asunder, and to cast them off his neck. He can feel the long delicate fingers cold and wet beneath his touch, and on the third finger of the left hand he can feel the ring which was his mother's – the golden serpent – the ring which he has always said he would know among a thousand by the touch alone. He knows it now!

His dead cousin's cold arms are round his neck – his dead cousin's wet hands are clasped upon his breast. He asks himself if he is mad. 'Up, Leo!' he shouts. 'Up, up, boy!' and the Newfoundland leaps to his shoulders – the dog's paws are on the dead hands, and the animal utters a terrific howl, and springs away from his master.

The student stands in the moonlight, the dead arms around his neck, and the dog at a little distance moaning piteously.

Presently a watchman, alarmed by the howling of the dog, comes into the square to see what is wrong.

In a breath the cold arms are gone.

He takes the watchman home to the hotel with him and gives him money; in his gratitude he could have given the man half his little fortune.

Will it ever come to him again, this embrace of the dead?

He tries never to be alone; he makes a hundred acquaintances, and shares the chamber of another student. He starts up if he is left by himself in the public room of the inn where he is staying, and runs into the street. People notice his strange actions, and begin to think that he is mad.

But, in spite of all, he is alone once more; for one night the public room being empty for a moment, when on some idle pretence he strolls into the street, the street is empty too, and for the second time he feels the cold arms round his neck, and for the second time, when he calls his dog, the animal shrinks away from him with a piteous howl.

After this he leaves Cologne, still travelling on foot – of necessity now, for his money is getting low. He joins travelling hawkers, he walks side by side with labourers, he talks to every foot-passenger he falls in with, and tries from morning till night to get company on the road.

At night he sleeps by the fire in the kitchen of the inn at which he stops; but do what he will, he is often alone, and it is now a common thing for him to feel the cold arms around his neck.

Many months have passed since his cousin's death – autumn, winter, early spring. His money is nearly gone, his health is utterly broken, he is the shadow of his former self, and he is getting near to Paris. He will reach that city at the time of the Carnival. To this he looks forward. In Paris, in Carnival time, he need never, surely, be alone, never feel that deadly caress; he may even recover his lost gaiety, his lost health, once more resume his profession, once more earn fame and money by his art.

How hard he tries to get over the distance that divides him from Paris, while day by day he grows weaker, and his step slower and more heavy!

But there is an end at last; the long dreary roads are passed. This is Paris, which he enters for the first time –

Paris, of which he has dreamed so much – Paris, whose million voices are to exorcise his phantom.

To him tonight Paris seems one vast chaos of lights, music, and confusion – lights which dance before his eyes and will not be still – music that rings in his ears and deafens him – confusion which makes his head whirl round and round.

But, in spite of all, he finds the opera-house, where there is a masked ball. He has enough money left to buy a ticket of admission, and to hire a domino to throw over his shabby dress. It seems only a moment after his entering the gates of Paris that he is in the very midst of all the wild gaiety of the opera-house ball.

No more darkness, no more loneliness, but a mad crowd, shouting and dancing, and a lovely Débardeuse hanging on his arm.

The boisterous gaiety he feels surely is his old light-heartedness come back. He hears the people round him talking of the outrageous conduct of some drunken student, and it is to him they point when they say this – to him, who has not moistened his lips since yesterday at noon, for even now he will not drink; though his lips are parched, and his throat burning, he cannot drink. His voice is thick and hoarse, and his utterance indistinct; but still this must be his old light-heartedness come back that makes him so wildly gay.

The little Débardeuse is wearied out – her arm rests on his shoulder heavier than lead – the other dancers one by one drop off.

The lights in the chandeliers one by one die out.

The decorations look pale and shadowy in that dim light which is neither night nor day.

A faint glimmer from the dying lamps, a pale streak

of cold grey light from the new-born day, creeping in through half-opened shutters.

And by this light the bright-eyed Débardeuse fades sadly. He looks her in the face. How the brightness of her eyes dies out! Again he looks her in the face. How white that face has grown! Again – and now it is the shadow of a face alone that looks in his.

Again – and they are gone – the bright eyes, the face, the shadow of the face. He is alone; alone in that vast saloon. Alone, and, in the terrible silence, he hears the echoes of his own footsteps in that dismal dance which has no music.

No music but the beating of his breast. The cold arms are round his neck – they whirl him round, they will not be flung off, or cast away; he can no more escape from their icy grasp than he can escape from death. He looks behind him – there is nothing but himself in the great empty *salle*; but he can feel – cold, deathlike, but Oh, how palpable! – the long slender fingers, and the ring which was his mother's.

He tries to shout, but he has no power in his burning throat. The silence of the place is only broken by the echoes of his own footsteps in the dance from which he cannot extricate himself. Who says he has no partner? The cold hands are clasped on his breast, and now he does not shun their caress. No! One more polka, if he drops down dead.

The lights are all out, and, half an hour after, the *gendarmes* come in with a lantern to see that the house is empty; they are followed by a great dog that they have found seated howling on the steps of the theatre. Near the principal entrance they stumble over the body of a student, who has died from want of food, exhaustion and the breaking of a blood-vessel.

R. H. BENSON

The Traveller

I am amazed, not that the Traveller returns from that Bourne, but that he returns so seldom.

The Pilgrim's Way

On one of these evenings as we sat together after dinner in front of the wide open fireplace in the central room of the house, we began to talk on that old subject – the relation of Science to Faith.

'It is no wonder,' said the priest, 'if their conclusions appear to differ, to shallow minds who think that the last words are being said on both sides, because their standpoints are so different. The scientific view is that you are not justified in committing yourself one inch ahead of your intellectual evidence: the religious view is that in order to find out anything worth knowing your faith must always be a little in advance of your evidence; you must advance *en échelon*. There is the principle of our Lord's promises. "Act as if it were true, and light will be given." The scientist on the other hand says, "Do not presume to commit yourself until light is given." The difference between the methods lies, of course, in the fact that Religion admits the heart and the whole man to the witness-box, while Science only admits the head – scarcely even the senses. Yet surely the evidence of experience is on the side of Religion. Every really great achievement is inspired by motives of the heart, and not of the head; by feeling and passion, not by a calculation of probabilities. And so are the mysteries of God

308

unveiled by those who carry them first by assault; "The Kingdom of Heaven suffereth violence; and the violent take it by force."

'For example,' he continued after a moment, 'the scientific view of haunted houses is that there is no evidence for them beyond that which may be accounted for by telepathy, a kind of thought-reading. Yet if you can penetrate that veneer of scientific thought that is so common now, you find that by far the larger part of mankind still believes in them. Practically not one of us really accepts the scientific view as an adequate one.'

'Have you ever had an experience of that kind yourself?' I asked.

'Well,' said the priest, smiling, 'you are sure you will not laugh at it? There is nothing commoner than to think such things a subject for humour; and that I cannot bear. Each such story is sacred to one person at the very least, and therefore should be to all reverent people.'

I assured him that I would not treat his story with disrespect.

'Well,' he answered, 'I do not think you will, and I will tell you. It only happened a very few years ago. This was how it began.

'A friend of mine was, and is still, in charge of a church in Kent, which I will not name; but it is within twenty miles of Canterbury. The district fell into Catholic hands a good many years ago. I received a telegram, in this house, a day or two before Christmas, from my friend, saying that he had been suddenly seized with a very bad attack of influenza, which was devastating Kent at that time; and asking me to come down, if possible at once, and take his place over Christmas. I had only lately given up active work owing to growing infirmity, but it was impossible to resist this appeal; so Parker packed my things and we went together by the next train.

'I found my friend really ill, and quite incapable of doing anything; so I assured him that I could manage perfectly, and that he need not be anxious.

'On the next day, a Wednesday and Christmas Eve, I went down to the little church to hear confessions. It was a beautiful old church, though tiny, and full of interesting things: the old altar had been set up again; there was a rood-loft with a staircase leading on to it; and an awmbry on the north of the sanctuary had been fitted up as a receptacle for the Most Holy Sacrament, instead of the old hanging pyx. One of the most interesting discoveries made in the church was that of the old confessional. In the lower half of the rood-screen, on the south side, a square hole had been found, filled up with an insertion of oak; but an antiquarian of the Alcuin Club, whom my friend had asked to examine the church, declared that this without doubt was the place where in the pre-Reformation times confessions were heard. So it had been restored, and put to its ancient use; and now on this Christmas Eve I sat within the chancel in the dim fragrant light, while penitents came and knelt outside the screen on the single step, and made their confessions through the old opening.

'I know this is a great platitude, but I never can look at a piece of old furniture without a curious thrill at a thing that has been so much saturated with human emotion; but, above all that I have ever seen, I think that this old confessional moved me. Through that little opening had come so many thousands of sins, great and little, weighted with sorrow; and back again, in Divine exchange for those burdens, had returned the balm of the Saviour's blood. "Behold! a door opened in heaven", through which that strange commerce of sin and grace may be carried on – grace pressed down and running over, given into the bosom in exchange for sin. O, *bonum commercium*!'

The priest was silent for a moment, his eyes glowing. Then he went on.

'Well, Christmas Day and the three following festivals passed away very happily. On the Sunday night after service, as I came out of the vestry, I saw a child waiting. She told me, when I asked her if she wanted me, that her father and others of her family wished to make their confessions on the following evening about six o'clock. They had had influenza in the house, and had not been able to come out before; but the father was going to work next day, as he was so much better, and would come, if it pleased me, and some of his children to make their confessions in the evening and their communions the following morning.

'Monday dawned, and I offered the Holy Sacrifice as usual, and spent the morning chiefly with my friend, who was now able to sit up and talk a good deal, though he was not yet allowed to leave his bed.

'In the afternoon I went for a walk.

'All the morning there had rested a depression on my soul such as I have not often felt; it was of a peculiar quality. Every soul that tries, however poorly, to serve God, knows by experience those heavinesses by which our Lord tests and confirms His own; but it was not like that. An element of terror mingled with it, as of impending evil.

'As I started for my walk along the high road this depression deepened. There seemed no physical reason for it that I could perceive. I was well myself, and the weather was fair; yet air and exercise did not affect it. I turned at last, about half-past three o'clock, at a milestone that marked sixteen miles to Canterbury.

'I rested there for a moment, looking to the south-east, and saw that far on the horizon heavy clouds were gathering; and then I started homewards. As I went I heard a faraway boom, as of distant guns, and I thought at first that there was some sea-fort to the south where artillery practice was being held; but presently I noticed that it was too irregular and prolonged for the report of a gun; and then it was with a sense of relief that I came to the conclusion it was a faraway thunderstorm, for I felt that the state of the atmosphere might explain away this depression that so troubled me. The thunder seemed to come nearer, pealed more loudly three or four times, and ceased.

'But I felt no relief. When I reached home a little after four Parker brought me in some tea, and I fell asleep afterwards in a chair before the fire. I was wakened after a troubled and unhappy dream by Parker bringing in my coat and telling me it was time to keep my appointment at the church. I could not remember what my dream was, but it was sinister and suggestive of evil, and, with the shreds of it still clinging to me, I looked at Parker with something of fear as he stood silently by my chair holding the coat.

'The church stood only a few steps away, for the garden and churchyard adjoined one another. As I went down carrying the lantern that Parker had lighted for me, I remember hearing far away to the south, beyond the village, the beat of a horse's hoofs. The horse seemed to be in a gallop, but presently the noise died away behind a ridge.

'When I entered the church I found that the sacristan had lighted a candle or two as I had asked him, and I could just make out the kneeling figures of three or four people in the north aisle.

'When I was ready I took my seat in the chair set beyond the screen, at the place I have described; and then, one by one, the labourer and his children came up and made their confessions. I remember feeling again, as on Christmas Eve, the strange charm of this old place of penitence, so redolent of God and man, each in his tenderest character of Saviour and penitent; with the red light burning like a luminous flower in the dark before me, to remind me of how God was indeed tabernacling with men, and was their God.

'Now I do not know how long I had been there, when again I heard the beat of a horse's hoofs, but this time in the village just below the churchyard; then again there fell a sudden silence. Then presently a gust of wind flung the door wide, and the candles began to gutter and flare in the draught. One of the girls went and closed the door.

'Presently the boy who was kneeling by me at that time finished his confession, received absolution and went down the church, and I waited for the next, not knowing how many there were.

'After waiting a minute or two I turned in my seat, and was about to get up, thinking there was no one else, when a voice whispered sharply through the hole a single sentence. I could not catch the words, but I supposed they were the usual formula for asking a blessing, so I gave the blessing and waited, a little astonished at not having heard the penitent come up.

'Then the voice began again.'

The priest stopped a moment and looked round, and I could see that he was trembling a little.

'Would you rather not go on?' I said. 'I think it disturbs you to tell me.'

'No, no,' he said; 'it is all right, but it was very dreadful – very dreadful.

'Well, the voice began again in a loud quick whisper, but the odd thing was that I could hardly understand a word; there were just phrases here and there, like the name of God and of our Lady, that I could catch. Then there were a few old French words that I knew; "*le roy*" came over and over again. Just at first I thought it must be some extreme form of dialect unknown to me; then I thought it must be a very old man who was deaf, because when I tried, after a few sentences, to explain that I could not understand, the penitent paid no attention, but whispered on quickly without a pause. Presently I could perceive that he was in a terrible state of mind; the voice broke and sobbed, and then almost cried out, but still in this loud whisper; then on the other side of the screen I could hear fingers working and moving uneasily, as if entreating admittance at some barred door. Then at last there was silence for a moment, and then plainly some closing formula was repeated, which gradually grew lower and ceased. Then, as I rose, meaning to come round and explain that I had not been able to hear, a loud moan or two came from the penitent. I stood up quickly and looked through the upper part of the screen, and there was no one there.

'I can give you no idea of what a shock that was to me. I stood there glaring, I suppose, through the screen down at the empty step for a moment or two, and perhaps I said something aloud, for I heard a voice from the end of the church.

' "Did you call, sir?" And there stood the sacristan, with his keys and lantern, ready to lock up.

'I still stood without answering for a moment, and then I spoke; my voice sounded oddly in my ears. "Is there anyone else, Williams? Are they all gone?" or something like that.

'Williams lifted his lantern and looked round the dusky church. "No, sir; there is no one."

'I crossed the chancel to go to the vestry, but as I was halfway, suddenly again in the quiet village there broke out the desperate gallop of a horse.

' "There! There!" I cried. "Do you hear that?"

'Williams came up the church towards me. "Are you ill, sir?" he said. "Shall I fetch your servant?"

'I made an effort and told him it was nothing; but he insisted on seeing me home: I did not like to ask him whether he had heard the gallop of the horse; for, after all, I thought, perhaps there was no connection between that and the voice that whispered.

'I felt very much shaken and disturbed; and after dinner, which I took alone of course, I thought I would go to bed very soon. On my way up, however, I looked into my friend's room for a few minutes. He seemed very bright and eager to talk, and I stayed very much longer than I had intended. I said nothing of what had happened in the church, but listened to him while he talked about the village and the neighbourhood. Finally, as I was on the point of bidding him good-night, he said something like this:

"Well, I mustn't keep you, but I've been thinking while you've been in church of an old story that is told by antiquarians about this place. They say that one of St Thomas à Becket's murderers came here on the very evening of the murder. It is his day today, you know, and that is what put me in mind of it, I suppose."

'While my friend said this, my old heart began to beat furiously; but, with a strong effort of self-control, I told him I should like to hear the story.

' "Oh! there's nothing much to tell," said my friend; "and they don't know who it's supposed to have been; but it is said to have been either one of the four knights, or one of the men-at-arms."

' "But how did he come here?" I asked, "and what for?"

' "Oh! he's supposed to have been in terror for his soul, and that he rushed here to get absolution, which, of course, was impossible."

' "But tell me," I said. "Did he come here alone, or how?"

' "Well, you know, after the murder they ransacked the Archbishop's house and stables; and it is said that this man got one of the fastest horses and rode like a madman, not knowing where he was going; and that he dashed into the village, and into the church where the priest was: and then afterwards, mounted again and rode off. The priest, too, is buried in the chancel somewhere, I believe. You see it's a very vague and improbable story. At the Gatehouse at Malling, too, you know, they say that one of the knights slept there the night after the murder."

'I said nothing more; but I suppose I looked strange, because my friend began to look at me with some anxiety, and then ordered me off to bed: so I took my candle and went.

'Now,' said the priest, turning to me, 'that is the story. I need not say that I have thought about it a great deal ever since: and there are only two theories which appear to me credible, and two others, which would no doubt be suggested, which appear to me incredible.

'First, you may say that I was obviously unwell: my previous depression and dreaming showed that, and therefore that I dreamt the whole thing. If you wish to think that – well, you must think it.

'Secondly, you may say, with the Psychical Research Society, that the whole thing was transmitted from my friend's brain to mine; that his was in an energetic, and mine in a passive state, or something of the kind.

'These two theories would be called "scientific", which term means that they are not a hair's-breadth in advance of the facts with which the intellect, a poor instrument at the best, is capable of dealing. And these two "scientific" theories create in their own turn a new brood of insoluble difficulties.

'Or you may take your stand upon the spiritual world, and use the faculties which God has given you for dealing with it, and then you will no longer be helplessly puzzled, and your intellect will no longer over-strain itself at a task for which it was never made. And you may say, I think, that you prefer one of two theories.

'First, that human emotion has a power of influencing or saturating inanimate nature. Of course this is only the old familiar sacramental principle of all creation. The expressions of your face, for instance, caused by the shifting of the chemical particles of which it is composed, vary with your varying emotions. Thus we might say that the violent passions of hatred, anger, terror, remorse, of this poor murderer, seven hundred years ago, combined to make a potent spiritual fluid that bit so deep into the very place where it was all poured out, that under certain circumstances it is reproduced. A phonograph, for example, is a very coarse parallel, in which the vibrations of sound translate themselves first into terms of wax, and then re-emerge again as vibrations when certain conditions are fulfilled.

'Or, secondly, you may be old-fashioned and simple, and say that by some law, vast and inexorable, beyond our perception, the personal spirit of the very man is chained to the place, and forced to expiate his sin again and again, year by year, by attempting to express his grief and to seek forgiveness, without the possibility of receiving it. Of course we do not know who he was; whether one of the knights who afterwards did receive absolution, which possibly was not ratified by God; or one of the men-at-arms who assisted, and who, as an anonymous chronicle says, "*sine confessione et viatico subito rapti sunt*".

'There is nothing materialistic, I think, in believing that spiritual beings may be bound to express themselves within limits of time and space; and that inanimate nature, as well as animate, may be the vehicles of the unseen. Arguments against such possibilities have surely, once for all, been silenced, for Christians at any rate, by the Incarnation and the Sacramental system, of which the whole principle is that the Infinite and Eternal did once, and does still, express itself under forms of inanimate nature, in terms of time and space.

'With regard to another point, perhaps I need not remind you that a thunderstorm broke over Canterbury on the day and hour of the actual murder of the Archbishop.'

A. V. Laider

I unpacked my things and went down to await luncheon. It was good to be here again in this little old sleepy hostel by the sea. Hostel I say, though it spelt itself without an 's' and even placed a circumflex above the 'o'. It made no other pretensions. It was very cosy indeed.

I had been here just a year before, in mid-February, after an attack of influenza. And now I had returned, after an attack of influenza. Nothing was changed. It had been raining when I left, and the waiter – there was but a single, very old waiter – had told me it was only a shower. That waiter was still here, not a day older. And the shower had not ceased.

Steadfastly it fell on to the sands, steadfastly into the iron-grey sea. I stood looking out at it from the windows of the hall, admiring it very much. There seemed to be little else to do. What little there was I did. I mastered the contents of a blue handbill which, pinned to the wall just beneath the framed engraving of Queen Victoria's Coronation, gave token of a concert that was to be held – or, rather, was to have been held some weeks ago – in the Town Hall for the benefit of the Life-Boat Fund. I looked at the barometer, tapped it, was not the wiser. I glanced at a pamphlet about our dying industries (a theme on which Mr Joseph Chamberlain was at that time trying to alarm us). I wandered to the letter-board.

These letter-boards always fascinate me. Usually

some two or three of the envelopes stuck into the cross-garterings have a certain newness and freshness. They seem sure they will yet be claimed. Why not? Why *shouldn't* John Doe, Esq., or Mrs Richard Roe turn up at any moment? I do not know. I can only say that nothing in the world seems to me more unlikely. Thus it is that these young bright envelopes touch my heart even more than do their dusty and sallowed seniors. Sour resignation is less touching than impatience for what will not be, than the eagerness that has to wane and wither. Soured beyond measure these old envelopes are. They are not nearly so nice as they should be to the young ones. They lose no chance of sneering and discouraging. Such dialogues as this are only too frequent:

A VERY YOUNG ENVELOPE: Something in me whispers that he will come today!

A VERY OLD ENVELOPE: He? Well, that's good! Ha, ha, ha! Why didn't he come last week, when *you* came? What reason have you for supposing he'll ever come *now*? It isn't as if he were a frequenter of the place. He's never been here. His name is utterly unknown here. You don't suppose he's coming on the chance of finding *you*?

A VERY YOUNG ENVELOPE: It may seem silly, but – something in me whispers –

A VERY OLD ENVELOPE: Something in *you*? One has only to look at you to see there's nothing in you but a note scribbled to him by a cousin. Look at *me*! There are three sheets, closely written, in *me*. The lady to whom I am addressed –

A VERY YOUNG ENVELOPE: Yes, sir, yes; you told me all about her yesterday.

A VERY OLD ENVELOPE: And I shall do so today and tomorrow and every day and all day long. That young lady was a widow. She stayed here many times. She was delicate, and the air suited her. She was poor, and the tariff was just within her means. She was lonely, and had need of love. I have in me for her a passionate avowal and strictly honourable proposal, written to her, after many rough copies, by a gentleman who had made her acquaintance under this very roof. He was rich, he was charming, he was in the prime of life. He had asked if he might write to her. She had flutteringly granted his request. He posted me to her the day after his return to London. I looked forward to being torn open by her. I was very sure she would wear me and my contents next to her bosom. She was gone. She had left no address. She never returned. This I tell you, and shall continue to tell you, not because I want any of your callow sympathy – no, *thank* you! – but that you may judge how much less than slight are the probabilities that you yourself –

But my reader has overheard these dialogues as often as I. He wants to know what was odd about this particular letter-board before which I was standing. At first glance I saw nothing odd about it. But presently I distinguished a handwriting that was vaguely familiar. It was mine. I stared, I wondered. There is always a slight shock in seeing an envelope of one's own after it has gone through the post. It looks as if it had gone through so much. But this was the first time I had ever seen an envelope of mine eating its heart out in bondage on a letter-board. This was outrageous. This was hardly to be believed. Sheer kindness had impelled me to write to 'A. V. Laider, Esq.', and this was the result! I hadn't minded receiving no answer. Only now, indeed, did I remember that I hadn't received one. In multitudinous London the memory of A. V. Laider and his trouble had soon passed from my mind. But – well, what a lesson not to go out of one's way to write to casual acquaintances!

My envelope seemed not to recognise me as its writer. Its gaze was the more piteous for being blank. Even so had I once been gazed at by a dog that I had lost and, after many days, found in the Battersea Home. 'I don't know who you are, but, whoever you are, claim me, take me out of this!' That was my dog's appeal. This was the appeal of my envelope.

I raised my hand to the letter-board, meaning to effect a swift and lawless rescue, but paused at sound of a footstep behind me. The old waiter had come to tell me that my luncheon was ready. I followed him out of the hall, not, however, without a bright glance across my shoulder to reassure the little captive that I should come back.

I had the sharp appetite of the convalescent, and this the sea air had whetted already to a finer edge. In touch with a dozen oysters, and with stout, I soon shed away the unreasoning anger I had felt against A. V. Laider. I became merely sorry for him that he had not received a letter which might perhaps have comforted him. In touch with cutlets, I felt how sorely he had needed comfort. And anon, by the big bright fireside of that small dark smoking-room where, a year ago, on the last evening of my stay here, he and I had at length spoken to each other, I reviewed in detail the tragic experience he had told me; and I fairly revelled in reminiscent sympathy with him.

A. V. Laider – I had looked him up in the visitors' book on the night of his arrival. I myself had arrived the day before, and had been rather sorry there was no one else staying here. A convalescent by the sea likes to have someone to observe, to wonder about, at meal-time. I was glad when, on my second evening, I found seated at the table opposite to mine another guest. I was the gladder because he was just the right kind of guest. He was enigmatic. By this I mean that he did not look soldierly or financial or artistic or anything definite at all. He offered a clean slate for speculation. And, thank heaven! he evidently wasn't going to spoil the fun by engaging me in conversation later on. A decently unsociable man, anxious to be left alone.

The heartiness of his appetite, in contrast with his extreme fragility of aspect and limpness of demeanour, assured me that he, too, had just had influenza. I liked him for that. Now and again our eyes met and were instantly parted. We managed, as a rule, to observe each other indirectly. I was sure it was not merely because he had been ill that he looked interesting. Nor did it seem to me that a spiritual melancholy, though I imagined him sad at the best of times, was his sole asset. I conjectured that he was clever. I thought he might also be imaginative. At first glance I had mistrusted him. A shock of white hair, combined with a young face and dark eyebrows, does somehow make a man look like a charlatan. But it is foolish to be guided by an accident of colour. I had soon rejected my first impression of my fellow-diner. I found him very sympathetic.

Anywhere but in England it would be impossible for two solitary men, howsoever much reduced by influenza, to spend five or six days in the same hostel and not exchange a single word. That is one of the charms of England. Had Laider and I been born and bred in any other land we should have become acquainted before the end of our first evening in the small smoking-room, and have found ourselves irrevocably committed to go on talking to each other throughout the rest of our visit. We might, it is true, have happened to like each other more than anyone we had ever met. This off-chance may have occurred to us both. But it counted for nothing against the certain surrender of quietude and liberty. We slightly bowed to each other as we entered or left the dining-room or smoking-room, and as we met on the wide-spread sands or in the shop that had a small and faded circulating library. That was all. Our mutual aloofness was a positive bond between us.

Had he been much older than I, the responsibility for our silence would of course have been his alone. But he was not, I judged, more than five or six years ahead of me, and thus I might without impropriety have taken it on myself to perform that hard and perilous feat which English people call, with a shiver, 'breaking the ice'. He had reason, therefore, to be as grateful to me as I to him. Each of us, not the less frankly because silently, recognised his obligation to the other. And when, on the last evening of my stay, the ice actually was broken there was no ill-will between us: neither of us was to blame.

It was a Sunday evening. I had been out for a long last walk and had come in very late to dinner. Laider had left his table almost directly after I sat down to mine. When I entered the smoking-room I found him reading a weekly review which I had bought the day before. It was a crisis. He could not silently offer nor could I have silently accepted, sixpence. It was a crisis. We faced it like men. He made, by word of mouth, a graceful apology. Verbally, not by signs, I besought him to go on reading. But this, of course, was a vain counsel of perfection. The social code forced us to talk now. We obeyed it like men. To reassure him that our position was not so desperate as it might seem, I took the earliest opportunity to mention that I was going away early next morning. In the tone of his 'Oh, are you?' he tried bravely to imply that he was sorry, even now, to hear that. In a way, perhaps, he really was sorry. We had got on so well together, he and I. Nothing could efface the memory of that. Nay, we seemed to be hitting it off even now. Influenza was not our sole theme. We passed from that to the afore-said weekly review, and to a correspondence that was raging therein on faith and reason.

This correspondence had now reached its fourth and penultimate stage – its Australian stage. It is hard to see why these correspondences spring up; one only knows that they do spring up, suddenly, like street crowds. There comes, it would seem, a moment when the whole English-speaking race is unconsciously bursting to have its say about some one thing – the split infinitive, or the habits of migratory birds, or faith and reason, or what-not. Whatever weekly review happens at such a moment to contain a reference, however remote, to the theme in question reaps the storm. Gusts of letters come in from all corners of the British Isles. These are presently reinforced by Canada in full blast. A few weeks later the Anglo-Indians weigh in. In due course we have the help of our Australian cousins. By that time, however, we of the mother country have got our second wind, and so determined are we to make the most of it that at last even the editor suddenly loses patience and says, 'This correspondence must now cease. – Ed.' and wonders why on earth he ever allowed anything so tedious and idiotic to begin.

I pointed out to Laider one of the Australian letters that had especially pleased me in the current issue. It was from 'A Melbourne Man', and was of the abrupt kind which declares that 'all your correspondents have been groping in the dark' and then settles the whole matter in one short sharp flash. The flash in this instance was 'Reason is faith, faith reason – that is all we know on earth and all we need to know.' The writer then enclosed his card and was, etc., 'A Melbourne Man'. I said to Laider how very restful it was, after influenza, to read anything that meant nothing whatsoever. Laider was inclined to take the letter more seriously than I, and to be mildly metaphysical. I said that for me faith and reason were two separate things, and as I am no good at metaphysics, however mild, I offered a definite example, to coax the talk on to ground where I should be safer.

'Palmistry, for example,' I said. 'Deep down in my heart I believe in palmistry.'

Laider turned in his chair. 'You believe in palmistry?'

I hesitated. 'Yes, somehow I do. Why? I haven't the slightest notion. I can give myself all sorts of reasons for laughing it to scorn. My common sense utterly rejects it. Of course the shape of the hand means something, is more or less an index of character. But the idea that my past and future are neatly mapped out on my palms – ' I shrugged my shoulders.

'You don't like that idea?' asked Laider in his gentle, rather academic voice.

'I only say it's a grotesque idea.'

'Yet you do believe in it?'

'I've a grotesque belief in it, yes.'

'Are you sure your reason for calling this idea "grotesque" isn't merely that you dislike it?'

'Well,' I said, with the thrilling hope that he was a companion in absurdity, 'doesn't it seem grotesque to *you*?'

'It seems strange.'

'You believe in it?'

'Oh, absolutely.'

'Hurrah!'

He smiled at my pleasure, and I, at the risk of re-entanglement in metaphysics, claimed him as standing shoulder to shoulder with me against 'A Melbourne Man'. This claim he gently disputed.

'You may think me very prosaic,' he said, 'but I can't believe without evidence.'

'Well, I'm equally prosaic and equally at a disadvantage: I can't take my own belief as evidence, and I've no other evidence to go on.'

He asked me if I had ever made a study of palmistry. I said I had read one of Desbarolles's books years ago, and one of Heron-Allen's. But, he asked, had I tried to test them by the lines on my own hands or on the hands of my friends? I confessed that my actual practice in palmistry had been of a merely passive kind – the prompt extension of my palm to anyone who would be so good as to 'read' it and truckle for a few minutes to my egoism. (I hoped Laider might do this.)

'Then I almost wonder,' he said, with his sad smile,

'that you haven't lost your belief, after all the nonsense you must have heard. There are so many young girls who go in for palmistry. I am sure all the five foolish virgins were "awfully keen on it" and used to say, "You can be led, but not driven," and, "You are likely to have a serious illness between the ages of forty and forty-five," and, "You are by nature rather lazy, but can be very energetic by fits and starts." And most of the professionals, I'm told, are as silly as the young girls.'

For the honour of the profession, I named three practitioners whom I had found really good at reading character. He asked whether any of them had been right about past events. I confessed that, as a matter of fact, all three of them had been right in the main. This seemed to amuse him. He asked whether any of them had predicted anything which had since come true. I confessed that all three had predicted that I should do several things which I had since done rather unexpectedly. He asked if I didn't accept this as, at any rate, a scrap of evidence. I said I could only regard it as a fluke – a rather remarkable fluke.

The superiority of his sad smile was beginning to get on my nerves. I wanted him to see that he was as absurd as I.

'Suppose,' I said – 'suppose, for the sake of argument, that you and I are nothing but helpless automata created to do just this and that, and to have just that and this done to us. Suppose, in fact, we *haven't* any free will whatsoever. Is it likely or conceivable that the Power which fashioned us would take the trouble to jot down in cipher on our hands just what was in store for us?'

Laider did not answer this question; he did but annoyingly ask me another.

'You believe in free will?'

'Yes, of course. I'll be hanged if I'm an automaton.'

'And you believe in free will just as in palmistry – without any reason?'

'Oh, no. Everything points to our having free will.'

'Everything? What, for instance?'

This rather cornered me. I dodged out, as lightly as I could, by saying: 'I suppose *you* would say it's written in my hand that I should be a believer in free will.'

'Ah, I've no doubt it is.'

I held out my palms. But, to my great disappointment, he looked quickly away from them. He had ceased to smile. There was agitation in his voice as he explained that he never looked at people's hands now. 'Never now – never again.' He shook his head as though to beat off some memory.

I was much embarrassed by my indiscretion. I hastened to tide over the awkward moment by saying that if *I* could read hands I wouldn't, for fear of the awful things I might see there.

'Awful things, yes,' he whispered, nodding at the fire.

'Not,' I said in self-defence, 'that there's anything very awful, so far as I know, to be read in *my* hands.'

He turned his gaze from the fire to me.

'You aren't a murderer, for example?'

'Oh, no,' I replied, with a nervous laugh.

'*I* am.'

This was more than awkward, it was a painful moment for me; and I am afraid I must have started or winced, for he instantly begged my pardon.

'I don't know,' he exclaimed, 'why I said it. I'm

usually a very reticent man. But sometimes – ' He pressed his brow. 'What you must think of me!'

I begged him to dismiss the matter from his mind.

'It's very good of you to say that; but – I've placed myself as well as you in a false position. I ask you to believe that I'm not the sort of man who is "wanted" or ever was "wanted" by the police. I should be bowed out of any police-station at which I gave myself up. I'm not a murderer in any bald sense of the word. No.'

My face must have perceptibly brightened, for, 'Ah,' he said, 'don't imagine I'm not a murderer at all. Morally, I am.' He looked at the clock. I pointed out that the night was young. He assured me that his story was not a long one. I assured him that I hoped it was. He said I was very kind. I denied this. He warned me that what he had to tell might rather tend to stiffen my unwilling faith in palmistry, and to shake my opposite and cherished faith in free will. I said, 'Never mind.' He stretched his hands pensively forward towards the fire. I settled myself back in my chair.

'My hands,' he said, staring at the backs of them, 'are the hands of a very weak man. I dare say you know enough of palmistry to see that for yourself. You notice the slightness of the thumbs and of the two "little" fingers. They are the hands of a weak and over-sensitive man – a man without confidence, a man who would certainly waver in an emergency. Rather Hamlet-ish hands,' he mused. 'And I'm like Hamlet in other respects, too: I'm no fool, and I've rather a noble disposition, and I'm unlucky. But Hamlet was luckier than I in one thing: he was a murderer by accident, whereas the murders that I committed one day fourteen years ago – for I must tell you it wasn't one murder, but many murders that

I committed – were all of them due to the wretched inherent weakness of my own wretched self.

'I was twenty-six – no, twenty-seven years old, and rather a nondescript person, as I am now. I was supposed to have been called to the Bar. In fact, I believe I *had* been called to the Bar. I hadn't listened to the call. I never intended to practise, and I never did practise. I only wanted an excuse in the eyes of the world for existing. I suppose the nearest I have ever come to practising is now at this moment: I am defending a murderer. My father had left me well enough provided with money. I was able to go my own desultory way, riding my hobbies where I would. I had a good stableful of hobbies. Palmistry was one of them. I was rather ashamed of this one. It seemed to me absurd, as it seems to you. Like you, though, I believed in it. Unlike you, I had done more than merely read a book about it. I had read innumerable books about it. I had taken casts of all my friends' hands. I had tested and tested again the points at which Desbarolles dissented from the gypsies, and – well, enough that I had gone into it all rather thoroughly, and was as sound a palmist as a man may be without giving his whole life to palmistry.

'One of the first things I had seen in my own hand, as soon as I had learned to read it, was that at about the age of twenty-six I should have a narrow escape from death – from a violent death. There was a clean break in the life-line, and a square joining it – the protective square, you know. The markings were precisely the same in both hands. It was to be the narrowest escape possible. And I wasn't going to escape without injury, either. That is what bothered me. There was a faint line connecting the break in the life-line with a star on the line of health. Against that star was another square. I was to recover from the injury, whatever it might be. Still, I didn't exactly look forward to it. Soon after I had reached the age of twenty-five, I began to feel uncomfortable. The thing might be going to happen at any moment. In palmistry, you know, it is impossible to pin an event down hard and fast to one year. This particular event was to be when I was about twenty-six; it mightn't be till I was twenty-seven; it might be while I was only twenty-five.

'And I used to tell myself it mightn't be at all. My reason rebelled against the whole notion of palmistry, just as yours does. I despised my faith in the thing, just as you despise yours. I used to try not to be so ridiculously careful as I was whenever I crossed a street. I lived in London at that time. Motor cars had not yet come in, but – what hours, all told, I must have spent standing on kerbs, very circumspect, very lamentable! It was a pity, I suppose, that I had no definite occupation – something to take me out of myself. I was one of the victims of private means. There came a time when I drove in four-wheelers rather than in hansoms, and was doubtful of four-wheelers. Oh, I assure you, I was very lamentable indeed.

'If a railway journey could be avoided, I avoided it. My uncle had a place in Hampshire. I was very fond of him and of his wife. Theirs was the only house I ever went to stay in now. I was there for a week in November, not long after my twenty-seventh birthday. There were other people staying there, and at the end of the week we all travelled back to London together. There were six of us in the carriage: Colonel

Elbourn and his wife and their daughter, a girl of seventeen; and another married couple, the Bretts. I had been at Winchester with Brett, but had hardly seen him since that time. He was in the Indian Civil, and was home on leave. He was sailing for India next week. His wife was to remain in England for some months, and then join him out there. They had been married five years. She was now just twenty-four years old. He told me that this was her age. The Elbourns I had never met before. They were charming people. We had all been very happy together. The only trouble had been that on the last night, at dinner, my uncle asked me if I still went in for "the gypsy business", as he always called it; and of course the three ladies were immensely excited, and implored me to "do" their hands. I told them it was all nonsense, I said I had forgotten all I once knew, I made various excuses; and the matter dropped. It was quite true that I had given up reading hands. I avoided anything that might remind me of what was in my own hands. And so, next morning, it was a great bore to me when, soon after the train started, Mrs Elbourn said it would be "too cruel" of me if I refused to do their hands now. Her daughter and Mrs Brett also said it would be "brutal"; and they were all taking off their gloves, and – well, of course I had to give in.

'I went to work methodically on Mrs Elbourn's hands, in the usual way, you know, first sketching the character from the backs of them; and there was the usual hush, broken by the usual little noises – grunts of assent from the husband, cooings of recognition from the daughter. Presently I asked to see the palms, and from them I filled in the details of Mrs Elbourn's character before going on to the events in her life. But while I talked I was calculating how old Mrs Elbourn might be. In my first glance at her palms I had seen that she could not have been less than twenty-five when she married. The daughter was seventeen. Suppose the daughter had been born a year later – how old would the mother be? Forty-three, yes. Not less than that, poor woman!'

Laider looked at me.

'Why "poor woman!" you wonder? Well, in that first glance I had seen other things than her marriage-line. I had seen a very complete break in the lines of life and of fate. I had seen violent death there. At what age? Not later, not possibly *later*, than forty-three. While I talked to her about the things that had happened in her girlhood, the back of my brain was hard at work on those marks of catastrophe. I was horribly wondering that she was still alive. It was impossible that between her and that catastrophe there could be more than a few short months. And all the time I was talking; and I suppose I acquitted myself well, for I remember that when I ceased I had a sort of ovation from the Elbourns.

'It was a relief to turn to another pair of hands. Mrs Brett was an amusing young creature, and her hands were very characteristic, and prettily odd in form. I allowed myself to be rather whimsical about her nature, and having begun in that vein, I went on in it, somehow, even after she had turned her palms. In those palms were reduplicated the signs I had seen in Mrs Elbourn's. It was as though they had been copied neatly out. The only difference was in the placing of them; and it was this difference that was the most horrible point. The fatal age in Mrs Brett's hands was – not past, no, for here *she* was. But she might have died when she was twenty-one. Twenty-three seemed to be the utmost span. She was twenty-four, you know.

'I have said that I am a weak man. And you will have good proof of that directly. Yet I showed a certain amount of strength that day – yes, even on that day which has humiliated and saddened the rest of my life. Neither my face nor my voice betrayed me when in the palms of Dorothy Elbourn I was again confronted with those same signs. She was all for knowing the future, poor child! I believe I told her all manner of things that were to be. And she had no future – none, none in *this* world – except –

'And then, while I talked, there came to me suddenly a suspicion. I wondered it hadn't come before. You guess what it was? It made me feel very cold and strange. I went on talking. But, also, I went on – quite separately – thinking. The suspicion wasn't a certainty. This mother and daughter were always together. What was to befall the one might any-where – anywhere – befall the other. But a like fate, in an equally near future, was in store for that other lady. The coincidence was curious, very. Here we all were together – here, they and I – I who was narrowly to escape, so soon now, what they, so soon now, were to suffer. Oh, there was an inference to be drawn. Not a *sure* inference, I told myself. And always I was talking, talking, and the train was swinging and swaying noisily along – to what? It was a fast train. Our carriage was near the engine. I was talking loudly. Full well I had known what I should see in the colonel's hands. I told myself I had not known. I told myself that even now the thing I dreaded was not sure to be. Don't think I was dreading it for myself. I wasn't so "lamentable" as all that – now. It was only of them that I thought – only for them. I hurried over the colonel's character and career; I was perfunctory. It was Brett's hands that I wanted. *They* were the hands that mattered. If *they* had the marks – Remember, Brett was to start for India in the coming week, his wife was to remain in England. They would be apart. Therefore –

'And the marks were there. And I did nothing – nothing but hold forth on the subtleties of Brett's character. There was a thing for me to do. I wanted to do it. I wanted to spring to the window and pull the communication-cord. Quite a simple thing to do. Nothing easier than to stop a train. You just give a sharp pull, and the train slows down, comes to a standstill. And the guard appears at your window. You explain to the guard.

'Nothing easier than to tell him there is going to be a collision. Nothing easier than to insist that you and your friends and every other passenger in the train must get out at once . . . There *are* easier things than this? Things that need less courage than this? Some of *them* I could have done, I dare say. This thing I was going to do. Oh, I was determined that I would do it – directly.

'I had said all I had to say about Brett's hands. I had brought my entertainment to an end. I had been thanked and complimented all round. I was quite at liberty. I was going to do what I had to do. I was determined, yes.

'We were near the outskirts of London. The air was grey, thickening; and Dorothy Elbourn had said: "Oh, this horrible old London! I suppose there's the same old fog!" And presently I heard her father saying something about "prevention" and "a short act of Parliament" and "anthracite". And I sat and listened and agreed and – '

Laider closed his eyes. He passed his hand slowly through the air.

'I had a racking headache. And when I said so, I was told not to talk. I was in bed, and the nurses were always telling me not to talk. I was in a hospital. I knew that; but I didn't know why I was there. One day I thought I should like to know why, and so I asked. I was feeling much better now. They told me by degrees that I had had concussion of the brain. I had been brought there unconscious, and had remained unconscious for forty-eight hours. I had been in an accident – a railway accident. This seemed to me odd. I had arrived quite safely at my uncle's place, and I had no memory of any journey since that. In cases of concussion, you know, it's not uncommon for the patient to forget all that happened just before the accident; there may be a blank for several hours. So it was in my case. One day my uncle was allowed to come and see me. And somehow, suddenly, at sight of him, the blank was filled in. I remembered, in a flash, everything. I was quite calm, though. Or I made myself seem so, for I wanted to know how the collision had happened. My uncle told me that the engine-driver had failed to see a signal because of the fog, and our train had crashed into a goods-train.

'I didn't ask him about the people who were with me. You see, there was no need to ask.

'Very gently my uncle began to tell me, but – I had begun to talk strangely, I suppose. I remember the frightened look of my uncle's face, and the nurse scolding him in whispers.

'After that, all a blur. It seems that I became very ill indeed, wasn't expected to live.

'However, I live.'

There was a long silence. Laider did not look at me, nor I at him. The fire was burning low, and he watched it.

At length he spoke: 'You despise me. Naturally. I despise myself.'

'No, I don't despise you; but – '

'You blame me.' I did not meet his gaze. 'You blame me,' he repeated.

'Yes.'

'And there, if I may say so, you are a little unjust. It isn't my fault that I was born weak.'

'But a man may conquer weakness.'

'Yes, if he is endowed with the strength for that.'

His fatalism drew from me a gesture of disgust.

'Do you really mean,' I asked, 'that because you didn't pull that cord, you *couldn't* have pulled it?'

'Yes.'

'And it's written in your hands that you couldn't?'

He looked at the palms of his hands.

'They are the hands of a very weak man,' he said.

'A man so weak that he cannot believe in the possibility of free will for himself or for anyone?'

'They are the hands of an intelligent man, who can weigh evidence and see things as they are.'

'But answer me: was it foreordained that you should not pull that cord?'

'It was foreordained.'

'And was it actually marked in your hands that you were not going to pull it?'

'Ah, well, you see, it is rather the things one *is* going to do that are actually marked. The things one *isn't* going to do – the innumerable negative things – how could one expect *them* to be marked?'

'But the consequences of what one leaves undone may be positive?'

'Horribly positive. My hand is the hand of a man who has suffered a great deal in later life.'

'And was it the hand of a man *destined* to suffer?'

'Oh, yes. I thought I told you that.'

There was a pause.

'Well,' I said, with awkward sympathy, 'I suppose all hands are the hands of people destined to suffer.'

'Not of people destined to suffer so much as *I* have suffered – as I still suffer.'

The insistence of his self-pity chilled me, and I harked back to a question he had not straightly answered.

'Tell me: was it marked in your hands that you were not going to pull that cord?'

Again he looked at his hands, and then, having pressed them for a moment to his face, 'It was marked very clearly,' he answered, 'in *their* hands.'

Two or three days after this colloquy there had occurred to me in London an idea – an ingenious and comfortable doubt. How was Laider to be sure that his brain, recovering from concussion, had *remembered* what happened in the course of that railway journey? How was he to know that his brain hadn't simply, in its abeyance, *invented* all this for him? It might be that he had never seen those signs in those hands. Assuredly, here was a bright loophole. I had forthwith written to Laider, pointing it out.

This was the letter which now, at my second visit, I had found miserably pent on the letter-board. I remembered my promise to rescue it. I arose from the retaining fireside, stretched my arms, yawned, and went forth to fulfil my Christian purpose. There was no one in the hall. The 'shower' had at length ceased. The sun had positively come out, and the front door had been thrown open in its honour. Everything along the seafront was beautifully gleaming, drying, shimmering. But I was not to be diverted from my errand. I went to the letter-board. And – my letter was not there! Resourceful and plucky little thing – it had escaped! I did hope it would not be captured and brought back. Perhaps the alarm had already been raised by the tolling of that great bell which warns the inhabitants for miles around that a letter has broken loose from the letter-board. I had a vision of my envelope skimming wildly along the coastline, pursued by the old, but active, waiter and a breathless pack of local worthies. I saw it outdistancing them all, dodging past coastguards, doubling on its tracks, leaping breakwaters, unluckily injuring itself, losing speed, and at last, in a splendour of desperation, taking to the open sea. But suddenly I had another idea. Perhaps Laider had returned?

He had. I espied afar on the sands a form that was recognisably, by the listless droop of it, his. I was glad and sorry – rather glad, because he completed the scene of last year; and very sorry, because this time we should be at each other's mercy: no restful silence and liberty for either of us this time. Perhaps he had been told I was here, and had gone out to avoid me while he yet could. Oh weak, weak! Why palter? I put on my hat and coat, and marched out to meet him.

'Influenza, of course?' we asked simultaneously.

There is a limit to the time which one man may

spend in talking to another about his own influenza; and presently, as we paced the sands, I felt that Laider had passed this limit. I wondered that he didn't break off and thank me now for my letter. He must have read it. He ought to have thanked me for it at once. It was a very good letter, a remarkable letter. But surely he wasn't waiting to answer it by post? His silence about it gave me the absurd sense of having taken a liberty, confound him! He was evidently ill at ease while he talked. But it wasn't for me to help him out of his difficulty, whatever that might be. It was for him to remove the strain imposed on myself.

Abruptly, after a long pause, he did now manage to say: 'It was – very good of you to – to write me that letter.' He told me he had only just got it, and he drifted away into otiose explanations of this fact. I thought he might at least say it was a remarkable letter; and you can imagine my annoyance when he said, after another interval, 'I was very much touched indeed.' I had wished to be convincing, not touching. I can't bear to be called touching.

'Don't you,' I asked, 'think it *is* quite possible that your brain invented all those memories of what – what happened before that accident?'

He drew a sharp sigh.

'You make me feel very guilty.'

'That's exactly what I tried to make you *not* feel!'

'I know, yes. That's why I feel so guilty.'

We had paused in our walk. He stood nervously prodding the hard wet sand with his walking-stick.

'In a way,' he said, 'your theory was quite right. But – it didn't go far enough. It's not only possible, it's a fact, that I didn't see those signs in those hands. I never examined those hands. They weren't there. *I* wasn't there. I haven't an uncle in Hampshire, even. I never had.'

I, too, prodded the sand.

'Well,' I said at length, 'I do feel rather a fool.'

'I've no right even to beg your pardon, but – '

'Oh, I'm not vexed. Only – I rather wish you hadn't told me this.'

'I wish I hadn't had to. It was your kindness, you see, that forced me. By trying to take an imaginary load off my conscience, you laid a very real one on it.'

'I'm sorry. But you, of your own free will, you know, exposed your conscience to me last year. I don't yet quite understand why you did that.'

'No, of course not. I don't deserve that you should. But I think you will. May I explain? I'm afraid I've talked a great deal already about my influenza, and I shan't be able to keep it out of my explanation. Well, my weakest point – I told you this last year, but it happens to be perfectly true that my weakest point – is my will. Influenza, as you know, fastens unerringly on one's weakest point. It doesn't attempt to undermine my imagination. That would be a forlorn hope. I have, alas! a very strong imagination. At ordinary times my imagination allows itself to be governed by my will. My will keeps it in check by constant nagging. But when my will isn't strong enough even to nag, then my imagination stampedes. I become even as a little child. I tell myself the most preposterous fables, and – the trouble is – I can't help telling them to my friends. Until I've thoroughly shaken off influenza, I'm not fit company for anyone. I perfectly realise this, and I have the good sense to go right away till I'm quite well again. I come here usually. It seems absurd, but I must confess I was sorry last year when

343

we fell into conversation. I knew I should very soon be letting myself go, or, rather, very soon be swept away. Perhaps I ought to have warned you; but – I'm a rather shy man. And then you mentioned the subject of palmistry. You said you believed in it. I wondered at that. I had once read Desbarolles's book about it, but I am bound to say I thought the whole thing very great nonsense indeed.'

'Then,' I gasped, 'it isn't even true that you believe in palmistry?'

'Oh, no. But I wasn't able to tell you that. You had begun by saying that you believed in palmistry, and then you proceeded to scoff at it. While you scoffed I saw myself as a man with a terribly good reason for *not* scoffing; and in a flash I saw the terribly good reason; I had the whole story – at least I had the broad outlines of it – clear before me.'

'You hadn't ever thought of it before?' He shook his head. My eyes beamed. 'The whole thing was sheer improvisation?'

'Yes,' said Laider, humbly, 'I am as bad as all that. I don't say that all the details of the story I told you that evening were filled in at the very instant of its conception. I was filling them in while we talked about palmistry in general, and while I was waiting for the moment when the story would come in most effectively. And I've no doubt I added some extra touches in the course of the actual telling. Don't imagine that I took the slightest pleasure in deceiving you. It's only my will, not my conscience, that is weakened after influenza. I simply can't help telling what I've made up, and telling it to the best of my ability. But I'm thoroughly ashamed all the time.'

'Not of your ability, surely?'

'Yes, of that, too,' he said, with his sad smile. 'I always feel that I'm not doing justice to my idea.'

'You are too stern a critic, believe me.'

'It is very kind of you to say that. You are very kind altogether. Had I known that you were so essentially a man of the world, in the best sense of that term, I shouldn't have so much dreaded seeing you just now and having to confess to you. But I'm not going to take advantage of your urbanity and your easy-going ways. I hope that some day we may meet somewhere when I haven't had influenza and am a not wholly undesirable acquaintance. As it is, I refuse to let you associate with me. I am an older man than you, and so I may without impertinence warn you against having anything to do with me.'

I deprecated this advice, of course; but for a man of weakened will he showed great firmness.

'You,' he said, 'in your heart of hearts, don't want to have to walk and talk continually with a person who might at any moment try to bamboozle you with some ridiculous tale. And I, for my part, don't want to degrade myself by trying to bamboozle anyone, especially one whom I have taught to see through me. Let the two talks we have had be as though they had not been. Let us bow to each other, as last year, but let that be all. Let us follow in all things the precedent of last year.'

With a smile that was almost gay he turned on his heel, and moved away with a step that was almost brisk. I was a little disconcerted. But I was also more than a little glad. The restfulness of silence, the charm of liberty – these things were not, after all, forfeit. My heart thanked Laider for that; and throughout the week I loyally seconded him in the system he had laid down for us. All was as it had been last year. We did not smile to each other, we merely bowed, when we entered or left the dining-room or smoking-room, and when we met on the widespread sands or in that shop which had a small and faded but circulating library.

Once or twice in the course of the week it did occur to me that perhaps Laider had told the simple truth at our first interview and an ingenious lie at our second. I frowned at this possibility. The idea of anyone wishing to be quit of *me* was most distasteful. However, I was to find reassurance. On the last evening of my stay I suggested, in the small smoking-room, that he and I should, as sticklers for precedent, converse. We did so, very pleasantly. And after a while I happened to say that I had seen this afternoon a great number of sea-gulls flying close to the shore.

'Sea-gulls?' said Laider, turning in his chair.

'Yes. And I don't think I had ever realised how extraordinarily beautiful they are when their wings catch the light.'

'Beautiful?' Laider threw a quick glance at me and away from me. 'You think them beautiful?'

'Surely.'

'Well, perhaps they are, yes; I suppose they are. But – I don't like seeing them. They always remind me of something – rather an awful thing – that once happened to me . . . '

VERNON LEE

A Wicked Voice

THEY have been congratulating me again today upon being the only composer of our days – of these days of deafening orchestral effects and poetical quackery – who has despised the new-fangled nonsense of Wagner, and returned boldly to the traditions of Handel and Gluck and the divine Mozart, to the supremacy of melody and the respect of the human voice.

O cursed human voice, violin of flesh and blood, fashioned with the subtle tools, the cunning hands, of Satan! O execrable art of singing, have you not wrought mischief enough in the past, degrading so much noble genius, corrupting the purity of Mozart, reducing Handel to a writer of high-class singing-exercises, and defrauding the world of the only inspiration worthy of Sophocles and Euripides, the poetry of the great poet Gluck? Is it not enough to have dishonoured a whole century in idolatry of that wicked and contemptible wretch the singer, without persecuting an obscure young composer of our days, whose only wealth is his love of nobility in art, and perhaps some few grains of genius?

And then they compliment me upon the perfection with which I imitate the style of the great dead masters; or ask me very seriously whether, even if I could gain over the modern public to this bygone style of music, I could hope to find singers to perform it. Sometimes, when people talk as they have been talking today, and laugh when I declare myself a follower of Wagner, I burst into a paroxysm of unintelligible, childish rage, and exclaim: 'We shall see that some day!'

Yes; some day we shall see! For, after all, may I not recover from this strangest of maladies? It is still possible that the day may come when all these things shall seem but an incredible nightmare; the day when *Ogier the Dane* shall be completed, and men shall know whether I am a follower of the great master of the Future or the miserable singing-masters of the Past. I am but half-bewitched, since I am conscious of the spell that binds me. My old nurse, far off in Norway, used to tell me that werewolves are ordinary men and women half their days, and that if, during that period, they become aware of their horrid transformation they may find the means to forestall it. May this not be the case with me? My reason, after all, is free, although my artistic inspiration be enslaved; and I can despise and loathe the music I am forced to compose, and the execrable power that forces me.

Nay, is it not because I have studied with the doggedness of hatred this corrupt and corrupting music of the Past, seeking for every little peculiarity of style and every biographical trifle merely to display its vileness, is it not for this presumptuous courage that I have been overtaken by such mysterious, incredible vengeance?

And meanwhile, my only relief consists in going over and over again in my mind the tale of my miseries. This time I will write it, writing only to tear up, to throw the manuscript unread into the fire. And yet, who knows? As the last charred pages shall crackle and slowly sink into the red embers, perhaps the spell may be broken, and I may possess once more my long-lost liberty, my vanished genius.

It was a breathless evening under the full moon, that implacable full moon beneath which, even more than beneath the dreamy splendour of noontide, Venice seemed to swelter in the midst of the waters, exhaling, like some great lily, mysterious influences, which make the brain swim and the heart faint – a moral malaria, distilled, as I thought, from those languishing melodies, those cooing vocalisations which I had found in the musty music-books of a century ago. I see that moonlight evening as if it were present. I see my fellow-lodgers of that little artists' boarding-house. The table on which they lean after supper is strewn with bits of bread, with napkins rolled in tapestry rollers, spots of wine here and there, and at regular intervals chipped pepper-pots, stands of toothpicks, and heaps of those huge hard peaches which nature imitates from the marble-shops of Pisa. The whole *pension*-full is assembled, and examining stupidly the engraving which the American etcher has just brought for me, knowing me to be mad about eighteenth-century music and musicians, and having noticed, as he turned over the heaps of penny prints in the square of San Polo, that the portrait is that of a singer of those days.

Singer, thing of evil, stupid and wicked slave of the voice, of that instrument which was not invented by the human intellect, but begotten of the body, and which, instead of moving the soul, merely stirs up the dregs of our nature! For what is the voice but the Beast calling, awakening that other Beast sleeping in the depths of mankind, the Beast which all great art has ever sought to chain up, as the archangel chains

up, in old pictures, the demon with his woman's face?
How could the creature attached to this voice, its
owner and its victim, the singer, the great, the real
singer who once ruled over every heart, be otherwise
than wicked and contemptible? But let me try and get
on with my story.

I can see all my fellow-boarders, leaning on the
table, contemplating the print, this effeminate beau,
his hair curled into *ailes de pigeon,* his sword passed
through his embroidered pocket, seated under a
triumphal arch somewhere among the clouds,
surrounded by puffy Cupids and crowned with laurels
by a bouncing goddess of fame. I hear again all the
insipid exclamations, the insipid questions about this
singer: 'When did he live? Was he very famous? Are
you sure, Magnus, that this is really a portrait?' etc.
And I hear my own voice, as if in the far distance,
giving them all sorts of information, biographical and
critical, out of a battered little volume called *The
Theatre of Musical Glory; or, Opinions upon the most
Famous Chapel-masters and Virtuosi of this Century,* by
Father Prosdocimo Sabatelli, Barnalite, Professor of
Eloquence at the College of Modena, and Member
of the Arcadian Academy, under the pastoral name of
Evander Lilybaean, Venice, 1785, with the approb-
ation of the Superiors. I tell them all how this singer,
this Balthasar Cesari, was nicknamed Zaffirino
because of a sapphire engraved with cabalistic signs
presented to him one evening by a masked stranger,
in whom wise folk recognised that great cultivator of
the human voice, the devil; how much more wonderful had been this Zaffirino's vocal gifts than those of
any singer of ancient or modern times; how his brief
life had been but a series of triumphs, petted by the

greatest kings, sung by the most famous poets, and finally, adds Father Prosdocimo, 'courted (if the grave Muse of history may incline her ear to the gossip of gallantry) by the most charming nymphs, even of the very highest quality'.

My friends glance once more at the engraving; more insipid remarks are made; I am requested – especially by the American young ladies – to play or sing one of this Zaffirino's favourite songs – 'For of course you know them, dear Maestro Magnus, you who have such a passion for all old music. Do be good, and sit down to the piano.' I refuse, rudely enough, rolling the print in my fingers. How fearfully this cursed heat, these cursed moonlight nights, must have unstrung me! This Venice would certainly kill me in the long run! Why, the sight of this idiotic engraving, the mere name of that coxcomb of a singer, have made my heart beat and my limbs turn to water like a lovesick hobbledehoy.

After my gruff refusal, the company begins to disperse; they prepare to go out, some to have a row on the lagoon, others to saunter before the cafés at St Mark's; family discussions arise, gruntings of fathers, murmurs of mothers, peals of laughing from young girls and young men. And the moon, pouring in by the wide-open windows, turns this old palace ball-room, nowadays an inn dining-room, into a lagoon, scintillating, undulating like the other lagoon, the real one, which stretches out yonder furrowed by invisible gondolas betrayed by the red prow-lights. At last the whole lot of them are on the move. I shall be able to get some quiet in my room, and to work a little at my opera of *Ogier the Dane*. But no! Conversation revives, and, of all things, about that singer, that

Zaffirino, whose absurd portrait I am crunching in my fingers.

The principal speaker is Count Alvise, an old Venetian with dyed whiskers, a great check tie fastened with two pins and a chain; a threadbare patrician who is dying to secure for his lanky son that pretty American girl, whose mother is intoxicated by all his mooning anecdotes about the past glories of Venice in general, and of his illustrious family in particular. Why, in heaven's name, must he pitch upon Zaffirino for his mooning, this old duffer of a patrician?

'Zaffirino, – ah yes, to be sure! Balthasar Cesari, called Zaffirino,' snuffles the voice of Count Alvise, who always repeats the last word of every sentence at least three times. 'Yes, Zaffirino, to be sure! A famous singer of the days of my forefathers; yes, of my forefathers, dear lady!' Then a lot of rubbish about the former greatness of Venice, the glories of old music, the former conservatoires, all mixed up with anecdotes of Rossini and Donizetti, whom he pretends to have known intimately. Finally, a story of course containing plenty about his illustrious family: 'My great grand-aunt, the Procuratessa Vendramin, from whom we have inherited our estate of Mistrà, on the Brenta' – a hopelessly muddled story, apparently, full of digressions, but of which that singer Zaffirino is the hero. The narrative, little by little, becomes more intelligible, or perhaps it is I who am giving it more attention.

'It seems,' says the Count, 'that there was one of his songs in particular which was called the "Husbands' Air" – *L' Aria dei Mariti* – because they didn't enjoy it quite as much as their better-halves . . . My grand-aunt, Pisana Renier, married to the Procuratore Vendramin, was a patrician of the old school, of the style that was getting rare a hundred years ago. Her virtue and her pride rendered her unapproachable. Zaffirino, on his part, was in the habit of boasting that no woman had ever been able to resist his singing, which, it appears, had its foundation in fact – the ideal changes, my dear lady, the ideal changes a good deal from one century to another! – and that his first song could make any woman turn pale and lower her eyes, the second make her madly in love, while the third song could kill her off on the spot, kill her for love, there under his very eyes, if he only felt inclined. My grand-aunt Vendramin laughed when this story was told her, refused to go to hear this insolent dog, and added that it might be quite possible by the aid of spells and infernal pacts to kill a *gentildonna*, but as to making her fall in love with a lackey – never! This answer was naturally reported to Zaffirino, who piqued himself upon always getting the better of anyone who was wanting in deference to his voice. Like the ancient Romans, *parcere subjectis et debellare superbos*. You American ladies, who are so learned, will appreciate this little quotation from the divine Virgil. While seeming to avoid the Procuratessa Vendramin, Zaffirino took the opportunity, one evening at a large assembly, to sing in her presence. He sang and sang and sang until the poor grand-aunt Pisana fell ill for love. The most skilful physicians were unable to explain the mysterious malady which was visibly killing the poor young lady; and the Procuratore Vendramin applied in vain to the most venerated Madonnas, and vainly promised an altar of silver, with massive gold candlesticks, to

353

SS Cosmas and Damian, patrons of the art of healing. At last the brother-in-law of the Procuratessa, Monsignor Almoro Vendramin, Patriarch of Aquileia, a prelate famous for the sanctity of his life, obtained in a vision of Saint Justina, for whom he entertained a particular devotion, the information that the only thing which could benefit the strange illness of his sister-in-law was the voice of Zaffirino. Take notice that my poor grand-aunt had never condescended to such a revelation.

'The Procuratore was enchanted at this happy solution; and his lordship the Patriarch went to seek Zaffirino in person, and carried him in his own coach to the Villa of Mistrà, where the Procuratessa was residing. On being told what was about to happen, my poor grand-aunt went into fits of rage, which were succeeded immediately by equally violent fits of joy. However, she never forgot what was due to her great position. Although sick almost unto death, she had herself arrayed with the greatest pomp, caused her face to be painted, and put on all her diamonds: it would seem as if she were anxious to affirm her full dignity before this singer. Accordingly she received Zaffirino reclining on a sofa which had been placed in the great ballroom of the Villa of Mistrà, and beneath the princely canopy; for the Vendramins, who had intermarried with the house of Mantua, possessed imperial fiefs and were princes of the Holy Roman Empire. Zaffirino saluted her with the most profound respect, but not a word passed between them. Only, the singer enquired from the Procuratore whether the illustrious lady had received the Sacraments of the Church. Being told that the Procuratessa had herself asked to be given extreme unction from the hands of her brother-in-law, he declared his readiness to obey the orders of His Excellency, and sat down at once to the harpsichord.

'Never had he sung so divinely. At the end of the first song the Procuratessa Vendramin had already revived most extraordinarily; by the end of the second she appeared entirely cured and beaming with beauty and happiness; but at the third air – the *Aria dei Mariti*, no doubt – she began to change frightfully; she gave a dreadful cry, and fell into the convulsions of death. In a quarter of an hour she was dead! Zaffirino did not wait to see her die. Having finished his song, he withdrew instantly, took post-horses, and travelled day and night as far as Munich. People remarked that he had presented himself at Mistrà dressed in mourning, although he had mentioned no death among his relatives; also that he had prepared everything for his departure, as if fearing the wrath of so powerful a family. Then there was also the extra-ordinary question he had asked before beginning to sing, about the Procuratessa having confessed and received extreme unction . . . No, thanks, my dear lady, no cigarettes for me. But if it does not distress you or your charming daughter, may I humbly beg permission to smoke a cigar?'

And Count Alvise, enchanted with his talent for narrative, and sure of having secured for his son the heart and the dollars of his fair audience, proceeds to light a candle, and at the candle one of those long black Italian cigars which require preliminary dis-infection before smoking.

. . . If this state of things goes on I shall just have to ask the doctor for a bottle; this ridiculous beating of my heart and disgusting cold perspiration have increased steadily during Count Alvise's narrative. To keep myself in countenance among the various idiotic commentaries on this cock-and-bull story of a vocal coxcomb and a vapouring great lady, I begin to unroll the engraving, and to examine stupidly the portrait of Zaffirino, once so renowned, now so forgotten. A ridiculous ass, this singer, under his triumphal arch, with his stuffed Cupids and the great fat winged kitchen maid crowning him with laurels. How flat and vapid and vulgar it is, to be sure, all this odious eighteenth century!

But he, personally, is not so utterly vapid as I had thought. That effeminate, fat face of his is almost beautiful, with an odd smile, brazen and cruel. I have seen faces like this, if not in real life, at least in my boyish romantic dreams, when I read Swinburne and Baudelaire, the faces of wicked, vindictive women. Oh, yes! he is decidedly a beautiful creature, this Zaffirino, and his voice must have had the same sort of beauty and the same expression of wickedness . . .

'Come on, Magnus,' sound the voices of my fellow-boarders, 'be a good fellow and sing us one of the old chap's songs; or at least something or other of that day, and we'll make believe it was the air with which he killed that poor lady.'

'Oh, yes! the *Aria dei Mariti*, the "Husbands' Air",' mumbles old Alvise, between the puffs at his impossible black cigar. 'My poor grand-aunt, Pisana Vendramin; he went and killed her with those songs of his, with that *Aria dei Mariti*.'

I feel senseless rage overcoming me. Is it that horrible palpitation (by the way, there is a Norwegian doctor, my fellow-countryman, at Venice just now) which is sending the blood to my brain and making me mad? The people round the piano, the furniture, everything together seems to get mixed and to turn into moving blobs of colour. I set to singing; the only thing which remains distinct before my eyes being the portrait of Zaffirino, on the edge of that boarding-house piano; the sensual, effeminate face, with its wicked, cynical smile, keeps appearing and disappearing as the print wavers about in the draught that makes the candles smoke and gutter. And I set to singing madly, singing I don't know what. Yes; I begin to identify it: 'tis the *Biondina in Gondoleta*, the only song of the eighteenth century which is still remembered by the Venetian people. I sing it, mimicking every old-school grace; shakes, cadences, languishingly swelled and diminished notes, and adding all manner of buffooneries, until the audience, recovering from its surprise, begins to shake with laughing; until I begin to laugh myself, madly, frantically, between the phrases of the melody, my voice finally smothered in this dull, brutal laughter . . . And then, to crown it all, I shake my fist at this long-dead singer, looking at me with his wicked woman's face, with his mocking, fatuous smile.

'Ah! you would like to be revenged on me also!' I exclaim. 'You would like me to write you nice roulades and flourishes, another nice *Aria dei Mariti*, my fine Zaffirino!'

That night I dreamed a very strange dream. Even in the big half-furnished room the heat and closeness were stifling. The air seemed laden with the scent of all manner of white flowers, faint and heavy in their intolerable sweetness: tuberoses, gardenias, and jasmines drooping I know not where in neglected vases. The moonlight had transformed the marble floor around me into a shallow, shining pool. On account of the heat I had exchanged my bed for a big old-fashioned sofa of light wood, painted with little nosegays and sprigs, like an old silk; and I lay there, not attempting to sleep, and letting my thoughts go vaguely to my opera of *Ogier the Dane*, of which I had long finished writing the words, and for whose music I had hoped to find some inspiration in this strange Venice, floating, as it were, in the stagnant lagoon of the past. But Venice had merely put all my ideas into hopeless confusion; it was as if there arose out of its shallow waters a miasma of long-dead melodies, which sickened but intoxicated my soul. I lay on my sofa watching that pool of whitish light, which rose higher and higher, little trickles of light meeting it here and there, wherever the moon's rays struck upon some polished surface; while huge shadows waved to and fro in the draught of the open balcony.

I went over and over that old Norse story: how the Paladin, Ogier, one of the knights of Charlemagne, was decoyed during his homeward wanderings from the Holy Land by the arts of an enchantress, the same who had once held in bondage the great Emperor Caesar and given him King Oberon for a son; how Ogier had tarried in that island only one day and one night, and yet, when he came home to his kingdom, he found all changed, his friends dead, his family dethroned, and not a man who knew his face; until at last, driven hither and thither like a beggar, a poor minstrel had taken compassion of his sufferings and given him all he could give – a song, the song of the prowess of a hero dead for hundreds of years, the Paladin Ogier the Dane.

The story of Ogier ran into a dream, as vivid as my

waking thoughts had been vague. I was looking no longer at the pool of moonlight spreading round my couch, with its trickles of light and looming, waving shadows, but the frescoed walls of a great saloon. It was not, as I recognised in a second, the dining-room of that Venetian palace now turned into a boarding-house. It was a far larger room, a real ballroom, almost circular in its octagon shape, with eight huge white doors surrounded by stucco mouldings, and, high on the vault of the ceiling, eight little galleries or recesses like boxes at a theatre, intended no doubt for musicians and spectators. The place was imperfectly lighted by only one of the eight chandeliers, which revolved slowly, like huge spiders, each on its long cord. But the light struck upon the gilt stuccoes opposite me, and on a large expanse of fresco, the sacrifice of Iphigenia, with Agamemnon and Achilles in Roman helmets, lappets, and knee-breeches. It discovered also one of the oil panels let into the mouldings of the roof, a goddess in lemon and lilac draperies, fore-shortened over a great green peacock. Round the room, where the light reached, I could make out big yellow satin sofas and heavy gilded consoles; in the shadow of a corner was what looked like a piano, and farther in the shade one of those big canopies which decorate the anterooms of Roman palaces. I looked about me, wondering where I was: a heavy, sweet smell, reminding me of the flavour of a peach, filled the place.

Little by little I began to perceive sounds; little, sharp, metallic, detached notes, like those of a mand-oline; and there was united to them a voice, very low and sweet, almost a whisper, which grew and grew and grew, until the whole place was filled with that exquisite vibrating note, of a strange, exotic, unique quality. The note went on, swelling and swelling. Suddenly there was a horrible piercing shriek, and the thud of a body on the floor, and all manner of smothered exclamations. There, close by the canopy, a light suddenly appeared; and I could see, among the dark figures moving to and fro in the room, a woman lying on the ground, surrounded by other women. Her blond hair, tangled, full of diamond sparkles which cut through the half-darkness, was hanging dishevelled; the laces of her bodice had been cut, and her white breast shone among the sheen of jewelled brocade; her face was bent forwards, and a thin white arm trailed, like a broken limb, across the knees of one of the women who were endeavouring to lift her. There was a sudden splash of water against the floor, more confused exclamations, a hoarse, broken moan, and a gurgling, dreaded sound . . . I awoke with a start and rushed to the window.

Outside, in the blue haze of the moon, the church and belfry of St George loomed blue and hazy, and the black hull and rigging, the red lights of a large steamer moored before them. From the lagoon rose a damp sea-breeze. What was it all? Ah! I began to understand: that story of old Count Alvise's, the death of his grand-aunt, Pisana Vendramin. Yes, it was about that I had been dreaming.

I returned to my room; I struck a light, and sat down to my writing-table. Sleep had become impossible. I tried to work at my opera. Once or twice I thought I had got hold of what I had looked for so long . . . But as soon as I tried to lay hold of my theme, there arose in my mind the distant echo of that voice, of that long note swelled slowly by insensible degrees, that long note whose tone was so strong and so subtle.

There are in the life of an artist moments when, still unable to seize his own inspiration, or even clearly to discern it, he becomes aware of the approach of that long-invoked idea. A mingled joy and terror warn him that before another day, another hour have passed, the inspiration shall have crossed the threshold of his soul and flooded it with its rapture. All day I had felt the need of isolation and quiet, and at nightfall I went for a row on the most solitary part of the lagoon. All things seemed to tell that I was going to meet my inspiration, and I waited its coming as a lover awaits his beloved.

I had stopped my gondola for a moment, and as I gently swayed to and fro on the water, all paved with moonbeams, it seemed to me that I was on the confines of an imaginary world. It lay close at hand, enveloped in luminous, pale blue mist, through which the moon had cut a wide and glistening path; out to sea, the little islands, like moored black boats, only accentuated the solitude of this region of moonbeams and wavelets; while the hum of the insects in orchards hard by merely added to the impression of untroubled silence. On some such seas, I thought, must the Paladin Ogier have sailed when about to discover that during that sleep at the enchantress's knees centuries had elapsed and the heroic world had set, and the kingdom of prose had come.

While my gondola rocked stationary on that sea of moonbeams, I pondered over that twilight of the heroic world. In the soft rattle of the water on the hull I seemed to hear the rattle of all that armour, of all those swords swinging rusty on the walls, neglected by the degenerate sons of the great champions of old. I had long been in search of a theme which I called the theme of the 'Prowess of Ogier'; it was to appear from time to time in the course of my opera, to develop at last into that song of the Minstrel, which reveals to the hero that he is one of a long-dead world. And at this moment I seemed to feel the presence of that theme. Yet an instant, and my mind would be overwhelmed by that savage music, heroic, funereal.

Suddenly there came across the lagoon, cleaving, chequering, and fretting the silence with a lace-work of sound even as the moon was fretting and cleaving the water, a ripple of music, a voice breaking itself in a shower of little scales and cadences and trills.

I sank back upon my cushions. The vision of heroic days had vanished, and before my closed eyes there seemed to dance multitudes of little stars of light, chasing and interlacing like those sudden vocalisations.

'To shore! Quick!' I cried to the gondolier.

But the sounds had ceased; and there came from the orchards, with their mulberry trees glistening in the moonlight, and their black swaying cypress-plumes, nothing save the confused hum, the monotonous chirp, of the crickets.

I looked around me: on one side empty dunes, orchards, and meadows, without house or steeple; on the other, the blue and misty sea, empty to where distant islets were profiled black on the horizon.

A faintness overcame me, and I felt myself dissolve. For all of a sudden a second ripple of voice swept over the lagoon, a shower of little notes, which seemed to form a little mocking laugh.

Then again all was still. This silence lasted so long that I fell once more to meditating on my opera. I lay in wait once more for the half-caught theme. But no. It was not that theme for which I was waiting and watching with bated breath. I realised my delusion when, on rounding the point of the Giudecca, the murmur of a voice arose from the midst of the waters, a thread of sound slender as a moonbeam, scarce audible, but exquisite, which expanded slowly, insensibly, taking volume and body, taking flesh almost and fire, an ineffable quality, full, passionate, but veiled, as it were, in a subtle, downy wrapper. The note grew stronger and stronger, and warmer and more passionate, until it burst through that strange and charming veil, and emerged beaming, to break itself in the luminous facets of a wonderful shake, long, superb, triumphant.

There was a dead silence.

'Row to St Mark's!' I exclaimed. 'Quick!'

The gondola glided through the long, glittering track of moonbeams, and rent the great band of yellow, reflected light, mirroring the cupolas of St Mark's, the lace-like pinnacles of the palace, and the slender pink belfry, which rose from the lit-up water to the pale and bluish evening sky.

In the larger of the two squares the military band was blaring through the last spirals of a *crescendo* of Rossini. The crowd was dispersing in this great open-air ballroom, and the sounds arose which invariably follow upon out-of-door music. A clatter of spoons and glasses, a rustle and grating of frocks and of chairs, and the click of scabbards on the pavement. I pushed my way among the fashionable youths contemplating the ladies while sucking the knob of their sticks; through the serried ranks of respectable families, marching arm in arm with their white-frocked young ladies close in front. I took a seat before Florian's, among the customers stretching themselves before departing, and the waiters hurrying to and fro, clattering their empty cups and trays. Two imitation Neapolitans were slipping their guitar and violin under their arm, ready to leave the place.

'Stop!' I cried to them; 'don't go yet. Sing me something – sing *La Camesella* or *Funiculì, funiculà* – no matter what, provided you make a row'; and as they screamed and scraped their utmost, I added, 'But can't you sing louder, d—n you! – sing louder, do you understand?'

I felt the need of noise, of yells and false notes, of something vulgar and hideous to drive away that ghost-voice which was haunting me.

Again and again I told myself that it had been some silly prank of a romantic amateur, hidden in the gardens of the shore or gliding unperceived on the lagoon; and that the sorcery of moonlight and sea mist had transfigured for my excited brain mere humdrum roulades out of exercises of Bordogni or Crescentini.

But all the same I continued to be haunted by that voice. My work was interrupted ever and anon by the attempt to catch its imaginary echo; and the heroic harmonies of my Scandinavian legend were strangely interwoven with voluptuous phrases and florid cadences in which I seemed to hear again that same accursed voice.

To be haunted by singing-exercises! It seemed too ridiculous for a man who professedly despised the art of singing. And still, I preferred to believe in that childish amateur, amusing himself with warbling to the moon.

One day, while making these reflections the hundredth time over, my eyes chanced to light upon the portrait of Zaffirino, which my friend had pinned against the wall. I pulled it down and tore it into half a dozen shreds. Then, already ashamed of my folly, I watched the torn pieces float down from the window, wafted hither and thither by the sea breeze. One scrap got caught in a yellow blind below me; the others fell into the canal, and were speedily lost to sight in the dark water. I was overcome with shame. My heart beat like bursting. What a miserable, unnerved worm I had become in this cursed Venice, with its languishing moonlights, its atmosphere as of some stuffy boudoir, long unused, full of old stuffs and potpourri!

That night, however, things seemed to be going better. I was able to settle down to my opera, and even to work at it. In the intervals my thoughts returned, not without a certain pleasure, to those scattered fragments of the torn engraving fluttering down to the water. I was disturbed at my piano by the hoarse voices and the scraping of violins which rose from one of those music-boats that station at night under the hotels of the Grand Canal. The moon had set. Under my balcony the water stretched black into the distance, its darkness cut by the still darker outlines of the flotilla of gondolas in attendance on the music-boat, where the faces of the singers, and the guitars and violins, gleamed reddish under the unsteady light of the Chinese lanterns.

'*Jammo, jammo; jammo, jammo, jà,*' sang the loud,

hoarse voices; then a tremendous scrape and twang, and the yelled-out burden: '*Funiculì, funiculà; funiculì, funiculà; jammo, jammo, jammo, jammo, jammo jà.*'

Then came a few cries of '*Bis, bis!*' from a neighbouring hotel, a brief clapping of hands, the sound of a handful of coppers rattling into the boat, and the oar-stroke of some gondolier making ready to turn away.

'Sing the *Camesella*,' ordered some voice with a foreign accent.

'No, no! *Santa Lucia.*'

'I want the *Camesella.*'

'No! *Santa Lucia*. Hi! sing *Santa Lucia* – d' you hear?'

The musicians, under their green and yellow and red lamps, held a whispered consultation on the manner of conciliating these contradictory demands. Then, after a minute's hesitation, the violins began the prelude of that once famous air, which has remained popular in Venice – the words written, some hundred years ago, by the patrician Gritti, the music by an unknown composer – *La Biondina in Gondoleta.*

That cursed eighteenth century! It seemed a malignant fatality that made these brutes choose just this piece to interrupt me.

At last the long prelude came to an end; and above the cracked guitars and squeaking fiddles there arose, not the expected nasal chorus, but a single voice singing below its breath.

My arteries throbbed. How well I knew that voice! It was singing, as I have said, below its breath, yet none the less it sufficed to fill all that reach of the canal with its strange quality of tone, exquisite, far-fetched.

They were long-drawn-out notes, of intense but

peculiar sweetness, a man's voice which had much of a woman's, but more even of a chorister's, but a chorister's voice without its limpidity and innocence; its youthfulness was veiled, muffled, as it were, in a sort of downy vagueness, as in a passion of tears withheld.

There was a burst of applause, and the old palaces re-echoed with the clapping. 'Bravo, bravo! Thank you, thank you! Sing again – please, sing again. Who can it be?'

And then a bumping of hulls, a splashing of oars, and the oaths of gondoliers trying to push each other away, as the red prow-lamps of the gondolas pressed round the gaily lit singing-boat.

But no one stirred on board. It was to none of them that this applause was due. And while everyone pressed on, and clapped and vociferated, one little red prow-lamp dropped away from the fleet; for a moment a single gondola stood forth black upon the black water, and then was lost in the night.

For several days the mysterious singer was the universal topic. The people of the music-boat swore that no one besides themselves had been on board, and that they knew as little as ourselves about the owner of that voice. The gondoliers, despite their descent from the spies of the old Republic, were equally unable to furnish any clue. No musical celebrity was known or suspected to be at Venice; and everyone agreed that such a singer must be a European celebrity. The strangest thing in this strange business was, that even among those learned in music there was no agreement on the subject of this voice: it was called by all sorts of names and described by all manner of incongruous adjectives;

people went so far as to dispute whether the voice belonged to a man or to a woman: everyone had some new definition.

In all these musical discussions I, alone, brought forward no opinion. I felt a repugnance, an impossibility almost, of speaking about that voice; and the more or less commonplace conjectures of my friends had the invariable effect of sending me out of the room.

Meanwhile my work was becoming daily more difficult, and I soon passed from utter impotence to a state of inexplicable agitation. Every morning I arose with fine resolutions and grand projects of work; only to go to bed that night without having accomplished anything. I spent hours leaning on my balcony, or wandering through the network of lanes with their ribbon of blue sky, endeavouring vainly to expel the thought of that voice, or endeavouring in reality to reproduce it in my memory; for the more I tried to banish it from my thoughts, the more I grew to thirst for that extraordinary tone, for those mysteriously downy, veiled notes; and no sooner did I make an effort to work at my opera than my head was full of scraps of forgotten eighteenth-century airs, of frivolous or languishing little phrases; and I fell to wondering with a bitter-sweet longing how those songs would have sounded if sung by that voice.

At length it became necessary to see a doctor, from whom, however, I carefully hid away all the stranger symptoms of my malady. The air of the lagoons, the great heat, he answered cheerfully, had pulled me down a little; a tonic and a month in the country, with plenty of riding and no work, would make me myself again. The old idler, Count Alvise, who had insisted on accompanying me to the physician's, immediately suggested that I should go and stay with his son, who was boring himself to death super-intending the maize harvest on the mainland: he could promise me excellent air, plenty of horses, and all the peaceful surroundings and the delightful occupations of a rural life – 'Be sensible, my dear Magnus, and just go quietly to Mistrà.'

Mistrà – the name sent a shiver all down me. I was about to decline the invitation, when a thought suddenly loomed vaguely in my mind.

'Yes, dear Count,' I answered; 'I accept your invitation with gratitude and pleasure. I will start tomorrow for Mistrà.'

The next day found me at Padua, on my way to the Villa of Mistrà. It seemed as if I had left an intolerable burden behind me. I was, for the first time since how long, quite light of heart. The tortuous, rough-paved streets, with their empty, gloomy porticoes; the ill-plastered palaces, with closed, discoloured shutters; the little rambling square, with meagre trees and stub-born grass; the Venetian garden-houses reflecting their crumbling graces in the muddy canal; the gardens without gates and the gates without gardens, the avenues leading nowhere; and the population of blind and legless beggars, of whining sacristans, which issued as by magic from between the flagstones and dust-heaps and weeds under the fierce August sun, all this dreariness merely amused and pleased me. My good spirits were heightened by a musical mass which I had the good fortune to hear at St Anthony's.

Never in all my days had I heard anything com-parable, although Italy affords many strange things in the way of sacred music. Into the deep nasal chanting of the priests there had suddenly burst a chorus of children, singing absolutely independent of all time and tune; grunting of priests answered by squealing of boys, slow Gregorian modulation interrupted by jaunty barrel-organ pipings, an insane, insanely merry jumble of bellowing and barking, mewing and cackling and braying, such as would have enlivened a witches' meeting, or rather some medieval Feast of Fools. And, to make the grotesqueness of such music still more fantastic and Hoffman-like, there was, besides, the magnificence of the piles of sculptured marbles and gilded bronzes, the tradition of the musical splendour for which St Anthony's had been famous in days gone by. I had read in old travellers, Lalande and Burney, that the Republic of St Mark had squandered immense sums not merely on the monuments and decoration, but on the musical establishment of its great cathedral of Terra Firma. In the midst of this ineffable concert of impossible voices and instruments, I tried to imagine the voice of Guadagni, the soprano for whom Gluck had written *Che farò senza Euridice*, and the fiddle of Tartini, that Tartini with whom the devil had once come and made music. And the delight in anything so absolutely, barbarously, grotesquely, fantastically incongruous as such a performance in such a place was heightened by a sense of profanation: such were the successors of those wonderful musicians of that hated eighteenth century!

The whole thing had delighted me so much, so very much more than the most faultless performance could have done, that I determined to enjoy it once more; and towards vesper-time, after a cheerful dinner with two bagmen at the inn of the Golden Star, and a pipe over the rough sketch of a possible cantata upon the music which the devil made for Tartini, I turned my steps once more towards St Anthony's.

The bells were ringing for sunset, and a muffled sound of organs seemed to issue from the huge, solitary church; I pushed my way under the heavy leathern curtain, expecting to be greeted by the grotesque performance of that morning.

I proved mistaken. Vespers must long have been over. A smell of stale incense, a crypt-like damp filled my mouth; it was already night in that vast cathedral. Out of the darkness glimmered the votive lamps of the chapels, throwing wavering lights upon the red polished marble, the gilded railing, and chandeliers, and plaquing with yellow the muscles of some sculptured figure. In a corner a burning taper put a halo about the head of a priest, burnishing his shining bald skull, his white surplice, and the open book before him. 'Amen,' he chanted; the book was closed with a snap, the light moved up the apse, some dark figures of women rose from their knees and passed quickly towards the door; a man saying his prayers before a chapel also got up, making a great clatter in dropping his stick.

The church was empty, and I expected every minute to be turned out by the sacristan making his evening round to close the doors. I was leaning against a pillar, looking into the greyness of the great arches, when the organ suddenly burst out into a series of chords, rolling through the echoes of the church: it seemed to be the conclusion of some service. And above the organ rose the notes of a voice; high, soft, enveloped in a kind of downiness, like a cloud of incense, and which ran through the mazes of a long cadence. The voice dropped into silence; with two thundering chords the organ closed in. All was silent. For a moment I stood leaning against one of the pillars of the nave; my hair was clammy, my knees sank beneath me, an enervating heat spread through my body; I tried to breathe more largely, to suck in the sounds with the incense-laden air. I was supremely happy, and yet as if I were dying; then suddenly a chill ran through me, and with it a vague panic. I turned away and hurried out into the open.

The evening sky lay pure and blue along the jagged line of roofs; the bats and swallows were wheeling about; and from the belfries all around, half drowned by the deep bell of St Anthony's, jangled the peal of the *Ave Maria*.

'You really don't seem well,' young Count Alvise had said the previous evening, as he welcomed me, in the light of a lantern held up by a peasant, in the weedy back garden of the Villa of Mistrà. Everything had seemed to me like a dream: the jingle of the horse's bells driving in the dark from Padua, as the lantern swept the acacia hedges with their wide yellow light; the grating of the wheels on the gravel; the supper-table, illuminated by a single petroleum lamp for fear of attracting mosquitoes, where a broken old lackey, in an old stable jacket, handed round the dishes among the fumes of onion; Alvise's fat mother gabbling dialect in a shrill, benevolent voice behind the bullfights on her fan; the unshaven village priest, perpetually fidgeting with his glass and foot, and sticking one shoulder up above the other. And now, in the afternoon, I felt as if I had been in this long, rambling, tumble-down Villa of Mistrà – a villa three-quarters of which was given

up to the storage of grain and garden tools, or to the
exercise of rats, mice, scorpions, and centipedes – all
my life; as if I had always sat there, in Count Alvise's
study, among the pile of undusted books on agriculture, the sheaves of accounts, the samples of grain
and silkworm seed, the ink-stains and the cigar ends;
as if I had never heard of anything save the cereal
basis of Italian agriculture, the diseases of maize, the
peronospora of the vine, the breeds of bullocks, and
the iniquities of farm labourers; with the blue cones of
the Euganean hills closing in the green shimmer of
plain outside the window.

After an early dinner, again with the screaming
gabble of the fat old Countess, the fidgeting and
shoulder-raising of the unshaven priest, the smell of
fried oil and stewed onions, Count Alvise made me
get into the cart beside him, and whirled me along
among clouds of dust, between the endless glister of
poplars, acacias, and maples, to one of his farms.

In the burning sun some twenty or thirty girls, in
coloured skirts, laced bodices, and big straw hats,
were threshing the maize on the big red-brick
threshing-floor, while others were winnowing the
grain in great sieves. Young Alvise III (the old one
was Alvise II: everyone is Alvise, that is to say, Lewis,
in that family; the name is on the house, the carts, the
barrows, the very pails) picked up the maize, touched
it, tasted it, said something to the girls that made
them laugh, and something to the head farmer that
made him look very glum; and then led me into a
huge stable, where some twenty or thirty white
bullocks were stamping, switching their tails, hitting
their horns against the mangers in the dark. Alvise III
patted each, called him by his name, gave him some

salt or a turnip, and explained which was the Mantuan breed, which the Apulian, which the Romagnolo, and so on. Then he bade me jump into the trap, and off we went again through the dust, among the hedges and ditches, till we came to some more brick farm buildings with pinkish roofs smoking against the blue sky. Here there were more young women threshing and winnowing the maize, which made a great golden Danae cloud; more bullocks stamping and lowing in the cool darkness; more joking, fault-finding, explaining, and thus through five farms, until I seemed to see the rhythmical rising and falling of the flails against the hot sky, the shower of golden grains, the yellow dust from the winnowing-sieves on to the bricks, the switching of innumerable tails and plunging of innumerable horns, the glistening of huge white flanks and foreheads, whenever I closed my eyes.

'A good day's work!' cried Count Alvise, stretching out his long legs with the tight trousers riding up over the Wellington boots. 'Mamma, give us some aniseed-syrup after dinner; it is an excellent restorative and precaution against the fevers of this country.'

'Oh! you've got fever in this part of the world, have you? Why, your father said the air was so good!'

'Nothing, nothing,' soothed the old Countess. 'The only thing to be dreaded are mosquitoes; take care to fasten your shutters before lighting the candle.'

'Well,' rejoined young Alvise, with an effort of conscience, 'of course there *are* fevers. But they needn't hurt you. Only, don't go out into the garden at night, if you don't want to catch them. Papa told me that you have fancies for moonlight rambles. It won't do in this climate, my dear fellow; it won't do. If you must stalk about at night, being a genius, take a turn inside the house; you can get quite exercise enough.'

After dinner the aniseed-syrup was produced, together with brandy and cigars, and they all sat in the long, narrow, half-furnished room on the first floor; the old Countess knitting a garment of uncertain shape and destination, the priest reading out the newspaper; Count Alvise puffing at his long, crooked cigar, and pulling the ears of a long, lean, dog with a suspicion of mange and a stiff eye. From the dark garden outside rose the hum and whirr of countless insects, and the smell of the grapes which hung black against the starlit, blue sky, on the trellis. I went to the balcony. The garden lay dark beneath; against the twinkling horizon stood out the tall poplars. There was the sharp cry of an owl; the barking of a dog; a sudden whiff of warm, enervating perfume, a perfume that made me think of the taste of certain peaches, and suggested white, thick, wax-like petals. I seemed to have smelt that flower once before: it made me feel languid, almost faint.

'I am very tired,' I said to Count Alvise. 'See how feeble we city folk become!'

But, despite my fatigue, I found it quite impossible to sleep. The night seemed perfectly stifling. I had felt nothing like at Venice. Despite the injunctions of the Countess I opened the solid wooden shutters, hermetically closed against mosquitoes, and looked out.

The moon had risen; and beneath it lay the big lawns, the rounded tree-tops, bathed in a blue, luminous mist, every leaf glistening and trembling in what seemed a heaving sea of light. Beneath the window was the long trellis, with the white shining piece of pavement under it. It was so bright that I could distinguish the green of the vine-leaves, the dull red of the catalpa flowers. There was in the air a vague scent of cut grass, of ripe American grapes, of that white flower (it must be white) which made me think of the taste of peaches, all melting into the delicious freshness of falling dew. From the village church came the stroke of one: Heaven knows how long I had been vainly attempting to sleep. A shiver ran through me, and my head suddenly filled as with the fumes of some subtle wine; I remembered all those weedy embankments, those canals full of stagnant water, the yellow faces of the peasants; the word malaria returned to my mind. No matter! I remained leaning on the window, with a thirsty longing to plunge myself into this blue moon-mist, this dew and perfume and silence which seemed to vibrate and quiver like the stars that strewed the depths of heaven. ... What music, even Wagner's, or of that great singer of starry nights, the divine Schumann, what music could ever compare with this great silence, with this great concert of voiceless things that sing within one's soul?

As I made this reflection, a note, high, vibrating, and sweet, rent the silence, which immediately closed around it. I leaned out of the window, my heart beating as though it must burst. After a brief space the silence was cloven once more by that note, as the darkness is cloven by a falling star or a firefly rising slowly like a rocket. But that time it was plain that the voice did not come, as I had imagined, from the garden, but from the house itself, from some corner of this rambling old villa of Mistrà.

Mistrà – Mistrà! The name rang in my ears, and I began at length to grasp its significance, which seems to have escaped me till then. 'Yes,' I said to myself, 'it is quite natural.' And with this odd impression of naturalness was mixed a feverish, impatient pleasure. It was as if I had come to Mistrà on purpose, and that I was about to meet the object of my long and weary hopes.

Grasping the lamp with its singed green shade, I gently opened the door and made my way through a series of long passages and of big, empty rooms, in which my steps re-echoed as in a church, and my light disturbed whole swarms of bats. I wandered at random, farther and farther from the inhabited part of the buildings.

This silence made me feel sick; I gasped as under a sudden disappointment.

All of a sudden there came a sound – chords, metallic, sharp, rather like the tone of a mandoline – close to my ear. Yes, quite close: I was separated from the sounds only by a partition. I fumbled for a door; the unsteady light of my lamp was insufficient for my eyes, which were swimming like those of a drunkard. At last I found a latch, and, after a moment's hesitation, I lifted it and gently pushed open the door. At first I could not understand what manner of place I was in. It was dark all round me, but a brilliant light blinded me, a light coming from below and striking the opposite wall. It was as if I had entered a dark box in a half-lighted theatre. I was, in fact, in something of the kind, a sort of dark hole with a high balustrade, half-hidden by an up-drawn curtain. I remembered those little galleries or recesses for the use of musicians or lookers-on which

exist under the ceiling of the ballrooms in certain old
Italian palaces. Yes; it must have been one like that.
Opposite me was a vaulted ceiling covered with gilt
mouldings, which framed great time-blackened
canvases; and lower down, in the light thrown up
from below, stretched a wall covered with faded
frescoes. Where had I seen that goddess in lilac and
lemon draperies foreshortened over a big, green peacock? For she was familiar to me, and the stucco
Tritons also who twisted their tails round her gilded
frame. And that fresco, with warriors in Roman
cuirasses and green and blue lappets, and knee-
breeches – where could I have seen them before? I
asked myself these questions without experiencing
any surprise. Moreover, I was very calm, as one is
calm sometimes in extraordinary dreams – could I be
dreaming?

I advanced gently and leaned over the balustrade.
My eyes were met at first by the darkness above me,
where, like gigantic spiders, the big chandeliers
rotated slowly, hanging from the ceiling. Only one
of them was lit, and its Murano-glass pendants, its
carnations and roses, shone opalescent in the light of
the guttering wax. This chandelier lighted up the
opposite wall and that piece of ceiling with the
goddess and the green peacock; it illumined, but far
less well, a corner of the huge room, where, in the
shadow of a kind of canopy, a little group of people
were crowding round a yellow satin sofa, of the same
kind as those that lined the walls. On the sofa, half-
screened from me by the surrounding persons, a
woman was stretched out: the silver of her
embroidered dress and the rays of her diamonds
gleamed and shot forth as she moved uneasily. And

immediately under the chandelier, in the full light, a man stooped over a harpsichord, his head bent slightly, as if collecting his thoughts before singing.

He struck a few chords and sang. Yes, sure enough, it was the voice, the voice that had so long been persecuting me! I recognised at once that delicate, voluptuous quality, strange, exquisite, sweet beyond words, but lacking all youth and clearness. That passion veiled in tears which had troubled my brain that night on the lagoon, and again on the Grand Canal singing the *Biondina*, and yet again, only two days since, in the deserted cathedral of Padua. But I recognised now what seemed to have been hidden from me till then, that this voice was what I cared most for in all the wide world.

The voice wound and unwound itself in long, languishing phrases, in rich, voluptuous *rifiorituras*, all fretted with tiny scales and exquisite, crisp shakes; it stopped ever and anon, swaying as if panting in languid delight. And I felt my body melt even as wax in the sunshine, and it seemed to me that I too was turning fluid and vaporous, in order to mingle with these sounds as the moonbeams mingle with the dew.

Suddenly, from the dimly lighted corner by the canopy, came a little piteous wail; then another followed, and was lost in the singer's voice. During a long phrase on the harpsichord, sharp and tinkling, the singer turned his head towards the dais, and there came a plaintive little sob. But he, instead of stopping, struck a sharp chord; and with a thread of voice so hushed as to be scarcely audible, slid softly into a long *cadenza*. At the same moment he threw his head backwards, and the light fell full upon the handsome, effeminate face, with its ashy pallor and big, black

brows, of the singer Zaffirino. At the sight of that
face, sensual and sullen, of that smile which was cruel
and mocking like a bad woman's, I understood – I
knew not why, by what process – that his singing *must*
be cut short, that the accursed phrase *must* never be
finished. I understood that I was before an assassin,
that he was killing this woman, and killing me also,
with his wicked voice.

I rushed down the narrow stair which led down
from the box, pursued, as it were, by that exquisite
voice, swelling, swelling by insensible degrees. I flung
myself on the door which must be that of the big
saloon. I could see its light between the panels. I
bruised my hands in trying to wrench the latch. The
door was fastened tight, and while I was struggling
with that locked door I heard the voice swelling,
swelling, rending asunder that downy veil which
wrapped it, leaping forth clear, resplendent, like the
sharp and glittering blade of a knife that seemed to
enter deep into my breast. Then, once more, a wail, a
death-groan, and that dreadful noise, that hideous
gurgle of breath strangled by a rush of blood. And
then a long shake, acute, brilliant, triumphant.

The door gave way beneath my weight, one half
crashed in. I entered. I was blinded by a flood of blue
moonlight. It poured in through four great windows,
peaceful and diaphanous, a pale blue mist of moonlight, and turned the huge room into a kind of sub-
marine cave, paved with moonbeams, full of shimmers,
of pools of moonlight. It was as bright as at midday,
but the brightness was cold, blue, vaporous, supernatural. The room was completely empty, like a great
hay-loft. Only, there hung from the ceiling the ropes
which had once supported a chandelier; and in a

corner, among stacks of wood and heaps of Indian corn, whence spread a sickly smell of damp and mildew, there stood a long, thin harpsichord, with spindle-legs, and its cover cracked from end to end.

I felt, all of a sudden, very calm. The one thing that mattered was the phrase that kept moving in my head, the phrase of that unfinished cadence which I had heard but an instant before. I opened the harpsichord, and my fingers came down boldly upon its keys. A jingle-jangle of broken strings, laughable and dreadful, was the only answer.

Then an extraordinary fear overtook me. I clambered out of one of the windows; I rushed up the garden and wandered through the fields, among the canals and the embankments, until the moon had set and the dawn began to shiver, followed, pursued for ever by that jangle of broken strings.

People expressed much satisfaction at my recovery. It seems that one dies of those fevers.

Recovery? But have I recovered? I walk, and eat and drink and talk; I can even sleep. I live the life of other living creatures. But I am wasted by a strange and deadly disease. I can never lay hold of my own inspiration. My head is filled with music which is certainly by me, since I have never heard it before, but which still is not my own, which I despise and abhor: little, tripping flourishes and languishing phrases, and long-drawn, echoing cadences.

O wicked, wicked voice, violin of flesh and blood made by the Evil One's hand, may I not even execrate thee in peace; but it is necessary that, at the moment when I curse, the longing to hear thee again should parch my soul like hell-thirst? And since I have satiated thy lust for revenge, since thou hast withered my life and withered my genius, is it not time for pity? May I not hear one note, only one note of thine, O singer, O wicked and contemptible wretch?

AMELIA B. EDWARDS

In the Confessional

The things of which I write befell – let me see, some
fifteen or eighteen years ago. I was not young then; I
am not old now. Perhaps I was about thirty-two; but
I do not know my age very exactly, and I cannot be
certain to a year or two one way or the other.

My manner of life at that time was desultory and
unsettled. I had a sorrow – no matter of what kind –
and I took to rambling about Europe; not certainly in
the hope of forgetting it, for I had no wish to forget,
but because of the restlessness that made one place
after another *triste* and intolerable to me.

It was change of place, however, and not excitement, that I sought. I kept almost entirely aloof from
great cities, Spas, and beaten tracks, and preferred for
the most part to explore districts where travellers and
foreigners rarely penetrated.

Such a district at that time was the Upper Rhine. I
was traversing it that particular summer for the first
time, and on foot; and I had set myself to trace the
course of the river from its source in the great Rhine
glacier to its fall at Schaffhausen. Having done this,
however, I was unwilling to part company with the
noble river; so I decided to follow it yet a few miles
farther – perhaps as far as Mayence, but at all events
as far as Basle.

And now began, if not the finest, certainly not the
least charming part of my journey. Here, it is true,
were neither Alps, nor glaciers, nor ruined castles

perched on inaccessible crags; but my way lay through
a smiling country, studded with picturesque hamlets,
and beside a bright river, hurrying along over swirling
rapids, and under the dark arches of antique covered
bridges, and between hillsides garlanded with vines.

It was towards the middle of a long day's walk
among such scenes as these that I came to Rheinfelden, a small place on the left bank of the river,
about fourteen miles above Basle.

As I came down the white road in the blinding
sunshine, with the vines on either hand, I saw the
town lying low on the opposite bank of the Rhine. It
was an old walled town, enclosed on the land side
and open to the river, the houses going sheer down to
the water's edge, with flights of slimy steps worn
smooth by the wash of the current, and overhanging
eaves, and little built-out rooms with penthouse roofs,
supported from below by jutting piles black with age
and tapestried with water-weeds. The stunted towers
of a couple of churches stood up from amid the brown
and tawny roofs within the walls.

Beyond the town, height above height, stretched a
distance of wooded hills. The old covered bridge,
divided by a bit of rocky island in the middle of the
stream, led from bank to bank – from Germany to
Switzerland. The town was in Switzerland; I, looking
towards it from the road, stood on Baden territory;
the river ran sparkling and foaming between.

I crossed, and found the place all alive in anticipation of a Kermess, or fair, that was to be held there
the next day but one. The townsfolk were all out in
the streets or standing about their doors; and there
were carpenters hard at work knocking up rows of
wooden stands and stalls the whole length of the

384

principal thoroughfare. Shop-signs in open-work of wrought iron hung over the doors. A runlet of sparkling water babbled down a stone channel in the middle of the street. At almost every other house (to judge by the rows of tarnished watches hanging in the dingy parlour windows), there lived a watchmaker; and presently I came to a fountain – a regular Swiss fountain, spouting water from four ornamental pipes, and surmounted by the usual armed knight in old grey stone.

As I rambled on thus (looking for an inn, but seeing none), I suddenly found that I had reached the end of the street, and with it the limit of the town on this side. Before me rose a lofty, picturesque old gate-tower, with a tiled roof and a little window over the archway; and there was a peep of green grass and golden sunshine beyond. The town walls (sixty or seventy feet in height, and curiously roofed with a sort of projecting shed on the inner side) curved away to right and left, unchanged since the Middle Ages. A rude wain, laden with clover and drawn by mild-eyed, cream-coloured oxen, stood close by in the shade.

I passed out through the gloom of the archway into the sunny space beyond. The moat outside the walls was bridged over and filled in – a green ravine of grasses and wild-flowers. A stork had built its nest on the roof of the gate-tower. The cicalas shrilled in the grass. The shadows lay sleeping under the trees, and a family of cocks and hens went plodding inquisitively to and fro among the cabbages in the adjacent field. Just beyond the moat, with only this field between, stood a little solitary church – a church with a wooden porch, and a quaint, bright-red steeple, and a church-yard like a rose-garden, full of colour and perfume, and scattered over with iron crosses wreathed with immortelles.

The churchyard gate and the church door stood open. I went in. All was clean, and simple, and very poor. The walls were whitewashed; the floor was laid with red bricks; the roof raftered. A tiny confessional like a sentry-box stood in one corner; the font was covered with a lid like a wooden steeple; and over the altar, upon which stood a pair of battered brass candlesticks and two vases of artificial flowers, hung a daub of the Holy Family, in oils.

All here was so cool, so quiet, that I sat down for a few moments and rested. Presently an old peasant woman trudged up the church-path with a basket of vegetables on her head. Having set this down in the porch, she came in, knelt before the altar, said her simple prayers, and went her way.

Was it not time for me also to go my way? I looked at my watch. It was past four o'clock, and I had not yet found a lodging for the night.

I got up, somewhat unwillingly; but, attracted by a tablet near the altar, crossed over to look at it before leaving the church. It was a very small slab, and bore a very brief German inscription to this effect:

To the Sacred Memory of
THE REVEREND PÈRE CHESSEZ

for twenty years the beloved
Pastor of this Parish.
Died April 16th, 1825. Aged 44.
He lived a saint; he died a martyr.

I read it over twice, wondering idly what story was wrapped up in the concluding line. Then, prompted by a childish curiosity, I went up to examine the confessional.

It was, as I have said, about the size of a sentry-box, and was painted to imitate old dark oak. On the one side was a narrow door with a black handle, on the other a little opening like a ticket-taker's window, closed on the inside by a faded green curtain.

I know not what foolish fancy possessed me, but, almost without considering what I was doing, I turned the handle and opened the door. Opened it – peeped in – found the priest sitting in his place – started back as if I had been shot – and stammered an unintelligible apology.

'I – I beg a thousand pardons,' I exclaimed. 'I had no idea – seeing the church empty – '

He was sitting with averted face, and clasped hands lying idly in his lap – a tall, gaunt man, dressed in a black soutane. When I paused, and not till then, he slowly, very slowly, turned his head, and looked me in the face.

The light inside the confessional was so dim that I could not see his features very plainly. I only observed that his eyes were large, and bright, and wild-looking, like the eyes of some fierce animal, and that his face, with the reflection of the green curtain upon it, looked lividly pale.

For a moment we remained thus, gazing at each other, as if fascinated. Then, finding that he made no reply, but only stared at me with those strange eyes, I stepped hastily back, shut the door without another word, and hurried out of the church.

I was very much disturbed by this little incident; more disturbed, in truth, than seemed reasonable, for my nerves for the moment were shaken. Never, I told myself, never while I lived could I forget that fixed attitude and stony face, or the glare of those terrible eyes. What was the man's history? Of what secret despair, of what lifelong remorse, of what wild unsatisfied longings was he the victim? I felt I could not rest till I had learned something of his past life.

Full of these thoughts, I went on quickly into the town, half running across the field, and never looking back. Once past the gateway and inside the walls, I breathed more freely. The wain was still standing in the shade, but the oxen were gone now, and two men were busy forking out the clover into a little yard close by. Having enquired of one of these regarding an inn, and being directed to the Krone, 'over against the Frauenkirche', I made my way to the upper part of the town, and there, at one corner of a forlorn, weed-grown marketplace, I found my hostelry.

The landlord, a sedate, bald man in spectacles, who, as I presently discovered, was not only an innkeeper but a clockmaker, came out from an inner room to receive me. His wife, a plump, pleasant body, took my orders for dinner. His pretty daughter showed me to my room. It was a large, low, white-washed room, with two lattice windows overlooking the marketplace, two little beds, covered with puffy red eiderdowns at the farther end, and an army of clocks and ornamental timepieces arranged along every shelf, table, and chest of drawers in the room. Being left here to my meditations, I sat down and counted these companions of my solitude.

Taking little and big together, Dutch clocks, cuckoo clocks, *châlet* clocks, skeleton clocks and *pendules* in ormolu, bronze, marble, ebony and alabaster cases, there were exactly thirty-two. Twenty-eight were going merrily. As no two among them were of the same opinion as regarded the time, and as several struck the quarters as well as the hours, the consequence was that one or other gave tongue about every five minutes. Now, for a light and nervous sleeper such as I was at that time, here was a lively prospect for the night!

Going downstairs presently with the hope of getting my landlady to assign me a quieter room, I passed two eight-day clocks on the landing, and a third at the foot of the stairs. The public room was equally well-stocked. It literally bristled with clocks, one of which played a spasmodic version of Gentle Zitella with variations every quarter of an hour. Here I found a little table prepared by the open window, and a dish of trout and a flask of country wine awaiting me. The pretty daughter waited upon me; her mother bustled to and fro with the dishes; the landlord stood by, and beamed upon me through his spectacles.

'The trout were caught this morning, about two miles from here,' he said, complacently.

'They are excellent,' I replied, filling him out a glass of wine, and helping myself to another. 'Your health, Herr Wirth.'

'Thanks, mein Herr – yours.'

Just at this moment two clocks struck at opposite ends of the room – one twelve, and the other seven. I ventured to suggest that mine host was tolerably well reminded of the flight of time; whereupon he explained that his work lay chiefly in the repairing and regulating line, and that at that present moment he had no less than one hundred and eighteen clocks of various sorts and sizes on the premises.

'Perhaps the Herr Engländer is a light sleeper,' said

his quick-witted wife, detecting my dismay. 'If so, we can get him a bedroom elsewhere. Not, perhaps, in the town, for I know no place where he would be as comfortable as with ourselves; but just outside the Friedrich's Thor, not five minutes' walk from our door.'

I accepted the offer gratefully.

'So long,' I said, 'as I ensure cleanliness and quiet, I do not care how homely my lodgings may be.'

'Ah, you'll have both, mein Herr, if you go where my wife is thinking of,' said the landlord. 'It is at the house of our pastor – the Père Chessez.'

'The Père Chessez!' I exclaimed. 'What, the pastor of the little church out yonder?'

'The same, mein Herr.'

'But – but surely the Père Chessez is dead! I saw a tablet to his memory in the chancel.'

'Nay, that was our pastor's elder brother,' replied the landlord, looking grave. 'He has been gone these thirty years and more. His was a tragical ending.'

But I was thinking too much of the younger brother just then to feel any curiosity about the elder; and I told myself that I would put up with the companionship of any number of clocks, rather than sleep under the same roof with that terrible face and those unearthly eyes.

'I saw your pastor just now in the church,' I said, with apparent indifference. 'He is a singular-looking man.'

'He is too good for this world,' said the landlady.

'He is a saint upon earth!' added the pretty Fräulein.

'He is one of the best of men,' said, more soberly, the husband and father. 'I only wish he was less of a saint. He fasts, and prays, and works beyond his strength. A little more beef and a little less devotion would be all the better for him.'

'I should like to hear something more about the life of so good a man,' said I, having by this time come to the end of my simple dinner. 'Come, Herr Wirth, let us have a bottle of your best, and then sit down and tell me your pastor's history!'

The landlord sent his daughter for a bottle of the 'green seal', and, taking a chair, said: 'Ach Himmel! mein Herr, there is no history to tell. The good father has lived here all his life. He is one of us. His father, Johann Chessez, was a native of Rheinfelden and kept this very inn. He was a wealthy farmer and vine-grower. He had only those two sons – Nicholas, who took to the church and became pastor of Feldkirche; and this one, Matthias, who was intended to inherit the business; but who also entered religion after the death of his elder brother, and is now pastor of the same parish.'

'But why did he "enter religion"? ' I asked. 'Was he in any way to blame for the accident (if it was an accident) that caused the death of his elder brother?'

'Ah Heavens! no!' exclaimed the landlady, leaning on the back of her husband's chair. 'It was the shock – the shock that told so terribly upon his poor nerves! He was but a lad at that time, and as sensitive as a girl – but the Herr Engländer does not know the story. Go on, my husband.'

So the landlord, after a sip of the 'green seal', con-tinued: 'At the time my wife alludes to, mein Herr, Johann Chessez was still living. Nicholas, the elder son, was in holy orders and established in the parish of Feldkirche, outside the walls; and Matthias, the younger, was a lad of about fourteen years old, and

lived with his father. He was an amiable good boy –
pious and thoughtful – fonder of his books than of the
business. The neighbour-folk used to say even then
that Matthias was cut out for a priest, like his elder
brother. As for Nicholas, he was neither more nor less
than a saint. Well, mein Herr, at this time there lived
on the other side of Rheinfelden, about a mile beyond
the Basel Thor, a farmer named Caspar Rufenacht
and his wife Margaret. Now Caspar Rufenacht was a
jealous, quarrelsome fellow; and the Frau Margaret
was pretty; and he led her a devil of a life. It was said
that he used to beat her when he had been drinking,
and that sometimes, when he went to fair or market,
he would lock her up for the whole day in a room at
the top of the house. Well, this poor, ill-used Frau
Margaret – '

'Tut, tut, my man,' interrupted the landlady. 'The
Frau Margaret was a light one!'

'Peace, wife! Shall we speak hard words of the
dead? The Frau Margaret was young and pretty, and
a flirt; and she had a bad husband, who left her too
much alone.'

The landlady pursed up her lips and shook her
head, as the best of women will do when the character
of another woman is under discussion. The innkeeper
went on.

'Well, mein Herr, to cut a long story short, after
having been jealous first of one and then of another,
Caspar Rufenacht became furious about a certain
German, a Badener named Schmidt, living on the
opposite bank of the Rhine. I remember the man
quite well – a handsome, merry fellow, and no saint;
just the sort to make mischief between man and wife.
Well, Caspar Rufenacht swore a great oath that, cost

what it might, he would come at the truth about his wife and Schmidt; so he laid all manner of plots to surprise them – waylaid the Frau Margaret in her walks; followed her at a distance when she went to church; came home at unexpected hours; and played the spy as if he had been brought up to the trade. But his spying was all in vain. Either the Frau Margaret was too clever for him, or there was really nothing to discover; but still he was not satisfied. So he cast about for some way to attain his end, and, by the help of the Evil One, he found it.'

Here the innkeeper's wife and daughter, who had doubtless heard the story a hundred times over, drew near and listened breathlessly.

'What, think you,' continued the landlord, 'does this black-souled Caspar do? Does he punish the poor woman within an inch of her life, till she confesses? No. Does he charge Schmidt with having tempted her from her duty, and fight it out with him like a man? No. What else then? I will tell you. He waits till the vigil of St Margaret – her saint's day – when he knows the poor sinful soul is going to confession; and he marches straight to the house of the Père Chessez – the very house where our own Père Chessez is now living – and he finds the good priest at his devotions in his little study, and he says to him: "Father Chessez, my wife is coming to the church this afternoon to make her confession to you."

' "She is," replies the priest.

' "I want you to tell me all she tells you," says Caspar; "and I will wait here till you come back from the church, that I may hear it. Will you do so?"

' "Certainly not," replies the Père Chessez. "You

393

must surely know, Caspar, that we priests are forbidden to reveal the secrets of the confessional."

' "That is nothing to me," says Caspar, with an oath. "I am resolved to know whether my wife is guilty or innocent; and know it I will, by fair means or foul."

' "You shall never know it from me, Caspar," says the Père Chessez, very quietly.

' "Then, by Heavens!" says Caspar, "I'll learn it for myself." And with that he pulls out a heavy horse-pistol from his pocket, and with the butt end of it deals the Père Chessez a tremendous blow upon the head, and then another, and another, till the poor young man lay senseless at his feet. Then Caspar, thinking he had quite killed him, dressed himself in the priest's own soutane and hat; locked the door; put the key in his pocket; and stealing round the back way into the church, shut himself up in the confessional.'

'Then the priest died!' I exclaimed, remembering the epitaph upon the tablet.

'Ay, mein Herr – the Père Chessez died; but not before he had told the story of his assassination, and identified his murderer.'

'And Caspar Rufenacht, I hope, was hanged?'

'Wait a bit, mein Herr, we have not come to that yet. We left Caspar in the confessional, waiting for his wife.'

'And she came?'

'Yes, poor soul! she came.'

'And made her confession?'

'And made her confession, mein Herr.'

'What did she confess?'

The innkeeper shook his head.

'That no one ever knew, save the good God and her murderer.'

'Her murderer!' I exclaimed.

'Ay, just that. Whatever it was that she confessed, she paid for it with her life. He heard her out, at all events, without discovering himself, and let her go home believing that she had received absolution for her sins. Those who met her that afternoon said she seemed unusually bright and happy. As she passed through the town, she went into the shop in the Mongarten Strasse, and bought some ribbons. About half an hour later, my own father met her outside the Basel Thor, walking briskly homewards. He was the last who saw her alive.

'That evening (it was in October, and the days were short), some travellers coming that way into the town heard shrill cries, as of a woman screaming, in the direction of Caspar's farm. But the night was very dark, and the house lay back a little way from the road; so they told themselves it was only some drunken peasant quarrelling with his wife, and passed on. Next morning Caspar Rufenacht came to Rheinfelden, walked very quietly into the Polizei, and gave himself up to justice.

' "I have killed my wife," said he. "I have killed the Père Chessez. And I have committed sacrilege."

'And so, indeed, it was. As for the Frau Margaret, they found her body in an upper chamber, well-nigh hacked to pieces, and the hatchet with which the murder was committed lying beside her on the floor. He had pursued her, apparently, from room to room; for there were pools of blood and handfuls of long light hair, and marks of bloody hands along the walls, all the way from the kitchen to the spot where she lay dead.'

'And so he was hanged?' said I, coming back to my original question.

'Yes, yes,' replied the innkeeper and his woman-kind in chorus. 'He was hanged – of course he was hanged.'

'And it was the shock of this double tragedy that drove the younger Chessez into the church?'

'Just so, mein Herr.'

'Well, he carries it in his face. He looks like a most unhappy man.'

'Nay, he is not that, mein Herr!' exclaimed the landlady. 'He is melancholy, but not unhappy.'

'Well, then, austere.'

'Nor is he austere, except towards himself.'

'True, wife,' said the innkeeper; 'but, as I said, he carries that sort of thing too far. You understand, mein Herr,' he added, touching his forehead with his forefinger, 'the good pastor has let his mind dwell too much upon the past. He is nervous – too nervous, and too low.'

I saw it all now. That terrible light in his eyes was the light of insanity. That stony look in his face was the fixed, hopeless melancholy of a mind diseased.

'Does he know that he is mad?' I asked, as the landlord rose to go.

He shrugged his shoulders and looked doubtful.

'I have not said that the Père Chessez is *mad*, mein Herr,' he replied. 'He has strange fancies sometimes, and takes his fancies for facts – that is all. But I am quite sure that he does not believe himself to be less sane than his neighbours.'

So the innkeeper left me, and I (my head full of the story I had just heard) put on my hat, went out into the marketplace, asked my way to the Basel Thor, and set off to explore the scene of the Frau Margaret's murder.

I found it without difficulty – a long, low-fronted, beetle-browed farmhouse, lying back a meadow's length from the road. There were children playing upon the threshold, a flock of turkeys gobbling about the barn-door, and a big dog sleeping outside his kennel close by. The chimneys, too, were smoking merrily. Seeing these signs of life and cheerfulness, I abandoned all idea of asking to go over the house. I felt that I had no right to carry my morbid curiosity into this peaceful home; so I turned away, and retraced my steps towards Rheinfelden.

It was not yet seven, and the sun had still an hour's course to run. I re-entered the town, strolled back through the street, and presently came again to the Friedrich's Thor and the path leading to the church. An irresistible impulse seemed to drag me back to the place.

Shudderingly, and with a sort of dread that was half longing, I pushed open the churchyard gate and went in. The doors were closed; a goat was browsing among the graves; and the rushing of the Rhine, some three hundred yards away, was distinctly audible in the silence. I looked round for the priest's house – the scene of the first murder; but from this side, at all events, no house was visible. Going round, however, to the back of the church, I saw a gate, a box-bordered path, and, peeping through some trees, a chimney and the roof of a little brown-tiled house.

This, then, was the path along which Caspar Rufenacht, with the priest's blood upon his hands and the priest's gown upon his shoulders, had taken his guilty way to the confessional! How quiet it all looked in the golden evening light! How like the church-path of an English parsonage!

I wished I could have seen something more of the house than that bit of roof and that one chimney. There must, I told myself, be some other entrance – some way round by the road! Musing and lingering thus, I was startled by a quiet voice close against my shoulder, saying: 'A pleasant evening, mein Herr!'

I turned, and found the priest at my elbow. He had come noiselessly across the grass, and was standing between me and the sunset, like a shadow.

'I – I beg your pardon,' I stammered, moving away from the gate. 'I was looking – '

I stopped in some surprise, and indeed with some sense of relief, for it was not the same priest that I had seen in the morning. No two, indeed, could well be more unlike, for this man was small, white-haired, gentle-looking, with a soft, sad smile inexpressibly sweet and winning.

'You were looking at my arbutus?' he said.

I had scarcely observed the arbutus till now, but I bowed and said something to the effect that it was an unusually fine tree.

'Yes,' he replied; 'but I have a rhododendron round at the front that is still finer. Will you come in and see it?'

I said I should be pleased to do so. He led the way, and I followed.

'I hope you like this part of our Rhine-country?' he said, as we took the path through the shrubbery.

'I like it so well,' I replied, 'that if I were to live anywhere on the banks of the Rhine, I should certainly choose some spot on the Upper Rhine between Schaffhausen and Basle.'

'And you would be right,' he said. 'Nowhere is the river so beautiful. Nearer the glaciers it is milky and turbid – beyond Basle it soon becomes muddy. Here we have it blue as the sky – sparkling as champagne. Here is my rhododendron. It stands twelve feet high, and measures as many in diameter. I had more than two hundred blooms upon it last spring.'

When I had duly admired this giant shrub, he took me to a little arbour on a bit of steep green bank overlooking the river, where he invited me to sit down and rest. From hence I could see the porch and part of the front of his little house; but it was all so closely planted round with trees and shrubs that no clear view of it seemed obtainable in any direction. Here we sat for some time chatting about the weather, the approaching vintage, and so forth, and watching the sunset. Then I rose to take my leave.

'I heard of you this evening at the Krone, mein Herr,' he said. 'You were out, or I should have called upon you. I am glad that chance has made us acquainted. Do you remain over tomorrow?'

'No; I must go on tomorrow to Basle,' I answered. And then, hesitating a little, I added: – 'you heard of me, also, I fear, in the church.'

'In the church?' he repeated.

'Seeing the door open, I went in – from curiosity – as a traveller; just to look round for a moment and rest.'

'Naturally.'

'I – I had no idea, however, that I was not alone there. I would not for the world have intruded – '

'I do not understand,' he said, seeing me hesitate. 'The church stands open all day long. It is free to everyone.'

'Ah! I see he has not told you!'

The priest smiled but looked puzzled.

'He? Whom do you mean?'

'The other priest, mon père – your colleague. I regret to have broken in upon his meditations; but I had been so long in the church, and it was all so still and quiet, that it never occurred to me that there might be someone in the confessional.'

The priest looked at me in a strange, startled way.

'In the confessional!' he repeated, with a catching of his breath. 'You saw someone – in the confessional?'

'I am ashamed to say that, having thoughtlessly opened the door – '

'You saw – what did you see?'

'A priest, mon père.'

'A priest! Can you describe him? Should you know him again? Was he pale, and tall, and gaunt, with long black hair?'

'The same, undoubtedly.'

'And his eyes – did you observe anything particular about his eyes?'

'Yes; they were large, wild-looking, dark eyes, with a look in them – a look I cannot describe.'

'A look of terror!' cried the pastor, now greatly agitated. 'A look of terror – of remorse – of despair!'

'Yes, it was a look that might mean all that,' I replied, my astonishment increasing at every word. 'You seem troubled. Who is he?'

But instead of answering my question, the pastor took off his hat, looked up with a radiant, awestruck face, and said: 'All-merciful God, I thank Thee! I thank Thee that I am not mad, and that Thou hast sent this stranger to be my assurance and my comfort!'

Having said these words, he bowed his head, and his lips moved in silent prayer. When he looked up again, his eyes were full of tears.

'My son,' he said, laying his trembling hand upon my arm, 'I owe you an explanation; but I cannot give it to you now. It must wait till I can speak more calmly – till tomorrow, when I must see you again. It involves a terrible story – a story peculiarly painful to myself – enough now if I tell you that I have seen the Thing you describe – seen It many times; and yet, because It has been visible to my eyes alone, I have doubted the evidence of my senses. The good people here believe that much sorrow and meditation have touched my brain. I have half believed it myself till now. But you – you have proved to me that I am the victim of no illusion.'

'But in Heaven's name,' I exclaimed, 'what do you suppose I saw in the confessional?'

'You saw the likeness of one who, guilty also of a double murder, committed the deadly sin of sacrilege in that very spot, more than thirty years ago,' replied the Père Chessez, solemnly.

'Caspar Rufenacht!'

'Ah! you have heard the story? Then I am spared the pain of telling it to you. That is well.'

I bent my head in silence. We walked together without another word to the wicket, and thence round to the churchyard gate. It was now twilight, and the first stars were out.

'Good-night, my son,' said the pastor, giving me his hand. 'Peace be with you.'

As he spoke the words, his grasp tightened – his eyes dilated – his whole countenance became rigid.

'Look!' he whispered. 'Look where it goes!'

I followed the direction of his eyes, and there, with a freezing horror which I have no words to describe, I saw – distinctly saw through the deepening gloom – a tall, dark figure in a priest's soutane and broad-brimmed hat, moving slowly across the path leading from the parsonage to the church. For a moment it seemed to pause – then passed on to the deeper shade, and disappeared.

'You saw it?' said the pastor.

'Yes – plainly.'

He drew a deep breath; crossed himself devoutly; and leaned upon the gate, as if exhausted.

'This is the third time I have seen it this year,' he said. 'Again I thank God for the certainty that I see a visible thing, and that His great gift of reason is mine unimpaired. But I would that He were graciously pleased to release me from the sight – the horror of it is sometimes more than I know how to bear. Good-night.'

With this he again touched my hand; and so, seeing that he wished to be alone, I silently left him. At the Friedrich's Thor I turned and looked back. He was still standing by the churchyard gate, just visible through the gloom of the fast deepening twilight.

I never saw the Père Chessez again. Save his own old servant, I was the last who spoke with him in this world. He died that night – died in his bed, where he was found next morning with his hands crossed upon his breast, and with a placid smile upon his lips, as if he had fallen asleep in the act of prayer.

As the news spread from house to house, the whole town rang with lamentations. The church-bells tolled; the carpenters left their work in the streets; the children, dismissed from school, went home weeping.

' 'Twill be the saddest Kermess in Rheinfelden tomorrow, mein Herr!' said my good host of the Krone, as I shook hands with him at parting. 'We have lost the best of pastors and of friends. He was a saint. If you had come but one day later, you would not have seen him!'

And with this he brushed his sleeve across his eyes, and turned away.

Every shutter was up, every blind down, every door closed, as I passed along the Friedrich's Strasse about midday on my way to Basle; and the few townsfolk I met looked grave and downcast. Then I crossed the bridge and, having shown my passport to the German sentry on the Baden side, I took one long, last farewell look at the little walled town as it lay sleeping in the sunshine by the river – knowing that I should see it no more.

AMBROSE BIERCE

The Moonlit Road

I

Statement of Joel Hetman, Jr

I am the most unfortunate of men. Rich, respected, fairly well educated and of sound health – with many other advantages usually valued by those having them and coveted by those who have them not – I sometimes think that I should be less unhappy if they had been denied me, for then the contrast between my outer and my inner life would not be continually demanding a painful attention. In the stress of privation and the need of effort I might sometimes forget the sombre secret ever baffling the conjecture that it compels.

I am the only child of Joel and Julia Hetman. The one was a well-to-do country gentleman, the other a beautiful and accomplished woman to whom he was passionately attached with what I now know to have been a jealous and exacting devotion. The family home was a few miles from Nashville, Tennessee, a large, irregularly built dwelling of no particular order of architecture, a little way off the road, in a park of trees and shrubbery.

At the time of which I write I was nineteen years old, a student at Yale. One day I received a telegram from my father of such urgency that in compliance with its unexplained demand I left at once for home. At the railway station in Nashville a distant relative awaited me to apprise me of the reason for my recall: my mother had been barbarously murdered – why and by whom none could conjecture, but the circumstances were these: my father had gone to Nashville, intending to return the next afternoon. Something prevented his accomplishing the business in hand, so he returned on the same night, arriving just before the dawn. In his testimony before the coroner he explained that having no latchkey and not caring to disturb the sleeping servants, he had, with no clearly defined intention, gone round to the rear of the house. As he turned an angle of the building, he heard a sound as of a door gently closed, and saw in the darkness, indistinctly, the figure of a man, which instantly disappeared among the trees of the lawn. A hasty pursuit and brief search of the grounds in the belief that the trespasser was someone secretly visiting a servant proving fruitless, he entered at the unlocked door and mounted the stairs to my mother's chamber. Its door was open, and stepping into black darkness he fell headlong over some heavy object on the floor. I may spare myself the details; it was my poor mother, dead of strangulation by human hands!

Nothing had been taken from the house, the servants had heard no sound, and excepting those terrible fingermarks upon the dead woman's throat – dear God! that I might forget them! – no trace of the assassin was ever found.

I gave up my studies and remained with my father, who, naturally, was greatly changed. Always of a sedate, taciturn disposition, he now fell into so deep a dejection that nothing could hold his attention, yet anything – a footfall, the sudden closing of a door – aroused in him a fitful interest; one might have called it an apprehension. At any small surprise of the senses he would start visibly and sometimes turn pale, then relapse into a melancholy apathy deeper than before. I suppose he was what is called a 'nervous wreck'. As to me, I was younger then than now – there is much in that. Youth is Gilead, in which is balm for every wound. Ah, that I might again dwell in that enchanted land! Unacquainted with grief, I knew not how to appraise my bereavement; I could not rightly estimate the strength of the stroke.

One night, a few months after the dreadful event, my father and I walked home from the city. The full moon was about three hours above the eastern horizon; the entire countryside had the solemn stillness of a summer night; our footfalls and the ceaseless song of the katydids were the only sound aloof. Black shadows of bordering trees lay athwart the road, which, in the short reaches between, gleamed a ghostly white. As we approached the gate to our dwelling, whose front was in shadow, and in which no light shone, my father suddenly stopped and clutched my arm, saying, hardly above his breath: 'God! God! what is that?'

'I hear nothing,' I replied.

'But see – see!' he said, pointing along the road, directly ahead.

I said: 'Nothing is there. Come, father, let us go in – you are ill.'

He had released my arm and was standing rigid and motionless in the centre of the illuminated road-way, staring like one bereft of sense. His face in the moonlight showed a pallor and fixity inexpressibly distressing. I pulled gently at his sleeve, but he had forgotten my existence. Presently he began to retire backward, step by step, never for an instant removing his eyes from what he saw, or thought he saw. I turned half round to follow, but stood irresolute. I do not recall any feeling of fear, unless a sudden chill was its physical manifestation. It seemed as if an icy wind had touched my face and enfolded my body from head to foot; I could feel the stir of it in my hair.

At that moment my attention was drawn to a light that suddenly streamed from an upper window of the house: one of the servants, awakened by what mysterious premonition of evil who can say, and in obedience to an impulse that she was never able to name, had lit a lamp. When I turned to look for my father he was gone, and in all the years that have passed no whisper of his fate has come across the borderland of conjecture from the realm of the unknown.

2

Statement of Caspar Grattan

Today I am said to live; tomorrow, here in this room, will lie a senseless shape of clay that all too long was I. If anyone lift the cloth from the face of that unpleasant thing it will be in gratification of a mere morbid curiosity. Some, doubtless, will go further and enquire, 'Who was he?' In this writing I supply the only answer that I am able to make – Caspar Grattan. Surely, that should be enough. The name has served my small need for more than twenty years of a life of unknown length. True, I gave it to myself, but lacking another I had the right. In this world one must have a name; it prevents confusion, even when it does not establish identity. Some, though, are known by numbers, which also seem inadequate distinctions.

One day, for illustration, I was passing along a street of a city, far from here, when I met two men in uniform, one of whom, half pausing and looking curiously into my face, said to his companion, 'That man looks like 767.' Something in the number seemed familiar and horrible. Moved by an uncontrollable impulse, I sprang into a side street and ran until I fell exhausted in a country lane.

I have never forgotten that number, and always it comes to memory attended by gibbering obscenity, peals of joyless laughter, the clang of iron doors. So I say a name, even if self-bestowed, is better than a number. In the register of the potter's field I shall soon have both. What wealth!

Of him who shall find this paper I must beg a little consideration. It is not the history of my life; the knowledge to write that is denied me. This is only a record of broken and apparently unrelated memories, some of them as distinct and sequent as brilliant beads upon a thread, others remote and strange, having the character of crimson dreams with interspaces blank and black – witch-fires glowing still and red in a great desolation.

Standing upon the shore of eternity, I turn for a last look landward over the course by which I came. There are twenty years of footprints fairly distinct, the impressions of bleeding feet. They lead through poverty and pain, devious and unsure, as of one staggering beneath a burden –

Remote, unfriended, melancholy, slow.

Ah, the poet's prophecy of Me – how admirable, how dreadfully admirable!

Backward beyond the beginning of this *via dolorosa* –

this epic of suffering with episodes of sin – I see nothing clearly; it comes out of a cloud. I know that it spans only twenty years, yet I am an old man.

One does not remember one's birth – one has to be told. But with me it was different; life came to me full-handed and dowered me with all my faculties and powers. Of a previous existence I know no more than others, for all have stammering intimations that may be memories and may be dreams. I know only that my first consciousness was of maturity in body and mind – a consciousness accepted without surprise or conjecture. I merely found myself walking in a forest, half-clad, footsore, unutterably weary and hungry. Seeing a farmhouse, I approached and asked for food, which was given me by one who enquired my name. I did not know, yet knew that all had names. Greatly embarrassed, I retreated, and night coming on, lay down in the forest and slept.

The next day I entered a large town which I shall not name. Nor shall I recount further incidents of the life that is now to end – a life of wandering, always and everywhere haunted by an over-mastering sense of crime in punishment of wrong and of terror in punishment of crime. Let me see if I can reduce it to narrative.

I seem once to have lived near a great city, a prosperous planter, married to a woman whom I loved and distrusted. We had, it sometimes seems, one child, a youth of brilliant parts and promise. He is at all times a vague figure, never clearly drawn, frequently altogether out of the picture.

One luckless evening it occurred to me to test my wife's fidelity in a vulgar, commonplace way familiar to everyone who has acquaintance with the literature of fact and fiction. I went to the city, telling my wife that I should be absent until the following afternoon. But I returned before daybreak and went to the rear of the house, purposing to enter by a door with which I had secretly so tampered that it would seem to lock, yet not actually fasten. As I approached it, I heard it gently open and close, and saw a man steal away into the darkness. With murder in my heart, I sprang after him, but he had vanished without even the bad luck of identification. Sometimes now I cannot even persuade myself that it was a human being.

Crazed with jealousy and rage, blind and bestial with all the elemental passions of insulted manhood, I entered the house and sprang up the stairs to the door of my wife's chamber. It was closed, but having tampered with its lock also, I easily entered and despite the black darkness soon stood by the side of her bed. My groping hands told me that although disarranged it was unoccupied.

'She is below,' I thought, 'and terrified by my entrance has evaded me in the darkness of the hall.'

With the purpose of seeking her I turned to leave the room, but took a wrong direction – the right one! My foot struck her, cowering in a corner of the room. Instantly my hands were at her throat, stifling a shriek, my knees were upon her struggling body; and there in the darkness, without a word of accusation or reproach, I strangled her till she died!

There ends the dream. I have related it in the past tense, but the present would be the fitter form, for again and again the sombre tragedy re-enacts itself in my consciousness – over and over I lay the plan, I suffer the confirmation, I redress the wrong. Then all is blank; and afterward the rains beat against the grimy window-panes, or the snows fall upon my scant attire, the wheels rattle in the squalid streets where my life lies in poverty and mean employment. If there is ever sunshine I do not recall it; if there are birds they do not sing.

There is another dream, another vision of the night. I stand among the shadows in a moonlit road. I am aware of another presence, but whose I cannot rightly determine. In the shadow of a great dwelling I catch the gleam of white garments; then the figure of a woman confronts me in the road – my murdered wife! There is death in the face; there are marks upon the throat. The eyes are fixed on mine with an infinite gravity which is not reproach, nor hate, nor menace, nor anything less terrible than recognition. Before this awful apparition I retreat in terror – a terror that is upon me as I write. I can no longer rightly shape the words. See! they –

Now I am calm, but truly there is no more to tell: the incident ends where it began – in darkness and in doubt.

Yes, I am again in control of myself: 'the captain of my soul'. But that is not respite; it is another stage and phase of expiation. My penance, constant in degree, is mutable in kind: one of its variants is tranquillity. After all, it is only a life-sentence. 'To Hell for life' – that is a foolish penalty: the culprit chooses the duration of his punishment. Today my term expires.

To each and all, the peace that was not mine.

*Statement of the late Julia Hetman,
through the medium Bayrolles*

I had retired early and fallen almost immediately into
a peaceful sleep, from which I awoke with that indefinable sense of peril which is, I think, a common
experience in that other, earlier life. Of its unmeaning
character, too, I was entirely persuaded, yet that did
not banish it. My husband, Joel Hetman, was away
from home; the servants slept in another part of the
house. But these were familiar conditions; they had
never before distressed me. Nevertheless, the strange
terror grew so insupportable that conquering my
reluctance to move I sat up and lit the lamp at my
bedside. Contrary to my expectation this gave me no
relief; the light seemed rather an added danger, for I
reflected that it would shine out under the door,
disclosing my presence to whatever evil thing might
lurk outside. You that are still in the flesh, subject to
horrors of the imagination, think what a monstrous
fear that must be which seeks in darkness security
from malevolent existences of the night. That is to
spring to close quarters with an unseen enemy – the
strategy of despair!

Extinguishing the lamp I pulled the bed-clothing
about my head and lay trembling and silent, unable
to shriek, forgetful to pray. In this pitiable state I
must have lain for what you call hours – with us there
are no hours, there is no time.

At last it came – a soft, irregular sound of footfalls
on the stairs! They were slow, hesitant, uncertain, as
of something that did not see its way; to my disordered

412

reason all the more terrifying for that, as the approach of some blind and mindless malevolence to which is no appeal. I even thought that I must have left the hall lamp burning and the groping of this creature proved it a monster of the night. This was foolish and inconsistent with my previous dread of the light, but what would you have? Fear has no brains; it is an idiot. The dismal witness that it bears and the cowardly counsel that it whispers are unrelated. We know this well, we who have passed into the Realm of Terror, who skulk in eternal dusk among the scenes of our former lives, invisible even to ourselves and one another, yet hiding forlorn in lonely places; yearning for speech with our loved ones, yet dumb, and as fearful of them as they of us. Sometimes the disability is removed, the law suspended: by the deathless power of love or hate we break the spell – we are seen by those whom we would warn, console, or punish. What form we seem to them to bear we know not; we know only that we terrify even those whom we most wish to comfort, and from whom we most crave tenderness and sympathy.

Forgive, I pray you, this inconsequent digression by what was once a woman. You who consult us in this imperfect way – you do not understand. You ask foolish questions about things unknown and things forbidden. Much that we know and could impart in our speech is meaningless in yours. We must communicate with you through a stammering intelligence in that small fraction of our language that you yourselves can speak. You think that we are of another world. No, we have knowledge of no world but yours, though for us it holds no sunlight, no warmth, no music, no laughter, no song of birds, nor any companionship. Oh God! what a thing it is to be a ghost, cowering and shivering in an altered world, a prey to apprehension and despair!

No, I did not die of fright: the Thing turned and went away. I heard it go down the stairs, hurriedly, I thought, as if itself in sudden fear. Then I rose to call for help. Hardly had my shaking hand found the doorknob when – merciful heaven! – I heard it returning. Its footfalls as it remounted the stairs were rapid, heavy and loud; they shook the house. I fled to an angle of the wall and crouched upon the floor. I tried to pray. I tried to call the name of my dear husband. Then I heard the door thrown open. There was an interval of unconsciousness, and when I revived I felt a strangling clutch upon my throat – felt my arms feebly beating against something that bore me backward – felt my tongue thrusting itself from between my teeth! And then I passed into this life.

No, I have no knowledge of what it was. The sum of what we knew at death is the measure of what we know afterward of all that went before. Of this existence we know many things, but no new light falls upon any page of that; in memory is written all of it that we can read. Here are no heights of truth overlooking the confused landscape of that dubitable domain. We still dwell in the Valley of the Shadow, lurk in its desolate places, peering from brambles and thickets at its mad, malign inhabitants. How should we have new knowledge of that fading past?

What I am about to relate happened on a night. We know when it is night, for then you retire to your houses and we can venture from our places of concealment to move unafraid about our old homes, to look in at the windows, even to enter and gaze upon

your faces as you sleep. I had lingered long near the
dwelling where I had been so cruelly changed to what
I am, as we do while any that we love or hate remain.
Vainly I had sought some method of manifestation,
some way to make my continued existence and
my great love and poignant pity understood by my
husband and son. Always if they slept they would
wake, or if in my desperation I dared approach them
when they were awake, would turn towards me
the terrible eyes of the living, frightening me by the
glances that I sought from the purpose that I held.

On this night I had searched for them without
success, fearing to find them; they were nowhere in
the house, nor about the moonlit lawn. For, although
the sun is lost to us forever, the moon, full-orbed or
slender, remains to us. Sometimes it shines by night,
sometimes by day, but always it rises and sets, as in
that other life.

I left the lawn and moved in the white light and
silence along the road, aimless and sorrowing.
Suddenly I heard the voice of my poor husband in
exclamations of astonishment, with that of my son in
reassurance and dissuasion; and there by the shadow
of a group of trees they stood – near, so near! Their
faces were towards me, the eyes of the elder man
fixed upon mine. He saw me – at last, at last, he saw
me! In the consciousness of that, my terror fled as a
cruel dream. The death-spell was broken: Love had
conquered Law! Mad with exultation I shouted – I
must have shouted, 'He sees, he sees: he will understand!' Then, controlling myself, I moved forward,
smiling and consciously beautiful, to offer myself to
his arms, to comfort him with endearments, and,
with my son's hand in mine, to speak words that

should restore the broken bonds between the living and the dead.

Alas! alas! his face went white with fear, his eyes were as those of a hunted animal. He backed away from me, as I advanced, and at last turned and fled into the wood – whither, it is not given to me to know.

To my poor boy, left doubly desolate, I have never been able to impart a sense of my presence. Soon he, too, must pass to this Life Invisible and be lost to me for ever.

HENRY JAMES

The Friends of the Friends

I find, as you prophesied, much that's interesting, but
little that helps the delicate question – the possibility
of publication. Her diaries are less systematic than I
hoped; she only had a blessed habit of noting and
narrating. She summarised, she saved; she seldom
appears indeed to have let a good story pass without
catching it on the wing. I allude of course not so
much to things she heard as to things she saw and
felt. She writes sometimes of herself, sometimes of
others, sometimes of the combination. It's under the
last rubric that she's usually most vivid. But it's not,
you'll understand, when she's most vivid that she's
always most publishable. To tell the truth she's fearfully indiscreet, or has at least all the material for
making *me* so. Take as an instance the fragment I
send you after dividing it for your convenience
into several small chapters. It's the contents of a thin
blank-book which I've copied out and which has the
merit of being nearly enough a rounded thing, an
intelligible whole. These pages evidently date from
years ago. I've read with liveliest wonder the statement they so circumstantially make and done my best
to swallow the prodigy they leave to be inferred. These
things would be striking, wouldn't they? to any reader;
but can you imagine for a moment my placing such a
document before the world, even though, as if she
herself desired the world should have the benefit of it,
she has given her friends neither names nor initials?

Have you any sort of clue to their identity? I leave her the floor.

1

I know perfectly of course that I brought it on myself; but that doesn't make it any better. I was the first to speak of her to him – he had never even heard her mentioned. Even if I had happened not to speak, someone else would have made up for it: I tried afterwards to find comfort in that reflection. But the comfort of reflections is thin: the only comfort that counts in life is not to have been a fool. That's a beatitude I shall doubtless never enjoy. 'Why you ought to meet her and talk it over' is what I immediately said. 'Birds of a feather flock together.' I told him who she was and that they were birds of a feather because if he had had in his youth a strange adventure she had had about the same time just such another. It was well known to her friends – an incident she was constantly called on to describe. She was charming clever pretty unhappy; but it was none the less the thing to which she had originally owed her reputation.

Being at the age of eighteen somewhere abroad with an aunt, she had had a vision of one of her parents at the moment of death. The parent was in England hundreds of miles away and so far as she knew neither dying nor dead. It was by day, in the museum of some great foreign town. She had passed alone, in advance of her companions, into a small room containing some famous work of art and occupied at that moment by two other persons. One of these was the old custodian; the second, before observing him, she took for a stranger, a tourist. She was merely conscious that he was bareheaded and seated on a bench. The instant her eyes rested on him however she beheld to her amazement her father, who, as if he had long waited for her, looked at her in singular distress and an impatience akin to reproach. She rushed to him with a bewildered cry, 'Papa, what *is* it?' but this was followed by an exhibition of still livelier feeling when on her movement he simply vanished, leaving the custodian and her relations, who were by that time at her heels, to gather round her in dismay. These persons, the official, the aunt, the cousins, were therefore in a manner witnesses of the fact – the fact at least of the impression made on her; and there was the further testimony of a doctor who was attending one of the party and to whom it was immediately afterwards communicated. He gave her a remedy for hysterics, but said to the aunt privately: 'Wait and see if something doesn't happen at home.' Something *had* happened – the poor father, suddenly and violently seized, had died that morning. The aunt, the mother's sister, received before the day was out a telegram announcing the event and requesting her to prepare her niece for it. Her niece was already prepared, and the girl's sense of this visitation remained of course indelible. We had all, as her friends, had it conveyed to us and had conveyed it creepily to each other. Twelve years had elapsed, and as a woman who had made an unhappy marriage and lived apart from her husband she had become interesting from other sources; but since the name she now bore was a name frequently borne, and since moreover her judicial separation, as things were going, could hardly count as a distinction, it was usual to qualify her as 'the one, you know, who saw her father's ghost'.

As for him, dear man, he had seen his mother's – so there you are! I had never heard of that till this occasion on which our closer, our pleasanter acquaintance led him, through some turn in the subject of our talk, to mention it and to inspire me in so doing with the impulse to let him know that he had a rival in the field – a person with whom he could compare notes. Later on his story became for him, perhaps because of my unduly repeating it, likewise a convenient worldly label; but it hadn't a year before been the ground on which he was introduced to me. He had other merits, just as she, poor thing, had others. I can honestly say that I was quite aware of them from the first – I discovered them sooner than he discovered mine. I remember how it struck me even at the time that his sense of mine was quickened by my having been able to match, though indeed not straight from my own experience, his curious anecdote. It dated, this anecdote, as hers did, from some dozen years before – a year in which, at Oxford, he had for some reason of his own been staying into the 'Long'. He had been in the August afternoon on the river. Coming back into his room while it was still distinct daylight he found his mother standing there as if her eyes had been fixed on the door. He had had a letter from her that morning out of Wales, where she was staying with her father. At the sight of him she smiled with extraordinary radiance and extended her arms to him, and then as he sprang forward and joyfully opened his own she vanished from the place. He wrote to her that night, telling her what had happened; the letter had been carefully preserved. The next morning he heard of her death. He was through this chance of our talk extremely struck with the little prodigy I was able to produce for him. He had never encountered another case. Certainly they ought to meet, my friend and he; certainly they would have something in common. I would arrange this, wouldn't I? – if *she* didn't mind; for himself he didn't mind in the least. I had promised to speak to her of the matter as soon as possible, and within the week I was able to do so. She 'minded' as little as he; she was perfectly willing to see him. And yet no meeting would occur – as meetings are commonly understood.

2

That's just half my tale – the extraordinary way it was hindered. This was the fault of a series of accidents; but the accidents, persisting for years, became, to me and to others, a subject of mirth with either party. They were droll enough at first, then they grew rather a bore. The odd thing was that both parties were amenable: it wasn't a case of their being indifferent, much less of their being indisposed. It was one of the caprices of chance, aided I suppose by some rather settled opposition of their interests and habits. His were centred in his office, his eternal inspectorship, which left him small leisure, constantly calling him away and making him break engagements. He liked society, but found it everywhere and took it at a run. She was on her side practically suburban: she lived at Richmond and never went 'out'. She was a woman of distinction, but not of fashion, and felt, as people said, her situation. Decidedly proud and rather whimsical, she lived her life as she had planned it. There were things one could do for her, but one couldn't make her come to one's parties. One went indeed a little more than seemed quite convenient to hers, which consisted of her cousin, a cup of tea and the view. The tea was good; but the view was familiar, though perhaps not, like the cousin – a disagreeable old maid who had been of the group at the museum and with whom she now lived – offensively so. This connection with an inferior relative, which had partly an economic motive – she proclaimed her companion a marvellous manager – was one of those little perversities we had to forgive her. Another was her estimate of the proprieties created by her rupture with her husband. That was extreme – many persons called it even morbid. She made no advances; she cultivated scruples; she suspected, or I should perhaps rather say she remembered, slights: she was one of the few women I've known whom the particular predicament had rendered modest rather than bold. Dear thing, she had some delicacy! Especially marked were the limits she set to possible attentions from men: it was always her thought that her husband only waited to pounce on her. She discouraged if she didn't forbid the visits of male persons not senile: she said she could never be too careful.

When I first mentioned to her that I had a friend whom fate had distinguished in the same weird way as herself I put her quite at liberty to say, 'Oh bring him out to see me!' I should probably have been able to bring him, and a situation perfectly innocent or at any rate comparatively simple would have been created. But she uttered no such word; she only said: 'I must meet him certainly; yes, I shall look out for him!' That caused the first delay, and meanwhile various things happened. One of them was that as time went on she made, charming as she was, more and more friends, and that it regularly befell that these friends were sufficiently also friends of his to bring him up in conversation. It was odd that without belonging, as it were, to the same world or, according to the horrid term, the same set, my baffled pair should have happened in so many cases to fall in with the same people and make them join in the droll chorus. She had friends who didn't know each other but who inevitably and punctually recommended *him*. She had also a sort of originality, the intrinsic interest, that led her to be kept by each of us as a private resource, cultivated jealously, more or less in secret, as a person one didn't meet in society, whom it was not for everyone – whom it was not for the vulgar – to approach, and with whom therefore acquaintance was particularly difficult and particularly precious. We saw her separately, with appointments and conditions, and found it made on the whole for harmony not to tell each other. Somebody had always a note from her still later than somebody else. There was some silly woman who for a long time, among the underprivileged, owed to three simple visits to Richmond a reputation for being intimate with 'lots of awfully clever out-of-the-way people'.

Everyone has had friends it has seemed a happy thought to bring together, and everyone remembers that his happiest thoughts have not been his greatest successes; but I doubt if there ever was a case in which the failure was in such direct proportion to the quantity of influence set in motion. It's really perhaps here the quantity of influence that was most remarkable. My lady and my gentleman pronounced it to me and others a subject for a roaring farce. The reason first given had with time dropped out of sight and fifty better ones flourished on top of it. They were so awfully alike: they had the same ideas and tricks and tastes, the same prejudices and superstitions and heresies; they said the same things and sometimes did them; they liked and disliked the same persons and places, the same books, authors and styles; there were touches of resemblance even in their looks and features. It established much of a propriety that they were in common parlance 'nice' and almost equally handsome. But the great sameness, for wonder and chatter, was their rare perversity in regard to being photographed. They were the only persons ever heard of who had never been 'taken' and who had a passionate objection to it. They just wouldn't be – no, not for anything anyone could say. I loudly complained of this; him in particular I had so vainly desired to be able to show on my drawing-room chimney-piece in a Bond Street frame. It was at any rate the very liveliest of all the reasons why they ought to know each other – all the lively reasons reduced to naught by the strange law that made them bang so many doors in each other's face, made them the buckets in the well, the two ends of the seesaw, the two parties in the State, so that when one was up the other was down, when one was out the other was in; neither by any possibility entering a house till the other had left it or leaving it all unawares till the other was at hand. They only arrived when they had been given up, which was also precisely when they departed. They were in a word alternate and incompatible; they missed each other with an inveteracy that could be explained only by its being preconcerted. It was however so far from preconcerted that it had ended – literally after several years – by disappointing and annoying them. I don't think their curiosity was lively till it had been proved utterly vain. A great deal was of course done to help them, but it merely laid wires for them to trip. To give examples I should have to have taken notes; but I happen to remember that neither had ever been able to dine on the right occasion. The right occasion for each was the occasion that would be wrong for the other. On the wrong one they were most punctual, and there were never any but the wrong ones. The very elements conspired and the constitution of man re-enforced them. A cold, a headache, a bereavement, a storm, a fog, an earthquake, a cataclysm, infallibly intervened. The whole business was beyond a joke.

Yet as a joke it had still to be taken, though one couldn't help feeling that the joke had made the situation serious, had produced on the part of each a consciousness, an awkwardness, a positive dread of the last accident of all, the only one with any freshness left, the accident that *would* bring them together. The final effect of its predecessors had been to kindle this instinct. They were quite ashamed – perhaps even a little of each other. So much preparation, so much frustration: what indeed could be good enough for it all to lead up to? A mere meeting would be mere flatness. Did I see them at the end of years, they often asked, just stupidly confronted? If they were bored by the joke they might easily be bored by something else. They made exactly the same reflections, and each in some manner was sure to hear of the other's. I really think it was this peculiar diffidence that finally con-trolled the situation. I mean that if they had failed for the first year or two because they couldn't help it, they kept up the habit because they had – what shall I

call it? – grown nervous. It really took some lurking
volition to account for anything both so regular and
so ridiculous.

3

When to crown our long acquaintance I accepted his
renewed offer of marriage, it was humorously said, I
know, that I had made the gift of his photograph a
condition. This was so far true that I refused to give
him mine without it. At any rate I had him at last, in
his high distinction, on the chimney-piece, where the
day she called to congratulate me she came nearer
than she had ever done to seeing him. He had in
being taken set her an example that I invited her to
follow; he had sacrificed his perversity – wouldn't she
sacrifice hers? She too must give me something on
my engagement – wouldn't she give me the companion-piece? She laughed and shook her head; she
had headshakes whose impulse seemed to come from
as far away as the breeze that stirs a flower. The
companion-piece to the portrait of my future husband
was the portrait of his future wife. She had taken her
stand – she could depart from it as little as she could
explain it. It was a prejudice, an *entêtement*, a vow –
she would live and die unphotographed. Now too she
was alone in that state: this was what she liked; it
made her so much more original. She rejoiced in the
fall of her late associate and looked for a long time at
his picture, about which she made no memorable
remark, though she even turned it over to see the
back. About our engagement she was charming – full
of cordiality and sympathy. 'You've known him even
longer than I've *not*,' she said, 'and that seems a very

long time.' She understood how we had jogged over
hill and dale and how inevitable it was that we should
now rest together. I'm definite about all this because
what followed is so strange that it's kind of a relief to
me to mark the point up to which our relations were
as natural as ever. It was I myself who in a sudden
madness altered and destroyed them. I see now that
she gave me no pretext and that I only found one in
the way she looked at the fine face in the Bond Street
frame. How then would I have had her look at it?
What I had wanted from the first was to make her
care for him. Well, that was what I still wanted – up
to the moment of her having promised me she would
on this occasion really aid me to break the silly spell
that had kept them asunder. I had arranged with him
to do his part if she would as triumphantly do hers. I
was on a different footing now – I was on a footing to
answer for him. I would positively engage that at five
on the following Saturday he should be on that spot.
He was out of town on pressing business, but, pledged
to keep his promise to the letter, would return on
purpose and in abundant time. 'Are you perfectly
sure?' I remember she asked, looking grave and considering: I thought she had turned a little pale. She
was tired, she was indisposed: it was a pity he was to
see her after all at so poor a moment. If he only *could*
have seen her five years before! However, I replied
that this time I was sure and that success therefore
depended simply on herself. At five o'clock on the
Saturday she would find him in a particular chair I
pointed out, the one in which he usually sat and in
which – though this I didn't mention – he had been
sitting when, the week before, he put the question of
our future to me in the way that had brought me

427

round. She looked at it in silence, just as she had looked at his photograph, while I repeated for the twentieth time that it was too preposterous one shouldn't somehow succeed in introducing one's dearest friend to one's second self. '*Am* I your dearest friend?' she asked with a smile that for a moment brought back her beauty. I replied by pressing her to my bosom; after which she said, 'Well, I'll come. I'm extraordinarily afraid, but you may count on me.'

When she left me I began to wonder what she was afraid of, for she had spoken as if she fully meant it. The next day, late in the afternoon, I had three lines from her: she had found on getting home the announcement of her husband's death. She hadn't seen him for seven years, but she wished me to know it in this way before I should hear of it in another. It made however in her life, strange and sad to say, so little difference that she would scrupulously keep her appointment. I rejoiced for her – I supposed it would make at least the difference of her having more money; but even in this diversion, far from forgetting she had said that she was afraid, I seemed to catch sight of a reason for her being so. Her fear, as the evening went on, became contagious, and the contagion took in my breast the form of a sudden panic. It wasn't jealousy – it was just the dread of jealousy. I called myself a fool for not having been quiet till we were man and wife. After that I should somehow feel secure. It was only a question of waiting another month – a trifle surely for people who had waited so long. It had been plain enough that she was nervous, and now she was free her nervousness wouldn't be less. What was it therefore but a sharp foreboding? She had been hitherto the victim of interference, but it was quite possible she would henceforth be the source of it. The victim in that case would be my simple self. What had the interference been but the finger of Providence pointing out a danger? The danger was of course for poor *me*. It had been kept at bay by a series of accidents unexampled in their frequency; but the reign of accidents was now visibly at an end. I had an intimate conviction that both parties would keep the tryst. It was more and more impressed on me that they were approaching, converging. They were like the seekers for the hidden object in the game of blindfold; they had one and the other begun to 'burn'. We had talked about breaking the spell; well, it would be effectually broken – unless indeed it should merely take another form and overdo their encounters as it had overdone their escapes. This was something I couldn't sit still for thinking of; it kept me awake – at midnight I was full of unrest. At last I felt there was only one way of laying the ghost. If the reign of accident was over I must just take up the succession. I sat down and wrote a hurried note which would meet him on his return and which as the servants had gone to bed I sallied forth bareheaded into the empty gusty street to drop into the nearest pillar-box. It was to tell him that I shouldn't be able to be at home in the afternoon as I had hoped and that he must postpone his visit until dinner-time. This was an implication that he would find me alone.

4

When accordingly at five she presented herself I naturally felt false and base. My act had been a momentary madness, but I had at least, as they say, to live up to it. She remained an hour; he of course never came; and I could only persist in my perfidy. I had thought it best to let her come; singular as this now seems to me, I held it diminished my guilt. Yet as she sat there so visibly white and weary, stricken with a sense of everything her husband's death had opened up, I felt a really piercing pang of pity and remorse. If I didn't tell her on the spot what I had done it was because I was too ashamed. I feigned astonishment – I feigned it to the end; I protested that if ever I had had confidence I had had it that day. I blush as I tell my story – I take it as my penance. There was nothing indignant I didn't say about him; I invented suppositions, attenuations; I admitted in stupefaction, as the hands of the clock travelled, that their luck hadn't turned. She smiled at this vision of their 'luck', but she looked anxious – she looked unusual: the only thing that kept me up was the fact that, oddly enough, she wore mourning – no great depths of crape, but simple and scrupulous black. She had in her bonnet three small black feathers. She carried a little muff of astrachan. This put me, by the aid of some acute reflection, in the right. She had written to me that the sudden event made no difference for her, but apparently it made as much difference as that. If she was inclined to the usual forms why didn't she observe that of not going out the next day or two to tea? There was someone she wanted so much to see that she couldn't wait until her husband was buried. Such a betrayal of eagerness made me hard and cruel enough to practise my odious deceit, though at the same time, as the hour waxed and waned, I suspected in her something deeper still than disappointment and something less successfully concealed. I mean a strange underlying relief, the soft low emission of the breath that comes when a danger is past. What happened as she spent her barren hour with me was that at last she gave him up. She let him go for ever. She made the most graceful joke of it that I've ever seen made of anything; but it was for all that a great date in her life. She spoke with mild gaiety of all the other vain times, the long game of hide-and-seek, the unprecedented queerness of such a relation. For it *was*, or had been, a relation, wasn't it, hadn't it? That was just the absurd part of it. When she got up to go I said to her that it was more of a relation than ever, but I hadn't the face after what had occurred to propose to her for the present another opportunity. It was plain that the only valid opportunity would be my accomplished marriage. Of course she would be at my wedding? It was even to be hoped that *he* would.

'If *I* am, he won't be!' – I remember the high quaver and the little break of her laugh. I admitted there might be something in that. The thing therefore was to get us safely married first. 'That won't help us. Nothing will help us!' she said as she kissed me farewell. 'I shall never, never see him!' It was with those words she left me.

I could bear her disappointment as I've called it; but when a couple hours later I received him at dinner I discovered I couldn't bear his. The way my manoeuvre might have affected him hadn't been particularly present to me; but the result of it was the first word of reproach that had ever dropped from him. I say 'reproach' because that expression is scarcely too strong for the terms in which he conveyed to me his surprise that under the extraordinary circumstances I shouldn't have found some means not to deprive him of such an occasion. I might really have managed either not to be obliged to go out or to let their meeting take place all the same. They would probably have got on, in my drawing-room, well enough without me. At this I quite broke down – I confessed my iniquity and the miserable reason of it. I hadn't put her off and I hadn't gone out; she had been there and, after waiting for him an hour, had departed in the belief that he had been absent by his own fault.

'She must think me a precious brute!' he exclaimed. 'Did she say of me' – and I remember the just perceptible catch of breath in his pause – 'what she had a right to say?'

'I assure you she said nothing that showed the least feeling. She looked at your photograph, she even turned round the back of it, on which your address happens to be inscribed. Yet it provoked her to no demonstration. She doesn't care as much as all that.'

'Then why were you afraid of her?'

'It wasn't of her I was afraid. It was of you.'

'Did you think that I'd be so sure to fall in love with her? You never alluded to such a possibility before,' he went on as I remained silent. 'Admirable person as you pronounced her, that wasn't the light in which you showed her to me.'

'Do you mean that if it *had* been you'd have managed by now to catch a glimpse of her? I didn't fear things then,' I added. 'I hadn't the same reason.'

He kissed me at this, and when I remembered that she had done so an hour or two before I felt for an instant as if he were taking from my lips the very pressure of hers. In spite of kisses the incident had shed a certain chill, and I suffered horribly from the sense that he had seen me guilty of a fraud. He had seen it only through my frank avowal, but I was as unhappy as if I had a stain to efface. I couldn't get over the manner of his looking at me when I spoke of her apparent indifference to his not having come. For the first time since I had known him he seemed to have expressed a doubt of my word. Before we parted I told him that I'd undeceive her – start the first thing in the morning for Richmond and there let her know that he had been blameless. At this he kissed me again. I'd expiate my sin, I said; I'd humble myself in the dust; I'd confess and ask to be forgiven. At this he kissed me once more.

5

In the train the next day this struck me as a good deal for him to have consented to; but my purpose was firm enough to carry me on. I mounted the long hill to where the view begins, and then I knocked at her door. I was a trifle mystified by the fact that her blinds were still drawn, reflecting that if in the stress of my compunction I had come early I had certainly yet allowed people time to get up.

'At home, mum? She has left home for ever.'

I was extraordinarily startled by this announcement of the elderly parlour-maid. 'She has gone away?'

'She's dead, mum, please.' Then as I gasped at the horrible word: 'She died last night.'

The loud cry that escaped me sounded even in my own ears like some harsh violation of the hour. I felt for the moment as if I had killed her; I turned faint and saw through a vagueness that woman hold out her arms to me. Of what next happened I've no recollection, nor of anything but my friend's poor stupid cousin, in a darkened room, after an interval that I suppose very brief, sobbing at me in a smothered accusatory way. I can't say how long it took for me to understand, to believe and then to press back with an immense effort that pang of responsibility which, superstitiously, insanely, had been at first almost all I was conscious of. The doctor, after the fact, had been superlatively wise and clear: he was satisfied of a long-latent weakness of the heart, determined probably years before by the agitations and terrors to which her marriage had introduced her. She had had in those days cruel scenes with her husband, she had been in fear of her life. All emotion, everything in the nature of anxiety and suspense had been after that to be strongly deprecated, as in her marked cultivation of a quiet life she was evidently well aware; but who could say that anyone, especially a 'real lady', might be successfully protected from *every* little rub? She had had one a day or two before in the news of her husband's death – since there were shocks of all kinds, not only those of grief and surprise. For that matter she had never dreamed of so near a release: it had looked uncommonly as if he would live as long as herself. Then in the evening, in town, she had manifestly had some misadventure: something must have happened there that it would be imperative to clear up. She had come back very late – it was past eleven o'clock, and on being met in the hall by her cousin, who was extremely anxious, had allowed she was tired and must rest a moment before mounting the stairs. They had passed together into the dining-room, her companion proposing a glass of wine and bustling to pour it out. This took but a moment, and when my informant turned round our poor friend had not had time to seat herself. Suddenly, with a small moan that was barely audible, she dropped upon the sofa. She was dead. What unknown 'little rub' had dealt her the blow? What concussion, in the name of wonder, *had* awaited her in town? I mentioned immediately the one thinkable ground of disturbance – her having failed to meet at my house, to which by invitation she had come at five o'clock, the gentleman I was to be married to, who had been accidentally kept away and with whom she had no acquaintance whatever. This obviously counted for little; but something else might easily have occurred: nothing in the London streets was more possible than an accident, especially an accident in those desperate cabs. What had she done, where had she gone on leaving my house? I had taken for granted that she had gone straight home. We both presently remembered that in her excursions to town she sometimes, for convenience, for refreshment, spent an hour or two at the 'Gentlewomen', the quiet little ladies' club, and I promised that it should be my first care to make at that establishment an earnest appeal. Then we entered the dim and dreadful chamber where she lay locked up in death and where, asking after a little to be left alone with her, I remained for half an hour. Death had made her, had kept her beautiful; but I felt above all, as I knelt at her bed, that it had made her, had kept her silent. It had turned the key on something I was concerned to know.

On my return from Richmond and after another duty had been performed I drove to his chambers. It was the first time, but I had often wanted to see them. On the staircase, which, as the house contained twenty sets of rooms, was unrestrictedly public, I met his servant, who went back with me and ushered me in. At the sound of my entrance he appeared in the doorway of a farther room, and the instant we were alone I produced my news: 'She's dead!'

'Dead?' He was tremendously struck, and I noticed he had no need to ask whom, in this abruptness, I meant.

'She died last evening – just after leaving me.'

He stared with the strangest expression, his own eyes searching mine as for a trap. 'Last evening – after leaving you?' He repeated my words in stupefaction. Then he brought out, so that it was in stupefaction I heard, 'Impossible! I saw her.'

'You "saw" her?'

'On that spot – where you stand.'

This called back to me after an instant, as if to help me take it in, the great warning of his youth. 'In the hour of death – I understand: as you so beautifully saw your mother.'

'Ah *not as* I saw my mother – not that way, not that way!' He was deeply moved by my news – far more moved, it was plain, than he would have been the day before: it gave me a vivid sense that, as I had then said to myself, there was indeed a relation between them and that he had actually been face to face with her. Such an idea, by its reassertion of his extraordinary privilege, would have suddenly presented him as painfully abnormal hadn't he vehemently insisted on the difference. 'I saw her living. I saw her to speak to her. I saw her as I see you now.'

It's remarkable that for a moment, though only for a moment, I found relief in the more personal, as it were, but also the more natural, of the two odd facts. The next, as I embraced this image of her having come to him on leaving me and of just what it accounted for in the disposal of her time, I demanded with a shade of harshness of which I was aware: 'What on earth did she come for?'

He had now had a moment to think – to recover himself and judge of effects, so that if it was still with excited eyes he spoke, he showed a conscious redness and made an inconsequent attempt to smile away the gravity of my words. 'She came just to see me. She came – after what had passed at your house – so that we *should*, nevertheless at last meet. The impulse seemed to me exquisite, and that was the way I took it.'

I looked round the room where she had been – where she had been and I never had till now. 'And was the way you took it the way she expressed it?'

'She only expressed it by being here and by letting me look at her. That was enough!' he cried with an extraordinary laugh.

I wondered more and more. 'You mean she didn't speak to you?'

'She said nothing. She only looked at me as I looked at her.'

'And you didn't speak either?'

He gave me again his painful smile. 'I thought of *you*. The situation was very delicate. I used the finest tact. But she saw she had pleased me.' He even repeated his dissonant laugh.

'She evidently "pleased" you!' Then I thought a moment. 'How long did she stay?'

'How can I say? It seemed twenty minutes, but it was probably a good deal less.'

'Twenty minutes of silence!' I began to have my definite view and now in fact quite to clutch at it. 'Do you know you're telling me a thing positively monstrous?'

He had been standing with his back to the fire; at this, with a pleading look, he came to me. 'I beseech you, dearest, to take it kindly.'

I could take it kindly, and I signified as much; but I couldn't somehow, as he rather awkwardly opened his arms, let him draw me to him. So there fell between us for an appreciable time the discomfort of a great silence.

6

He broke it by presently saying: 'There's absolutely no doubt of her death?'

'Unfortunately no. I've just risen from my knees by the bed where they've laid her out.'

He fixed his eyes hard on the floor; then he raised them to mine. 'How does she look?'

'She looks – at peace.'

He turned away again while I watched him; but after a moment he began: 'At what hour then – ?'

'It must have been near midnight. She dropped as she reached her house – from an affection of the heart which she knew herself and her physician knew her to have, but of which, patiently, bravely, she had never spoken to me.'

He listened intently and for a minute was unable to speak. At last he broke out with an accent of which the almost boyish confidence, the really sublime simplicity, rings in my ears as I write: 'Wasn't she *wonderful*!' Even at the time I was able to do it justice enough to answer that I had always told him so; but the next minute, as if after speaking he had caught a glimpse of what he might have made me feel, he went on quickly: 'You can easily understand that if she didn't get home till midnight – '

I instantly took him up. 'There was plenty of time for you to have seen her? How so,' I asked, 'when you didn't leave my house until late? I don't remember the very moment – I was preoccupied. But you know that though you said you had lots to do you sat for some time after dinner. She, on her side, was all the evening at the "Gentlewomen", I've just come from there – I've ascertained. She had tea there; she remained a long long time.'

'What was she doing there all that long long time?'

I saw him eager to challenge at every step my account of the matter; and the more he showed this the more I was moved to emphasise that version, to prefer with apparent perversity an explanation which only deepened the marvel and the mystery, but which, of the two prodigies it had to choose from, my reviving jealousy found easiest to accept. He stood there pleading with a candour that now seems to me beautiful for the privilege of having in spite of supreme defeat known the living woman; while I, with a passion I wonder at today, though it still smoulders in a manner in its ashes, could only reply that, through a strange gift shared by her with his mother and on her own side equally hereditary, the miracle of his youth had been renewed for him, the miracle of hers for her. She had been to him – yes, and by an impulse as charming as he liked; but oh she hadn't been in the body! It was a simple question of evidence. I had had, I maintained, a definite statement of what she had done – most of the time – at the little club. The place was almost empty, but the servants had noticed her. She had sat motionless in a deep chair by the drawing-room fire; she had leaned back her head, she had closed her eyes, she had seemed softly to sleep.

'I see. But till what o'clock?'

'There,' I was obliged to answer, 'the servants fail me a little. The portress in particular is unfortunately a fool, even though she too is supposed to be a gentlewoman. She was evidently at that period of time, without a substitute and against regulations, absent for some little time from the cage in which it's her business to watch the comings and goings. She's muddled, she palpably prevaricates; so I can't positively, from her observation, give you an hour. But it was remarked towards half-past ten that our poor friend was no longer in the club.'

It suited him down to the ground. 'She came straight here, and from here she went straight to the train.'

'She couldn't have run it so close,' I declared. 'That was a thing she particularly never did.'

'There was no need of running it close, my dear – she had plenty of time. Your memory's at fault about my having left you late: I left you, as it happens, unusually early. I'm sorry my stay with you seemed long, for I was back here by ten.'

'To put yourself into your slippers,' I retorted, 'and fall asleep in your chair. You slept till morning – you saw her in a dream!' He looked at me in silence and with sombre eyes – eyes that showed me he had some irritation to repress. Presently I went on: 'You had a visit, at an extraordinary hour, from a lady – *soit*: nothing in the world's more probable. But there are ladies and ladies. How in the name of goodness, if she was unannounced and dumb and you had into the bargain never seen the least portrait of her – how could you identify the person we're speaking of?'

'Haven't I to absolute satiety heard her described? I'll describe her for you in every particular.'

'Don't!' I cried with a promptness that made him laugh once more. I coloured at this, but I continued: 'Did your servant introduce her?'

'He wasn't here – he's always away when he's wanted. One of the features of this big house is that from the street-door the different floors are accessible practically without challenge. My servant makes love to a young person employed in the rooms above these, and he had a long bout of it last evening. When he's out on that job he leaves my outer door, on the staircase, so much ajar as to enable him to slip back without a sound. The door only requires a little push. She pushed it – that simply took a little courage.'

'A little? It took tons! And it took all sorts of impossible calculations.'

'Well, she had them – she made them. Mind you, I don't deny for a moment,' he added, 'that it was very very wonderful!'

Something in his tone kept me a time from trusting myself to speak. At last I said: 'How did she come to know where you live?'

'By remembering the address on the little label the shop-people happily left sticking to the frame I had had made for my photograph.'

'And how was she dressed?'

'In mourning, my own dear. No great depths of crape, but simple and scrupulous black. She had in her bonnet three small black feathers. She carried a little muff of astrachan. She has near the left eye,' he continued, 'a tiny vertical scar – '

I stopped him short. 'The mark of a caress from her husband.' Then I added: 'How close you must have been to her!' He made no answer to this, and I thought he blushed, observing which I broke straight off. 'Well, goodbye.'

'You won't stay a little?' He came to me again tenderly, and this time I suffered him. 'Her visit had its beauty,' he murmured as he held me, 'but yours has a greater one.'

I let him kiss me, but I remembered, as I had remembered the day before, that the last kiss she had given, as I supposed, in this world had been for the lips he touched. 'I'm life, you see,' I answered. 'What you saw last night was death.'

'It was life – it was life!'

He spoke with a soft stubbornness – I disengaged myself. We stood looking at each other hard. 'You describe the scene – so far as you describe it at all – in terms that are incomprehensible. She was in the room before you knew it?'

'I looked up from my letter-writing – at that table under the lamp I had been wholly absorbed in it – and she stood before me.'

'Then what did you do?'

'I sprang up with an ejaculation, and she, with a smile, laid her finger, ever so warningly, yet with a delicate dignity, to her lips. I knew it meant silence, but the strange thing was that it seemed immediately to explain and justify her. We at any rate stood for a time that, as I told you, I can't calculate, face to face. It was just as you and I stand now.'

'Simply staring?'

442

He shook an impatient head. 'Ah! *we're* not staring!'

'Yes, but we're talking.'

'Well, *we* were – after a fashion.' He lost himself in the memory of it. 'It was as friendly as this.' I had on my tongue's end to ask if that was saying much for it, but I made the point instead that what they had evidently done was gaze in mutual admiration. Then I asked if recognition of her had been immediate. 'Not quite,' he replied, 'for of course I didn't expect her; but it came to me long before she went who she was – who she could only be.'

I thought a little. 'And how did she at last go?'

'Just as she arrived. The door was open behind her and she passed out.'

'Was she rapid – slow?'

'Rather quick. But looking behind her,' he smiled to add. 'I let her go, for I perfectly knew I was to take it as she wished.'

I was conscious of exhaling a long vague sigh. 'Well, you must take it now as *I* wish – you must let *me* go.'

At this he drew near me again, detaining and persuading me, declaring with all due gallantry that I was a very different matter. I'd have given anything to have been able to ask him if he had touched her, but the words refused to form themselves: I knew to the last tenth of a tone how horrid and vulgar they'd sound. I said something else – I forget exactly what; it was feebly tortuous and intended, meanly enough, to make him tell me without my putting the question. But he didn't tell me; he only repeated, as from a glimpse of the propriety of soothing and consoling me, the sense of his declaration of some minutes before – the assurance that she was indeed exquisite, as I had always insisted, but that I was his 'real' friend

443

and his very own for ever. This led me to reassert, in the spirit of my previous rejoinder, that I had at least the merit of being alive; which in turn drew from him again the flash of contradiction I dreaded. 'Oh *she* was alive! She was, she was!'

'She was dead, she was dead!' I asseverated with an energy, a determination it should *be* so, which comes back to me now almost as grotesque. But the sound of the word as it rang out filled me suddenly with horror, and all the natural emotion the meaning of it might have evoked in other conditions gathered and broke in a flood. It rolled over me that here was a great affection quenched and how much I had loved and trusted her. I had a vision at the same time of the lonely beauty of her end. 'She's gone – she's lost to us for ever!' I burst into sobs.

'That's exactly what I feel,' he exclaimed, speaking with extreme kindness and pressing me to him for comfort. 'She's gone; she's lost to us for ever: so what does it matter now?' He bent over me, and when his face had touched mine I scarcely knew if it were wet with my tears or his own.

7

It was my theory, my conviction, it became, as I may say, my attitude, that they had still never 'met'; and it was just on this ground I felt it generous to ask him to stand with me at her grave. He did so very modestly and tenderly, and I assumed, though he himself clearly cared nothing for the danger, that the solemnity of the occasion, largely made up of persons who had known them both and had a sense of the long joke, would sufficiently deprive his presence of all light association. On the question of what had happened the evening of her death little more passed between us; I had been taken by a horror of the element of evidence. On either hypothesis it was gross and prying. He on his side lacked producible corroboration – everything, that is, but a statement of his house-porter, on his own admission a most casual and intermittent personage – that between the hours of ten o'clock and midnight no less than three ladies in deep black had flitted in and out of the place. This proved far too much; we had neither of us any use for three. He knew I considered I had accounted for every fragment of her time, and we dropped the matter as settled; we abstained from further discussion. What *I* knew however was that he abstained to please me rather than because he yielded to my reasons. He didn't yield – he was only indulgent; he clung to his interpretation because he liked it better. He liked it better, I held, because it had more to say to his vanity.

That, in a similar position, wouldn't have been its effect on me, though I had doubtless quite as much; but these are things of individual humour and as to which no person can judge for another. I should have supposed it more gratifying to be the subject of one of those inexplicable occurrences that are chronicled in thrilling books and disputed about at learned meetings; I could conceive, on the part of a being just engulfed in the infinite and still vibrating with human emotion, of nothing more fine and pure, more high and august, than such an impulse of reparation, of admonition, or even of curiosity. *That* was beautiful, if one would, and I should in his place have thought more of myself for being so distinguished and so selected. It was public that he had already, that he had long figured in that light, and what was such a fact itself but almost a proof? Each of the strange visitations contributed to establishing the other. He had a different feeling; but he had also, I hasten to add, an unmistakable desire not to make a stand or, as they say, a fuss about it. I might believe what I liked – the more so that the whole thing was in a manner a mystery of my producing. It was an event of my history, a puzzle of my consciousness, not of his; therefore he would take about it any tone that struck me as convenient. We had both at all events other business on hand; we were pressed with preparations for our marriage.

Mine were assuredly urgent, but I found as the days went on that to believe what I 'liked' was to believe what I was more and more intimately convinced of. I found also that I didn't like it so much as that came to, or that the pleasure at all events was far from being the cause of my conviction. My obsession, as I may really call it and as I began to perceive, refused to be elbowed away, as I had hoped, by my sense of paramount duties. If I had a great deal to do I had still more to think of, and the moment came when my occupations were gravely menaced by my thoughts. I see it all now, I feel it, I live it over. It's terribly void of joy, it's full indeed to overflowing of bitterness; and yet I must do myself justice – I couldn't have been other than I was. The same strange impressions, had I to meet them again, would produce the same deep anguish, the same sharp doubts, the same still sharper certainties. Oh it's all easier to remember than to write, but even could I retrace the business hour by hour, could I find terms for the inexpressible, the ugliness and pain would quickly stay my hand. Let me then note very simply and briefly that a week before our wedding-day, three weeks after her death, I knew in all my fibres that I had something very serious to look in the face and that if I was to make the effort I must make it on the spot and before another hour should elapse. My unextinguished jealousy – that was the Medusa mask. It hadn't died with her death, it had lividly survived, and it was fed by suspicions unspeakable. They *would* be unspeakable today, that is, if I hadn't felt the sharp need of uttering them at the time. This need took possession of me – to save me, as it seemed, from my fate. When once it had done so I saw – in the urgency of the case, the diminishing hours and shrinking interval – only one issue, that of absolute promptness and frankness. I could at least not do him the wrong of delaying another day; I could at least treat my difficulty as too fine for any subterfuge. Therefore very quietly, but none the less abruptly and hideously, I put it before him on a certain evening that we must reconsider our situation and recognise that it had completely altered.

He stared bravely. 'How in the world altered?'

'Another person has come between us.'

He took but an instant to think. 'I won't pretend not to know whom you mean.' He smiled in pity for my aberration, but he meant to be kind. 'A woman dead and buried!'

'She's buried, but she's not dead. She's dead for the world – she's dead for me. But she's not dead for you.'

'You hark back to the different construction we put on her appearance that evening?'

'No,' I answered, 'I hark back to nothing. I've no need of it. I've more than enough with what's before me.'

'And pray, darling, what may that be?'

'You're completely changed.'

'By that absurdity?' he laughed.

'Not so much by that one as by other absurdities that have followed it.'

'And what may *they* have been?'

We had faced each other fairly, with eyes that didn't flinch; but his had a dim strange light, and my certitude triumphed in his perceptible paleness. 'Do you really pretend,' I asked, 'not to know what they are?'

'My dear child,' he replied, 'you describe them too sketchily!'

I considered a moment. 'One may well be embarrassed to finish the picture! But from that point of view – and from the beginning – what was ever more embarrassing than your idiosyncrasy?'

He invoked his vagueness – a thing he always did beautifully. 'My idiosyncrasy?'

'Your notorious, your peculiar power.'

He gave a great shrug of impatience, a groan of overdone disdain. 'Oh my peculiar power!'

'Your accessibility to forms of life,' I coldly went on, 'your command of impressions, appearances, contacts, closed – for our gain or our loss – to the rest of us. That was originally a part of the deep interest with which you inspired me – one of the reasons I was amused, I was indeed positively proud, to know you. It was a magnificent distinction; it's a magnificent distinction still. But of course I had no prevision then of the way it would operate now; and even had that been the case I should have had none of the extraordinary way of which its action would affect me.'

'To what in the name of goodness,' he pleadingly enquired, 'are you fantastically alluding?' Then as I remained silent, gathering a tone for my charge, 'How in the world *does* it operate?' he went on; 'and how in the world are you affected?'

'She missed you for five years,' I said, 'but she never misses you now. You're making it up!'

'Making it up?' He had begun to turn from white to red.

'You see her – you see her: you see her every night!' He gave a loud sound of derision, but I felt it ring false. 'She comes to you as she came that evening,' I declared; 'having tried it she found she liked it!' I was able, with God's help, to speak without blind passion or vulgar violence; but those were the exact words – and far from 'sketchy' they then appeared to me – that I uttered. He had turned away in his laughter, clapping his hands at my folly, but in an instant he faced me again with a change of expression that struck me. 'Do you dare to deny,' I then asked, 'that you habitually see her?'

He had taken the line of indulgence, of meeting me halfway and kindly humouring me. At all events he to my astonishment suddenly said: 'Well, my dear, what if I do?'

'It's your natural right: it belongs to your constitution and to your wonderful if not perhaps quite enviable fortune. But you'll easily understand that it separates us. I unconditionally release you.'

'Release me?'

'You must choose between me and her.'

He looked at me hard. 'I see.' Then he walked away a little, as if grasping what I had said and thinking how he had best treat it. At last he turned on me afresh. 'How on earth do you know such an awfully private thing?'

'You mean because you've tried so hard to hide it? It *is* awfully private, and you may believe that I shall never betray you. You've done your best, you've acted your part, you've behaved, poor dear! loyally and admirably. Therefore I've watched you in silence, playing my part too; I've noted every drop in your voice, every absence in your eyes, every effort in your indifferent hand: I've waited till I was utterly sure and miserably unhappy. How can you hide it when you're abjectly in love with her, when you're sick almost to death with the joy of what she gives you?' I checked his quick protest with a quicker gesture. 'You love her as you've never loved, and, passion for passion, she gives it straight back. She rules you, she holds you, she has you all! A woman, in such a case as mine, divines and feels and sees; she's not a dull dunce who has to be "credibly informed". You come to me mechanically, compunctiously, with the dregs of your tenderness and the remnant of your life. I can renounce you, but I can't share you: the best of you is hers, I know what it is and freely give you up to her for ever!'

He made a gallant fight, but it couldn't be patched up; he repeated his denial, he retracted his ad-mission, he ridiculed my charge, of which I freely granted him moreover the indefensible extravagance. I didn't pretend for a moment that we were talking of common things; I didn't pretend for a moment that he and she were common people. Pray, if they *had* been, how should I ever have cared for them? They had enjoyed a rare extension of being and they had caught me up in their flight; only I couldn't breathe in such air and I promptly asked to be set down. Everything in the facts was monstrous, and most of all my lucid perception of them; the only thing allied to nature and truth was my having to act on that perception. I felt after I had spoken in this sense that my assurance was complete; nothing had been wanting to it but the sight of my effect on him. He disguised indeed the effect in a cloud of chaff, a diversion that gained him time and covered his retreat. He challenged my sincerity, my sanity, almost my humanity, and that of course widened our breach and confirmed our rupture. He did everything in short but convince me either that I was wrong or that he was unhappy: we separated and I left him to his inconceivable communion.

He never married, any more than I've done. When six years later, in solitude and silence, I heard of his death I hailed it as a direct contribution to my theory. It was sudden, it was never properly accounted for, it was surrounded by circumstances in which – for oh I took them to pieces! – I distinctly read an intention, the mark of his own hidden hand. It was the result of a long necessity, of an unquenchable desire. To say exactly what I mean, it was a response to an irresistible call.

JEROME K. JEROME

Silhouettes

I fear I must be of a somewhat gruesome turn of
mind. My sympathies are always with the melancholy
side of life and nature. I love the chill October days,
when the brown leaves lie thick and sodden underneath your feet, and a low sound as of stifled sobbing
is heard in the damp woods – the evenings in late
autumn time, when the white mist creeps across the
fields, making it seem as though old Earth, feeling the
night air cold to its poor bones, were drawing ghostly
bedclothes round its withered limbs. I like the twilight
of the long grey street, sad with the wailing cry of the
distant muffin man. One thinks of him, as, strangely
mitred, he glides by through the gloom, jangling his
harsh bell, as the High Priest of the pale spirit of
Indigestion, summoning the devout to come forth and
worship. I find a sweetness in the aching dreariness of
Sabbath afternoons in genteel suburbs – in the evil-
laden desolateness of waste places by the river, when
the yellow fog is stealing inland across the ooze and
mud, and the black tide gurgles softly round worm-
eaten piles.

I love the bleak moor, when the thin long line of the
winding road lies white on the darkening heath, while
overhead some belated bird, vexed with itself for being
out so late, scurries across the dusky sky, screaming
angrily. I love the lonely, sullen lake, hidden away in
mountain solitudes. I suppose it was my childhood's
surroundings that instilled in me this affection for

sombre hues. One of my earliest recollections is of a
dreary marshland by the sea. By day, the water stood
there in wide, shallow pools. But when one looked in
the evening they were pools of blood that lay there.

It was a wild, dismal stretch of coast. One day, I
found myself there all alone – I forget how it came
about – and, oh, how small I felt amid the sky and
the sea and the sandhills! I ran, and ran, and ran,
but I never seemed to move; and then I cried, and
screamed, louder and louder, and the circling sea-
gulls screamed back mockingly at me. It was an
'unken' spot, as they say up North.

In the far back days of the building of the world, a
long, high ridge of stones had been reared up by the
sea, dividing the swampy grassland from the sand.
Some of these stones – 'pebbles', so they called them
round about – were as big as a man, and many as big
as a fair-sized house; and when the sea was angry –
and very prone he was to anger by that lonely shore,
and very quick to wrath; often have I known him
sink to sleep with a peaceful smile on his rippling
waves, to wake in fierce fury before the night was
spent – he would snatch up giant handfuls of these
pebbles and fling and toss them here and there, till
the noise of their rolling and crashing could be heard
by the watchers in the village far off.

'Old Nick's playing at marbles tonight,' they would
say to one another, pausing to listen. And then the
women would close tight their doors, and try not to
hear the sound.

Far out to sea, by where the muddy mouth of the
river yawned wide, there rose ever a thin white line of
surf, and underneath those crested waves there dwelt
a very fearsome thing, called the Bar. I grew to hate

453

and be afraid of this mysterious Bar, for I heard it spoken of always with bated breath, and I knew that it was very cruel to fisher folk, and hurt them so sometimes that they would cry whole days and nights together with the pain, or would sit with white scared faces, rocking themselves to and fro.

Once when I was playing among the sandhills, there came by a tall, grey woman, bending beneath a load of driftwood. She paused when nearly opposite to me, and, facing seaward, fixed her eyes upon the breaking surf above the Bar. 'Ah, how I hate the sight of your white teeth!' she muttered; then turned and passed on.

Another morning, walking through the village, I heard a low wailing come from one of the cottages, while a little farther on a group of women were gathered in the roadway, talking. 'Ay,' said one of them, 'I thought the Bar was looking hungry last night.'

So, putting one and the other together, I concluded that the 'Bar' must be an ogre, such as a body reads of in books, who lived in a coral castle deep below the river's mouth, and fed upon the fishermen as he caught them going down to the sea or coming home.

From my bedroom window, on moonlight nights, I could watch the silvery foam, marking the spot beneath where he lay hid; and I would stand on tip-toe, peering out, until at length I would come to fancy I could see his hideous form floating below the waters. Then, as the little white-sailed boats stole by him, tremblingly, I used to tremble too, lest he should suddenly open his grim jaws and gulp them down; and when they had all safely reached the dark, soft sea beyond, I would steal back to the bedside, and pray to God to make the Bar good, so that he would give up eating the poor fishermen.

Another incident connected with that coast lives in my mind. It was the morning after a great storm – great even for that stormy coast – and the passion-worn waters were still heaving with the memory of a fury that was dead. Old Nick had scattered his marbles far and wide, and there were rents and fissures in the pebbly wall such as the oldest fisherman had never known before. Some of the hugest stones lay tossed a hundred yards away, and the waters had dug pits here and there along the ridge so deep that a tall man might stand in some of them, and yet his head not reach the level of the sand.

Round one of these holes a small crowd was pressing eagerly, while one man, standing in the hollow, was lifting the few remaining stones off something that lay there at the bottom. I pushed my way between the straggling legs of a big fisher lad, and peered over with the rest. A ray of sunlight streamed down into the pit, and the thing at the bottom gleamed white. Sprawling there among the black pebbles it looked like a huge spider. One by one the last stones were lifted away, and the thing was left bare, and then the crowd looked at one another and shivered.

'Wonder how he got there,' said a woman at length; 'somebody must ha' helped him.'

'Some foreign chap, no doubt,' said the man who had lifted off the stones; 'washed ashore and buried here by the sea.'

'What, six foot below the water-mark, wi' all they stones atop of him?' said another.

'That's no foreign chap,' cried a grizzled old woman, pressing forward. 'What's that that's aside him?'

Someone jumped down and took it from the stone where it lay glistening, and handed it up to her, and she clutched it in her skinny hand. It was a gold earring, such as fishermen sometimes wear. But this was a somewhat large one, and of rather unusual shape.

'That's young Abram Parsons, I tell 'ee, as lies down there,' cried the old creature, wildly. 'I ought to know. I gave him the pair o' these forty year ago.'

It may be only an idea of mine, born of after brooding upon the scene. I am inclined to think it must be so, for I was only a child at the time, and would hardly have noticed such a thing. But it seems to my remembrance that as the old crone ceased, another woman in the crowd raised her eyes slowly, and fixed them on a withered, ancient man, who leant upon a stick, and that for a moment, unnoticed by the rest, these two stood looking strangely at each other.

From these sea-scented scenes, my memory travels to a weary land where dead ashes lie, and there is blackness – blackness everywhere. Black rivers flow between black banks; black, stunted trees grow in black fields; black withered flowers by black wayside. Black roads lead from blackness past blackness to blackness; and along them trudge black, savage-looking men and women; and by them black, old-looking children play grim, unchildish games.

When the sun shines on this black land, it glitters black and hard; and when the rain falls a black mist rises towards heaven, like the hopeless prayer of a hopeless soul.

By night it is less dreary, for then the sky gleams with a lurid light, and out of the darkness the red flames leap, and high up in the air they gambol and writhe – the demon spawn of that evil land, they seem.

Visitors who came to our house would tell strange tales of this black land, and some of the stories I am inclined to think were true. One man said he saw a young bulldog fly at a boy and pin him by the throat. The lad jumped about with much sprightliness, and tried to knock the dog away. Whereupon the boy's father rushed out of the house, hard by, and caught his son and heir roughly by the shoulder. 'Keep still, thee young —, can't 'ee!' shouted the man angrily; 'let 'un taste blood.'

Another time, I heard a lady tell how she had visited a cottage during a strike, to find the baby, together with the other children, almost dying for want of food. 'Dear, dear me!' she cried, taking the wee wizened mite from the mother's arms, 'but I sent you down a quart of milk, yesterday. Hasn't the child had it?'

'Theer weer a little coom, thank 'ee kindly, ma'am,' the father took upon himself to answer; 'but thee see it weer only just enow for the poops.'

We lived in a big lonely house on the edge of a wide common. One night, I remember, just as I was reluctantly preparing to climb into bed, there came a wild ringing at the gate, followed by a hoarse, shrieking cry, and then a frenzied shaking of the iron bars.

Then hurrying footsteps sounded through the house, and the swift opening and closing of doors; and I slipped back hastily into my knickerbockers and ran out. The women folk were gathered on the stairs, while my father stood in the hall, calling to them to be quiet. And still the wild ringing of the bell continued, and, above it, the hoarse, shrieking cry.

My father opened the door and went out, and we could hear him striding down the gravel path, and we clung to one another and waited.

After what seemed an endless time, we heard the heavy gate unbarred, and quickly clanged to, and footsteps returning on the gravel. Then the door opened again, and my father entered, and behind him a crouching figure that felt its way with its hands as it crept along, as a blind man might. The figure stood up when it reached the middle of the hall, and mopped its eyes with a dirty rag that it carried in its hand; after which it held the rag over the umbrella-stand and wrung it out, as washerwomen wring out clothes, and the dark drippings fell into the tray with a dull, heavy splut.

My father whispered something to my mother, and she went out towards the back; and, in a little while, we heard the stamping of hoofs – the angry plunge of a spur-startled horse – the rhythmic throb of the long, straight gallop, dying away into the distance.

My mother returned and spoke some reassuring words to the servants. My father, having made fast the door and extinguished all but one or two of the lights, had gone into a small room on the right of the hall; the crouching figure, still mopping that moisture from its eyes, following him. We could hear them talking there in low tones, my father questioning, the other voice thick and interspersed with short panting grunts.

We on the stairs huddled closer together, and, in the darkness, I felt my mother's arm steal round me and encompass me, so that I was not afraid. Then we waited, while the silence round our frightened whispers thickened and grew heavy till the weight of it seemed to hurt us.

At length, out of its depths, there crept to our ears a faint murmur. It gathered strength like the sound of the oncoming of a wave upon a stony shore, until it broke in a Babel of vehement voices just outside. After a few moments, the hubbub ceased, and there came a furious ringing – then angry shouts demanding admittance.

Some of the women began to cry. My father came out into the hall, closing the room door behind him, and ordered them to be quiet, so sternly that they were stunned into silence. The furious ringing was repeated; and, this time, threats mingled among the hoarse shouts. My mother's arm tightened around me, and I could hear the beating of her heart.

The voices outside the gate sank into a low confused mumbling. Soon they died away altogether, and the silence flowed back.

My father turned up the hall lamp, and stood listening.

Suddenly, from the back of the house, rose the noise of a great crashing, followed by oaths and savage laughter.

My father rushed forward, but was borne back; and, in an instant, the hall was full of grim, ferocious faces. My father, trembling a little (or else it was the shadow cast by the flickering lamp), and with lips tight pressed, stood confronting them; while we women and children, too scared to even cry, shrank back up the stairs.

What followed during the next few moments is, in my memory, only a confused tumult, above which my father's high, clear tones rise every now and again, entreating, arguing, commanding. I see nothing distinctly until one of the grimmest of the faces thrusts itself before the others, and a voice which, like Aaron's rod, swallows up all its fellows, says in deep, determined bass, 'Coom, we've had enow chatter, master. Thee mun give 'un up, or thee mun get out o' th' way an' we'll search th' house for oursel'.'

Then a light flashed into my father's eyes that kindled something inside me, so that the fear went out of me, and I struggled to free myself from my mother's arm, for the desire stirred me to fling myself down upon the grimy faces below, and beat and stamp upon them with my fists. Springing across the hall, he snatched from the wall where it hung an ancient club, part of a trophy of old armour, and planting his back against the door through which they would have to pass, he shouted, 'Then be damned to you all, he's in this room! Come and fetch him out.'

(I recollect that speech well. I puzzled over it, even at that time, excited though I was. I had always been told that only low, wicked people ever used the word 'damn', and I tried to reconcile things, and failed.)

The men drew back and muttered among themselves. It was an ugly-looking weapon, studded with iron spikes. My father held it secured to his hand by a chain, and there was an ugly look about him also, now, that gave his face a strange likeness to the dark faces round him.

But my mother grew very white and cold, and underneath her breath she kept crying, 'Oh, will they never come – will they never come?' and a cricket somewhere about the house began to chirp.

Then all at once, without a word, my mother flew down the stairs, and passed like a flash of light through the crowd of dusky figures. How she did it I could never understand, for the two heavy bolts had both been drawn, but the next moment the door stood wide open; and a hum of voices, cheery with the anticipation of a period of perfect bliss, was borne in upon the cool night air.

My mother was always very quick of hearing.

Again, I see a wild crowd of grim faces, and my father's, very pale, among them. But this time the faces are very many, and they come and go like faces in a dream. The ground beneath my feet is wet and sloppy, and a black rain is falling. There are women's faces in the crowd, wild and haggard, and long skinny arms stretch out threateningly towards my father, and shrill, frenzied voices call out curses on him. Boys' faces also pass me in the grey light, and on some of them there is an impish grin.

I seem to be in everybody's way; and to get out of it, I crawl into a dark, draughty corner and crouch there among cinders. Around me, great engines fiercely strain and pant like living things fighting beyond their strength. Their gaunt arms whirl madly above me, and the ground rocks with their throbbing. Dark figures flit to and fro, pausing from time to time to wipe the black sweat from their faces.

The pale light fades, and the flame-lit night lies red upon the land. The flitting figures take strange shapes. I hear the hissing of wheels, the furious clanking of iron chains, the hoarse shouting of many voices, the hurrying tread of many feet; and, through all, the wailing and weeping and cursing that never seem to cease. I drop into a restless sleep, and dream that I have broken a chapel window, stone-throwing, and have died and gone to hell.

At length, a cold hand is laid upon my shoulder, and I awake. The wild faces have vanished and all is silent now, and I wonder if the whole thing has been a dream. My father lifts me into the dog-cart, and we drive home through the chill dawn.

My mother opens the door softly as we alight. She does not speak, only looks her question. 'It's all over, Maggie,' answers my father very quietly, as he takes off his coat and lays it across a chair; 'we've got to begin the world afresh.'

My mother's arms steal up about his neck; and I, feeling heavy with a trouble I do not understand, creep off to bed.

The Glass of Supreme Moments

Lucas Morne sat in his college rooms, when the winter afternoon met the evening, depressed and dull. There were various reasons for his depression. He was beginning to be a little nervous about his health. A week before he had run second in a mile race, the finish of which had been a terrible struggle; ever since then any violent exertion or excitement had brought on symptoms which were painful, and to one who had always been strong, astonishing. He had felt them early that afternoon, on coming from the river. Besides, he was discontented with himself. He had had several visitors in his rooms that afternoon, who were better than he was, men who had enthusiasms and had found them satisfying. Lucas had a moderate devotion to athletics, but no great enthusiasm. Neither had he the finer perceptions. Neither was he a scholar. He was just an ordinary man, and reputed to be a good fellow.

His visitors had drunk his tea, talked of their own enthusiasms, and were now gone. Nothing is so unclean as a used teacup; nothing is so cold as toast which has once been hot, and the concrete expression of dejection is crumbs. Even Lucas Morne, who had not the finer perceptions, was dimly conscious that his room had become horrible, and now flung open the window. One of the men – a large, clumsy man – had been smoking mitigated Latakia; and Latakia has a way of rolling itself all round the atmosphere and kicking. Lucas seated himself in his easiest chair.

His rooms were near the chapel, and he could hear the organ. The music and the soft fall of the darkness were soothing; he could hardly see the used teacups now; the light from the gas-lamp outside came just a little way into the room, shyly and obliquely.

Well, he had not noticed it before, but the fireplace had become a staircase. He felt too lazy to wonder much at this. He would, he thought, have the things all altered back again on the morrow. It would be worthwhile to sell the staircase, seeing that its steps were fashioned of silver and crystal. Unfortunately he could not see how much there was of it, or whither it led. The first five steps were clear enough; he felt convinced that the workmanship of them was Japanese. But the rest of the staircase was hidden from his sight by a grey veil of mist. He found himself a little angry, in a severe and strictly logical way, that in these days of boasted science we could not prevent a piece of fog, measuring ten feet by seven, from coming in at an open window and sitting down on a staircase which had only just begun to exist, and blotting out all but five steps of it in its very earliest moments. He allowed that it was a beautiful mist; its colour changed slowly from grey to rose, and then back again from rose to grey; fireflies of silver and gold shot through it at intervals; but it was a nuisance, because he wanted to see the rest of the staircase, and it prevented him. Every moment the desire to see more grew stronger. At last he determined to shake off his laziness, and go up the staircase and through the mist into the something beyond. He felt sure that the something beyond would be beautiful – sure with the certainty which was nothing to do with logical conviction.

It seemed to him that it was with an effort that he brought himself to rise from the chair and walk to the foot of that lovely staircase. He hesitated there for a moment or two, and as he did so he heard the sound of footsteps, high up, far away, yet coming nearer and nearer, with light music in the sound of them. Someone was coming down the staircase. He listened eagerly and excitedly. Then through the grey mist came a figure robed in grey.

It was the figure of a woman – young, with wonderful grace in her movements. Her face was veiled, and all that could be seen of her as she paused on the fifth step was the soft dark hair that reached to her waist, and her arms – white wonders of beauty. The rest was hidden by the grey veil and the long grey robe, that left, however, their suggestion of classical grace and slenderness. Lucas Morne stood looking at her tremulously. He felt sure, too, that she was looking at him, and that she could see through the folds of the thin grey veil that hid her face. She was the first to speak. Her voice in its gentleness and delicacy was like the voice of a child; it was only afterwards that he heard in it the under-thrill which told of more than childhood.

'Why have you not come? I have been waiting for you, you know, up there. And this is the only time,' she added.

'I am very sorry,' he stammered. 'You see – I never knew the staircase was there until today. In fact – it seems very stupid of me – but I always thought it was a fireplace. I must have been dreaming, of course. And then this afternoon I thought, or dreamed, that a lot of men came in to see me. Perhaps they really did come; and we got talking, you know – '

'Yes,' she said, with the gentlest possible interruption. 'I *do* know. There was one man, Fynsale, large, ugly, clumsy, a year your senior. He sat in that chair over there, and sulked, and smoked Latakia. I rather like the smell of Latakia. He especially loves to write or to say some good thing; and at times he can do it. Therefore you envy him. Then there was Blake. Blake is an athlete, like yourself, but is just a little more successful. Yes, I know you are good, but Blake is very good. You were tried for the Varsity – Blake was selected. He and Fynsale both have delight in ability, and you envy both. There was that dissenting little Paul Reece. He is not exactly in your set, but you were at school with him, and so you tolerate him. How good he is, for all his insignificance and social defects! Blake knows that, and kept a guard on his talk this afternoon. He would not offend Paul Reece for worlds. Paul's belief gives him earnestness, his earnestness leads him to self-sacrifice, and self-sacrifice is deep delight to him. You have more ability than Paul Reece, but you cannot reach that kind of enthusiastic happiness, and therefore you envy him. I could say similar things of the other men. It was because they made you vaguely dissatisfied with yourself that they bored you. You take pleasure – a certain pleasure – in athletics, and that pleasure would become an enthusiastic delight if you were a little better at them. Some men could get the enthusiastic delight out of as much as you can do, but your temperament is different. I know you well. You are not easily satisfied. You are not clever, but you are – ' She paused, but without any sign of embarrassment.

'What am I?' he asked eagerly. He felt sure that it would be something good, and he was not less vain than other men.

'I do not think I will say – not now.'

'But who are you?' His diffidence and stammering had vanished beneath her calm, quiet talk. 'You must let me at least ask that. Who are you? And how do you know all this?'

'I am a woman, but not an earth-woman. And the chief difference between us is that I know nearly all the things you do not know, and you do not know nearly all the things that I know. Sometimes I forget your ignorance – do not be angry for a word; there is no other for it, and it is not your fault. I forgot it just now when I asked you why you had not come to me up the staircase of silver and crystal, through the grey veil where the fireflies live, and into that quiet room beyond. This is the only time; tomorrow it will not be possible. And I have – ' Once more she paused. There was a charm for Lucas Morne in the things which she did not say. 'Your room is dark,' she continued, 'and I can hardly see you.'

'I will light the lamp,' said Lucas hurriedly, 'and – and won't you let me get you some tea?' He saw, as soon as he had said it, how unspeakably ludicrous this proffer of hospitality was. He almost fancied a smile, a moment's shimmer of little white teeth, beneath the long grey veil. 'Or shall I come now – at once,' he added.

'Come now; I will show you the mirror.'

'What is that?'

'You will understand when you see it. It is the glass

of supreme moments. I shall tell you about it. But come.'

She looked graceful, and she suggested the most perfect beauty as she stood there, a slight figure against the background of grey mist, which had grown luminous as the room below grew darker. Lucas Morne went carefully up the five steps, and together they passed through the grey, misty curtain. He was wondering what the face was like which was hidden beneath that veil; would it be possible to induce her to remove the veil? He might, perhaps, lead the conversation thither – delicately and subtly.

'A cousin of mine,' he began, 'who has travelled a good deal, once told me that the women of the East – '

'Yes,' she said, and her voice and way were so gentle that it hardly seemed like an interruption; 'and so do I.'

He felt very much anticipated; for a moment he was driven back into the shy and stammering state. There were only a few more steps now, and then they entered through a rosy curtain into a room, which he supposed to be 'that quiet room beyond', of which she had spoken.

It was a large room, square in shape. The floor was covered with black and white tiles, with the exception of a small square space in the centre, which looked like silver, and over which a ripple seemed occasionally to pass. She pointed it out to him. 'That,' she said, 'is the glass of the supreme moments.' There were no windows, and the soft light that filled the room seemed to come from that liquid silver mirror in the centre of the floor. The walls, which were lofty, were hung with curtains of different colours, all subdued, dreamy, reposeful. These colours were repeated in the painting of the ceiling. In a recess at the farther end of the room there were seats on which one could sleep. There was a faint smell of syringa in the air, making it heavy and drowsy. Now and then one heard faintly, as if afar off, the great music of an organ. Could it, he found himself wondering, be the organ of the college chapel? It was restful and pleasant to hear. She drew him to one of the seats in the recess, and once more pointed to the mirror.

'All the ecstasy in the world lies reflected there. The supreme moments of each man's life – the scene, the spoken words – all lie there. Past and present, and future – all are there.'

'Shall I be able to see them?'

'If you will.'

'And how?'

'Bend over the mirror, and say the name of the man or woman into whose life you wish to see. You only have to want it, and it will appear before your eyes. But there are some lives which have no supreme moments.'

'Commonplace lives?'

'Yes.'

Lucas Morne walked to the edge of the mirror and knelt down looking into it. The ripple passed to and fro over the surface. For a moment he hesitated, doubting for whom he should ask; and then he said in a low voice: 'Are there supreme moments in the life of Blake – Vincent Blake, the athlete?' The surface of the mirror suddenly grew still, and in it rose what seemed a living picture.

He could see once more the mile race in which he had been defeated by Blake. It was the third and last lap; and he himself was leading by some twenty yards, for Blake was waiting. There was a vast crowd of spectators, and he could hear every now and then the dull sound of their voices. He saw Vincent Blake slightly quicken his pace, and marked his own plucky attempt to answer it; he saw, too, that he had very little left in him. Gradually Blake drew up, until at a hundred yards from the finish there were not more than five yards between the two runners. Then he noticed his own fresh attempt. There were some fifty yards of desperate fighting, in which neither seemed to gain or lose an inch on the other. The voices of the excited crowd rose to a roar. And then – then Blake had it his own way. He saw himself passed a yard from the tape.

'Blake has always just beaten me,' he said savagely as he turned from the mirror.

He went back to his seat. 'Tell me,' he said, 'does that picture really represent the supreme moments of Blake's life?'

'Yes,' answered the veiled woman, 'he will have nothing quite like the ecstasy which he felt at winning that race. He will marry, and have children, and his married life will be happy, but the happiness will not be so intense. There is an emotion-meter outside this room, you know, which measures such things.'

'Now if one wanted to bet on a race,' he began. Then he stopped short. He had none of the finer perceptions, but it did not take these to show him that he was becoming a little inappropriate. 'I will look again at the mirror,' he added after a pause. 'I am afraid, though, that all this will make me more discontented with myself.'

Once more he looked into the glass of supreme

moments. He murmured the name of Paul Reece, the good little dissenter, his old schoolfellow. It was not in the power of accomplishment that Paul Reece excelled Lucas Morne, but only in the goodness and spirituality of his nature. As he looked, once more a picture formed on the surface of the mirror. It was of the future this time.

It was a sombre picture of the interior of a church. Through the open door one saw the snow falling slowly into the dusk of a winter afternoon. Within, before the richly decorated altar, flickered the little ruby flames of hanging lamps. On the walls, dim in the dying light, were painted the stations of the Cross. The fragrance of the incense smoke still lingered in the air. He could see but one figure, bowed, black-robed, before the altar. 'And is this Paul Reece – who was a dissenter?' he asked himself, knowing that it was he. Someone was seated at the organ, and the cry of the music was full of appeal, and yet full of peace; '*Agnus Dei, qui tollis peccata mundi!*'

Then the picture died away, and once more the little ripple moved too and fro over the surface of the liquid silver mirror. Lucas went back again to his place. The veiled woman was leaning backward, her small white hands linked together. She did not speak, but he was sure that she was looking at him – looking at him intently. Slowly it came to him that there was in this woman a subtle, mastering attraction which he had never known before. And side by side with this thought there still remained the feeling which had filled him as he witnessed the supreme moments of Paul Reece, a paradoxical feeling which was half rest-lessness and half peace.

'I do not know if I envy Paul,' he said, 'but if so, it

is not the envy which hurts. I shall never be like him. I can't feel as he does. It's not in me. But this picture did not make me angry as the other did.' He looked steadfastly at the graceful, veiled figure, and added in a lower tone: 'When I spoke of the travels of my cousin a little while ago – over Palestine, and Turkey, and thereabouts, you know – I had meant to lead up to the question, as you saw. I had meant to ask if you would put away your veil and let me see your face. And there are many things which I want to know about you. May I not stay here by your side and talk?'

'Soon, very soon I will talk with you, and after that you shall see me. What do you think, then, of the glass of supreme moments?'

'It is wonderful. I only feared the sight of the exquisite happiness in others would make me more discontented. At first you seemed to think that I was too dissatisfied.'

'Do not be deceived. Do not think that these supreme moments are everything; for that life is easiest which is gentle, level, placid, and has no supreme moments. There is a picture in the life of your friend Fynsale which I wish you to see. Look at it in the mirror, and then I shall have something to tell you.'

Lucas did as he was bidden. The mirror showed him a wretched, dingy room – sitting-room and bedroom combined – in a lodging house. At a little rickety table, pushed in front of a very small fire, Fynsale sat writing by lamplight. The lamp was out of order apparently. The combined smell of lamp and Latakia was poignant. There was a pile of manuscript before him, and on the top of it he was placing the sheet he had just written. Then he rose from his chair, folded his arms on the mantelpiece, and bent down, with his head on his hands, looking into the fire. It was an uncouth attitude of which, Lucas remembered, Fynsale had been particularly fond when he was at college.

When the picture had passed, Lucas looked round, and saw that the veiled woman had left the recess, and was now standing by his side. 'I do not understand this,' he said. 'How can those be the supreme moments in Fynsale's life? He looked poor and shabby, and the room was positively wretched. Where does the ecstasy come in?'

'He has just finished his novel; and he is quite madly in love with it. Some of it is very good, and some of it – from merely physical reasons – is very bad; he was half-starved when he was writing it, and it is not possible to write very well when one is half-starved. But he loves it. I am speaking of all this as if, like the picture of it, it was present; although, of course, it has not happened yet. But I will tell you more. I will show you, in this case at least, what these moments of ecstasy are worth. Some of Fynsale's book, I have said, is very good, and some of it is very bad; but none of it is what people want. He will take it to publisher after publisher, and they will refuse it. After three years it will at last be published, and it will not succeed in the least. And all through these years of failure he will recall from time to time the splendid joy he felt at finishing that book, and how glad he was that he had made it. The thought of that past ecstasy will make the torture all the worse.'

'Perhaps, then, after all, I should be glad that I am commonplace?' said Lucas.

'It does not always follow, though, that the common-place people have commonplace lives. There have been men who have been so ordinary that it hurt one to have anything to do with them, and yet the gods have made them come into poetry.'

Once more Lucas fancied that a smile with magic in it might be fluttering under that grey veil. Every moment the fascination of this woman, whose face he had not seen, and with whom he had spoken for so short a time, grew stronger on him. He did not know from whence it came, whether it lay in the grace of her figure and her movements, or in the beauty of her long dark hair, or in the music of her voice, or in that subtle, indefinable way in which she seemed to show him that she cared for him deeply. The room itself, quiet, mystical, restful, dedicated to the ecstasy of the world, had its effect upon his senses. More than ever before he felt himself impressed, tremulous with emotion. He knew that she saw how, in spite of himself, the look of adoration would come into his eyes.

And suddenly, she, whom but a moment before he had imagined to be smiling at her own light thoughts, seemed swayed by a more serious impulse.

'You must be comforted, though, and be angry with yourself no longer. For you are *not* commonplace, because you know that you *are* commonplace. It is something to have wanted the right things, although the gods have given you no power to attain them, nor even the wit and words to make your want eloquent.' Her voice was deeper, touched with the under-thrill.

'This,' he said, 'is the second time you have spoken of the gods – and yet we are in the nineteenth century.'

'Are we? I am very old and very young. Time is nothing to me; it does not change me. Yesterday in Italy each grave and stream spoke of divinity: "*Non omnis moriar*," sang one in confidence, "*Non omnis moriar!*" I heard his voice, and now he is passed and gone from the world.'

'We read him still,' said Lucas Morne, with a little pride. He was not intending to take the classical tripos, but he had with the help of a translation read that ode from which she was quoting. She did not heed his interruption in the least. She went on speaking –

'And today in England there is but little which is sacred; yet here, too, my work is seen; and here, too, as they die, they cry: "I shall not die, but live!" '

'You will think me stupid,' said Lucas Morne, a little bewildered, 'but I really do not understand you. I do not follow you. I cannot see to what you refer.'

'That is because you do not know who I am. Before the end of today I think we shall understand each other well.'

There was a moment's pause, and then Lucas Morne spoke again.

'You have told me that even in the lives of commonplace people there are sometimes supreme moments. I had scarcely hoped for them, and you have bidden me not to desire them. Shall I – even I – know what ecstasy means?'

'Yes, yes; I think so.'

'Then let me see it, as I saw the rest pictured in the mirror.' He spoke with some hesitation, his eyes fixed on the tiled floor of the room.

'That need not be,' she answered, and she hardly seemed to have perfect control over the tones of her voice now. 'That need not be, Lucas Morne, for the supreme moments of your life are here, here and now.'

He looked up, suddenly and excitedly. She had flung back the grey veil over her long, dark hair, and stood revealed before him, looking ardently into his eyes. Her face was paler than that of average beauty; the lips, shapely and scarlet, were just parted; but the eyes gave the most wonderful charm. They were like flames at midnight – not the soft, grey eyes that make men better, but the passionate eyes that make men forget honour, and reason, and everything. She stretched out both hands towards him, impulsively, appealingly. He grasped them in his own. His own hands were hot, burning; every nerve in them tingled with excitement. For a moment he held her at arm's length, looking at her, and said nothing. At last he found words –

'I knew that you would be like this. I think that I have loved you all my life. I wish that I might be with you for ever.'

There was a strange expression on her face. She did not speak, but she drew him nearer to her.

'Tell me your name,' he said.

'Yesterday, where that poet lived – that confident poet – they called me Libitina; and here, today, they call me Death. My name matters not, if you love me. For to you alone have I come thus. For the rest, I have done my work unseen. Only in this hour – only in this hour – was it possible.'

He had hardly heeded what she said. He bent down over her face.

'Stay!' she said in a hurried whisper, 'if you kiss me you will die.'

He smiled triumphantly. 'But I shall die kissing you,' he said. And so their lips met. Her lips were scarlet, but they were icy cold.

*

The captain of the football team had just come out of evening chapel, his gown slung over his arm, his cap pulled over his eyes, looking good-tempered, and strong, and jolly, but hardly devotional. He saw the window of Morne's rooms open – they were on the ground floor – and looked in. By the glow of the failing fire he saw what he thought was Lucas Morne seated in a lounge chair. He called to him, but there was no answer. 'The old idiot's asleep,' he said to himself, as he climbed in at the window. 'Wake up, old man,' he cried, as he put his hand on the shoulder of Lucas Morne's body, and swung it forward; 'wake up, old man.'

The body rolled forward and fell sideways to the ground heavily and clumsily. It lay there motionless.

RICHARD MARSH

The Fifteenth Man

It was not until we were actually in the field, and were about to begin to play, that I learnt that the Brixham men had come one short. It seemed that one of their men had been playing in a match the week before – in a hard frost, if you please! and, getting pitched on to his head, had broken his skull nearly into two clean halves. That is the worst of playing in a frost; you are nearly sure to come to grief. Not to ordinary grief, either, but a regular cracker. It was hard lines on the Brixham team. Some men always are getting themselves smashed to pieces just as a big match is due! The man's name was Joyce, Frank Joyce. He played half-back for Brixham, and for the county too – so you may be sure Lance didn't care to lose him. Still, they couldn't go and drag the man out of the hospital with a hole in his head big enough to put your fist into. They had tried to get a man to take his place, but at the last moment the substitute had failed to show.

'If we can't beat them – fifteen to their fourteen! – I think we'd better go in for challenging girls' schools. Last year they beat us, but this year, as we've one man to the good, perhaps we might manage to pull it off.'

That's how Mason talked to us, as if *we* wanted them to win! Although they were only fourteen men, they could play. I don't think I ever saw a team who were stronger in their forwards. Lance, their captain, kicked off; Mason, our chief, returned. Then one of their men, getting the leather, tried a run. We downed him, a scrimmage was formed, then, before we knew it, they were rushing the ball across the field. When it did show, I was on it like a flash. I passed to Mason. But he was collared almost before he had a chance to start. There was another turn at scrimmaging, and lively work it was, especially for us who had the pleasure of looking on. So, when again I got a sight of it, I didn't lose much time. I had it up, and I was off. I didn't pass; I tried a run upon my own account. I thought that I was clear away. I had passed the forwards; I thought that I had passed the field, when, suddenly, someone sprang at me, out of the fog – it was a little thick, you know – caught me round the waist, lifted me off my feet, and dropped me on my back. That spoilt it! Before I had a chance of passing they were all on top of me. And again the ball was in the scrimmage.

When I returned to my place behind I looked to see who it was had collared me. The fellow, I told myself, was one of their half-backs. Yet, when I looked at their halves, I couldn't make up my mind which of them it was.

Try how we could – although we had the best of the play – we couldn't get across their line. Although I say it, we all put in some first-rate work. We never played better in our lives. We all had run after run, the passing was as accurate as if it had been mechanical, and yet we could not do the trick. Time after time, just as we were almost in, one of their men put a stop to our little game, and spoilt us. The funny part of the business was that, either owing to the fog, or to our stupidity, we could not make up our minds which of their men it was.

At last I spotted him. Mason had been held nearly on their goal line. I took it. I passed to Mason. I thought he was behind, when – he was collared and thrown.

'Joyce!' I cried. 'Why, I thought that you weren't playing.'

'What are you talking about?' asked one of their men. 'Joyce isn't playing.'

I stared.

'Not playing! Why, it was he who collared Mason.'

'Stuff!'

I did not think the man was particularly civil. It was certainly an odd mistake which I had made. I was just behind Mason when he was collared, and I saw the face of the man who collared him. I could have sworn it was Frank Joyce!

'Who was that who downed you just now?' I asked of Mason, directly I had the chance.

'Their half-back.'

Their half-back! Their halves were Tom Wilson and Granger. How could I have mistaken either of them for Joyce?

A little later Giffard was puzzled.

'One of their fellows plays a thundering good game, but, do you know, I can't make out which one of them it is.'

'Do you mean the fellow who keeps collaring.'

'That's the man!'

The curious part of it was that I never saw the man except when he was collaring.

'The next time,' said Giffard, when, for about the sixth time, he had been on the point of scoring, 'if I don't get in, I'll know the reason why. I'll kill that man.'

It was all very well to talk about our killing him. It looked very much more like his killing us. Mason passed the word that if there was anything like a chance we were to drop. The chance came immediately afterwards. They muffed somehow in trying to pass. Blaine got the leather. He started to run.

'Drop,' yelled Mason.

In fog, and from where Blaine was, dropping a goal was out of the question. He tried the next best thing – he tried to drop into touch. But the attempt was a failure. The kick was a bad one – the ball was as heavy as lead, so that there was not much kick in it – and as it was coming down one of their men, appearing right on the spot, caught it, dropped a drop which was a drop, sent the ball right over our heads, and as near as a toucher over the bar.

Just then the whistle sounded.

'Do you know,' declared Ingall, as we were crossing over, 'I believe they're playing fifteen men.'

Mason scoffed.

'Do you think, without giving us notice, they would play fifteen when they told us they were only playing fourteen?'

'Hanged if I don't count them!' persisted Ingall.

He did, and we all did. We faced round and reckoned them up. There were only fourteen, unless one was slinking out of sight somewhere in the dim recesses of the fog, which seemed scarcely probable. Still Ingall seemed dissatisfied.

'They're playing four three-quarters,' whispered Giffard, when the game restarted.

So they were – Wheeler, Pendleton, Marshall, and another. Who the fourth man was I couldn't make out. He was a big, strapping fellow, I could see that; but the play was so fast that more than that I couldn't see.

'Who is the fourth man?'

'Don't know; can't see his face. It's so confound-edly foggy!'

It was foggy; but still, of course, it was not foggy enough to render a man's features indistinguishable at the distance of only a few feet. All the same, some-how or other he managed to keep his face concealed from us. While Giffard and I had been whispering they had been packing in. The ball broke out our side. I had it. I tried to run. Instantly I saw that fourth three-quarter rush at me. As he came I saw his face. I was so amazed that I stopped dead. Putting his arms about me he held me as in a vice.

'Joyce!' I cried.

Before the word was out of my mouth half a dozen of their men had hold of the ball.

'Held! held!' they screamed.

'Down!' I gasped.

And it was down, with two or three of their men on top of me. They were packing the scrimmage before I had time to get fairly on my feet again.

'That was Joyce who collared me!' I exclaimed.

'Pack in! pack in!' shouted Mason from behind.

And they did pack in with a vengeance. Giffard had the ball. They were down on him; it was hammer and tongs. But through it all we stuck to the leather. They downed us, but not before we had passed it to a friend. Out of it came Giffard, sailing along as though he had not been swallowing mud in pailfuls. I thought he was clear – but no! He stopped short, and dropped the ball! – dropped it, as he stood there, from his two hands as though he were a baby! They asked no questions. They had it up; they were off with it, as though they meant to carry it home. They carried it, too, all the way – almost! It was in disagreeable propinquity to our goal by the time that it was held.

'Now then, Brixham, you've got it!'

That was what they cried.

'Steyning! Steyning! All together!'

That was what we answered. But though we did work all together, it was as much as we could manage.

'Where's Giffard?' bellowed Mason.

My impression was that he had remained like a signpost rooted to the ground. I had seen him standing motionless after he had dropped the ball, and even as the Brixham men rushed past him. But just then he put in an appearance.

'I protest!' he cried.

'What about?' asked Mason.

'What do they mean by pretending they're not playing Frank Joyce when all the time they are?'

'Oh, confound Frank Joyce! Play up, do. You've done your best to give them the game already. Steady, Steyning, steady. Left, there, left. Centre, steady!'

We were steady. We were more than steady. Steadiness alone would not have saved us. We all played forward. At last, somehow, we got the ball back into something like the middle of the field. Giffard kept whispering to me all the time, even in the hottest of the rush.

'What lies, pretending that they're not playing Joyce!' Here he had a discussion with the ball, mostly on his knees. 'Humbug about his being in the hospital!'

We had another chance. Out of the turmoil, Mason was flying off with a lead. It was the first clear start he had that day. When he has got that it is catch him who catch can! As he pelted off the fog, which kept coming and going, all at once grew thicker. He had passed all their men. Of ours, I was the nearest to him. It looked all the world to a china orange that we were going to score at last, when, to my disgust, he reeled, seemed to give a sort of spring, and then fell right over on to his back! I did not understand how he had managed to do it, but I supposed that he had slipped in the mud. Before I could get within passing distance the Brixham men were on us, and the ball was down.

'I thought you'd done it that time.'

I said this to him as the scrimmage was being formed. He did not answer. He stood looking about him in a hazy sort of way, as though the further proceedings had no interest for him.

'What's the matter? Are you hurt?'

He turned to me.

'Where is he?' he asked.

'Where's who?'

I couldn't make him out. There was quite a curious look upon his face.

'Joyce!'

Somehow, as he said this, I felt a trifle queer. It was his face, or his tone, or something. 'Didn't you see him throw me?'

I didn't know what he meant. But before I could say so we had another little rough and tumble – one go up and the other go down. A hubbub arose. There was Ingall shouting.

'I protest! I don't think this sort of thing's fair play.'

'What sort of thing?'

'You said you weren't playing Joyce.'

'*Said* we weren't! We aren't.'

'Why, he just took the ball out of my hands! Joyce, where are you?'

'Yes, where is he?'

Then they laughed. Mason intervened.

'Excuse me, Lance; we've no objection to your playing Joyce, but why do you say you aren't?'

'I don't think you're well. I tell you that Frank Joyce is at this moment lying in Brixham hospital.'

'He just now collared me.'

I confess that when Mason said that I was a trifle staggered. I had distinctly seen that he had slipped and fallen. No one had been within a dozen yards of him at the time. Those Brixham men told him so – not too civilly.

'Do you fellows mean to say,' he roared, 'that Frank Joyce didn't just now pick me up and throw me?'

I struck in.

'I mean to say so. You slipped and fell. My dear fellow, no one was near you at the time.'

He sprang round at me.

'Well, that beats anything!'

'At the same time,' I added, 'it's all nonsense to talk about Joyce being in Brixham hospital, because, since half-time at any rate, he's been playing three-quarter.'

'Of course he has,' cried Ingall. 'Didn't I see him?'

'And didn't he collar me?' asked Giffard.

The Brixham men were silent. We looked at them, and they at us.

'You fellows are dreaming,' said Lance. 'It strikes me that you don't know Joyce when you see him.'

'That's good,' I cried, 'considering that he and I were five years at school together.'

'Suppose you point him out then?'

'Joyce!' I shouted. 'You aren't ashamed to show your face, I hope?'

'Joyce!' they replied, in mockery. 'You aren't bashful, Joyce?'

He was not there. Or we couldn't find him, at any rate. We scrutinised each member of the team; it was really absurd to suppose that I could mistake any of them for Joyce. There was not the slightest likeness.

Dryall appealed to the referee.

'Are you sure nobody's sneaked off the field?'

'Stuff!' he said. 'I've been following the game all the time, and know every man who's playing, and Joyce hasn't been upon the ground.'

'As for his playing three-quarter, Pendleton, Marshall, and I have been playing three-quarter all the afternoon, and I don't think that either of us is very much like Joyce.'

This was Tom Wilson.

'You've been playing four three-quarters since we crossed over.'

'Bosh!' said Wilson.

That was good, as though I hadn't seen the four with my own eyes.

'Play!' sang out the referee. 'Don't waste any more time.'

We were at it again. We might be mystified. There was something about the whole affair which was certainly mysterious to me. But we did not intend to be beaten.

'They're only playing three three-quarters now,' said Giffard.

So they were. That was plain enough. I wondered if the fourth man had joined the forwards. But why should they conceal the fact that they had been playing four?

One of their men tried a drop. Mason caught it, ran, was collared, passed – wide to the left – and I was off. The whole crowd was in the centre of the field. I put on the steam. Lance came at me. I dodged, he missed. Pendleton was bearing down upon me from the right. I outpaced him. I got a lead. Only Rivers, their back, was between the Brixham goal and me. He slipped just as he made his effort. I was past. I was only a dozen yards to the goal. Nothing would stop me now. I was telling myself that the only thing left was the shouting, when, right in front of me, stood – Joyce! Where he came from I have not the least idea. Out of nothing, it seemed to me. He stood there, cool as a cucumber, waiting – as it appeared – until I came within his reach. His sudden appearance baulked me. I stumbled. The ball slipped from beneath my arm. I saw him smile. Forgetting all about the ball, I made a dash at him. The instant I did so he was gone!

I felt a trifle mixed. I heard behind me the roar of voices. I knew that I had lost my chance. But, at the moment, that was not the trouble. Where had Joyce come from? Where had he gone?

'Now then, Steyning! All together, and you'll do it!'

I heard Mason's voice ring out above the hubbub.

'Brixham, Brixham!' shouted Lance. 'Play up!'

'Joyce or no Joyce,' I told myself, 'hang me if I won't do it yet!'

I got on side. Blaine had hold of the leather. They were on him like a cartload of bricks. He passed to Giffard.

'Don't run back!' I screamed.

They drove him back. He passed to me. They were

on the ball as soon as I was. They sent me spinning. Somebody got hold of it. Just as he was off I made a grab at his leg. He went down on his face. The ball broke loose. I got on to my feet. They were indulging in what looked to me very much like hacking. We sent the leather through, and Lance was off! Their fellows backed him up in style. They kept us off until he had a start. He bore off to the right. Already he had shaken off our forwards. I saw Mason charge him. I saw that he sent Mason flying. I made for him. I caught him round the waist. He passed to Pendleton. Pendleton was downed. He lost the ball. Back it came to me, and I was off!

I was away before most of them knew what had become of the leather. Again there was only Rivers between the goal and me. He soon was out of the reckoning. The mud beat him. As he was making for me down he came upon his hands and knees. I had been running wide till then. When he came to grief I centred. Should I take the leather in, or drop?

'Drop!' shouted a voice behind.

That settled me. I was within easy range of the goal. I ought to manage the kick. I dropped – at least, I tried to. It was only a try, because, just as I had my toe against the ball, and was in the very act of kicking, Joyce stood right in front of me! He stood so close that, so to speak, he stood right on the ball. It fell dead, it didn't travel an inch. As I made my fruitless effort, and was still poised upon one leg, placing his hand against my chest, he pushed me over backwards. As I fell I saw him smile – just as I had seen him smile when he had baulked me just before.

I didn't feel like smiling. I felt still less like smiling when, as I yet lay sprawling, Rivers, pouncing on the ball, dropped it back into the centre of the field. He was still standing by me when I regained my feet. He volunteered an observation.

'Lucky for us you muffed that kick.'

'Where's Joyce?' I asked.

'Where's who?'

'Joyce.'

He stared at me.

'I don't know what you're driving at. I think you fellows must have got Joyce on the brain.'

He returned to his place in the field. I returned to mine. I had an affectionate greeting from Giffard.

'That's the second chance you've thrown away. Whatever made you muff that kick?'

'Giffard,' I asked, 'do you think I'm going mad?'

'I should think you've gone.'

I could not – it seems ridiculous, but I could not ask if he had seen Joyce. It was so evident that he had not. And yet, if I had seen him, he must have seen him too. As he suggested – I must have gone mad!

The play was getting pretty rough, the ground was getting pretty heavy. We had churned it into a regular quagmire. Sometimes we went above the ankle in liquid mud. As for the state that we were in!

One of theirs had the ball. Half a dozen of ours had hold of him.

'Held! held!' they yelled.

'It's not held,' he gasped.

They had him down, and sat on him. Then he owned that it was held.

'Let it through,' cried Mason, when the leather was in scrimmage.

Before our forwards had a chance they rushed it through. We picked it up; we carried it back. They rushed it through again. The tide of battle swayed, now to this side, now to that. Still we gained. Two or three short runs bore the ball within punting distance of their goal. We more than retained the advantage. Yard by yard we drove them back. It was a match against time. We looked like winning if there was only time enough. At last it seemed as though matters had approached something very like a settlement. Pendleton had the ball. Our men were on to him. To avoid being held he punted. But he was charged before he really had a chance. The punt was muddled. It was a catch for Mason. He made his mark – within twenty yards of their goal! There is no better dropkick in England than Alec Mason. If from a free kick at that distance he couldn't top their bar, we might as well go home to bed.

Mason took his time. He judged the distance with his eye. Then, paying no attention to the Brixham forward, who had stood up to his mark, he dropped a good six feet on his own side of it. There was an instant's silence. Then they raised a yell; for as the ball left Mason's foot one of their men sprang at him, and, leaping upwards, caught the ball in the air. It was wonderfully done! Quick as lighting, before we had recovered from our surprise, he had dropped the ball back into the centre of the field.

'Now then, Brixham,' bellowed Lance.

And they came rushing on. They came on too! We were so disconcerted by Mason's total failure that they got the drop on us. They reached the leather before our back had time to return. It was all we could do to get upon the scene of action quickly enough to prevent their having the scrimmage all to themselves. Mason's collapse had put life into them as much as, for the moment, it had taken it out of us. They carried the ball through the scrimmage as though our forwards were not there.

'Now then, Steyning, you're not going to let them beat us!'

As Mason held his peace I took his place as fugleman.

But we could not stand against them – we could not – in scrimmage or out of it. All at once they seemed to be possessed. In an instant their back play improved a hundred per cent. One of their men, in particular, played like Old Nick himself. In the excitement – and they were an exciting sixty seconds – I could not make out which one of them it was; but he made things lively. He as good as played us single-handed; he was always on the ball; he seemed to lend their forwards irresistible impetus when it was in the scrimmage. And when it was out of it, wasn't he just upon the spot. He was ubiquitous – here, there, and everywhere. And at last he was off. Exactly how it happened is more than I can say, but I saw that he had the ball. I saw him dash away with it. I made for him. He brushed me aside as though I were a fly. I was about to start in hot pursuit when someone caught me by the arm. I turned – in a trifle of a rage. There was Mason at my side.

'Never mind that fellow. Listen to me.' These were funny words to come from the captain of one's team at the very crisis of the game. I both listened and looked. Something in the expression of his face quite startled me. 'Do you know who it was who spoilt my kick? It was either Joyce or – Joyce's ghost.'

Before I was able to ask him what it was he meant there arose a hullaballoo of shouting. I turned just in time to see the fellow, who had run away with the leather, drop it, as sweetly as you please, just over our goal. They had won! And at that moment the whistle sounded – they had done it just on time!

The man who had done the trick turned round and faced us. He was wearing a worsted cap, such as brewers wear. Taking it off, he waved it over his head. As he did so there was not a man upon the field who did not see him clearly, who did not know who he was. He was Frank Joyce! He stood there for a moment before us all, and then was gone.

'Lance,' shouted the referee, 'here's a telegram for you.'

Lance was standing close to Mason and to me. A telegraph boy came pelting up. Lance took the yellow envelope which the boy held out to him. He opened it.

'Why! what!' Through the mud upon his face he went white, up to the roots of his hair. He turned to us with startled eyes. 'Joyce died in Brixham Hospital nearly an hour ago. The hospital people have tele-graphed to say so.'

CHARLOTTE RIDDELL

The Old House in Vauxhall Walk

1

'Houseless – homeless – hopeless!'

Many a one who had before him trodden that same street must have uttered the same words – the weary, the desolate, the hungry, the forsaken, the waifs and strays of struggling humanity that are always coming and going, cold, starving and miserable, over the pavements of Lambeth Parish; but it is open to question whether they were ever previously spoken with a more thorough conviction of their truth, or with a feeling of keener self-pity, than by the young man who hurried along Vauxhall Walk one rainy winter's night, with no overcoat on his shoulders and no hat on his head.

A strange sentence for one-and-twenty to give expression to – and it was stranger still to come from the lips of a person who looked like and who was a gentleman. He did not appear either to have sunk very far down in the good graces of Fortune. There was no sign or token which would have induced a passer-by to imagine he had been worsted after a long fight with calamity. His boots were not worn down at the heels or broken at the toes, as many, many boots were which dragged and shuffled and scraped along the pavement. His clothes were good and fashionably cut, and innocent of the rents and patches and tatters that slunk wretchedly by, crouched in doorways, and

493

held out a hand mutely appealing for charity. His face was not pinched with famine or lined with wicked wrinkles, or brutalised by drink and debauchery, and yet he said and thought he was hopeless, and almost in his young despair spoke the words aloud.

It was a bad night to be about with such a feeling in one's heart. The rain was cold, pitiless and increasing. A damp, keen wind blew down the cross streets leading from the river. The fumes of the gas works seemed to fall with the rain. The roadway was muddy; the pavement greasy; the lamps burned dimly; and that dreary district of London looked its very gloomiest and worst.

Certainly not an evening to be abroad without a home to go to, or a sixpence in one's pocket, yet this was the position of the young gentleman who, without a hat, strode along Vauxhall Walk, the rain beating on his unprotected head.

Upon the houses, so large and good – once inhabited by well-to-do citizens, now let out for the most part in floors to weekly tenants – he looked enviously. He would have given much to have had a room, or even part of one. He had been walking for a long time, ever since dark in fact, and dark falls soon in December. He was tired and cold and hungry, and he saw no prospect save of pacing the streets all night.

As he passed one of the lamps, the light falling on his face revealed handsome young features, a mobile, sensitive mouth, and that particular formation of the eyebrows – not a frown exactly, but a certain draw of the brows – often considered to bespeak genius, but which more surely accompanies an impulsive organisation easily pleased, easily depressed, capable of suffering very keenly or of enjoying fully. In his short life he had not enjoyed much, and he had suffered a good deal. That night, when he walked bareheaded through the rain, affairs had come to a crisis. So far as he in his despair felt able to see or reason, the best thing he could do was to die. The world did not want him; he would be better out of it.

The door of one of the houses stood open, and he could see in the dimly lighted hall some few articles of furniture waiting to be removed. A van stood beside the kerb, and two men were lifting a table into it as he, for a second, paused.

'Ah,' he thought, 'even those poor people have some place to go to, some shelter provided, while I have not a roof to cover my head, or a shilling to get a night's lodging.' And he went on fast, as if memory were spurring him, so fast that a man running after had some trouble to overtake him.

'Master Graham! Master Graham!' this man exclaimed, breathlessly; arid, thus addressed, the young fellow stopped as if he had been shot.

'Who are you that know me?' he asked, facing round.

'I'm William; don't you remember William, Master Graham? And, Lord's sake, sir, what are you doing out a night like this without your hat?'

'I forgot it,' was the answer; 'and I did not care to go back and fetch it.'

'Then why don't you buy another, sir? You'll catch your death of cold; and besides, you'll excuse me, sir, but it does look odd.'

'I know that,' said Master Graham grimly; 'but I haven't a halfpenny in the world.'

'Have you and the master, then – ' began the man, but there he hesitated and stopped.

'Had a quarrel? Yes, and one that will last us our lives,' finished the other, with a bitter laugh.

'And where are you going now?'

'Going! Nowhere, except to seek out the softest paving stone, or the shelter of an arch.'

'You are joking, sir.'

'I don't feel much in a mood for jesting either.'

'Will you come back with me, Master Graham? We are just at the last of our moving, but there is a spark of fire still in the grate, and it would be better talking out of this rain. Will you come, sir?'

'Come! Of course I will come,' said the young fellow, and, turning, they retraced their steps to the house he had looked into as he passed along.

An old, old house, with long, wide hall, stairs low, easy of ascent, with deep cornices to the ceilings, and oak floorings, and mahogany doors, which still spoke mutely of the wealth and stability of the original owner, who lived before the Tradescants and Ashmoles were thought of, and had been sleeping far longer than they, in St Mary's churchyard, hard by the archbishop's palace.

'Step upstairs, sir,' entreated the departing tenant; 'it's cold down here, with the door standing wide.'

'Had you the whole house, then, William?' asked Graham Coulton, in some surprise.

'The whole of it, and right sorry I, for one, am to leave it; but nothing else would serve my wife. This room, sir,' and with a little conscious pride, William, doing the honours of his late residence, asked his guest into a spacious apartment occupying the full width of the house on the first floor.

Tired though he was, the young man could not repress an exclamation of astonishment.

'Why, we have nothing so large as this at home, William,' he said.

'It's a fine house,' answered William, raking the embers together as he spoke and throwing some wood upon them; 'but, like many a good family, it has come down in the world.'

There were four windows in the room, shuttered close; they had deep, low seats, suggestive of pleasant days gone by; when, well-curtained and well-cushioned, they formed snug retreats for the children, and sometimes for adults also; there was no furniture left, unless an oaken settle beside the hearth, and a large mirror let into the panelling at the opposite end of the apartment, with a black marble console table beneath it, could be so considered; but the very absence of chairs and tables enabled the magnificent proportions of the chamber to be seen to full advantage, and there was nothing to distract the attention from the ornamented ceiling, the panelled walls, the old-world chimney-piece so quaintly carved, and the fire-place lined with tiles, each one of which contained a picture of some scriptural or allegorical subject.

'Had you been staying on here, William,' said Coulton, flinging himself wearily on the settle, 'I'd have asked you to let me stop where I am for the night.'

'If you can make shift, sir, there is nothing as I am aware of to prevent you stopping,' answered the man, fanning the wood into a flame. 'I shan't take the key back to the landlord till tomorrow, and this would be better for you than the cold streets at any rate.'

'Do you really mean what you say?' asked the other eagerly. 'I should be thankful to lie here; I feel dead beat.'

'Then stay, Master Graham, and welcome. I'll fetch a basket of coals I was going to put in the van, and make up a good fire, so that you can warm yourself; then I must run round to the other house for a minute or two, but it's not far, and I'll be back as soon as ever I can.'

'Thank you, William; you were always good to me,' said the young man gratefully. 'This is delightful,' and he stretched his numbed hands over the blazing wood, and looked round the room with a satisfied smile.

'I did not expect to get into such quarters,' he remarked, as his friend in need reappeared, carrying a half-bushel basket full of coals, with which he proceeded to make up a roaring fire. 'I am sure the last thing I could have imagined was meeting with anyone I knew in Vauxhall Walk.'

'Where were you coming from, Master Graham?' asked William curiously.

'From old Melfield's. I was at his school once, you know, and he has now retired, and is living upon the proceeds of years of robbery in Kennington Oval. I thought, perhaps he would lend me a pound, or offer me a night's lodging, or even a glass of wine; but, oh dear, no. He took the moral tone, and observed he could have nothing to say to a son who defied his father's authority. He gave me plenty of advice, but nothing else, and showed me out into the rain with a bland courtesy, for which I could have struck him.'

William muttered something under his breath which was not a blessing, and added aloud: 'You are better here, sir, I think, at any rate. I'll be back in less than half an hour.'

Left to himself, young Coulton took off his coat,

and shifting the settle a little, hung it over the end to
dry. With his handkerchief he rubbed some of the
wet out of his hair; then, perfectly exhausted, he lay
down before the fire and, pillowing his head on his
arm, fell fast asleep.

He was awakened nearly an hour afterwards by the
sound of someone gently stirring the fire and moving
quietly about the room. Starting into a sitting posture,
he looked around him, bewildered for a moment, and
then, recognising his humble friend, said laughingly:
'I had lost myself; I could not imagine where I was.'

'I am sorry to see you here, sir,' was the reply; 'but
still this is better than being out of doors. It has come
on a nasty night. I brought a rug round with me that,
perhaps, you would wrap yourself in.'

'I wish, at the same time, you had brought me
something to eat,' said the young man, laughing.

'Are you hungry, then, sir?' asked William, in a
tone of concern.

'Yes; I have had nothing to eat since breakfast. The
governor and I commenced rowing the minute we sat
down to luncheon, and I rose and left the table. But
hunger does not signify; I am dry and warm, and can
forget the other matter in sleep.'

'And it's too late now to buy anything,' soliloquised
the man; 'the shops are all shut long ago. Do you
think, sir,' he added, brightening, 'you could manage
some bread and cheese?'

'Do I think – I should call it a perfect feast,'
answered Graham Coulton. 'But never mind about
food tonight, William; you have had trouble enough,
and to spare, already.'

William's only answer was to dart to the door and
run downstairs. Presently he reappeared, carrying in

one hand bread and cheese wrapped up in paper, and in the other a pewter measure full of beer.

'It's the best I could do, sir,' he said apologetically. 'I had to beg this from the landlady.'

'Here's to her good health!' exclaimed the young fellow gaily, taking a long pull at the tankard. 'That tastes better than champagne in my father's house.'

'Won't he be uneasy about you?' ventured William, who, having by this time emptied the coals, was now seated on the inverted basket, looking wistfully at the relish with which the son of the former master was eating his bread and cheese.

'No,' was the decided answer. 'When he hears it pouring cats and dogs he will only hope I am out in the deluge, and say a good drenching will cool my pride.'

'I do not think you are right there,' remarked the man.

'But I am sure I am. My father always hated me, as he hated my mother.'

'Begging your pardon, sir; he was over fond of your mother.'

'If you had heard what he said about her today, you might find reason to alter your opinion. He told me I resembled her in mind as well as body; that I was a coward, a simpleton, and a hypocrite.'

'He did not mean it, sir.'

'He did, every word. He does think I am a coward, because I – I – ' And the young fellow broke into a passion of hysterical tears.

'I don't half like leaving you here alone,' said William, glancing round the room with a quick trouble in his eyes; 'but I have no place fit to ask you to stop, and I am forced to go myself, because I am night watchman, and must be on at twelve o'clock.'

'I shall be right enough,' was the answer. 'Only I mustn't talk any more of my father. Tell me about yourself, William. How did you manage to get such a big house, and why are you leaving it?'

'The landlord put me in charge, sir; and it was my wife's fancy not to like it.'

'Why did she not like it?'

'She felt desolate alone with the children at night,' answered William, turning away his head; then added, next minute: 'Now, sir, if you think I can do no more for you, I had best be off. Time's getting on. I'll look round tomorrow morning.'

'Good-night,' said the young fellow, stretching out his hand, which the other took as freely and frankly as it was offered. 'What should I have done this evening if I had not chanced to meet you?'

'I don't think there is much chance in the world, Master Graham,' was the quiet answer. 'I do hope you will rest well, and not be the worse for your wetting.'

'No fear of that,' was the rejoinder, and the next minute the young man found himself all alone in the Old House in Vauxhall Walk.

2

Lying on the settle, with the fire burnt out, and the room in total darkness, Graham Coulton dreamed a curious dream. He thought he awoke from deep slumber to find a log smouldering away upon the hearth, and the mirror at the end of the apartment reflecting fitful gleams of light. He could not understand how it came to pass that, far away as he was from the glass, he was able to see everything in it; but he resigned himself to the difficulty without astonishment, as people generally do in dreams.

Neither did he feel surprised when he beheld the outline of a female figure seated beside the fire, engaged in picking something out of her lap and dropping it with a despairing gesture.

He heard the mellow sound of gold, and knew she was lifting and dropping sovereigns. He turned a little so as to see the person engaged in such a singular and meaningless manner, and found that, where there had been no chair on the previous night, there was a chair now, on which was seated an old, wrinkled hag, her clothes poor and ragged, a mob cap barely covering her scant white hair, her cheeks sunken, her nose hooked, her fingers more like talons than aught else as they dived down into the heap of gold, portions of which they lifted but to scatter mournfully.

'Oh! my lost life,' she moaned, in a voice of the bitterest anguish. 'Oh! my lost life – for one day, for one hour of it again!'

Out of the darkness – out of the corner of the room where the shadows lay deepest – out from the gloom abiding near the door – out from the dreary night, with their sodden feet and wet dripping from their heads, came the old men and the young children, the worn women and the weary hearts, whose misery that gold might have relieved, but whose wretchedness it mocked.

Round that miser, who once sat gloating as she now sat lamenting, they crowded – all those pale, sad shapes – the aged of days, the infant of hours, the sobbing outcast, honest poverty, repentant vice; but one low cry proceeded from those pale lips – a cry for help she might have given, but which she withheld.

They closed about her, all together, as they had done singly in life; they prayed, they sobbed, they entreated; with haggard eyes the figure regarded the poor she had repulsed, the children against whose cry she had closed her ears, the old people she had suffered to starve and die for want of what would have been the merest trifle to her; then, with a terrible scream, she raised her lean arms above her head, and sank down – down – the gold scattering as it fell out of her lap, and rolling along the floor, till its gleam was lost in the outer darkness beyond.

Then Graham Coulton awoke in good earnest, with the perspiration oozing from every pore, with a fear and an agony upon him such as he had never before felt in all his existence, and with the sound of the heart-rending cry – 'Oh! my lost life' – still ringing in his ears.

Mingled with all, too, there seemed to have been some lesson for him which he had forgotten, that, try as he would, eluded his memory, and which, in the very act of waking, glided away.

He lay for a little thinking about all this, and then, still heavy with sleep, retraced his way into dreamland once more.

It was natural, perhaps, that, mingling with the strange fantasies which follow in the train of night and darkness, the former vision should recur, and the young man ere long found himself toiling through scene after scene wherein the figure of the woman he had seen seated beside a dying fire held principal place.

He saw her walking slowly across the floor munching a dry crust – she who could have purchased all the luxuries wealth can command; on the hearth, contemplating her, stood a man of commanding presence, dressed in the fashion of long ago. In his eyes there was a dark look of anger, on his lips a curling smile of disgust, and somehow, even in his sleep, the dreamer understood it was the ancestor to the descendant he beheld – that the house put to mean uses in which he lay had never so far descended from its high estate, as the woman possessed of so pitiful a soul, contaminated with the most despicable and insidious vice poor humanity knows, for all other vices seem to have connection with the flesh, but the greed of the miser eats into the very soul.

Filthy of person, repulsive to look at, hard of heart as she was, he yet beheld another phantom, which, coming into the room, met her almost on the threshold, taking her by the hand, and pleading, as it seemed, for assistance. He could not hear all that passed, but a word now and then fell upon his ear. Some talk of former days; some mention of a fair young mother – an appeal, as it seemed, to a time when they were tiny brother and sister, and the accursed greed for gold had not divided them. All in vain; the hag only answered him as she had answered the children, and the young girls, and the old people in his former vision. Her heart was as invulnerable to natural affection as it had proved to human sympathy. He begged, as it appeared, for aid to avert some bitter misfortune or terrible disgrace, and adamant might have been found more yielding to his prayer. Then the figure standing on the hearth changed to an angel, which folded its wings mournfully over its face, and the man, with bowed head, slowly left the room.

Even as he did so the scene changed again; it was night once more, and the miser wended her way upstairs. From below, Graham Coulton fancied he watched her toiling wearily from step to step. She had aged strangely since the previous scenes. She moved with difficulty; it seemed the greatest exertion for her to creep from step to step, her skinny hand traversing the balusters with slow and painful deliberateness. Fascinated, the young man's eyes followed the progress of that feeble, decrepit woman. She was solitary in a desolate house, with a deeper blackness than the darkness of night waiting to engulf her.

It seemed to Graham Coulton that after that he lay for a time in a still, dreamless sleep, upon awaking from which he found himself entering a chamber as sordid and unclean in its appointments as the woman of his previous vision had been in her person. The poorest labourer's wife would have gathered more comforts around her than that room contained. A four-poster bedstead without hangings of any kind – a blind drawn up awry – an old carpet covered with dust, and dirt on the floor – a rickety washstand with all the paint worn off it – an ancient mahogany dressing-table, and a cracked glass spotted all over – were all the objects he could at first discern, looking at the room through that dim light which oftentimes obtains in dreams.

By degrees, however, he perceived the outline of someone lying huddled on the bed. Drawing nearer, he found it was that of the person whose dreadful presence seemed to pervade the house. What a terrible sight she looked, with her thin white locks scattered over the pillow, with what were mere remnants of blankets gathered about her shoulders, with her claw-like fingers clutching the clothes, as though even in sleep she was guarding her gold!

An awful and a repulsive spectacle, but not with

half the terror in it of that which followed. Even as the young man looked he heard stealthy footsteps on the stairs. Then he saw first one man and then his fellow steal cautiously into the room. Another second, and the pair stood beside the bed, murder in their eyes.

Graham Coulton tried to shout – tried to move, but the deterrent power which exists in dreams only tied his tongue and paralysed his limbs. He could but hear and look, and what he heard and saw was this: aroused suddenly from sleep, the woman started, only to receive a blow from one of the ruffians, whose fellow followed his lead by plunging a knife into her breast.

Then, with a gurgling scream, she fell back on the bed, and at the same moment, with a cry, Graham Coulton again awoke, to thank heaven it was but an illusion.

3

'I hope you slept well, sir.' It was William, who, coming into the hall with the sunlight of a fine bright morning streaming after him, asked this question: 'Had you a good night's rest?'

Graham Coulton laughed, and answered: 'Why, faith, I was somewhat in the case of Paddy, "who could not slape for dhraming". I slept well enough, I suppose, but whether it was in consequence of the row with my dad, or the hard bed, or the cheese – most likely the bread and cheese so late at night – I dreamt all the night long, the most extraordinary dreams. Some old woman kept cropping up, and I saw her murdered.'

'You don't say that, sir?' said William nervously.

'I do, indeed,' was the reply. 'However, that is all gone and past. I have been down in the kitchen and had a good wash, and I am as fresh as a daisy, and as hungry as a hunter; and, oh, William, can you get me any breakfast?'

'Certainly, Master Graham. I have brought round a kettle, and I will make the water boil immediately. I suppose, sir' – this tentatively – 'you'll be going home today?'

'Home!' repeated the young man. 'Decidedly not. I'll never go home again till I return with some medal hung to my coat, or a leg or arm cut off. I've thought it all out, William. I'll go and enlist. There's a talk of war; and, living or dead, my father shall have reason to retract his opinion about my being a coward.'

'I am sure the admiral never thought you anything of the sort, sir,' said William. 'Why, you have the pluck of ten!'

'Not before him,' answered the young fellow sadly.

'You'll do nothing rash, Master Graham; you won't go 'listing, or aught of that sort, in your anger?'

'If I do not, what is to become of me?' asked the other. 'I cannot dig – to beg I am ashamed. Why, but for you, I should not have had a roof over my head last night.'

'Not much of a roof, I am afraid, sir.'

'Not much of a roof!' repeated the young man. 'Why, who could desire a better? What a capital room this is,' he went on, looking around the apartment, where William was now kindling a fire; 'one might dine twenty people here easily!'

'If you think so well of the place, Master Graham,

507

you might stay here for a while, till you have made up your mind what you are going to do. The landlord won't make any objection, I am very sure.'

'Oh! nonsense; he would want a long rent for a house like this.'

'I dare say; *if he could get it*,' was William's significant answer.

'What do you mean? Won't the place let?'

'No, sir. I did not tell you last night, but there was a murder done here, and people are shy of the house ever since.'

'A murder! What sort of a murder? Who was murdered?'

'A woman, Master Graham – the landlord's sister; she lived here all alone, and was supposed to have money. Whether she had or not, she was found dead from a stab in her breast, and if there ever was any money, it must have been taken at the same time, for none ever was found in the house from that day to this.'

'Was that the reason your wife would not stop here?' asked the young man, leaning against the mantelshelf, and looking thoughtfully down on William.

'Yes, sir. She could not stand it any longer; she got that thin and nervous no one would have believed it possible; she never saw anything, but she said she heard footsteps and voices, and then when she walked through the hall, or up the staircase, someone always seemed to be following her. We put the children to sleep in that big room you had last night, and they declared they often saw an old woman sitting by the hearth. Nothing ever came my way,' finished William, with a laugh; 'I was always ready to go to sleep the minute my head touched the pillow.'

'Were not the murderers discovered?' asked
Graham Coulton.

'No, sir; the landlord, Miss Tynan's brother, had
always lain under the suspicion of it – quite wrong-
fully, I am very sure – but he will never clear himself
now. It was known he came and asked her for help a
day or two before the murder, and it was also known
he was able within a week or two to weather whatever
trouble had been harassing him. Then, you see,
the money was never found; and, altogether, people
scarce knew what to think.'

'Humph!' ejaculated Graham Coulton, and he took
a few turns up and down the apartment. 'Could I go
and see this landlord?'

'Surely, sir, if you had a hat,' answered William,
with such a serious decorum that the young man burst
out laughing.

'That is an obstacle, certainly,' he remarked, 'and I
must make a note do instead. I have a pencil in my
pocket, so here goes.'

Within half an hour from the dispatch of that note
William was back again with a sovereign; the land-
lord's compliments, and he would be much obliged if
Mr Coulton could 'step round'.

'You'll do nothing rash, sir,' entreated William.

'Why, man,' answered the young fellow, 'one may
as well be picked off by a ghost as a bullet. What is
there to be afraid of?'

William only shook his head. He did not think his
young master was made of the stuff likely to remain
alone in a haunted house and solve the mystery it
assuredly contained by dint of his own unassisted
endeavours. And yet when Graham Coulton came
out of the landlord's house he looked more bright

d gay than usual, and walked up the Lambeth
oad to the place where William awaited his return,
humming an air as he paced along.

'We have settled the matter,' he said. 'And now if
the dad wants his son for Christmas, it will trouble
him to find him.'

'Don't say that, Master Graham, don't,' entreated
the man, with a shiver; 'maybe after all it would have
been better if you had never happened to chance upon
Vauxhall Walk.'

'Don't croak, William,' answered the young man;
'if it was not the best day's work I ever did for myself
I'm a Dutchman.'

During the whole of that forenoon and afternoon,
Graham Coulton searched diligently for the missing
treasure Mr Tynan assured him had never been discovered. Youth is confident and self-opinionated, and
this fresh explorer felt satisfied that, though others
had failed, he would be successful. On the second
floor he found one door locked, but he did not pay
much attention to that at the moment, as he believed
if there was anything concealed it was more likely to
be found in the lower than the upper part of the
house. Late into the evening he pursued his researches
in the kitchen and cellars and old-fashioned cup-
boards, of which the basement had an abundance.

It was nearly eleven, when, engaged in poking about
among the empty bins of a wine cellar as large as a
family vault, he suddenly felt a rush of cold air at his
back. Moving, his candle was instantly extinguished,
and in the very moment of being left in darkness he
saw, standing in the doorway, a woman, resembling
her who had haunted his dreams overnight.

He rushed with outstretched hands to seize her,

but clutched only air. He relit his candle, and closely examined the basement, shutting off communication with the ground floor ere doing so. All in vain. Not a trace could he find of any living creature – not a window was open – not a door unbolted.

'It is very odd,' he thought, as, after securely fastening the door at the top of the staircase, he searched the whole upper portion of the house, with the exception of the one room mentioned.

'I must get the key of that tomorrow,' he decided, standing gloomily with his back to the fire and his eyes wandering about the drawing-room, where he had once again taken up his abode.

Even as the thought passed through his mind, he saw standing in the open doorway a woman with white dishevelled hair, clad in mean garments, ragged and dirty. She lifted her hand and shook it at him with a menacing gesture, and then, just as he was darting towards her, a wonderful thing occurred.

From behind the great mirror there glided a second female figure, at the sight of which the first turned and fled, uttering piercing shrieks as the other followed her from storey to storey.

Sick almost with terror, Graham Coulton watched the dreadful pair as they fled upstairs past the locked room to the top of the house.

It was a few minutes before he recovered his self-possession. When he did so, and searched the upper apartments, he found them totally empty.

That night, ere lying down before the fire, he carefully locked and bolted the drawing-room door; before he did more he drew the heavy settle in front of it, so that if the lock were forced no entrance could be effected without considerable noise.

or some time he lay awake, then dropped into a
ep sleep, from which he was awakened suddenly by
noise as if of something scuffling stealthily behind
ne wainscot. He raised himself on his elbow and
listened, and, to his consternation, beheld seated at
the opposite side of the hearth the same woman he
had seen before in his dreams, lamenting over her
gold.

The fire was not quite out, and at that moment
shot up a last tongue of flame. By the light, transient
as it was, he saw that the figure pressed a ghostly
finger to its lips, and by the turn of its head and the
attitude of its body seemed to be listening.

He listened also – indeed, he was too much
frightened to do aught else; more and more distinct
grew the sounds which had aroused him, a stealthy
rustling coming nearer and nearer – up and up it
seemed, behind the wainscot.

'It is rats,' thought the young man, though, indeed,
his teeth were almost chattering in his head with fear.
But then in a moment he saw what disabused him of
that idea – *the gleam of a candle or lamp through a crack
in the panelling.* He tried to rise, he strove to shout –
all in vain; and, sinking down, remembered nothing
more till he awoke to find the grey light of an early
morning stealing through one of the shutters he had
left partially unclosed.

For hours after his breakfast, which he scarcely
touched, long after William had left him at midday,
Graham Coulton, having in the morning made a long
and close survey of the house, sat thinking before the
fire, then, apparently having made up his mind, he
put on the hat he had bought, and went out.

When he returned the evening shadows were

darkening down, but the pavements were full of people going marketing, for it was Christmas Eve, and all who had money to spend seemed bent on shopping.

It was terribly dreary inside the old house that night. Through the deserted rooms Graham could feel that ghostly semblance was wandering mournfully. When he turned his back he knew she was flitting from the mirror to the fire, from the fire to the mirror; but he was not afraid of her now – he was far more afraid of another matter he had taken in hand that day.

The horror of the silent house grew and grew upon him. He could hear the beating of his own heart in the dead quietude which reigned from garret to cellar.

At last William came; but the young man said nothing to him of what was in his mind. He talked to him cheerfully and hopefully enough – wondered where his father would think he had got to, and hoped Mr Tynan might send him some Christmas pudding. Then the man said it was time for him to go, and when he and Mr Coulton went downstairs to the hall-door, he remarked the key was not in it.

'No,' was the answer, 'I took it out today, to oil it.'

'It wanted oiling,' agreed William, 'for it worked terribly stiff.' Having uttered which truism he departed.

Very slowly the young man retraced his way to the drawing-room, where he only paused to lock the door on the outside; then taking off his boots he went up to the top of the house, where, entering the front attic, he waited patiently in darkness and in silence.

It was a long time, or at least it seemed long to him, before he heard the same sound which had aroused

on the previous night – a stealthy rustling – then
ush of cold air – then cautious footsteps – then the
iet opening of a door below.

It did not take as long in action as it has required to
tell. In a moment the young man was out on the
landing and had closed a portion of the panelling on
the wall which stood open; noiselessly he crept back
to the attic window, unlatched it, and sprung a rattle,
the sound of which echoed far and near through the
deserted streets, then rushing down the stairs, he
encountered a man who, darting past him, made for
the landing above; but perceiving the way of escape
closed, fled down again, to find Graham struggling
desperately with his fellow.

'Give him the knife – come along,' he said savagely;
and next instant Graham felt something like a hot
iron through his shoulder, and then heard a thud, as
one of the men, tripping in his rapid flight, fell from
the top of the stairs to the bottom.

At the same moment there came a crash, as if the
house was falling, and faint, sick and bleeding, young
Coulton lay insensible on the threshold of the room
where Miss Tynan had been murdered.

When he recovered he was in the dining-room, and
a doctor was examining his wound.

Near the door a policeman stiffly kept guard. The
hall was full of people; all the misery and vagabondism
the streets contain at that hour was crowding in to see
what had happened.

Through the midst two men were being conveyed
to the station-house; one, with his head dreadfully
injured, on a stretcher, the other handcuffed, uttering
frightful imprecations as he went.

After a time the house was cleared of the rabble,

the police took possession of it, and Mr Tynan was sent for.

'What was that dreadful noise?' asked Graham feebly, now seated on the floor, with his back resting against the wall.

'I do not know. Was there a noise?' said Mr Tynan, humouring his fancy, as he thought.

'Yes, in the drawing-room, I think; the key is in my pocket.'

Still humouring the wounded lad, Mr Tynan took the key and ran upstairs.

When he unlocked the door, what a sight met his eyes! The mirror had fallen – it was lying all over the floor shivered into a thousand pieces; the console table had been borne down by its weight, and the marble slab was shattered as well. But this was not what claimed his attention. Hundreds, thousands of gold pieces were scattered about, and an aperture behind the glass contained boxes filled with securities and deeds and bonds, the possession of which had cost his sister her life.

'Well, Graham, and what do you want?' asked Admiral Coulton that evening as his eldest born appeared before him, looking somewhat pale but otherwise unchanged.

'I want nothing,' was the answer, 'but to ask your forgiveness. William has told me all the story I never knew before; and, if you let me, I will try to make it up to you for the trouble you have had. I am provided for,' went on the young fellow, with a nervous laugh; 'I have made my fortune since I left you, and another man's fortune as well.'

hink you are out of your senses,' said the Admiral
tly.

No, sir, I have found them,' was the answer; 'and I
an to strive and make a better thing of my life than
should ever have done had I not gone to the Old
louse in Vauxhall Walk.'

'Vauxhall Walk! What is the lad talking about?'

'I will tell you, sir, if I may sit down,' was Graham
Coulton's answer, and then he told this story.